playgroUnd
of
LOST
toYs

"Usually at least once in a person's childhood we lose an object that at the time is invaluable and irreplaceable to us, although it is worthless to others. Many people remember that lost article for the rest of their lives. Whether it was a lucky pocketknife, a transparent plastic bracelet given to you by your father, a toy you had longed for and never expected to receive, but there it was under the tree on Christmas... it makes no difference what it was. If we describe it to others and explain why it was so important, even those who love us smile indulgently because to them it sounds like a trivial thing to lose. Kid stuff. But it is not. Those who forget about this object have lost a valuable, perhaps even crucial memory. Because something central to our younger self resided in that thing. When we lost it, for whatever reason, a part of us shifted permanently."

—JONATHAN CARROLL, winner of the World Fantasy Award, the British Fantasy Award, the Bram Stoker Award and the French Grand Prix de l'Imaginaire.

playgroUnd
of
LOSt
toYs

Edited by Colleen Anderson and Ursula Pflug

The Exile Book of Anthology Series
Number Eleven

EXILE
editions

Library and Archives Canada Cataloguing in Publication

Playground of lost toys / edited by Colleen Anderson and Ursula Pflug.

(The Exile book of anthology series ; number eleven)
Issued in print and electronic formats.
ISBN 978-1-55096-502-5 (paperback).--ISBN 978-1-55096-503-2 (epub).--
ISBN 978-1-55096-504-9 (mobi).--ISBN 978-1-55096-505-6 (pdf)

1. Short stories, Canadian (English). 2. Canadian fiction (English)--
21st century. 3. Toys--Fiction. 4. Children--Fiction. I. Anderson, Colleen,
editor II. Pflug, Ursula, 1958-, editor III. Series: Exile book of anthology
series ; no. 11

PS8323.T68P53 2015   C813'.0108353   C2015-906498-8
                                                   C2015-906499-6

Design and Composition by Mishi Uroboros
Typeset in Fairfield, U73 and Akzidenz Grotesk fonts at Moons of Jupiter Studios

Published by Exile Editions Ltd ~ www.ExileEditions.com
144483 Southgate Road 14 – GD, Holstein, Ontario, N0G 2A0
Printed and Bound in Canada in 2015, by Marquis Books

We gratefully acknowledge the Canada Council for the Arts,
the Government of Canada through the Canada Book Fund ,
the Ontario Arts Council, and the Ontario Media Development Corporation
for their support toward our publishing activities.

Conseil des Arts   Canada Council
du Canada   for the Arts

Canadä

ONTARIO ARTS COUNCIL
CONSEIL DES ARTS DE L'ONTARIO
an Ontario government agency
un organisme du gouvernement de l'Ontario

Ontario
Ontario Media Development
Corporation

Canadian Sales: The Canadian Manda Group, 664 Annette Street,
Toronto ON M6S 2C8   www.mandagroup.com   416 516 0911

North American and international distribution, and U.S. sales:
Independent Publishers Group, 814 North Franklin Street,
Chicago IL 60610   www.ipgbook.com   toll free: 1 800 888 4741

To all the children we used to be.

CONTENTS

INTRODUCTION
WE ARE MADE OF MEMORIES
COLLEEN ANDERSON

The genesis of the theme for *Playground of Lost Toys* happened when Ursula and I attended World Fantasy Con in Toronto. Several people were reminiscing about Show and Tell and toys we had as children. I mentioned the Roman coin my mother had, that I took to school, but watching it sink through layers of snow was part of the fascination. I remembered a toy fridge I played with, which was replaced with a newer version replete with plastic vegetables, but it was never as cherished as the first one.

We love a particular toy or are fascinated with some innocuous item where an adult cannot fathom its worth. We wax nostalgic over these toys long into our adult lives. Chris Kuriata's opening tale tags into the zany ads we once read in magazines and comics, while Joe Davies' "The Compass" touches on the mysterious wonder of gifts, no matter how simple, and DVS Duncan shows us in "Treasure" that inescapable loss of enchantment when we grow into the responsibilities of adulthood.

We are made up of memories. The deeds and events of our past inform our present and design our future. We act and react based on perceiving a glass coloured by yesteryear. While the magical make-believes of our innocence can entertain us for hours as in Melissa Yuan-Innes' story, there are the creatures under the bed, the scary dolls, the hideous ventriloquist dummies – toys that create a sinister mien in the shadowy hours.

Playground of Lost Toys embraces toys and games that bring redemption and condemnation such as Nathan Adler's "The Ghost Rattle" or Claude Lalumière's "Less than Katherine." The future, the world of what-ifs, can be as equally disconcerting in Meagan Whan's "The Die" or Shane Simmons' "When the Trains Run on Time."

Many of the stories in this anthology have a toy or game that is important to the character, but yet it is the lessons and the journeys they take these people on that give meaning. A hundred colourful toys sitting on a shelf do not come to life until they are claimed and given their own histories. Some pastimes are those of adults for we all seek escape from an ordered and mundane world, but the results can save us as in Lisa Carreiro's "Makour," while in Geoff Cole's "Wheatiesfields in Fall," the obsessive game dooms us. Even the gods have their own contests, deftly told in Alex C. Renwick's "Between the Branches of the Nine."

The most powerful form of playing is that which takes place in the playground of thoughts, where we create with our imaginations, before toys were ever created. Dominik Parisien's "Goodbye is a Mouthful of Water" and Catherine MacLeod's "Hide and Seek" look at the games of the mind, in very different situations.

Not every story can be mentioned here but like a Tickle Trunk, they are worthy for exploring the past and the future. And like Pandora's Box, there are many emotions that will be revealed in their telling.

INTRODUCTION
DREAM-EATING RABBITS
MAY OR MAY NOT BE REAL
URSULA PFLUG

As I write this we are almost finished, and it has been tough – *Lost Toys* is a mesmerizing theme not just for editors but for writers and we could easily have filled two books. In our early correspondence, Colleen and I agreed to stay away from the stereotype, and while the creepy doll was a lost toy we saw all too often, so was the worn rabbit stuffie with strange powers. In the end we chose just two doll stories and one rabbit stuffie story.

In Christine Daigle's "Of Dandelions and Magic," the reliability not just of the narrator but of memory itself is a linchpin. When we converse with parents and siblings and children, and their version of events is a little different from ours, do we alter our memories? When we (and I've discussed this one with so many writers!) fictionalize a story that actually happened to us, do we alter the memory? It's impossible to know, but Daigle's story isn't the only one which investigates these questions, natural ones for a Lost Toys anthology which will, by necessity, include many stories about memory.

Protagonist Shauna's mother suffers from dementia. "I was never sure your rabbit was real," she says more than once, and we too wonder. Was the dream-eating rabbit real, or was it a companion the lonely child invented, because she needed Patches so much – so much indeed – that a worn stuffed rabbit could never be enough?

In the end we aren't either – sure whether the rabbit was real – and I'm not sure it matters. I think these liminal stories are some of my favourites – the ones where dream-eating rabbits may or may not be real – or, as in Kate Story's "Show and Tell," a childhood doll reappears in a high school gymnasium on the night of a fundraiser. It isn't really possible that the doll remained in the cubby for so many years – but *it's as good as if she did*. Perhaps it's even the most unreliable narrators, the very young, the traumatized and the elderly who best understand this important truth.

Sometimes healing requires a journey through time and memory to recover pieces of ourselves we had to let go of, because we weren't yet strong enough to do the hard work of reintegration. But we're older now, and we can go back. The doll and the rabbit become our guides, leading us on a journey of retrieval. The lost toy helps us to find the lost child, our inner child we left behind long ago at the locus of trauma.

It will be obvious to some readers that I'm a fan of Joseph Campbell and Clarissa Pinkola Estes – but we *are* on a journey in which we are the heroes of our own tale, a narrative that's perilous, unbelievable, frightening, hilarious, touching and transcendent, either alternately or all at once. Much like the stories in *Playground of Lost Toys*.

I have mentioned a couple of our many wonderful tales by name because they illustrate a point I wanted to make about stories as psychological journeys. There are other comments I'd include if there was space: about beautiful prose, about technological agility, and about humour.

We hope you take as much pleasure in these stories as we did.

FUN THINGS FOR AGES 8 TO 10

Chris Kuriata

Hey Kids! Magazine Vol. 2, Issue 23

Hey, kids! Did you know you can use an old tape recorder to tell the future? It's true. This fortune telling act is sure to entertain the whole family! It's easy and fun!

You will need:

A tape recorder. Check the basement for Mom and Dad's old ghetto blaster. Even an answering machine will work.

A recordable audio cassette tape. Your folks are sure to have a whole shoebox full of tapes they used to record songs off the radio back in the old days. If you can't find any blank cassettes, use a pre-recorded one. If you cover the holes on the top with some masking tape, you can record over it

8-10 dead bugs. Check the windowsill for flies, or ask Mom and Dad to unscrew the kitchen light fixture, where you are sure to find all kinds of dusty moths inside. (NOTE: You must not use worms or butterflies.)

MAKING YOUR TAPE:

First, just before bedtime, set up your ghetto blaster in a room that's had lots of blood spilled in it. If your house is old, this could be any room. Lots of people lived here before your family, and the floorboards of the kitchen and living room are covered in thousands of invisible drops from arguments and jealous rages that took place long before even your parents were born. If your house is new, set up your ghetto blaster in the bathroom.

Next, cover your bugs with a piece of paper and roll them with a bottle. The older they are, the easier they will grind into dust. Sweep up the bug dust and sprinkle it into the tape slot. Be sure to wash your hands before rubbing your eyes!

With the bathroom light off, stare into the mirror. Let your mouth hang open. When your vision adjusts to the dark, you will faintly be able to see your face. Don't move your eyes. When you stare at your face in a dark mirror, your reflection distorts until you look fake like a wax mannequin or a corpse. Whisper, "Tell me, tell me, tell me," over and over until your words mix up like in a tongue twister!

Now, insert your tape and press the REC button (usually red). Depending on its age and condition, the ghetto blaster may make a loud grinding noise. Run back to your bedroom and get under the covers. Some tapes can record for a long time, almost as much as an hour, so you will have to be patient.

Try really hard to fall asleep. If you stay awake too long, you will feel a great weight pressing on your stomach or back when your visitor arrives. DO NOT OPEN YOUR EYES. Your visitor may give you a good sniffing to make sure you are asleep or jam its fingers inside your mouth and tap its rings against your teeth. There may be a funny odour, like the smell of pennies. Continue pretending to be asleep until morning.

When the sun rises, you may retrieve your tape. If the touch of your night visitor was rubbery, like fat fingertips, proceed to step 7. If the touch of your night visitor was cold and scratchy, like hands made of sticks, you must destroy the tape and start over. Don't just throw the tape into the garbage. If someone finds your tape and plays it you will be in BIG TROUBLE. Instead, take the tape to the park and pull out the insides. Be patient, there can be as much as 443 feet of tape (That's almost the height of THREE Niagara Falls!) Pull all the tape out and loop it through the trees. It will sparkle in the sun like Christmas tinsel. Have fun. A grown-up may yell at you, saying the tape is bad for the environment – squirrels or birds will get tangled up in it and choke – but they're just a goddamn liar. Unless you've chickened out like a little cry-baby, repeat steps 1-5 to prepare a new tape.

Bring the tape to school and show it to your science teacher. She will have big magnets, ones strong enough to pick up heavy weights like a roll of quarters. If your science teacher refuses to help you, you'll have to sneak into the science room during lunch hour. Don't worry, none of the other teachers like your science teacher very much and she spends lunch sitting alone in her car, so the coast will be clear. Sandwich your tape between two big magnets A cassette tape is covered in a magnetic dust that captures sound waves and allows you to play it back. Right now, your tape is full of the sound of the grinding mechanism of the ghetto blaster. Your science teacher's big magnets will pull these annoying sounds right off your tape, leaving only the voice of your visitor and the many secrets it whispered during the night. Your visitor's voice is too strong to be sucked out. (NOTE: If you are caught fooling around inside the science room, you will probably get in trouble and have to sit in the office but that is okay. The kids at school who see you sitting in the office will think you are pretty neat. Kids respect those with the balls to not always do what the grown-ups say.)

Your special tape is now ready for playing!

SHOWTIME:

After supper, gather the whole family in the living room. To make yourself look like a showman/girl, cut yourself a top hat out of black construction paper and wrap tinfoil around the head of a hairbrush for a microphone. You might even want to paint a moustache under your nose with Mom's eyeliner. (Make sure to ask permission).

Invite someone from the audience (get them to relax with a big round of applause) to press the PLAY button on the ghetto blaster. You'll enjoy the funny look of surprise on their face when a voice on the tape tells them a prediction about their future. Especially when they hear a scary prediction.

TIPS:

The voice on the tape recorder may use big or ancient words, so it is a good idea to have a thick dictionary handy for looking up head scratchers like "puerperium," "fistula" or "honorificabilitudinitatibus."

Remember, it is your job as master of ceremonies to keep everyone having a good time. As exciting as it is to hear predictions, some people may be frightened by their glimpse into the future. Encourage the audience to focus on the good predictions instead of dwelling on the nasty ones. If they become angry or start crying, remind them there is no way of knowing when their prediction will come to pass. It could be tomorrow, it could be in fifty years! (Except for the prediction about Grandma. That one is coming true soon).

If anyone decides to call an early end to the show it will probably be your dad. He doesn't like things that make Mom or your sister cry. He will accuse you of having recorded yourself saying all these horrible things about accidents and violations. He'll try to pull the tape out of the ghetto blaster and smash it, but you must not let him do that. YOU MUST PLAY THE TAPE TO THE END! Because if you don't, then brother, I wouldn't want to be you.

As you get close to the end of the tape that funny penny odour will begin to fill the house and you'll feel the visitor's weight pressing on your back. (Be careful not to fall down.) The final prediction on the tape must be fulfilled immediately; otherwise BAD THINGS will happen to everyone in the room. Bad things that will be everlasting. If the tape says, "A handsome gentlemen will give Mom flowers," have Dad rush out to the garden and snatch a few azaleas for her. Make sure he does it quickly. You don't have a lot of time before the visitor appears. If the tape says, "Your sister will receive her first kiss," there is no time to be bashful; either you or your brother better pucker up and plant one on her. Usually, the final prediction will be easy to fulfill, but sometimes it will prove to be a little harder. So be prepared to think fast. If the tape says, "Mom will lose a finger," know that although the pinkie is the smallest, it is second only to the thumb in importance for maintaining hand function. Mom will be better off losing the first finger on her non-dominant hand, so make sure you chop off that one. If the final prediction says, "The family home burns to the ground," don't worry – the dollhouse in your sister's room will suffice. But if the final prediction says, "Your neighbour's home burns to the ground," you'll want to get the fire spreading into their walls quickly. If the fire department arrives before the structure collapses, things will get unpleasant before very long. The visitor is unmerciful, and once raising its ire, you can only hope there is no afterlife.

(Why not use the tape to tell fortunes at your next Cub Scout Jamboree or school talent show? Send the funniest, most outrageous predictions to us at: Hey Kids! Shipman Publications, 190 Queenston Street, Suite 104, Shipman, ON. *The top three predictions will be published in an upcoming issue: First Place Junior Reporter will receive $3, Second Place $2, Third Place $1.)*

THE COMPASS

Joe Davies

When I picture the two of us crashing our way through the tall grass, I see it from the outside, as witness rather than participant. With some effort I can squeeze myself back in the shoes where I belong – following Arthur under the full gaze of the sun as he parts the way, compass in one hand, bending the grass to the side with the other – though seeing it this way feels strangely inauthentic.

In a way, Arthur was my first love, a boy so hopelessly lost in his own sorrows, heartsick at the dissolution of his family. We shared the kind of unwitting connection that can flare up between two eleven-year-old boys. Everyone I've become close with since has been a girl or a woman, but always more complicated than it feels it ought to have been. I had no idea at the time how rare it was, my friendship with Arthur. If I had, I might never have been so cruel to him.

He lived two blocks away, one block closer than me to the school where we met. When he'd joined our class partway through November he was given the seat next to mine and I was asked to help him settle in. To say I was "asked" means I was "told," but it was no trouble. Quite the opposite. Some connections you feel right away. Something about his open expression, the directness of his eyes when they fixed on mine. To this day I don't know how to describe it. Without uttering a word, he was saying, "Here I am." I looked into those eyes and was dragged in. We became inseparable. Skating, playing Stratego, watching television, going to the corner store, having sleepovers at my place – always it was my place. For a little over six months our companionship was scarcely interrupted.

The day Arthur lost the compass we were at a conservation area north of the city. It was something my family did at the time – go for a Sunday drive – and Arthur had come with us. There was always room in the station wagon for him, though it meant squishing four of us into the back seat – me, Arthur, my two older sisters, Bianca and Carmen. This was before anyone cared much about seat belts. I think my father enjoyed seeing the back seat so full, and my mother could never have left Arthur behind. I imagine she felt badly for him, a single child, his mother having run off, his father unable to play the roles of both parents.

Arthur was teased at school about his mother having left. He shrugged it off where he could, but I think it cut him deeply. He had pictures of her. She wasn't what I'd call pretty, but there was the same directness about her expression, and a kind of cheerfulness.

At Christmas that year there'd been a package for him. It had come from the west coast, from his mother. Inside was a spy kit, poorly made. The binoculars fell apart within a week. The decoder and magic ears soon followed. The only piece that endured was the compass, and it went everywhere with Arthur in his shirt pocket. He had it with us when our family drive stopped at the conservation area that Sunday in May.

◀ ▶

My mother hadn't packed a picnic exactly but knew never to leave the house without food if my father was behind the wheel. Depending on how he was feeling and how much gas was in the tank, a Sunday drive could last anywhere from three-quarters of an hour to five.

We'd been to the conservation area before. I have no idea what it was called or if it was even meant to be used the way it was. There were no picnic tables and no proper place to park, just a few spaces carved out at the side of the road. The main attraction was the view. It was in the bottom of a small, flat valley, with trees to either side, but opened out at one end to offer a narrow view of the city to the south.

When we got there that day it was clear my father wanted to stay a while. He promptly sat himself against the trunk of a maple, pulled his hat over his eyes and fell asleep.

"Piece of kielbasa?" said my mother, who had reached into her bag of food and produced a short coil of meat.

The blanket was spread out and we took our places. There was meat and cheese and hunks of bread, a couple of oranges and a bottle of tap water that we passed around. When my father woke from his nap he had some coffee from a thermos and asked why there were no cookies. My mother was famous for her gingersnaps and oatmeal squares, both of which disappeared in quantity if my father ever figured out where they were being hidden. My mother dropped a box of Girl Guide cookies on the blanket and said, "There," as if it was partial proof he wasn't good enough for her either.

"See what I get?" he asked, looking around at all of us with a smile. "Cookies baked by little girls who don't know what a grown man is capable of eating or not eating."

"No little girl ever touched those cookies except to bring them to our door," said my mother.

"Then why do they sell them?" asked my father.

My mother shrugged.

"I'll tell you why," offered my father. "They sell them to get rid of them." He reached down and opened the box, saying, "Who wants one?" and offered them around. We all took a couple and my father saw that Arthur held something in his hand.

"What's that you got there?" he asked.

Arthur showed him.

"Here," said my father, and held out his hand.

Arthur passed it to him.

"A compass."

"Of course it's a compass," said my mother. "You can see it's a compass. We can all see it's a compass."

"What? Do you use it to find your way around that dark and mysterious neighbourhood of ours?"

"No," said Arthur, looking away, as if embarrassed. But I could see he was enjoying the attention. I doubted he was ever teased this way at home. I doubted he was noticed much at all.

"But you know how to use it, yeah?"

Arthur pulled at the grass beside him and nodded.

"You boys want a little challenge? You want me to send you off on a little adventure?" As my father said this he was reaching into his own shirt pocket where he always kept a little pad and the stump of a pencil. "Let's see how close you can get to landing right back on this spot."

He scribbled on his pad for a minute, then handed it across to us.

"And no cheating."

We looked at the paper, then back at him.

"What is it?" asked my mother, and she and my sisters crowded in to see what my father had done.

It was a diagram with numbers scratched in and around it.

"Pass it back," said my father. "Here. This is your heading. See, you start by going south by southeast. That direction." He pointed over his shoulder. "And this, this is the number of paces. You have to count them to make sure you get it right. When you've done that, you take your bearings again and look, see? You go off to the west, again counting your paces. If you follow it all exactly, follow your heading while keeping the needle pointing north, you should end up right back here."

Arthur was looking at my father like there was a spark inside him that had suddenly been ignited.

"But you already know how to use it, don't you?"

"Don't get them lost," said my mother, wrapping up the cheese.

"I know how to use it," said Arthur.

"Good boy," said my dad. "Now off you go and count your paces. Have fun. We'll see you in half an hour."

"Can I see the compass?" asked my mother. When she had it in her hand she held it flat and looked down at it, then jiggled it. "It's just a toy," she said, glancing at my father. "The needle's sticky. It doesn't…"

"So they get lost. So what? Who wants 'em back, anyway?"

"I get his room," said my sister Carmen.

"I get his baseball cards," said my sister Bianca.

"You get nothing," said my father, "either of you. It's all mine," and he tousled my hair. "Now go! Here, I'll help you with the first step. You see? You sight something along that line, along your bearing, and you head for that. It's easy. When you get there you take another sighting and head for the next thing. See that big tree there? That one next to it, to the left, that's on the line you want to follow. So go, the both of you. Get out of here. Scram."

Like most of my memories from that far back, that day now seems as if it happened to someone else, as if I'm in possession of someone else's memory. If it's because of the fifty years that have fallen between, then they are fifty years that have spun me out of my own shoes.

I'm a grandfather now. Only just. My first-born had a daughter eight weeks ago. They're in Europe, in Spain, and I have no appetite for travel these days, not even to meet my first grandchild. And there's a feeling I haven't shared with anyone, a feeling that I'd only be in the way and not really wanted. And yet, had I gone when I first felt I should, I would never have seen Arthur again.

It happened by e-mail. I didn't recognize the sender, and the subject line, "Is it you?" was suspect enough that I nearly deleted the message unopened. It turned out to be from Arthur's partner, a man named Nelson, and it informed me that Arthur was dying. Among other things, he was suffering from a bone disease that made him so brittle he could no longer stand. Nelson understood it had been a long time, so long that perhaps I had no interest in coming to Arthur's bedside, especially when we'd known each other for only a relatively short while and such a long time ago. Still, I had been asked for specifically. It had taken weeks to find me and Arthur's remaining time was expected to be short, perhaps days.

I e-mailed to say I would come. It was halfway across the province, but I set out as soon as I could, climbing into my car the following morning and patting my shirt pocket to be sure of the compass.

◀ ▶

My first girlfriend came as a bit of a surprise to me. One minute we were walking home through town together, the next we were kissing in the alleyway next to her apartment building. I thought I knew how being with someone else was supposed to work, the kinds of things you were supposed to do, and it was good for a while, but didn't turn out how I expected. In the end we fell out.

I've felt an ache over the years. It's followed me through all the partners I've had. I've felt a love that seems to come closer to compassion than anything resembling the romantic ideal of connecting with a soulmate, something closer to a mutual recognition that we are both in the unenviable position of wanting to be loved, without having actually found it. My first marriage lasted a little over a year, the second almost eight. The compromising necessary to make anything work only seems to get harder the older I get. And for the longest time I had no idea how difficult I could be to get along with. In the past week I have thought back a great deal to the uncomplicated days of being eleven, and the closeness I felt to Arthur.

The first leg of our short excursion that Sunday in May was to be five hundred paces. After about two hundred we reached the tree my father had pointed out. Beneath it, in the shade, Arthur put the compass in the palm of his hand and shook it

a little, then shook it again. The needle did not want to cooperate.

"Does it always do that?" I asked.

Arthur shook his head.

I looked back in the direction we'd come and said, "Well,
if we just keep going in a straight line we should be okay."

Arthur squinted at me. It was a look that was probably
only meant to say, "Okay. Let's do that." But because of the
years in between I stand now looking over my own shoulder
at him, a spectator to my own experiences, and it has now
come to mean all sorts of other things, unquestionably ideal-
ized. In his look, he says, "You and me. This is the moment,
beautiful precisely because it could just as easily be forgotten.
And honestly, when will there ever be another chance to feel
this comfortable in our own skins?"

Young me, I pointed across the field. "See the break in the
trees over there?" I asked.

"Yes."

"Let's head for there."

We started out. At first the grass was short enough we
walked next to one another. Arthur put a hand on my shoulder. I put mine on his. As the grass got taller and thicker we
moved closer to each other and were side by side.

As I remember this I hover slightly above and to one side,
looking down. I see the moment when we break apart and
Arthur moves ahead. I see him turning over his shoulder to
say to me, "It's working again," and he holds it flat in one hand
while parting the grass in front with the other.

We stalked across that field in full sun, and in my memory of it, it goes on much longer than it ever could have. We
picked as direct a path as we could, all the time counting our

paces. Getting across would only have been a matter of minutes, but I have it as an almost static event, an occurrence that goes on and on. The air so still it's like being in the silence of a vacuum. First, Arthur steps though the parted grass, then I do, following on his heels. And this is repeated over and over, the same steps taken then retaken as our small frames negotiate the unending path we are making towards the gap in the trees, repeated as if it is impossible for me to imagine a moment more unaffected. But however much I slow it down, we always reach the line of trees. Once through, and a few paces the other side, up a slight rise, we reached our five hundred paces.

We halted. The view of the city was particularly good, and would have shown a much simpler, more modest skyline than today's.

"It's stuck again," said Arthur, and he shook it.

"Maybe it's not going to work so well if you always carry it around."

He shook it again. "There," he said, pointing down the rise. "That's west."

"It's all right," I said. "We're not going to get lost."

"Yeah, but it's working now."

"Okay," I said. We sighted a bit of open field on the other side of the little valley and headed for that. Halfway across we realized we'd forgotten to count steps, but we both knew it didn't matter. "Should we go back and start counting?"

"Nah," said Arthur. We were, by then, simply out for a hike.

We had just crossed a pile of stones when out of the blue Arthur said over his shoulder, "I'm going to live with Mother."

"What?" I said, not sure I'd heard correctly.

"She asked me to come out west, my mother. She wants me to go live with her."

"Oh," I said. It was all I could think to say. But immediately I was thinking about what it was going to be like for me, him going away. I thought about recess, about being out in the playground on my own. There'd been a few times, a handful at least, where I'd stood up for Arthur when others had taunted him about the situation with his mother. His need had made me strong, and I wondered who I'd be with him gone. I thought of us on my living room carpet, watching hockey, or sitting on my back steps eating popcorn, and a long list of other things we'd done together.

He turned to me and said, "I should go, shouldn't I?"

When I said nothing in return, it was as if I'd said what he didn't need to hear: No, he should stay. I would miss him.

Almost as if in answer to that, he said, "Life is very strange, isn't it?"

Again, I found nothing to say.

"Want to see something really weird?" he asked, and he held out his compass where I could see it, then drew back his arm as far as he could and launched the compass into the sky, south towards the city.

I watched it fly in a long slow arc out into the depths of the grass, thinking how final a move it was, since even if we looked for an hour we'd likely never find it.

When it had fallen I turned to him and laughed at the suddenness and rashness of the thing.

He shook his head and said, "Now, do you want to see the strangest thing?"

"What?" I said.

He stuck his hand into his shirt pocket and pulled out what looked to be an identical compass.

"You had two?" I asked.

"No," he said. "It's the same one."

"What? You threw something else? I saw it go."

"I can't lose it," he said. "No matter what I do, no matter what happens to it, I can stomp it to pieces, but as soon as I do, and as soon as I look away, it comes back to me." And he patted his shirt pocket.

He threw it again. And again. Each time it came back to his shirt pocket.

It was a trick. I knew it must be a trick. Because there was no such thing as real magic. I was old enough by then to be certain of that. But each time I watched as he drew his arm back and the thing flew off into the air and came down somewhere far off in the grass, and each time there was Arthur pulling the thing out of his pocket.

After about the sixth or seventh time Arthur put a hand on my shoulder and said it was okay, he'd had a hard time believing it at first too, but there it was. What could you do? The thing just always came back to him.

I stared at him, incredulous. The truth of it seemed to be what Arthur and my eyes were telling me, but nothing else about it made any sense. I cast about thinking what to make of it. Part of me wondered why. Why was it doing this? Why Arthur? And why was it making me so mad? Was I jealous? And what could I possibly have to be jealous about? I think my mind knew better than to try and settle the how of it. That, at least, seemed beyond the effort of thinking about.

For a minute Arthur stood there smiling at me, tossing the thing up in the air and catching it. It was as if he was at a loss himself to understand something, as if he was wondering how it was I could be so bewildered by the thing instead of simply standing there marvelling.

Eventually he put the compass back in his pocket and without a word we began to walk again.

I said, "We should change direction again, I think," and Arthur drew the compass from his pocket and worked out our new heading. He pointed up along the west side of the valley and said, "How about that dead tree there? Just to the right?"

I nodded, but as he was about to return the compass to his pocket I said, "Throw it again." By the look on his face it was as if I had said to him, "Yes. We are still friends. We will always be friends."

He threw the thing a ways up the slope, to the left. I heard it clatter off something and a moment later he produced it from his pocket.

"Well, how about that," I said, and we carried on making our way through the grass.

It was the little belt of saplings we had to walk through that undid us. I was walking in front, holding back the branches as we went so they wouldn't snap back in Arthur's face, but once or twice I miscalculated and he got lashed. I offered to let him take the lead again and he did. Almost immediately a large branch whipped back and caught me on the cheek, just below the eye. I'm sure now that he didn't mean it but at the time I felt inclined to believe he did. Why we had bothered to walk that way at all, I don't know. We weren't counting our steps and were only loosely following my father's design.

A little further ahead we hit open ground. We began walking side by side again, but weren't talking. I didn't see what it was, but Arthur stumbled on something and the compass leapt from his hand. I picked it up from the ground in front of me and held it out for him. He looked off and away, as if saying to me, "You have a turn. Throw it." I did. I pulled back my arm and lobbed the compass like I was going for the record. I watched as it flipped about in the sky, then grew smaller and eventually came down in some bushes, somewhere just the other side of a split-rail fence.

Arthur's hand immediately went to his shirt pocket and I knew at once something was wrong. Arthur patted himself all over, but it was no good. This time it had not come back.

I felt to blame, there was no question, and out of this grew the name-calling. On Arthur's part, I'm sure it simply grew out of the unfairness, and I had been the vehicle. But once we got started things quickly got out of hand, and I know for a fact that I even repeated most of the mean things I'd heard said at recess, the very things about his mother that I had defended him against. I won't put here what was said. I am forever ashamed.

When we got back to the blanket my mother had spread, it was clear to all my family that something was not right.

My mother said, "What happened?" and was told simply that the compass had been lost. Nothing else was said about it. My mother handed us some cookies, my father wore a look that said, "Gee, what tough luck," and we climbed into the car.

The drive home was one of the last times I saw Arthur. In a matter of days he was gone, and I heard nothing from him till we had a Christmas card that told nothing more than the generic holiday wishes it claimed to share. There was an address on the envelope, but I could never bring myself to write.

It was in the car ride home that day that I discovered the compass had come to me. Idiot that I was, I hadn't thought to check my own pockets. The shirt I wore hadn't any, but at some point on the drive into town I realized I was sitting on something uncomfortable. I reached back to the seat of my pants and felt the shape of a small circle. At first I thought it was a Girl Guide cookie, but judged right away that it was too large and too firm to be that. I was too pigheaded to give it back.

◄ ►

When I finally reached the long-term care facility where Arthur was, I didn't recognize the person in the bed. For several hours that afternoon I was alone with him in that dark impersonal space. He didn't know who I was and barely acknowledged my presence. His eyes opened and he spoke a few words, none of which arranged themselves into any sense. He was pretty much gone already.

At some point I took the compass from my shirt pocket and folded it into his hand, but his grip was loose and he dropped it over the edge of the bed, where it landed on the floor with a clatter. I knew enough to look away, and when I checked, the compass had found its way into the pocket of his dressing gown.

I patted him on the shoulder and left.

HIDE AND SEEK

Catherine MacLeod

My father could have taught Leonard Porter quite a lot about making people invisible.

My mother could have taught him everything.

I could teach him myself, but offering advice he hasn't asked for would be rude. I've been a guest in the Porters' home for almost a year. Their hospitality has been flawless. The fact that they don't actually know I'm in their house is no excuse for bad manners.

He'll just have to do it the hard way.

All great scientists have their obsessions. Dr. Porter's is cracking the secret of making people invisible. I don't understand why he wants to do that, unless it's simply to be the first, but he seems to have made a good start. His notes are very clear. To make an object invisible, he will have to bend light around it. If light never reflects off the object, it will never be seen. It will cast no shadow. There will be no sign that it ever existed.

That I understand perfectly.

Mother would have approved.

◀ ▶

Mother believed that courtesy was next to godliness. Her bible was *Modern Manners*, by Miss Amelia Gray, copyright

1898. A little out of date in the age of the Internet, but as Miss Gray writes, "Good manners never go out of style."

Mother quoted her until I had the book memorized.

She told me, "A good guest has no sense of self-importance."

She told me, "Every child is a guest in his parents' home."

She told me, "Children should be seen and not heard." Then she added, "And, in your case, unseen would be good, too."

Who was I to argue with godliness? I was an obliging boy, eager to please. From that day on I stayed out of her sight, always quiet, keeping to the dark corners – behaviour my father had learned years before. Mother so thoroughly ignored us that being unseen became ordinary, like breathing.

Invisibility is easier when people don't *want* to see you. Cooperation is appreciated. Mother took down the mirrors so we couldn't even see ourselves. Going unseen required humility, I thought. Being invisible was an act of virtue.

It was also an asset on the rare times I ventured outside the house. I'd always loved playing hide-and-seek with the other neighbourhood children. I knew the rules of the game as well as I knew Mother's; they were alike in many ways. I followed them to the letter. I was silent and still. I moved quietly into dark spaces, reminding myself that I was undeserving of notice, and changed hiding places after the seekers had passed.

Their glances slid past me, seeing only another shade of shadow.

The last game we played was memorable. When they ran home to their suppers, leaving me in the park, obviously forgotten, I knew I had won. I had become master of the game.

It would have been impolite to disturb Mother with the news, but surely she would have been pleased to see Miss Gray proven right.

After a time I truly believe she forgot I was in the house.

Certainly the people who bought it after her death didn't suspect.

They found me to be an excellent guest: they didn't find me at all.

As far as I know, my father is still there. I can't imagine him anywhere else. But then again, I can't imagine him at all. To this day I have no idea what he looked like. I left a month after the new owners came, packing a few necessities and the indispensable *Modern Manners*. Its final chapter, "Manners on the Move," would take me out into the world with confidence. In it, Miss Gray wrote of the professional houseguest, a visitor whose charm and comforting presence makes him welcome in home after home. After my mother's intensive training I felt I was more than up to the task.

Indeed, I thought it quite possible that being a guest was my calling.

And so I went unnoticed in home after home, year after year. At first I preferred bigger houses. They have so many dark corners. If no light touches me, I remain unseen; if I'm in one shadow, I don't cast another. Servants are paid not to see too much, and the hosts simply walk past me, daydreaming, or chatting on their cells, ignoring me wonderfully.

A rich host has so many *things* to think about that a few are bound to escape his attention. Like the sweater he looked for last night, today folded on the closet shelf where it's supposed to be. The last slice of cake he doesn't remember eating. Turning the television on to a channel he doesn't usually watch.

The flicker of movement in his peripheral vision that he dismisses as tiredness.

That warm itch like a breath on the back of his neck.

I don't mind that he ignores it. A good guest doesn't wish to intrude.

He also doesn't wish to criticize his hosts, so let me just *whisper* that mansions and whirlwind parties can become tiring after a while. That there's a certain malaise that comes with being in perpetual transit. That perhaps it was homesickness that made me long for the intimacy of family life. For a place where the phrase, *Make yourself at home* goes without saying.

I think the Porters may be the hosts I've waited for all my life.

◀ ▶

Denise Porter is the most beautiful woman I've ever seen. She has dark hair and darker eyes. She moves like a dancer. But she does very little to enhance her looks. At first I thought she was indifferent to her appearance, but have come to realize she simply doesn't know how lovely she is.

Certainly her husband doesn't seem to notice.

The vendor at the newsstand where I first saw her noticed, though. She returned his smile and answered her cell as she paid for the morning papers. She paid me no mind as I looked through the magazines. I was just one more face on a crowded street. I was the paradox of being invisible in plain sight.

"Hello? Hi, Marcy. Sure, I'm still up for dinner tomorrow night. Where do you want to meet this time? Oh, please, Leonard won't even know I'm gone. It's like we're playing hide-and-seek and he can't be bothered looking for me, even when I'm right in front of him."

Her mention of hide-and-seek intrigued me. So few people reference the game anymore. Even fewer understand its complexities.

Curious, I followed her home, keeping a comfortable distance between us until she approached the house. Then I walked in the door behind her, stepped into the closet as she shook the wrinkles out of her coat, froze as she hung it in front of me. She walked away singing an old song that had been a favourite of Mother's. I took it as a good sign.

Denise is a charming hostess. She has fresh flowers delivered every day, leaves snacks in the fridge, doesn't notice extra towels in the wash. She's an excellent cook. A good guest eats lightly, but can reasonably expect a well-prepared meal. Of course, he also washes his own dishes. Doing small household tasks to lighten his hosts' workload is a must. A guest who doesn't is simply a parasite.

I'm pleased to be of some small service to my hostess. I brush the dog, bring home fresh milk, take the garbage out – and always keep in mind that getting back in will require some care.

I have my own key – most people are surprisingly unconcerned when they lose theirs – but I'm still not sure of the security code. I'd hate to trouble the police unnecessarily. They tend to be blunt about the finer points of etiquette.

I always look forward to coming home. Denise is an avid reader, which pleases me to no end. The house has thousands of books, including many of the classics. Finally, I have a chance to read all of H.G. Wells. Along with other small comforts, a good host will always provide reading material to amuse his guest.

I especially enjoy Denise's journal. Most entries focus on trivia, what she's done that day, who she's seen. But the entries about her husband are enlightening and poignant. She knows about his affair. Not the other woman's name, or exactly when she became a problem, but she knows she's out there. She surmises correctly that she's one of his university students. Having once been one herself, she sees the possibilities.

A few entries are even thought-provoking. On a recent page she wrote, *When we first met, Leonard said I had an elegant name, but I can't remember the last time he used it.*

That one gave me pause. It made me wonder if I have a name. I can't remember Mother ever calling me by one. I must have wondered back then, too, but, no, I wouldn't have asked. A good guest doesn't ask too many questions.

Denise doesn't ask many, either. But at odd moments she stops to draw a shuddering breath, as if some knowledge is choking her. She obviously has no wish to be invisible.

The professor obviously doesn't care what she wishes. I've stood behind him in his workshop countless times as he told his girlfriend yes, he could see her tonight, his wife wouldn't even know he was gone.

She knew. She knows he turns to her only when his pretty student is unavailable. She closes her eyes when they have sex, as if it hurts to look at him. She closes them even when she's alone. She closes them with some frequency. I appreciate the effort.

A good guest can expect to be entertained.

◀ ▶

I would never dream of opening the medicine chest or snooping through the safe. I would never sift through the software he installs every time he buys a new laptop. But it's only polite to show an interest in something left in plain sight. Professor Porter's invisibility device looks like a heavy gold bracelet, each link adorned with a control button made of garnet. It is an exquisite, and somewhat disturbing, combination of science and art.

I can't comprehend his notes anymore, but I understand his journal only too well. He's going to give the bracelet to Denise for her birthday, making her his test subject.

He's not sure the effects can be reversed.

In his early notes he writes, *A man who is invisible will also be blind. If light doesn't reflect off him, it will never be absorbed by his retinas.*

The way *he* does it, yes.

I see some irony here.

Leonard Porter, who expects his device to bring him worldwide notice, doesn't see what's been going on under his nose.

Last week, on the first anniversary on my arrival in the house, Denise finished reading a new mystery novel. I was sure she wouldn't mind if I borrowed it. She closed the cover at midnight, dropped it on the floor, turned out the light. I listened to her breathing, an unexpectedly lonely sound. When it was deep and steady I picked up the book.

Her hand slipped off the mattress. Her knuckles tapped me on the head. She made nonsensical soothing sounds and scratched my scalp as I eased away.

"What?" her husband muttered.

"Dog's unnera bed."

"'Kay."

I held my breath, my heart racing. Partly because being discovered would have been gauche. Mostly because I couldn't remember ever having been touched before. It was…*wonderful*. The most beautiful burning. I stayed awake all night, staring at Denise's pale hand where it rested on the edge of the blanket. Longing to feel her touch again, but not daring to reach out.

I slipped away at daybreak. Denise had forgotten to set the timer on the coffee maker again. I turned it on, and took a blueberry muffin back to the guestroom as the smell of coffee woke them up. I sat, trembling and haunted, thinking of the hostess gifts I'd given her. The extra flowers tucked into the daily deliveries. The violet-scented soaps left in the back of her bureau drawers to be found accidentally. A box of her favourite tea, discovered in the cupboard when she thought she'd run out. I enjoyed her sweet, startled smiles. I wanted so desperately to make her happy.

As evening fell my thoughts put themselves in order.

When had good manners turned to courtship?

And when had I gone mad enough to even think about… ?

Before I could finish that thought I went down to the kitchen. I stood behind her as she peeled the vegetables for dinner. I *was* insane, I thought – and reached out to stroke her hair anyway. It was the softest thing I'd ever touched.

She tensed, but didn't turn around. "Leonard, you scared me."

I hummed a faint non-sound and brushed her hair aside to caress the back of her neck. She hummed back, then stepped away to check the roast in the oven. I faded out the door.

I know it's a terrible breach of decorum to want what my host hasn't offered.

But then again, he's already thrown it away.

◄ ►

A good guest doesn't interfere in his hosts' personal affairs. Miss Amelia Gray is very clear on this point. But she could hardly expect me to stand back and watch my hostess come to harm.

Leonard and I wait until Denise leaves for her monthly dinner with Marcy. We wait for his girlfriend to arrive at the kitchen door, where she'll be unseen from the street. We follow her downstairs and wait for her to finish admiring the bracelet.

She actually seems to understand some of the theory behind the device, which marks her as intelligent, if not necessarily smart. She's clearly besotted with this man who wants to replace his wife with a newer model, the same way he updates his tech.

She clearly agrees it's the right thing to do.

I watch as he takes her in Denise's bed then return to his workshop to take what I need.

An hour before Denise is due home, the girlfriend leaves, declining his offer to call a cab. It's a nice night for a walk, she says, and she'll be careful.

I follow her home, keeping a comfortable distance between us until she approaches her building. I walk in the door behind her, noting the apartment number on her mailbox, taking the stairs as she rides the elevator, and pivot around her as she locks herself in.

I walk back home in the dark and wait on the steps, sliding inside as Leonard leaves for work in the morning.

It's done.

I'm happy that Denise's last few journal entries mention Leonard's new attentiveness. *How gentle his touch has become.* She has no way of knowing how agitated he'll become as the day goes on. When his pretty student doesn't show up for class. When he discovers that both his bracelet and his notebooks are missing.

When he realizes, he doesn't dare call the police or draw attention to himself.

When he finds the notebooks in her apartment, but can't find the bracelet. Or her.

When he realizes he never will.

He'll be away tonight, planning what to do in a situation where nothing can be done. Wondering how to hide his wrongdoings; seeking a solution to a convoluted problem.

I will be in bed with Denise, kissing the skin that smells like violets. I am still the master of the game, as she is the master of me. I will never stop courting her. One day, when she opens her eyes, she will be grateful for my devotion. A good guest never stops making himself welcome.

I can't help but think Mother would be pleased.

SHOW AND TELL

Kate Story

I came late to the dance. I arrived hoping Marnie would already be there. I'd almost asked her if she wanted to go together, but I'd said nothing and now, I arrived alone.

The building still left me feeling queasy; it smelled the same. The interior walls were painted cinder blocks, glossed in brighter colours than in my day. But the school office looked the same. I remembered being sent there to get the strap for daydreaming, after being warned to pay attention three times, like in a fairy tale. Here on the island, back in the seventies in any case, there were penalties for fantasy; or maybe it was just that the teacher disliked me in particular.

But that was then. Now, twenty years later, I could hear music pumping from the gym and I saw the flash of colours; someone had rented a disco ball. I heard laughter, adult laughter. That was nice, right? Different. This was different.

I went into the gym and moved directly to the special-event licensed table, bought a beer, and surveyed the room. I'd had a sick feeling that some of my old classmates might show up this night, come back to...I don't know. Torture me. I gave myself a mental shake. I hadn't seen any of them in almost two decades. They had no way of knowing that I was even here.

My old elementary school had been slated for demolition, an event I anticipated with dark and vengeful pleasure. In the interim, some enterprising spark had arranged for the building to be rented out to community groups, and here we were, the fundraising committee for the dragon boat team, dancing at the seventies-themed event and, well, raising funds. Joining the team was how I'd met Marnie. She was the steerer, and fierce, yelling instructions from her adaptive seat in the stern. Also, Marnie was gay, although she and I had never talked about this.

I looked for her now, some beer safely inside me. She wasn't hard to spot. She'd found patch-pocket flares, a groovy open-necked shirt, and rainbow socks with toes. She'd decorated her wheelchair with those plastic straw things we used to put on our bicycle wheels so they made a vaguely musical noise. Out on the dance floor, she was carving it up.

I drank the beer too fast and joined her, admiring her rainbow-toed socks. After two dances – to "Dancing Queen" and the song from the Star Wars cantina – Stevie Wonder came on. "Sir Duke."

"Sometimes I feel like I'm living the wrong life."

That just came out. Things like that happen sometimes. I immediately regretted saying it, but it was too late.

"It's because we're in your old school, isn't it?"

This made me smile. Marnie knew me well enough at this point to grasp that my thoughts were usually only tenuously related to external stimulus; the thought was something I generated out of the spastic weirdness of my own brain. Suddenly I didn't feel like talking about wrong lives any more. "Never mind."

Marnie, I'd learned over the past month, hated *never minds* beyond all things, and teased me and poked at me until I elaborated. And indeed, part of me may have begun and then feebly tried to end the conversation on purpose. Because there was something *about* having Marnie pay attention to me.

"That there's some other life that's supposed to be yours," I yelled over Stevie, "but you've taken a wrong turn and the life you're supposed to be living is going on without you. The conscious *here* you."

"The conscious here me?" She executed a nifty spin in her chair.

"The you that, in this particular narrative, drags on, making the best of it, but…it isn't your life."

"But if you're here, then it's your life." She was taking this seriously. "Multiple universes?"

I kept dancing.

"Maybe it's not about universes," she proposed. "Maybe it's a narrative, like you said. Maybe it's what you choose to remember."

Which was pretty perceptive, because I had difficulty remembering all kinds of things.

The song after Stevie was "Don't Give Up on Us," slow. I got self-conscious and left Marnie to go get another beer. Got trapped by the guy who helped organize everything: he'd lost his wife to cancer and seemed determined to talk to me. All the time. "Why don't you like Santok?" Marnie had demanded, because really, Santok was nice and good-looking and his wife had been gone for five years so it wasn't creepy or anything.

I didn't tell Marnie that I'd never really dated. Just had sex. Not even good sex. I didn't tell her that I hated sex, but I seemed to want to have it all the time, with men I didn't like who didn't like me. I didn't tell her, or Santok, that I was trying not to do that anymore.

So I extricated myself from the nice, flirtatious, Marnie-approved man, and that's when I decided to take a walk around my old elementary school. Before it was consigned to dust forever, damn it to hell.

◄ ►

Walking down the darkened hallway, I realized my face was stretched in a weird, teeth-baring grimace. I gave my cheek a slap, trying for a reset. My mainlander grandmother used to whack the back of my hand every time I made a face – scrunch up my nose, for example, or purse my lips. Crossing my eyes, encouraged in my brothers as amusing, was of course forbidden. Let's not even bring up sticking out my tongue. She didn't tell me that if the wind changed, my face would stick that way, which is what my Newfoundland relatives all said. My mainland grandmother said it was "unattractive."

I wasn't a little girl who understood "attractive" except that I suspected I wasn't.

And neither was Saucy Doll. But I wanted her, and so did thousands of other little girls. Saucy Doll had a glamour about her, some kind of power. The ads made her seem like someone fun, companionable. Someone who could change things.

But she was ugly. Innocuously ugly, with blue eyes and blond hair before Karla Homolka sinisterized that combination, and even she hasn't, in the end, succeeded. A pink dress, with a gingham undershirt. Her go-to expression was eyes wide, lips parted in that semi-pornographic expression female dolls often model. But the whole point of her was this: you would take her left arm and pump it up and down, and as you did, her face would change.

Saucy Doll had several expressions. You had to go through them all, in the same order every time. The arm didn't move smoothly – it made a rattling, mechanical noise with every pump. Eyes rolled to the left, lips parted even further. A faintly alarming creaking noise as the semi-flexible rubber of her face stretched, the mechanism beneath just faintly perceptible. Then there'd be a sort of click, and her lips would snap closed as her eyes moved to the right.

When that one was done, she'd snap back to her original position, blue eyes staring straight into mine. Next, she'd wink her right eye. Her left cheek would begin to hitch up; after her right eye snapped back open (and it never went back up all the way, just stayed partly closed with her improbably black eyelashes curling up, lending her an eerie resemblance – one I recognized even then – to my mother after one too many evening ryes), the left eye would begin to close, and the hitch of the cheek continued, so that by the time she winked with her left eye she looked demented. It was a relief when that one returned to normal.

Her next trick was a sort of proto-yawn, with eyes closed (usually they didn't close simultaneously; we're talking serious Uncanny Valley here). Then her eyes hitched to the left, and her lips compressed. Jowls appeared, and a sort of uh-oh-what-have-I-done expression. But she snapped out of that and back to happy-neutral pretty quick, closed her eyes, and smiled. That expression reminded me of pictures of saints, usually just as they were about to die.

Her eyes would then pop open, and be crossed.

That was the last expression, and of course my favourite. Then the cycle began again, with several awkward, stiff

pumps of her arm. There was an inescapably jerky, masturba-
tory quality to the action.

I knew that because I'd seen the boy next door mastur-
bate. Bob was vastly old, thirteen. About a week after Saucy
came into my life, he got me to take off my pants and show
him my places, and after we'd gone through this a few times
he asked me if I wanted to see his.

I didn't, but I didn't say so.

And that's when I saw this masturbation thing for the first
time.

Before these incidents, I'd been an enthusiastic little mas-
turbator myself, although I didn't know that's what I was
doing. I'd straddle my spool-carved maple bed's footboard and
ride it until my hair was damp with sweat. I had an image in
my mind of a big field full of beautiful, giant flowers. The
flowers opened and opened and opened, under a lovely soft
blue sky.

I stopped that after the boy next door started looking at my
parts. I didn't like riding any more. And after seeing him mas-
turbate I stopped remembering that I'd ever done anything
like ride the bed or think of flowers.

I told my mother what had happened with Bob, and she
said not to tell anybody, especially my father, and to stop playing with him. So, the next time Bob asked me to play with
him I said I was busy. Playing with dolls was better.

Soon after, Saucy's face grew stiffer. It became harder to
make her change. And one of the cats got at her and left
bite marks all over her soft, rubbery face. Her hair grew
matted, and her dress became grubby. I will never know
what possessed me to bring her to Grade One Show and
Tell.

Maybe it was because I always forgot. The very first Show and Tell day, I was alerted to the fact too late, after my father had already delivered me, terribly early, on his way to work – just like he did every morning, and I'd stand around in the rain or cold or sun or whatever, because in those days teachers kept the school barricaded against all children until ten minutes to nine – so there I was watching all the other kids arrive, and all of them carried toys, including the horrible spectacle of Jessica, the rich girl, whose rapaciousness was legendary, with a stuffed panda bigger than she was. I felt literally sick. I'd forgotten Show and Tell day. Jessica had a giant fucking *panda* And then my scrabbling mind remembered that I was wearing my ring. I wore it every day – my mainland grandparents had given it to me. So, that day, I showed the ring. It wasn't a giant panda but it was something.

The second time I forgot Show and Tell (I want to say it was every Wednesday but I'd be making that up), I tried the ring again.

"You already showed and telled that," Jessica said.

"Yeah," said Monty, and I felt betrayed, because I'd thought Monty was my friend.

"I forgot," I mumbled, and sat back down, face hot and red.

Maybe I brought Saucy that third Show and Tell because she happened to be near the door as my father hustled me out to the car, and I happened to remember. It seems unlikely. There was no earthly reason I'd ever remember Show and Tell. I had trouble remembering that kind of thing, and my parents weren't into remembering for me. Maybe she wanted to go to school with me and somehow planted the suggestion in my mind, although telepathy wasn't one of her powers that I was aware of.

In any case, she came with me and I showed her.

"What happened to her face?" Monty, faithless friend, pointed at Saucy's mutilated visage.

"My cat," I whispered.

"She's ugly!" Jessica jeered. This week, she'd brought a doll almost as tall as me, with white-blond hair, a red dress trimmed with silver lace, and a rhinestone necklace.

"Saucy Doll! I have one of those!" screeched Heather Two (there were four Heathers in our class and three Cathys).

"So do I, and so does my cousin!" shrieked Cathy Three.

"Yes, Heather, Jessica, Monty, Cathy, we let every person have their show and tell and don't interrupt," said the teacher.

It shook me a bit that Heather Two and Cathy Three and Cathy Three's cousin had one. I'd thought I was the only person in all of Newfoundland with a Saucy Doll. But hey, I was up in front of forty-five beady-eyed kids and I'd better show and tell.

It went very well because of the faces. Everyone really liked the last one, the cross-eyed one, and because I was so nervous and wrenched Saucy through them at breakneck speed, everyone insisted that I do it all a second time, and when I was done it raised a general cheer.

I realized the second time around that I went through the faces myself as Saucy did them. Weird. Luckily nobody could see that because I kept my head down.

And luckily nobody noticed that I didn't tell the story of how I got Saucy. She'd just appeared in my life. I had no memory of opening a box and finding her, no memory of a parent or grandparent making some comment about her, or a brother trying to steal her or write on her face with a marker. Only the cat seemed to have noticed her.

She was not and then she was in my life. Kind of how she showed up at school for Show and Tell.

But maybe there was no real mystery to it. Like I said, I had trouble remembering all kinds of things. I forgot, then, to bring her home. She lived in my classroom cubbyhole for weeks. Occasionally, at recess or lunch, I'd reach in and pump her arm, taking her through her paces. She got even stiffer. Her right eye was permanently half-closed, despite my attempts at dolly physio, a fruitless nudging of it with my finger.

Finally one day she just stuck, in a terrible no-expression expression, in between.

I shoved her behind a bunch of stuff and forgot her.

Things kept going downhill after that. Suffice it to say that Monty's defection was just the beginning; soon, anybody who'd ever been nice to me or even just tolerated my presence at school turned on me.

Every now and again, at recess, a crowd of girls would form and take me to the bathroom where they made me stick my head in a toilet and lick the water like a dog, while Jessica and all of the Heathers and two of the Cathys looked on. That lasted for the rest of Grade One and most of Grade Two, when it fell out of fashion, and instead I spent my recesses watching them eat my lunch. They made requests. If I didn't come with what they wanted they'd kick and slap me. It was hard to pro-cure store-bought stuff because my parents didn't give me money for that kind of thing. I became adept at stealing small amounts of change. And my grades dropped because I was hungry. So that was recess.

At lunchtime people mostly just left me alone. It was a relief. I'd read. I had little else to do, my lunch having already been consumed by the others.

In Grade Six Monty shoved me into the boys' bathroom and made me suck his dick.

But Grade Six isn't forever. Right?

◀ ▶

Twenty years later here I was, fundraising for breast cancer research. Twenty years of my life felt as small and far away as a foreign city viewed through the small end of a telescope. Finishing school, university in Toronto, various arts admin jobs that I never liked as well as I should have, a string of liaisons with people I never cared about as much as I should have. My mother's breast cancer diagnosis. Flying home on the negative momentum of a job contract ending and the demise of yet another bad-boyfriend "relationship." And then my mother died. It gutted me.

I joined the dragon boat team, I came to the dance, and now I was walking down a dark hallway, the sound of merriment fading behind me. I had never been in the building at night before. It gave the whole place a hallucinatory quality, like the midpoint in a horror movie.

I started at the Grade Six end of the building, and worked my way down the hall, peering through the windows of the classroom doors. Grade Six, Grade Five, Grade Four, all in a row. They had a room, empty now, labelled LIBRARY. That was an improvement; when I'd gone to school, we'd had only a pitiful selection of books in each individual classroom.

There was a drinking fountain, weirdly low on the wall. Right. We'd been shorter.

Past the entrance to the gym. "Car Wash," disco lights flashing warm into the empty hallway. I heard Marnie and the others laughing and shrieking. Three more classrooms to go.

Grade Two, then Grade Three, which had always, weirdly, been out of sequence. The horrible desks had been replaced by tables and detachable chairs. Evidently class sizes had diminished – well, of course they had; that's one of the reasons this place was getting torn down. No children any more, like some child-collecting Pied Piper had drained our entire society.

It was the work of a moment to approach the door of my Grade One classroom, grasp the knob, find it unlocked, and walk inside.

It looked the same. Same desks, with chairs attached. The room was crammed full of them, just as in my day when there were over forty of us in one class. This room, unlike the others, hadn't been updated.

There was a lesson still on the board: math. Additions and subtractions.

At the back still ranged the row of hooks for our coats, and stacks of cubbyholes where we'd stash our lunches and such every day.

My cubbyhole had been the one on the bottom around the corner. A mobile chalkboard had been shoved across it; I pulled it out, dislodging a warren's worth of dust bunnies, got down on my knees, and peered into the darkness of the cubby.

It was full, and I took each item out, holding it up to the faint pulsing disco light to see: two textbooks, a pencil, a sweater and a pair of pink socks just the right size for an undersized girl around age six, some discarded lunch bags, an apple that had seen better days, a yellow mitten. I remembered that mitten. My aunt had knit me the pair and I'd promptly lost one, and felt so guilty that I'd kept the survivor in the cubby, where it tortured my conscience every time I looked at it.

I dug around some more. A book I'd brought from home: *Where the Wild Things Are*. Loved that book. The wrappers to a Flakie and a Butterfinger: plunder for the other kids.

At the very back, something hard and round, the size of a large grapefruit, with something attached to it that felt like a Brillo pad. I hauled on it and the other stuff shifted and slid.

Saucy's head, followed by her body.

Even in the shuddering light from the gym I could see how ugly she was. Her arm was raised in a left-handed Heil Hitler salute and there was dirt smeared across her pocked face. Right eye half-closed, mouth tense in the beginning of some kind of grimace.

I took her hand and pumped her arm, knowing she was broken, but what the hell.

Her face moved! Twenty years of neglect had returned the powers of movement to Saucy.

Some part of my brain was, of course, trying to deal with the utter impossibility of this cubbyhole being full of my stuff, and an apple that had seen better days but not *over twenty years* of better days. Most of me was looking at Saucy and her weird, wide, preternaturally blue eyes.

Look left. Look right. Wink right. Wink left, and grimace. Yawn, look left, uh-oh-what-have-I-done? Happy-neutral-pretty. Closed eyes: saint. Pop open: crossed eyes.

I almost laughed.

I took her through the sequence again.

When I got to the yawn, I yawned too. And then remembered how I'd realized that day at Show and Tell, the day before everything got even worse, that I mirrored Saucy's face when she went through her sequence. And I was doing it again now, and I hadn't even noticed. I mirrored the doll, or did the doll mirror me? On what sick cellular level were Saucy and I communing?

The song in the gym had changed to "Tonight's the Night." Rod Stewart's hoarse voice rang down the hall, singing the creepy, happy lyrics.

I pumped Saucy's arm in time to the music. Might as well go through it again. Third time's the charm, as Gandalf said.

As our eyes rolled to the left, the room flooded with light.

And I remembered the spool bed. Remembered riding it. Man, I used to ride that thing. Kid pleasure, nothing attached to it, no outcomes, no shame, except I suppose I knew not to do it in front of anybody. How could I have forgotten that?

Mechanically, I kept the doll's arm in motion. Her mouth clicked, my lips snapped closer together. The light died, and the music got quieter as well. It wasn't "Tonight's the Night." It was Supertramp. Strange to change a song in the middle like that.

The doll's eyes moved right, and so did mine. When they got so far over that it felt like they'd spin around inside my head, there was another flash of light and Supertramp morphed into slidey guitar and harp, an organ, swelling strings. "Tonight's the Night."

I laughed. And remembered flowers: huge, house-sized flowers, opening and opening and opening in an endless vista of unfolding beauty. Pleasure, pleasure, pleasure, on and on as far as the eye could see or the body experience. Falling through pleasure.

Snap.

Saucy stared straight into my eyes. The music dimmed, morphed, was not what I'd thought.

The wink came next, right eye. I knew it. I kept going.

Wink.

Light.

Tonight's the night.

Cathy One had been nice to me. That's right. Nice. She'd been the one to tell the others to stop making me drink the toilet water. That it made them disgusting pigs. She was fearless; she didn't care that they might turn on her. And what's weirder, they *had* stopped. Moved on to the lunches, but whatever.

Snap. Silence. The school was dark now, no music, no disco light, no laughter. I was crouched in the classroom, alone. And I knew that I was truly, profoundly alone. The world had stopped turning. I felt certain that if I put the doll down and went to the gym, there'd be nobody there. All would be dark. And if I went out in the world, nobody would be there either. It'd be the seventies again, my childhood, but empty, dark. Between.

I hung onto the doll's damn arm and pumped it. I didn't need to see her; I knew the sequence, could hear her creaking as the skin on her damaged face squeezed, morphed, our cheeks hitching up, right eye opening, left eye closing, that demented wink, the one I hated…

Light, music, tonight's the night. I remembered in Grade Six getting Monty to fuck off with the lunchtime penis-sucking in the boys' washroom. He'd made me do it by threatening me with something, something I couldn't remember. But it had terrified me. Something…telling something he knew about me. Whatever, I couldn't remember. But if I'd just do something for him…and it went on for a while. Maybe a month? I couldn't remember. A month is a long time when you're eleven. And finally I'd gotten him to fuck off with…or had I? It had stopped?

Snap.

Silence.

Creak, creak went the arm.

Yawn.

I yawned right along with the doll, invisible in the darkness.

Tonight's the night.

My ears popped, light flooded the room.

Cathy One and I, kissing. That's what Monty had threatened to tell. That Cathy One and I were dykes. She'd felt so good to kiss, soft, like something, like nibbling something, like flowers. She'd had breasts already, and she not only let me touch them, she wanted me to touch them.

I stayed there for a time, letting that memory wash through me, to Rod Stewart's scratchy voice. Memory, I call it, although it felt like some kind of braided *déjà vu*. There was a life, my life, where I'd never kissed Cathy One and Monty hadn't had to threaten me with anything. No, I'd just been so scared and checked out and unprotected that anyone could make me do anything. And there was another life where he'd threatened me and I'd crumbled. And another where…

Snap.

Uh-oh-what-have-I-done expression. Ugly, ugly doll. Ugly face, one I'd always hated so much I loved it. It fascinated me. Compressing lips, tight, tighter, edges of mouth turning down, eyes looking left, looking wide.

What you have done, Saucy, is pull my life into tonight's the night. There was another story now, *déjà vu*, already seen, one where I told Monty to fuck off and then he'd grabbed my hair and smashed my head off the sink. My head had rung and there'd been stars, but I'd twisted around and punched him in the balls, hard, really hard, three times, until he'd let go of my hair and folded onto the floor, staring at me, hands between his legs.

"Touch me again and I'll cut it off," and I'd walked backwards out of the boys' bathroom, and I'd never had to go in there again.

"She's crazy," Monty had told everybody but I didn't care, because Cathy One and I were friends, forever.

Snap.

Saint.

She'd died. I didn't want this thing, this memory or, or whatever it was. Bullshit story, alternate universe, whatever anyone wanted to call it. All gay people have to have tragic lives or something? Bullshit. But it wouldn't go away, tonight's the night. She'd died, something, what? Car accident, that was it. Her family had had an open casket and my mother had brought me to the funeral and said, "You don't have to look." I could tell she was disturbed, thought Cathy One's family must be crazy, but I'd understood why when I saw Cathy's mother standing by the coffin, stroking and stroking Cathy's hair. It was so you'd understand that she was truly dead.

Didn't really look like Cathy. Cathy never really was that much of a saint. A car accident couldn't kill her. But when I saw that smiling, closed-eye saint in the box, I knew she was dead.

Snap.

Silence. And dark.

Did I want to go on? The eyes of the doll would open crossed. Doubles, blurs, lack of distinction, everything bleeding into everything else. Maybe I could just stay here, in this place where I'd had a friend, and she'd died, and yes I'd been fucked up and fucked around but I'd pushed back too. I'd been able to find pleasure too. The flower had kept opening.

That was better; this was better, this place, right? I liked this story better.

Tonight's the night.

When the light and music flooded in, I looked down and yeah, the doll's eyes were crossed. But mine weren't. I could see just fine. I could hear that song, "Tonight's the Night." It had just started. I knew Marnie would probably dance, in a friendly fashion, with one of the guys, both of them hamming it up because Marnie was funny that way, could make you laugh.

Marnie made *me* laugh.

As one said, when a child, *I like you. Want to be friends?*

Meaning, *When I'm around you I want to get to know you, better and better and better. You are more interesting than anybody else on the face of this earth. I think of you all the time, whether you are around or not. You make me scared and happy. I want to show you things and I want to tell you things.*

I walked out of the empty classroom, down the hall to the gym. I found Marnie, sitting on the side with her rainbow-socked feet, and I asked her to dance to that slow, terrible, ridiculous, unsuitable tonight's the night song, and she said yes. I sat in an ordinary chair next to her decorated one with wheels, and we put our arms around each other, and we danced.

THE DIE

Meagan Whan

It might've been overlooked if not for the way the sun shimmered on its surface. Elizabeth stuffed her toonie gardening gloves into the back pocket of her skinny jeans. Plucking it from a spade full of fragrant dark earth, she held it between thumb and forefinger as if it were a jewel, tilting her head back to let light under the brim of her hat. After a moment, she realized it was an unnatural diamond-shaped die: twelve facets, six upper and six lower.

Elizabeth tucked the die into her blouse pocket. She finished planting the pansies, then dusted off the front garden's wooden border. She collected a pile of flattened pizza boxes, tucking them under her arm, and grabbed a stack of disposable red cups. A stray flip-flop hooked over her pinkie, she backed into the door, forcing it open.

She dropped the load onto the kitchen table, the last furnishing from the building's previous life as a home, before the Victorian had been vivisected into eight bedrooms and a communal living space. Her stomach rumbled. She washed her hands, patted them dry, and searched in vain for a piece of fruit. The only other option was toast, which would mean opening the colicky fridge; any disturbance sent it into a fit of growling hacks.

Madison shuffled into the kitchen in a pair of slippers, yoga pants and tangerine bra. Her phone peeped out from her cleavage. An earbud trailed against Madison's shoulder; Elizabeth heard the tinny voice of a man lecturing about proper patient restraint.

Madison munched from a bag of trail mix, while surfing horoscopes on her phone. She flopped down at the table, tossing a handful of mix into her mouth. "I don't know how you can be out there in this heat."

"I'm going to make the place respectable," Elizabeth said.

"Impossible."

"Habitable then."

Madison glanced at Elizabeth. "Running-from-the-paparazzi hat, Jackie O glasses, I know what that shit means."

Elizabeth bent closer to the junk she'd brought in. She hadn't meant to be so obvious, had thought her application of concealer artful. "Is this your flip flop? Speak now or forever lose it."

Madison shrugged. "It's probably Shelby's, she's tossing from her most recent Chris bust-up."

At least she and Jake didn't break up every time they disagreed.

Madison frowned. "Should we lock the doors?"

It wasn't Jake's fault he couldn't handle alcohol; she should've known better than to argue with him when he'd been drinking. Elizabeth threw the flip-flop into the bottom of the big metal garbage can, and swept everything else, everyone's trash inside, burying the lonely sole.

"We could change the locks – that would be an excellent thing to do," Madison said.

Elizabeth bristled. "Jake wouldn't hurt people. I know he'll sober up." Except he had hurt her, a small voice said, but he'd make amends for the punch. "He always does."

"Yeah, perfect, Elizabeth. If I were you, the next time you hear 'Libby. Libby, baby,'" she shook her head, dislodging the earbud, "I'd borrow my brother's baseball bat."

"It's complicated."

"Emptiest response in the English language," Madison said, shoving her chair. She gripped the chair back, the skin under her nails blooming from white to pink. "Do you want anything from my tote bag pharmacy?"

"I want your trail mix."

◀ ▶

Elizabeth's second-floor bedroom overlooked the sliver of a backyard. A sickle moon shone through the naked window, highlighting the bruise she studied in the dresser mirror.

Thick blond hair and dimpled chin, envy of all who'd seen him. The ghost of high school she'd never escaped: full of quick compliments and quicker moods, qualities part of the Rubik's Cube known as Jake. He seemed a part of her, as much as the shape of her eyes or the crooked curve of her foot. She pressed a package of peas to her face; the magical relief of numbness spread through her cheek.

Elizabeth had meant to take out the die at supper to show everyone, but it seemed too personal, almost equal to flashing. Using a Kleenex, she cleaned off the twelve facets. Roman numerals were etched onto the black surface. A book on the fundamentals of HTML balanced on her lap; she spun the die as if it were a top. It whirled around and around, a tiny black storm cell.

The die fell over with a noticeable click. It reminded her of the acceptance of a key, the turn of a lock.

Elizabeth, padding down the hall, glanced at Madison's open door.

"Beth." Jake hopscotched in the doorway, trying to get into his jeans, his boxers unbuttoned. "It didn't mean anything." He gave up on the pants, jeans pooling around his ankles. His hands, smelling of soap and roses, reached out to cradle her face. Bewildered, she backed into the stair rail.

"What happened to your cheek, Beth?"

"How drunk are you?" she whispered.

Madison slunk into the doorway in a tangerine baby doll. "It wasn't personal." Light glinted off a crystal stud in her left nostril. She gave Jake a push into the hall, flashed her teeth, and slammed the door.

Elizabeth blanched, dropping the die; it thumped dully against the hallway carpeting.

◀ ▶

Madison's door was still closed. Elizabeth glanced around the now empty hall. She touched her forehead and cheeks, expecting to feel either intense cold or intense heat; her skin felt normal. A small cry escaped her. She sat on the carpet, back against the stair railing, head hanging between her knees. The position made her shoulders ache. Blood rushed to her crown. Head pulsing, Elizabeth got up and turned Madison's doorknob.

Glass shattered. The neck of a beer bottle rolled across the floor banging against the leg of the bed; the broken body of the bottle spun. Elizabeth stepped across the threshold, flicking on the lamp over the desk. A notched baseball bat lay across a trio of dusty anatomy books and a stack of tarot cards. She touched the smooth grain of the bat's shaft; Madison didn't have a nose ring; Madison wasn't here. Above the desk, a city map had been tacked to the corkboard, circles marked in blue pen, stars marked in red pen. Newspaper clippings, web printouts, matte photographs were taped to the wall, a shrine to an obsession.

A photograph caught her eye. She ripped it down, angling the photo under the light. The quality was poor, taken from a surveillance camera in a bus or train station, but she recognized him. "Jake." The beard under his lip was thicker, bangs shaggier. He didn't seem like the Jake in the boxers who had been in Madison's room, or her Jake either.

She stepped back, scanning the wall, finding her own photo. Wild hair, cagey eyes; it was the kind of photograph seen in a tabloid, the late-night news, a wanted poster. Elizabeth forced her gaze to the hallway, which still looked the same and to the die, lying where she'd dropped it. She touched the upward facing facet; it felt different, warmer, as if it had a heart of coal.

She couldn't handle looking back in that room. She flipped the die in the air, catching it in her palm.

◄ ►

A kazoo went off. Music was playing. She stared down into a hive of activity on the first floor. They'd appeared so quickly? But no, she was the one who'd suddenly appeared. Balloons floated freely among the partygoers. As she descended the stairs, she saw Chris's teammates, dressed as servers, carrying trays of sewing needles. Someone popped a balloon; sparkling silver confetti misted the air, catching in her hair and eyelashes. A placard on the end table read: Happy Engagement Shelby & Chris!! The announcement was bookended by photos of the happy couple. An explosion of green confetti fell over her. Shelby and Chris got happiness and what did she get?

Elizabeth's gaze caught Madison's. An overwhelming sense of wrongness, of displacement, filled her. She pushed her way through the crowd, running to the front door. The balloons continued to pop. Crimson sparkles lit her fleeing back.

Her pansies didn't exist. The front garden didn't exist; it had been filled in with crushed white stones. Elizabeth nearly stumbled into the street when Madison emerged from the house. An orange tulle fascinator bobbed on her head. "Wait. Do you know me?"

"Do you know me?" Elizabeth asked.

"Lizzy."

"Madison."

"No, I'm Elizabeth."

"No, I'm Maddy."

"You're not from here."

"You're not from here."

"I found this   "

"—in the garden."

"In the cadaver. And I knew—"

"—knew it was mine," Elizabeth said.

The die on Maddy's palm was identical to Elizabeth's, yet she knew if they were to fall together, she would somehow be able to identify her own.

"What's happening? What is this place? Do you know?"

"Don't you? Twelve is a perfect number, the product of the Earth multiplied by the Heavens. This is just one side. Where did you start?" Maddy asked.

"I don't know."

"Neither do I."

"But you stayed here."

Maddy's hand balled into a fist. "She doesn't live in this place, not this Maddy; she's on a different track. And I've been afraid, so afraid. Too afraid to cast the die."

"You must want to go home. Twelve is a finite number, not like pi."

Maddy shook her head. She pulled Elizabeth into a hug. "We were never friends on my side, and we're not really friends here. What about…"

"Sort of."

"I hope there's a side where we're really truly friends." She let Elizabeth go. "Good luck."

Elizabeth rolled the die.

◀ ▶

The pansies were the first thing Elizabeth noticed, even before the absence of music, the absence of Maddy. Her pansies, evidence of life in the dirt. Her heart constricted, as she stepped into the kitchen, silent in the way of sleeping places. She tugged open the fridge and it gave a shivering hack. Home; her heart beat.

Elizabeth ventured into the living room. The first-floor lights were out, but the recessed ones in the upper hallway glowed softly. She sighed, and then cursed as she stepped on something. A business card poked into her foot, sticking up at an angle from the floorboard. It was for a New Age shop on Queen Street. She tried to remember it, couldn't quite, and then did. Madison had started work there, a few days ago.

An argument erupted in the upper hallway. She instinc-
tively retreated into the deeper shadows. Jake's voice, slurred
with drink. Her own voice, tempered with exhaustion.
Elizabeth didn't belong, not here; she'd been wrong. A part of
her wanted to see them, needed to see them; she'd leave in a
minute, maybe two. They were treading heavily in the hallway,
moving quickly. The pitch of their voices rose into a mingled
screaming. Elizabeth feared stepping too far into the light.

It happened too fast. Elizabeth couldn't be sure: acciden-
tal or intentional. She saw herself tumble, thudding down the
stairs. Sprawled with a loud crack at the foot. Head turned at
an impossible angle. Jake slumped at the top of the stairs. He
wept, the sound too coarse to be a comfort.

Elizabeth gasped. A five-year-old boy whimpered and
crawled out from behind a chair. Barefoot, he was dressed in
Spider-Man PJs. A toy car fell from one hand.

The boy stared at Elizabeth. She hesitated. She was in the
shape of his eyes, the crooked curve of his feet. She held her
arms open and he came running. He smelled of bath time and
grape popsicles.

"Those were always my favourite," she said.

Her hands fisted. They were empty except for the business card. She pawed at the ground, though she knew she
wouldn't have put the die down.

The boy touched her forehead, her ears, and her cheeks
methodically, as if looking for the zipper.

Jake would conquer his shock, soon. She saw the rest of
the story unfolding: distraught young man kills wife, then
child, before taking his own life. Elizabeth drew an afghan off
the couch to cover the boy's head, to protect him from the
scene. He clung to her neck as she backed away. A few more

steps and she'd be in the kitchen; then there'd be the door, and then freedom. His bare, pretty, crooked foot bumped a vase Elizabeth didn't recognize. She counted to ten under her breath.

"Liz." Jake loped down the stairs two at a time and skidded around the body, sliding on sweaty feet. "Liz."

His blond hair was shorn; the cut made his face severe. He reached out, hesitantly, as if he thought her a spectre.

"Stay away."

"You can't take him." Jake's eyes glistened. "It's not right. We need to be together."

Elizabeth eased backwards. "No."

"It's okay, Liz-Bear. I can make it right. I know what to do. I can do it too," he said, eyes shining with a maniacal love.

Elizabeth ran.

"Wait for me, Liz-Bear, I'm coming with you!"

She kicked open the kitchen door and shot into the street. The afghan fluttered in the oncoming headlights. Brakes squealed. A taxi driver cursed her while she shoved the boy into the backseat. "Drive," she cried, throwing herself in beside the boy.

The driver hit the gas. "Women's shelter?"

She couldn't focus, thoughts scattering like billiard balls.

"What's your name?" she asked the boy.

He wagged a finger at her. "You know."

Elizabeth supposed she did have a relative idea, and she knew then where they were headed; looking at the orange font on the business card, she told the driver to take them to Queen Street. Maybe luck was with her and she'd landed in the world where she and Madison were really truly friends. She watched Jake disappear from view in the mirror and didn't miss him.

THE FOOD OF MY PEOPLE

Candas Jane Dorsey

Reenie's dad worked on the rigs. Before the accident he was only home one week in six or eight. He was working so they could have a good future, Reenie's mom said. Reenie loved him dearly but sort of the same way she loved certain library books she took out from the Bookmobile when it came around, but knew she couldn't keep forever, that she had to share with the others whose dates were stamped in the back by Jan the librarian.

Right after the accident, Reenie was only allowed to see him through a glass window, where he lifted two fingers in a tiny wave, and Reenie would spread her fingers on the glass and watch the bandaged stranger with a nervous smile. Reenie's mom could go in the room, with special clothes on. But they didn't go very often, because Reenie's mom, Lori, had to work at the dollar store.

Lori took her hand one day and they went over to the next door of the row house where they lived, and Lori rang the doorbell.

"Hang on, I'm coming!" The door opened, and Reenie looked up with awe at the woman in the calf-length cotton pants and the floral top. She'd never seen anyone as big around as she was tall like that. Lori was tiny – Reenie was already almost up to her shoulder, and, Lori said, gaining on her every day – and thin as a rail, and wore thin jeans, cowboy boots and shirts with little pearl snaps that Reenie loved to touch and, since she went to school, to count. Lori said when Reenie was a big girl she could have one of them shirts. This big woman wore what seemed like enough flowered chintz to make a sail and float her away.

"Well, hi there!" the woman said, looking down at Reenie, then up at her mom.

"I'm Lori Gervais from next door," her mom said.

"Everybody calls me Cubbie, at least everybody polite." The woman laughed out loud, at which certain parts of her shook in an alarming way, as if there was something alive under her skin. Reenie shrank behind her mom and held on tight.

"I was wondering if you knew someone who could take care of my girl at noon and after school while I go to work?"

The woman – Cubbie – looked down at her and smiled. "Hello, Renée, honey," she said, and Reenie went cold with a mixture of fear and delight. Not even Lori called her by her real name. She thought nobody but her and her mama and daddy knew it. And how did *the lady* know it?

"Reenie's daddy is French," said Lori. "Say hello to Mrs. Cubbie."

"Just Cubbie," said Cubbie. "My husband was Jake Cubb, godrestisoul, but since I been looking like a beach ball, I been called Cubbie by everybody, adult, child or dog."

"Hello, Cubbie," Reenie – Renée – said bravely. "I'm six."

"Well, that's a wonder," said Cubbie, smiling at her, and then to Lori, "She can come to me."

"I can't pay you much," said Lori, looking aside.

"I don't want your money," said Cubbie. "Noon hour don't work for me, so you send Renée to school with her lunch in a bag. When she gets home she can come right here. Make me a sugar pie now and again, we'll call it even."

There was some back-and-forth about that, but by the time it was over they found themselves sitting at Cubbie's kitchen table, eating homemade doughnuts rolled in cinnamon and table sugar. Lori was telling Cubbie about the dollar store.

Renée had no idea that people made doughnuts. She thought they came from Tim Horton.

That was the start of it.

◄ ►

The next day, Reenie's mom walked her to school like always. "Now you eat your lunch in the lunchroom, and remember to go next door to Auntie Cubbie when you go home."

Reenie remembered.

That day Cubbie said they were going to put together a jig-saw puzzle. Cubbie showed Renée a box with little bits of picture jumbled up inside, with some of the pieces upside down, and some of them with their little stubby fingers tangled up with each other. Then she showed the lid, and said how the jumbly bits all fit together and made that picture that was on the lid.

The whole idea was amazing to Renée. How did she get almost halfway to the age of seven without hearing about this thing?

"Don't you have them in that school you go to?" Cubbie asked.

Renée tried to explain about the school kind of puzzle, with only ten or twenty-six pieces, made of wood, no box-with-a-picture-on, and educational.

"Don't look so sad. Not your fault that school is kinda backward!" Cubbie laughed and jiggled. "These ones are what regular people do, not educational so much."

Not only did Cubbie have a whole cupboard full, some of them in old, worn boxes with old-fashioned pictures on them, but she had a special felt cloth she put on the table before-hand. "Got it from Sara Martin." Renée knew she meant the Sara Martin catalogue from which Lori got the set of three nesting stainless steel bowls, and the special support bra for well-endowed women to prevent backache and that would last for five years guaranteed.

"You choose the picture you like," said Cubbie. Renée put her finger on a big red dot with no detail.

"That one's a little tough for a starter," said Cubbie, "and I usually save it for a special time. You never know when you might have a tricky problem, and if nothing else, making one of these clears your thoughts. But for a first-timer with noth-ing much on her mind, you best pick something a mite easier."

Renée picked a puppy dog in a basket, and fell into a trance of shape and colour until Cubbie said, "That's enough for today." She rolled the whole puzzle up in the tablecloth, presto, and tucked it up on the shelf above the puzzles, push-ing back a crocheted afghan in pink, yellow and lime green. "I bet you're hungry."

They went behind the kitchen island and Cubbie showed Renée how to make Jell-O. She wouldn't let Renée near the hot water but, after the ice cubes were in, Cubbie let her stir it. The Jell-O was orange. Cubbie mixed in a can of fruit cocktail, and put it all in a fancy copper dish she called a mold. Renee loved how the ice made a flat little tinkle against the Jell-O mold, but even more she loved how when the Jell-O was hardened and turned out on the plate, the fruit cocktail pieces floated in an orange sky, a sky that jiggled like Cubbie's laughing folds and tasted like Kool-Aid.

The next day when Lori dropped Reenie off at school, they both went to the office. "I hear you got Frenchimmersion here," said Lori. "Reenie's daddy is French and I want to put her in that." The principal called another teacher from outside the door, a fancy-looking lady with dyed hair. This was the Frenchimmersion teacher, call-me-Madame, who looked at Reenie's admission card and said, in a voice with the same music in it as her dad's voice, "So, Renée, you wan' to come wit' us an' learn *français*, eh?"

"Yes, ma'am," said Renée. So from that day on she went to Madame's classroom, and things got strange. She had to do everything *en français*. Count, ask to go to the bathroom, everything. Some of the kids knew how *parler français* real good, but Renée was, like most, slow and stumbly.

"I don't want to go," she said to Cubbie. "Two kids make fun of me. I was smart in my other class. I got all correct on my worksheet. I got to work on the computer. In French-immersion they only have three computers at the back, and we have to sit around in a circle and talk *Français*. I hate it."

"Why do you think your mom put you in there?" Cubbie said, not mean, not agreeing with Renée or disagreeing, just asking. Renée shook her head, trying not to cry.

"Well, tell you what, honey," Cubbie went on. "You sit down there with some of this delicious Jell-O and finish off that puzzle, and think on the answer."

Cubbie unrolled the puzzle, with its finished edges and mysterious middle, and Renée was so instantly absorbed that she hardly noticed how she finished her Jell-O.

There was one piece with two fingers of pink and the rest of it white. It reminded her of her father, in his peculiar suit of bandages. She laid the piece down in the centre space and started looking for another white and pink piece. She thought about how her father would come home from the rigs and call for her by her real name. He'd say what he always said, "*Viens-tu, ma petite chou!*" and when she came running, he'd call out, "*Bonjour, bonjour, ma petite Renée.*" He'd lift her up so she could see over his shoulder to the top of the fridge, that magic secret place only her dad could reach. His tattooed arms were strong and he'd bounce her up and down until she shrieked.

Wait a minute. Here was another pink bit. It was the puppy's nose! And Renée remembered that the teacher said, "*Bonjour*" too. "*Bonjour*" was *français* and *français* was French… "*Ma petite chou*" was "*My little darling…*"

A little white puppy sat in a nasty pink basket. Renée liked the puppy, but if she had a puppy like that, she'd let it sleep on her pillow, not put it in a basket like an Easter egg. The puzzle was done and Renée's dish was empty.

"Cubbie, can I have more Jell-O? *S'il vous plaît?*"

Cubbie laughed. "See there, *ma petite*, I told you puzzles would help." It turned out that Cubbie knew how to speak French too. Maybe it was just what people did, but nobody knew in her old school, like nobody knew about proper jigsaw puzzles. She had to come to the city for that. So Renée would figure it out, and teach her mother too, and when Daddy got better… but there her thoughts hit a rock and turned aside. She put her nose back into the Jell-O.

Well, it wasn't that easy. Like her mom said: "Reenie, nothing in life comes easy." There was so much to learn all over again. A whole new set of numbers before she could count. A whole new set of words. A bunch of sounds she'd never made before. "Put your mouth like an O and say E," said Madame, which made Renée's mouth sore at first.

Celeste and Marie-Claire ragged on her, but Madame and Lori and Cubbie all said, don't rag back, be a better person. That was easier said than done, as Cubbie would say, but Renée worked at it. The weeks went on, some of them slow, and some fast. Every day Reenie worked at school, then came to Cubbie and played, did a little puzzle, ate some cookies or a piece of pineapple upside-down cake, then went home with Lori.

Sometimes they went on the bus to see Renée's daddy. They had to go a long way in the big hospital, up two elevators. Now they let Reenie in too if she put on the gowns and gloves, but she couldn't hug him. She said, *"Je t'aime, Papa!"* from across the room, and from inside the bandages her daddy said, *"Très bien, ma petite chou! Je t'aime aussi!"* and waved his two pink fingers at her. Lori would say something like, "You stay and tell your dad what you're doing in school. I'm just going to talk to the staff," and Reenie would try to think of a story from school that didn't involve being teased or forgetting *un mot en français*. Sometimes she told him about Cubbie. He would murmur a word or two.

One day he said, "Not much happens here. It's pretty much same old, same old."

After they left, Lori was usually pretty quiet. Reenie could relate to that. She was learning it was better to be quiet when she was worried about something – especially what she was starting to think of as *same-old same-old* worry. Because even worrying got boring sometimes, though she didn't think she could explain that to her mom, so she didn't try.

◄ ►

One Saturday, the doctor met Lori in her dad's room. Lori said, "Reenie, you go sit on that chair outside a minute," and she and the doctor talked in low voices, standing beside her dad's bed. When they were done, Lori came out and said, "Just say hello to your father and then we'll go, kiddo. He's real tired today." So Renée said, "*Je t'aime, Papa!*" in a tiny voice, and her dad waved his fingers at her, and then Lori and Reenie went home.

On Monday, Renée wasn't concentrating and got three wrong on her math sheet. After school she ran to Cubbie's with a sick stomach, and held out the sheet with its red red ink.

"You put that by for now, and let's try to make *crêpes* tonight," Cubbie said. "Maybe if it works out we can make dinner for your mom. Me, I never made these yet, so it's gonna be a special adventure. Meanwhile, you go see what kind of puzzle you want to start up."

Soon she was deep in a picture of a mom in a long blue dress holding a little baby. The lady and the baby had gold plates behind their heads. Reenie was trying to do the border first, like Cubbie taught her, but she had found the face of the mom, so she carefully cleared a place on the felt right around where she thought the face should go. It went on well from there. It was a pretty easy puzzle, actually.

She heard Cubbie say, "You look like you been rode hard and put away wet. You sit down there by Renée and put a few

pieces in that there puzzle." Reenie looked up in surprise to
see Lori, her face tired and flat under her makeup. The metal
legs of the bridge chair scraped on the linoleum as Lori pulled
it out. She sat down at the side of the table with a sigh.

"It's a mom, like you," said Reenie. "Pretty."

Lori laughed. "More famous than me, that's for sure. You
know, we had that picture in church when I was little."

Lori and Ren, Reenie's dad, had had one of their special
discussions about church. Ren said he didn't know what
Reenie's grandparents would have thought if they saw Reenie
was growing up without going to church. Lori said that if he
wanted her to go so bad he could stay home and take her.
Then Ren said that he was working to give them a better life,
and Lori said Reenie was turning out just fine and Ren said
he couldn't argue with that, that's for sure, and they went
back to cooking hot dogs on the grill. That was back home in
Fahler; well, back in their *old* home. This was home now.

"Fahler's the honey capital of Canada," said Renée to
Cubbie.

"Well, that's a wonder," said Cubbie. "You both were born
up there, then?"

"Yep, just a little honey from Fahler," said Lori. "The kids
used to tease me about that until I cried. I was so glad to
shake the dust of that place off my feet, and then damned if
I didn't end up back there with Ren. Pardon my French."

"How come 'pardon my French' means 'sorry I swore'?"
asked Reenie. "Because in Frenchimmersion nobody swears.
Except the teacher said Celeste said a bad thing when she
called me stupid. But Mommy, I *am*..." Reenie's lip trembled
despite herself. She got down and ran to get her backpack.
"Here's my test. I got three wrong. I'm sorry." She began to

sob. Lori reached out and put an arm around her shoulder, gathered her in.

"Those damn kids. Are you crying just because of three wrong in subtraction?"

"I promised…to be good while Daddy was in hospital."

Lori looked up at Cubbie. It seemed to Reenie that Lori didn't know what to say. What Cubbie said didn't really make sense either. "You're not much more than a kid yourself. Give yourself a break."

Lori took Renée's chin and turned her face so they could see each other's eyes. "Reenie, honey, I just didn't want any temper tantrums, I didn't mean you couldn't make a mistake or two. Everybody makes a mistake or two. You shoulda seen me today trying to add up all the stuff this one old lady had in her cart. I had to do it three times. She was mad as he…heck at me, but I got it right in the end. That's all that matters, kiddo."

"Well," said Reenie. "That's a wonder." She wiped her eyes and nose on her sleeve. "Okay. You gonna help me with my jig-saw?"

Lori laughed her little laugh, more like a snort. "You don't like the weather, wait five minutes," she said.

"Cubbie's making *crêpes*."

"I haven't had *crêpes*" – her mom said it more like *craypse* – "since I was knee-high to a grasshopper. My granny used to make them."

"Well, it's my first time, so don't expect granny quality," said Cubbie. "But it's worth a try. All else fails, we'll have a Kraft Dinner."

"I never tried to make them myself, me," Lori said, rummaging in the box for blue dress pieces. "They hard?"

The upshot was that Renée finished her puzzle alone while Cubbie and Lori learned how to make *crêpes*.

When it was time, Cubbie let Reenie set the yellow Arborite kitchen table. Reenie put out the pink plastic place mats and carried three sets of knives and forks – Cubbie called them "silverware" and they were brighter and paler than the knives and forks Lori had got from the dollar store. Then they all sat down and ate the *crêpes*. They were basically to pancakes what Lori was to Cubbie, and then with stuff all wrapped up in them. They were good.

"Reenie's named after her daddy," Lori said between bites. "His name is René too, without the extra 'e' at the end. But everybody calls him Ken." Reenie didn't know that. She sat very quietly. "Ken's in the burn unit over at the University Hospital. He got caught in a blowout. He was lucky. The other three didn't make it."

Reenie didn't understand that. "Like I didn't make three questions on my arithmetic?"

"That's not what I meant, hon," said Lori.

"What did you mean?"

Lori looked at Cubbie. Finally she said, "It means they were too badly hurt, sweetie. They died."

Renée didn't ask out loud. Was Ken going to die?

◄ ►

The next day after school it was time to choose a new puzzle. Reenie was looking at the pictures, and she was trying to choose between some dogs dressed up in people clothes, and a Where's Waldo, when Cubbie came up behind her.

"I think you should start on this one today," she said, reaching up to a higher shelf of the puzzle closet. She handed

Renée a puzzle box that had "1000 PIECES" printed on the side.

"That's a lot of pieces," said Reenie.

"One thousand," said Cubbie. "But if you put your mind to it, you can do it all right."

The picture on the box was of some people working. There were a lot of pipes and rails around them. A lot of the puzzle was different colours of grey. "It looks hard," said Reenie.

"It is hard," said Cubbie. "If things were different, maybe you could work up to it slower, but from what your mom said last night, we don't have that kind of time."

"Can you help me?"

Cubbie shook her head. "No, honey. If I helped you, it wouldn't work, and you don't want that."

"I guess not."

"Trust me, honey, that's the right answer. Just start the way I showed you, with the edges first. It's just one piece at a time, just like the other ones."

The edges of this jigsaw were just as hard as the middles of other puzzles. By the end of the first day she hadn't even found all the edge pieces, and the parts that she had found and put together didn't join up. When Lori came, Reenie went home dispiritedly, and after their dinner, bologna and cheese sandwiches because Lori was tired, Reenie did homework. They had started multiplication, which had a special chant with it called the times tables. She had to write out her one- and two- and three-times tables. She suddenly realized when she got to the threes that there was a pattern that made them easier and easier. She took a new piece of paper and wrote them out in good.

"Look, Mom!" she said. "They're pretty!"

"That's good, kiddo," said Lori. Reenie put her homework in her backpack.

Lori hugged her. "See, you'll be acing that arithmetic stuff in no time."

"Mom, it's called *mathematiques!*"

"Kid, it's called bedtime."

The next afternoon as she sat down to the puzzle table, she saw the piece with the eyes right away. They were just a bit like how her daddy's eyes looked when he smiled down at her. She reached out for the piece. It felt warm. She knew it should go right in the middle. She knew she should finish the border first, but instead she placed the eyes piece in the middle of the felt, and looked back into the box. She remembered the pink pieces of the other puzzle. Would pink pieces in this one be easier to find?

Reenie thought for a minute. She hardly noticed Cubbie bringing her a glass of lemonade. She sipped it while she stirred her finger around in the box. The pieces were all every which way. That wasn't right. There was only a picture on one side. She looked at the table.

"Cubbie, how big is this puzzle? I mean, is it as big as the table?"

"Oh, no, there's plenty of room around a puzzle that size." Cubbie went back to her baking. It was chocolate chip day, but Renée hadn't even remembered to ask for batter. She got up on her knees on the chair and leaned over the table.

"You be careful you don't tip over!" Cubbie called from the sink without even looking.

"Well, that's a wonder!" Renée said to herself, but she didn't get down. She tilted the box and carefully poured out all the pieces onto the table. Then she began to turn all of them over onto their cardboard backs so the colours faced up. As she did, she looked for the face-coloured pieces – lots of different face colours from pink like her dad to brown. She put all those pieces over on the left side of where she had put her daddy's eyes, where the middle of the puzzle was going to be.

After a bit, she noticed that she could also sort the other colours into colour families at the same time, grey and black and blue and even some green she hadn't noticed before, so she went back and did that. She also started to put all the edge pieces over on the right edge of the table.

This took a long time. She sat down and sipped her lemonade. Two chocolate chip cookies on a plate had appeared on the other bridge chair when she wasn't looking, so she ate one while she looked at the face pieces.

After the cookie was done, she reached out and finished the middle face. The more she looked at it, the more she thought he looked like her daddy. Then she realized that the green pieces were the colour of his shirt. She remembered from before the accident. He had more than one of those shirts and he wore them every workday. She realized for the first time that there was a patch with his name embroidered into it, René, sewn on just above the left pocket.

The other people had green shirts too, with name patches: "Sam" and "Nadine" and "Jeff." Their faces looked sad to Renée, even though they were smiling. Were they the ones who "didn't make it?" Were they sad because they were dead? Maybe it was Reenie who was sad because they were dead. She would be sad if her dad were dead, that's for sure.

"She's right patient, that one," said Cubbie.

"Reenie is?" said her mom, sounding surprised. Reenie hadn't noticed her come in, but she couldn't stop now. The pieces of the puzzle were starting to make sense. Lori picked up the cookie plate and absently ate the cookie while she started looking for edge pieces. But Reenie kept doing the middle.

"Were Jeff and Nadine and Sam friends of Daddy?" Renée asked as she worked.

"How'd you know that, baby?"

"Says on their shirts," said Renée. "See?"

"Those are a bit like the rig company shirts," said Lori. "But these are blue."

"Green," said Renée.

"So they are," said Lori.

After their tuna melt and soup Renée went to bed early, she was so tired! "Well, that's a wonder!" Lori said, and came and kissed her goodnight. But when she was in bed, in the grey darkness that was never quite black because of all the city lights, Renée couldn't sleep for a while, worrying about stuff.

By Friday Reenie was so tired when she went to school that Lori had to tell her three times to hurry up. Finally Lori grabbed her hand and hurried her along. Why on earth was she such a slowpoke? When it was her turn to answer, Madame had to ask her twice. When Reenie came in to Cubbie's, Cubbie said, "What's your daddy's favourite kind of pie?"

"Saskatoon," said Renée. "Why?"

"While you're finishing that jigsaw, I think I'll bake me a saskatoon pie. You and your mom and I can have a piece when she comes to get you tonight. Can't hurt."

"Can you come talk to me?"

"You just work away there, and I'll work away in here. Pie's kinda labour-intensive."

When her mom came to Cubbie's door, Reenie didn't hear the knock. She was deep into the pieces of her daddy. By supper, Renée had finished all the face and his left arm, but his right arm was only half there, and the legs still weren't done.

Cubbie had added extra macaroni and grated cheese to a Kraft Dinner to make it stretch, and had cut one of the saskatoon pies for their dessert. Reenie could hardly concentrate on finishing her Kraft Dinner for the enticing smell of the pie sitting there above her dinner plate, but she was good and ate every bite of macaroni first.

"We can't keep coming over here to eat," said Lori. "We'll eat you out of house and home."

"If I can't make Kraft Dinner for my friends now and again, it's a pretty poor home," said Cubbie comfortably, clearing the plates to the counter. "Keep your fork."

Renée licked every bit of cheese off the fork before she took the first bite of pie. Usually she liked to start at the crust end and work her way down to the tip, saving the best part for last. But today she very slowly and carefully lined up her fork across the tip so it was perfectly even, then gently pressed. The triangle that tilted onto her fork was as perfect as she could make it. She put it into her mouth and it melted on her tongue as if it were something else besides pie: air or water or blood or *mathematiques*.

"We should go home right after the dishes," said Lori. She was eating her pie the same way, slowly and gently. "I'm sure Reenie has homework."

Before Reenie could protest, Cubbie said, "Let her bide for tonight and work on her puzzle. She's that worried about her dad."

"I am too," said Lori.

After the last bite of the saskatoon pie, Reenie remembered to ask to be excused before she got down and went back to the puzzle on the bridge table. She put three or four pieces in fast, and Lori came and helped her a bit with background, then went off to the kitchen to dry dishes for Cubbie.

There was a really hard part on her dad's right leg that wasn't coming clear. Renée looked through all the pieces that were left. What she needed wasn't there.

"Cubbie, there are some bits missing!"

"Maybe they got stuck in the box," Cubbie said. "Look in the lid too. And check if they fell on the floor."

Reenie found two pieces stuck in the corner of the box lid where it had split a little, and one sticking up from the pile of the shag carpet right by the fern stand beside the puzzle table. That almost did it. Then she found the one with the right thumb on it, on the floor way over underneath the coffee table. Now how did it get there? She imagined it scuttling over on its little puzzle feet while they were having dinner. She giggled as she turned it all four ways. There! It fit! That was it for the hand and legs! There were only a few more pieces...

Renée sighed with relief. The puzzle was done. Then she blinked at Lori and Cubbie. They were sitting on the couch watching TV. The clock above the couch had both hands pointing to the nine. That was wrong! That was fifteen minutes past her bedtime! Reenie walked over and sat by her mom, drooping against her shoulder.

"My goodness, kiddo, we better get you home!" Lori said. Reenie was so sleepy she wanted her mom to hoist her up, but Lori said, "Oof, you're too big! You have to use your own feet."

"Take the rest of the pie," urged Cubbie. "Have it for breakfast."

Reenie giggled at the idea.

"Nothing like saskatoon pie to round out a healthy breakfast," said Lori. "Why not? Ren loves this pie more than almost anything."

"Except you two," said Cubbie.

They did have pie for breakfast. The phone rang while they were eating it. Lori came back from the call grinning. "Put your coat on, kiddo," she said jubilantly. "We're going to see your daddy! He took a turn for the better last night!" She hugged Reenie.

As they went out, Cubbie was on her porch, hanging her delicates wash on a wooden rack that unfolded like an accordion.

"Cubbie, we're going to see my daddy!" said Reenie. Cubbie hugged them, then left her hand on Renée's shoulder to hold her back as Lori started away. "You did well this week," she said quietly.

"You made the pie," said Renée.

"You did well," Cubbie repeated. "Your daddy is going to be fine now. You can stop worrying."

"Hurry up, Reenie, we'll miss the bus!" Lori called. She ran.

◀ ▶

It was all winter before her daddy could come home, and when he did, he leaned on crutches and was thin as a rake, Cubbie said – but he was home.

. Reenie and Cubbie didn't talk much about what happened. All Cubbie said was, "When my Mr. Cubb was first sick, I did the red dot. I put on my grandmother's girdle, and I'll tell you, *that* was a stretch, more ways than one. I had my mother's floral polyester dress, and I bought support pantyhose in an egg from Vic's Super Drugs. But we had ten more good years together."

"What was *his* favourite pie?"

"Flapper," Cubbie said, and let out that big laugh that set all her rolls to quivering again. "Me, I like a good bread pudding. That's easy to make. Flapper pie, now, takes a meringue topping and cream filling, easy to mess those up. The only easy thing is the graham wafer crumb crust."

◀ ▶

Time settled down and quit stretching out, so it went on in a relaxed and happy way for a few years without seeming to take as long as those few months had taken. Renée's dad went to vocational retraining and became a health-and-safety officer, which Renée thought was a pretty strange kind of a thing – didn't everybody want health and safety? She and Cubbie talked that over one day.

"Accidents happen," said Cubbie. "But they don't have to always happen. Things can be done." Reenie thought of the puzzles and pie, and smiled a little. She learned to make bread pudding with Cubbie and Lori, and later attended to the making of flapper pie, and all four of them ate it.

One June day when Lori came to tell Reenie it was time to come home, Cubbie said, "You have some time tomorrow? I'd like us to make an angel food cake, and maybe you all could pop over for supper Friday."

"What's the occasion?" Lori joked.

"It's my eightieth birthday," said Cubbie, "and I thought the four of us might want to celebrate a tad."

"No way you're eighty!" said Lori.

"I sure am!" Cubbie laughed and set her rolls to quivering, but Renée noticed then, and the next day as they all worked in Cubbie's kitchen, that there weren't as many rolls as there used to be, and more wrinkles. Under Cubbie's arm when she reached up to get down the multi-coloured sprinkles for the angel food, a fold of skin now swung, and her neck was wattled. The world swung a little too, and settled down in a new path. Cubbie was eighty years old!

As she stirred seven-minute icing on the stove (Cubbie said store icing in a tub was the devil's work, and if the day came that she couldn't scratch-build icing for a cake, she might as well be in her grave), Lori said, "You know, Reenie's old enough now to stay late after school, or come home and let herself in. You don't have to be bothered with her if you don't want."

Reenie held her breath. But Cubbie said, "Let her come. She's no trouble. She earns her keep."

◀ ▶

One day in January, Renée came in all bundled up and unwound the scarf she was wearing. She and Lori had made it themselves, after Cubbie taught them to knit, and Renée's dad even took a turn. It was made of three balls of wool of three different colours, and was a little wonky here and there, but it wrapped around four times with room to tie, so Reenie liked it.

Cubbie was working in the kitchen, and Reenie went to help her turn the chocolate chip cookies out onto the cooling rack. She knew how to make them herself now.

Suddenly Cubbie sat down, hard, on the easy chair she kept in the kitchen, and said, "Renée, please take those cookies out and then turn off the oven."

"But there's more..." Renée looked at the shade of Cubbie's face, and turned off the oven.

"You need to get my phone and call 911 for me, honey," Cubbie said. Renée called, and when the operator told her to, she brought the cordless phone to Cubbie so Cubbie could have a word with the lady at the other end. Before you could say Jack Robinson, Cubbie's house was cluttered up with paramedics – Pete and Kate, by their name tags – fussing with a stretcher and making the place seem very small. When they helped Cubbie up from the chair, Renée sat down in her warm spot, mostly to stay out of the way, but also because it seemed like the last warm spot in the kitchen.

Cubbie on the stretcher under a beige blanket made a mound like bread dough until paramedic Pete raised the head end so Reenie could see her face again.

"Hold on a sec," Cubbie said as they began to wheel her out. "Kate, dear, you're tall. Reach up there on top of the fridge and get down that cookie jar? Just put it on the table there." Paramedic Kate carefully lifted down the cookie jar. It was shaped like a mother cat in a storybook with a hat and a shawl, and matched the salt and pepper set that always sat on Cubbie's table.

"Renée, you look in there and find my spare key. You come in and out like usual, and keep my plants watered too, if you don't mind."

"Okay, Cubbie."

"Go home now and stay there, tell your folks what happened. She'll be fine," Cubbie said to the paramedics. "Go get me my purse, Renée, honey, I'll need it."

Renée ran to Cubbie's lacy bedroom to get the worn red leather purse, and brought it to the stretcher. Cubbie put her arm around her and kissed her cheek.

"You did real good," she said. "Don't worry, now. I'll call when I know what's what."

After they left, Renée carefully lifted off the cookie jar lid – it was the whole of the cat's head, which was a bit uncanny. Inside were a lot of bits of paper – mostly crochet patterns and recipes, plus Cubbie's pair of embroidery scissors shaped like a crane, and a key ring with two keys hanging from it, labelled *FRONT* and *BACK* on bits of white tape. She put it on the table.

Then she turned the oven back on and used two teaspoons to put out the last batch of cookies onto a baking sheet. While they baked, she licked out and washed up the batter bowl, and while they were on the cookie rack, she washed and put away the cookie sheets. She stacked the cooled cookies, separating the layers with waxed paper, into one of Cubbie's cookie tins, the one with the peacock on the lid. She washed the cooling rack and put it away. She watered the plants, and looked around the house. Everything was the way it should be.

She turned out the lights and, taking the cookie tin, her coat and scarf and mitts, and her school backpack, she locked up after herself and went home to wait for Ren and Lori.

They ate two chocolate chip cookies each while they waited for news. Lori put the rest in the freezer against a special occasion.

◀ ▶

As had happened with Renée's father years earlier, Cubbie's stay in hospital seemed to get longer the more optimistically the doctors talked. Lori and Ren and Renée visited her quite a bit. Cubbie seemed to get thinner in the bed, smaller, older, a stranger walking away down a long road. Renée looked around at some of the other old folks on the same ward and realized that this is how it happens.

It was like looking backwards through binoculars into her parents' future, and her own. She didn't like it.

The day Cubbie had been in hospital exactly three months, when Reenie went over to water Cubbie's plants she went to the puzzle cupboard. She and Cubbie hadn't done many puzzles the last little while. The one she wanted wasn't on the shelves she could reach. She went and got the kitchen stool and climbed up to reach the top shelf. It was right at the back, at the bottom.

With trepidation, she took down the red dot puzzle. She carefully put all the other boxes back, climbed down, and put the kitchen stool in its place. She went back home and got the chocolate chip cookies out of the freezer. She put two on Cubbie's Bunnykins plate to defrost. She rolled out the felt cloth onto the bridge table, put the puzzle box in the cloth, and opened the lid.

This was a puzzle that had to be worked from the outside in. It had 2500 pieces, and every one of them red. In the end, it would be just a big round red dot. Even finding the edges took days, let alone placing them.

It was the hardest thing. With her dad, it had been putting back something that wanted to get better anyway, just

giving a little shove. With the red puzzle, it was just the opposite. She was fighting something back, something immature
and growing that just wanted to be alive, to be everywhere, to
eat and eat no matter who else went hungry. She had to fight
the energy these uncontrolled cells had.

Renée had to fight herself, too. She had to fight the
shame she felt that her younger self had been like that, so
hungry in her heart. She had to fight her guilt that she hadn't
noticed Cubbie getting thinner and sicker in time to work on
it earlier, when it would have been easier. But she fought.
Every day she added more pieces.

One day, Ren was home early so Renée asked him to help
her make a bread pudding for dinner. She was so tired.

"We can have it for dinner, and take some of the leftovers
up to Cubbie," she said. "She told me she hates that hospital
food."

"Renée, *ma chou*, I don't think she'll be able to eat any.
She's pretty sick, you know."

"Why does she have to be sick, anyway?"

"It's entropy. We French have a saying about it, you know.
Tout passé, tout lasse, tout casse. It means that—"

"I know what it means, Papa, I'm in French immersion,
OK?"

"No need to be rude, *p'tite*."

"*Je m'excuse, Papa*. But let's just try, OK?"

So they did try, and ate the pudding for supper with Kraft
Dinner. "Comfort food," said Lori.

"Cubbie food," said Reenie.

The next day at the hospital, Cubbie was sitting up in
a chair. She took the lid off the Tupperware, took her
Rogers silver-plate spoon that Renée had brought, and

ate almost all of the bread pudding. "That was just fine, girl."

"Daddy helped me cut the bread," said Renée. "We buttered it with real butter."

"You learned what I taught you pretty good. You know, I'm leaving you my things. You might need them later, when you grow up."

"You need them *now*, Cubbie!" Reenie protested. She was afraid of entropy, but she needed to know. "Cubbie, did we use it all up? You know, on Daddy?"

Cubbie looked at her sharply. "It don't work that way, child. It's like water. It just flows down."

"So it's always there?"

"If you can get at it, it sure is."

Renée went home to her puzzle. Every day that week Cubbie sat up in a chair. Renée began to think that she might be able to manage. At night she couldn't sleep, dogged by shadows in her room made by the lights as cars whooshed by on the service road outside. Seemed like there were more cars than Renée had ever noticed, but then again, she usually slept better.

All week she worked on the spiralling closing eye of the puzzle, until by Friday suppertime she was at the centre.

The hole for the last piece was heart-shaped: not heart like a greeting card, but shaped like the actual heart in the Heart Association brochure on Cubbie's TV table. But there were no more pieces on the table. She reached into the box and felt around. The box was empty.

The heart of the puzzle was missing.

It wasn't in the box. It wasn't on the floor. She looked all through the living room and down beside all the couch cushions. She took every puzzle out of the puzzle cupboard and opened the boxes one at a time, rummaged through the pieces of each one before she put it back. The centre piece wasn't there either.

All weekend she searched Cubbie's house. She went through Cubbie's bedroom, feeling like a trespasser, but driven to it. She searched the lavender-smelling drawers, even under their shelf-paper lining. She took all the sensible shoes out of the bottom of the closet and searched behind them. She glimpsed red at the back of the closet but it wasn't the puzzle piece. It was a beautiful pair of red open-toed high-heeled pumps that she couldn't imagine Cubbie ever wearing. Among the clothes, the swatch of red she saw in a garment bag at the side wasn't the puzzle piece but a red velvet evening gown with a strapless sweetheart bodice and a full skirt. She had always known there was more to Cubbie than met the eye. Cubbie couldn't die now, she just couldn't die. Cubbie was a bundle of life; this was the proof she always had been. How could death come for her so soon? The lady in the next bed at the hospital was ninety-nine, and still telling stories. It wasn't fair.

Reenie searched the spare room, the bathroom with its shelf of scented bath oils, the mud room, and the porch. She searched the basement with its toolbox and good wood. Nothing.

Finally she searched her own room at home, in case some-how she'd tracked the piece back when she came home one time.

Rien. Nothing.

By Sunday afternoon when it was time to go over to the hospital Renée was ready to cry at the drop of a hat. At least she didn't need her winter coat. It was the first nice spring day.

"Maybe she's too tired to go," Lori said to Ren. "She spent all weekend doing housework over there, and she has school tomorrow."

"Let her go, *cherie*," said Ren. "Her heart fairly beats on our Cubbie."

Renée thought about this all the way over on the LRT. Hearts and heartbeats – difficult and complicated and a terrible challenge. When she got to Cubbie's room Cubbie was back in bed. She had an oxygen tank on one side and a drip-controlling machine on the other, and on its IV stand was clamped a box full of monitors that were hooked up to a plastic pincher on Cubbie's finger.

"Hello, my loves." Cubbie hugged Lori, and Ren awkwardly bent over for his own hug. They talked a few minutes about the kind of things they always did. If it hadn't been for the beeps and humming of the machines, it would have been calming.

Then Cubbie beckoned Renée closer. "Come over here so I can hug you! Lori and Ren, why don't you go get a coffee so I can talk to my girl?"

Renée wended her way between the equipment and approached the hospital bed with its metal edges. Cubbie took her hand. Her warm comforting grip was the same, even though she looked flat as an empty plastic bag, lying there covered only by a single white sheet. Her crocheted afghan was folded on the chair.

"Are you cold, Cubbie?" Renée said. "Do you need your afghan?"

"My lovely Renée," said Cubbie. "Don't worry, I'm fine."

"I'm doing the red puzzle for you," whispered Renée, finally telling her secret. "I've done it all, but one piece is missing."

Cubbie winked at her. "That's why I've been feeling so good. Thank you, child."

Then she did a strange thing. She opened her mouth and stuck out her tongue at Renée.

On her tongue was the last piece from the heart of the puzzle.

"Oh, give it back," begged Renée. "Please! It's the last one…"

But even as she watched, the red puzzle piece, the triangular three-legged one from the very heart of the round red puzzle, began to dissolve, and lose its edges. It soaked into Cubbie's tongue until nothing was left but a bright red stain, as if Cubbie had been sucking on those red Valentine cinnamon hearts. Cubbie closed her mouth and swallowed, smiling as if around a sweet taste.

Reenie began to cry.

Cubbie squeezed her hand gently. "I'm an old woman," she said. "A person can't live forever."

"But Papa…he…we…"

"It wasn't the right time for him. We just helped the Universe see that. But for me, it's the right time. It happens to everyone."

"I don't like it!"

"The Universe never asked us if we do or we don't. It is what it is."

"It is what it is… ?"

"That's my girl. Give me a kiss goodbye, now, Reenie. You won't see me again."

It was the first time Cubbie had ever used Renée's nick-name.

Renée squeezed Cubbie's hand hard and leaned in to kiss her pale, frail, wrinkled cheek. Cubbie kissed Renée on both cheeks and smiled at her. "Now, my girl. Don't forget all I taught you."

"Oh, Cubbie," said Renée. She put Cubbie's hand up to her cheek, where both their hands got wet with Renée's tears.

She was just pulling herself back together when Lori and Ren came back from the coffee machine with their covered paper cups. "Come on, Reenie," said her mom. "Cubbie has to rest now. We can see her again next Saturday." Lori couldn't help it. She didn't know.

"Bye-bye, dear," said Cubbie. "You know I love you. Remember."

"Goodbye, Cubbie," said Renée. "I love you too. I won't forget. I promise."

She didn't cry all the way home, but she felt like it. The only reason that she didn't was Lori and Ren didn't know what was going to happen, and Renée didn't know how to explain it to them.

They were very practical people. It had been a trial to her and Cubbie sometimes.

◀ ▶

When Renée and her parents got home, Renée went next door. She had to water the plants, she said.

Through the wall she could hear her parents talking, but not what they were saying. Cubbie always said these places had walls like paper.

She walked slowly to the table with the red puzzle on it, the proof of her failure to save Cubbie's life, the puzzle with the heart missing.

But that's not what she saw. The puzzle lay there complete, the heart-shaped centre piece in place as if she had never searched all of Cubbie's row house and theirs too, trying to find it, as if she'd never seen it dissolve on Cubbie's tongue and be swallowed.

She walked forward slowly and reached out her hand to touch the piece. It was smoothly fitted in, as if by Cubbie's gentle, precise hand. It felt warm.

"Cubbie," she whispered. "I'll remember everything. Everything. I promise."

Through the wall, she heard the phone ringing, the call from the hospital.

CHAYA AND LOONY-BOY

Rati Mehrotra

One monsoon evening when the clouds hung low over the old city, I was banished by my grandmother to the dark and dusty attic at the top of our tall, crumbling house. It was all Chaya's fault. She'd broken a glass tray from Mumbai, the one that was reserved for special occasions. As always, the blame had fallen on my ten-year-old shoulders.

Clutching Chaya in one hand, I trudged up the winding staircase, my grandmother chivvying me from behind. "Hurry up," she said, poking me with her favourite walnut stick. "The attic ghost must be very hungry. He hasn't eaten a fat little girl like you for ages. We mustn't keep him waiting."

"What ghost?" I said, stopping just short of the attic door. "The ghost is in the cellar cupboard downstairs, not in the attic." I knew this because on one memorable occasion I had been locked in the cellar, and heard the ghost rattling the cupboard, moaning to be let out. Chaya and I spent the hour of our punishment hugging each other and promising to be good, if only the ghost would stay inside the cupboard.

"There are ghosts everywhere," said my grandmother, pushing me inside the attic. "That is why you must behave nicely, like a well-mannered child, not a glass-breaking hooligan. Then maybe they won't notice you." She bolted the door and I was left alone, listening to her footsteps going down the creaky staircase.

I shook Chaya. "This is all because of you!" I shouted. Some *doll* she turned out to be. She'd arrived in the mail one morning with a birthday card from my father, who was in the navy. At the time, I'd stroked her silky black hair, marvelled at her smooth brown skin, and fingered the blue dress, prettier than anything I owned. Now her hair was matted and the dress torn – she never let me comb her hair or mend her frock.

"You're always getting me into trouble," I told her. "Act more like a doll sometimes," knowing even as I said it that it would rile her.

"I'm not a doll, so why should I act like one?" snapped Chaya, wriggling out of my grasp. "Be quiet or the attic ghost will hear you. Let's not wake him up."

We'd never been up here by ourselves before. I followed Chaya on tiptoe to the lone window. She climbed up to sit on the dusty ledge. A gloomy twilight filtered in through the window's grimy pane; I was relieved that at least it wasn't pitch-dark, like the cellar.

We were in a large room cluttered with the assorted junk of half a century or more. Whenever my grandmother couldn't make up her mind whether to keep something or throw it out, it usually found its way into the attic – trunks of old clothes, shelves stuffed with tattered books, broken lamps, bundles of old letters, their ink fading into oblivion. And somewhere, of course, the ghost that hid and sighed and waited to make its move.

I tried to open the window but it was stuck. I pressed my face against it and looked down. I could see all the way to the courtyard on the second floor, with its lemon tree, rose bushes, tulsi, and marigold plants that my grandmother watered without fail every evening. There might be a drought, the wind from the desert could blow hot and dry across the plains, and water rationed out to the rest of us, but the Goddess forbid that the plants should go thirsty.

I hated those plants. Gran loved them more than she loved any of us. Sometimes, I used to sneak up to the second floor after dark and tear off a few leaves and, if I was feeling particularly wronged, a couple of flowers as well. I would crush them in my hand feeling triumphant, smelling the sweet smell of flowery death. Then I would steal back down, lock myself in the bathroom and wash my hands for a long time.

A dark shape scurried across the floor and I yelped. Chaya glared at me out of her one good eye – the other had been poked out by a neighbour boy during a nasty fight we'd had – and said, "It's just a rat."

"Just a rat?" I squeaked. "I hate rats! Let's get out of here."

"Are you *scared?*" mocked Chaya.

Thumpthumpthump. Chaya and I leapt. Several books had slid off a shelf and now lay on the floor in a grey, ragged heap. Somewhere, something scratched itself. A noxious smell stole into the attic – a mix of rotting fruit and open drains.

"You're right," said Chaya. "I think we'd better leave."

Easier said than done. I ran to the door my grandmother had shut so firmly, and jiggled it. Nothing gave. I could picture the other side so clearly – the peeling blue paint of the door, the rusted iron bolt, the framed and garlanded picture of Krishna, the steps winding down to the relative safety of the courtyard with the plants and the lemon tree. I banged against the door in frustration and mounting panic.

Chaya put her hands on her hips. "It's no use trying that door," she said. "We can't break it down, and if we did, Gran would kill us. How about *this* door?"

And that was how we got out of the attic. You see, there was another door at the opposite end of the room, narrow, almost invisible with dust. It was hardly ever used anymore, and led the wrong way, *up* instead of down, but anything was better than being locked up with the attic ghost. We dragged an old tin trunk to the door. I climbed on the trunk and Chaya climbed on my shoulders. She removed the iron chain from the hook at the top. Something wetly sniffed my neck and I screamed – then the door opened and we shot out to freedom and fresh air.

The door banged shut behind us. We picked ourselves up and my breathing returned to normal. I rubbed the back of my neck; that had been too close. Another minute and I'd have felt *teeth*.

"Isn't this fun?" said Chaya.

"What fun?" I grumbled, but despite myself, I was excited. We were in the upper courtyard, a forbidden place. A short, steep flight of steps in one corner led to the flat roof above.

The roofs of all the houses in our crowded street were joined together, so it was possible for an agile person to jump from one house to the next. On our left lived a large and quarrelsome family that often took its disputes to my grandmother to resolve. On our right lived a cross old woman and her mad son. We knew he was mad because he occasionally emitted blood-curdling howls, and he never left the house. We called him Loony-boy.

There was a time when my whole family used to spend winter afternoons in the upper courtyard of the house. The adults used to play cards and eat peanuts, while I read comics. Then one day a monkey bit my great-grandmother and she had to get six rabies shots. Not long after, a thief jumped onto our roof after climbing a water pipe in the quarrelsome family's house, and made off with our shoes, slippers and blankets while we slept out in the open. It was now absolutely forbidden to come up here at all, let alone in the dark. I couldn't even imagine the punishment for it.

I circled the courtyard to make sure there were no monkeys or humans about.

"Come on, silly. There's no one here," said Chaya. She ran up the stairs to the rooftop, her torn frock billowing behind her.

I didn't know what to be more afraid of, my grandmother's wrath when she discovered how we had escaped, the ghost in the attic who must be disappointed that we got away, or the monkeys, bats and thieves who frequented the rooftops on our street. But I followed Chaya, determined not to show my unease.

When I reached the rooftop, no one was in sight. The wind blew softly and a lone star peeped out from behind the clouds. The rooftop was small and empty, surrounded by a brick barrier. There was no place to hide.

"Chaya!" I called, trying to keep the anxiety from my voice. The things of the dusk can smell your fear; they can hear it in your voice. If you're frightened, it's best not to let them know. So I sang a bit, a couple of lines from my favourite song: *Uncle Moon, where do you go, when the sun slips into the sky; Uncle Moon, see you soon, day is coming, bye-bye.* I skipped around, trying to look and feel happy, like I didn't care I was alone in a place I wasn't supposed to be.

A weak voice wafted from the other side of the brick railing, "Here. I'm here."

I rushed over to the railing and peered down. Chaya was lying at the bottom of the rooftop stairs in the courtyard of the neighbouring house, her leg twisted under her.

"What happened? Are you hurt?" I cried.

"Not much," said Chaya, straightening her leg out. "I leaned too far and toppled over. But I don't think I can walk. You'll have to come and get me."

My heart gave a lurch. This, of course, was the house where Loony-boy lived. "Can't you somehow get yourself up the stairs to the roof?" I asked. "Then I could lean over and haul you up over the railing."

Chaya didn't deign to respond. She gazed at me, her blank, beloved face giving no clue to what she was thinking. She was just a few metres from me, but it could have been the other end of the world. There was no way I was going to jump over the railing to Loony-boy's house to rescue her, and she knew it. My knees shook. The darkness had deepened, and I wanted to be safe downstairs curled up with a book, my aunts arguing over which television program to watch, my grandfather playing chess with himself, and my great-grandmother chanting in the prayer house.

"I'll tell Gran what happened," I said. "She'll get you out. Or maybe I can go look for a rope in the attic and use that to pull you up."

At that moment we heard footsteps coming up from the neighbour's attic. Chaya froze and I slunk low behind the railing. The door creaked open and a soft yellow light flooded the courtyard. Loony-boy stepped out into the light.

My heart constricted as I remembered all the horrible stories about this house. According to one story, the old woman was haunted by a demon during her pregnancy, so her son was born all wrong in the head. Another story claimed he was an English professor who was driven to insanity when his wife and child died in a train accident. Still others said there was no madman at all, and it was the old woman herself who howled in the night.

Chaya's voice came sharp and clear, "Hello, Amar. You smell a bit. When did you last have a bath?"

I couldn't believe my ears. Chaya never, ever tried to talk to grownups, even crazy ones. It just never worked. I peeked over the railing. Loony-boy stood below me, near Chaya. He had a smooth, round face and curly black hair. He would have looked like a child except that he was huge, taller than my grandfather and fatter than our milkman. He bent down and picked Chaya up by her injured leg. She gave a small scream.

Before I knew what I was doing, I was over that railing and tumbling down the stairs to the courtyard as fast as my stubby legs could carry me. I skidded to a halt before Loony-boy and panted, "Give her back to me."

He cradled Chaya and gave me a blank stare. My heart thudded against my ribcage. I had never seen Loony-boy up close before. Chaya lay limply in his arms with her head turned towards me, and a crooked little smile on her face. Like she had known this would happen, had in fact planned it.

"Give her back to me at once," I shouted. "You're hurting her." I stretched out my arms, meaning to snatch her back.

But Loony-boy stepped back, and his eyes grew big and wet. He clutched Chaya to his chest, raised his face to the sky, and roared. "AAWWHHAAHHAAAAWWA!" I put my hands over my ears to block the desolate sound. I should have run then, but I was rooted to the spot, terrified and fascinated.

"AAWWHHAAHHAAAAWWA!" he roared again and then a more subdued, "Aaahhhhhaaahhhoooh?" He fell silent and we eyed each other.

"Hello?" I said.

"Hooohhho?" whispered Loony-boy.

"I'm sorry if I frightened you," I said softly. "I just want my friend back." I pointed to Chaya.

Loony-boy did not step back but neither did he loosen his grip on Chaya. He just stood there with his head cocked to one side as if he was trying hard to understand something. And suddenly my fear of him vanished. I felt all his loss, his incomprehension. Here was someone even more in need of a friend than I.

Footsteps creaked up the staircase to the courtyard and a querulous voice shouted, "Where have you got to now, you good-for-nothing hulk? Must I chase you everywhere? How many times have I told you not to come up here!"

Loony-boy gulped and a look of fear crossed his face. He wrapped his arms around Chaya, hugging her to his chest.

"Run!" hissed Chaya. "If that witch finds you here, you're a goner for sure."

"But what about you?" I protested.

"Don't worry about me," she said. "I'll be safe with Amar."

How did she know Loony-boy's name? I had no time to ask, for at that moment the door banged open. I raced up the stairs and vaulted over the roof, not even waiting to see what the old woman would do to Loony-boy – no, to *Amar* – and to Chaya. I ran down the stairs to our own attic and locked myself in. I lay panting on the floor, hoping the old woman hadn't seen me, and praying the attic ghost wouldn't eat me.

Perhaps it had already eaten that evening, for it contented itself with pulling my hair and throwing away my slippers. In any other circumstance, that would have been enough to make me scream, but I was too far gone to care.

My grandmother came for me a little later, asking if I'd learned my lesson. I could hardly form coherent words, but I must have satisfied her, for I was allowed to leave the attic and rejoin the adults downstairs.

I sneaked up to the roof whenever I could in the months that followed. I heard Amar now and then, emitting his sad, peculiar noises. But I never saw Chaya again. I missed her with an ache that grew sharper with time, as I understood she was not coming back – had never intended to come back.

Even Amar's noises went away after a while – people said that he had died and been carted away to a special morgue reserved for mad dead people.

But I know otherwise. I know that somewhere in that ancient house besides ours, Chaya holds Amar's hand and leads him to adventures in fantastic worlds, like she led me.

THE GHOST RATTLE

Nathan Adler

Clay Cutter, Dare Theremin, and Tyler Kendrars were bored. It was Cutter who first came up with the idea.

"I heard this story about an old Indian burial ground out by Ghost Lake," Clay said. "This woman went out there and took all these pictures – and when she got the film developed – there were these ghostly figures in all the photos."

"That's just an urban legend," Tyler said over the noise of the little pen-motor. "There isn't even a graveyard out there." The sewing needle rose and fell as it punctured Theremin's flesh, the salvaged toy motor buzzing as it delivered blue ink into the lower layers of the epidermis. There wasn't anywhere to get a tattoo in town, so they made their own; something to pass the time.

"There is one out on the reserve," Clay said.

"There's hardly anyone out there this time of year," Theremin said, wincing as the needle went in. "We should check it out."

"I don't know." Tyler wiped away blood welling up on Theremin's shoulder blade, so he could see the image as he created it.

"It isn't just any graveyard – it's an Indian burial ground," Theremin pointed out.

"So?" Tyler asked, pulling the blue latex gloves tighter. "Haven't you seen any horror movies? *Poltergeist? Pet Sematary? The Amityville Horror?*"

"How does it look?" Theremin asked, trying to look over his shoulder.

"It looks like shit," Tyler said, smiling at his handiwork.

"How hard could it be to draw a skull?" Theremin asked. "You draw two eye cavities, a hole for the nose, and some grinning teeth."

When the tattoo was finished, they hopped on their skidoos and took off for the ice road. Local folks used the frozen surface of the lake in the winter because it was a more direct route than the road, which weaved its way through multiple obstacles – swamps, rivers, and rocky promontories.

The shortest distance between two points is a straight line.

Most likely this excursion would turn out to be a pointless trek, but it was as good an excuse as any for an adventure. The skidoo tracks they followed led them past an area that was clearly still being used as a burial ground. Newer marble headstones and wooden crosses mixed together with older structures made of wood, mausoleums standing on stilts, like little houses for the dead held up by scaffolding.

They left their skidoos, engines cooling like silenced chainsaws. A few crows cawed to each other in the stark canopy overhead. Some of the branches held human-shaped bundles, like Egyptian mummies wrapped in leather shrouds. Maybe it was the desiccated meat the birds were after, and the boys were intruding upon the meal. The trees creaked, sounding like voices, as if complaining of the burden they carried in their arms, or maybe it was the dead themselves that spoke.

"Whoa," Tyler whispered, "This place is creepy."

"Of course it's creepy," Clay said, also keeping his voice hushed. "It's a graveyard."

They spread out, picking their way through the cemetery, examining older wooden structures, and avoiding the newer dead; those with names and dates inscribed on polished stone. The platforms only had the occasional pictograph or clan symbol carved into lumber, but age could be assessed by the level of disrepair. Some had clearly been maintained; others had long since fallen into ruin. Many of the little houses held pouches, bowls, dolls, and other trinkets adorning them like decorations, or offerings for the departed.

Tyler wandered further into the darkness of the trees, picking his way across the pitted ground. He tripped, stepping into a cavity where a coffin had collapsed under ground, leaving behind a depression. The marker for the grave had long since mouldered away.

"An arrowhead!" he heard Cutter exclaim, as he sat cradling his twisted ankle, his eyes now level with a smaller mausoleum, where an ancient and faded toy rattle rested on a ledge beneath the overhang of the pointed roof. Tyler made out a racing stripe of red paint, and some faded blue stars. He picked up the rattle and gave it a few shakes, listening to the sound of the beads shifting around inside, like waves lapping rhythmically against the shore of Ghost Lake.

Tyler smiled, charmed by the discovery. He collected old children's toys and noisemakers to use as supporting instruments – they were perfect on background tracks, looping to create distinctive beats. Tyler slipped the rattle into his pocket, and went to check on the others.

"You could use that to shave!" Theremin was saying.

"Not unless I want to slice my face apart," Cutter replied, standing up. "Come on. Let's get out of here. This place is starting to give me the creeps."

"Ooh, now look who's scared," Tyler sneered, and Theremin snickered.

"It's *supposed* to be creepy; it's a burial ground. Besides, why do I want to hang out in a cemetery all day? There's plenty of time for that later – like when I'm dead."

They trudged silently back to the trail and mounted their skidoos. Now familiar with the route, they made quicker progress and parted halfway back to reach their separate homes.

◀ ▶

Tyler Kendrars met his friends on the path the next day. They trudged lethargically to their Monday morning classes, snow crunching beneath their boots.

"Can I have a puff?" Theremin asked Cutter, holding out his hand. They always shared a smoke when one of them was out.

"I'm not smoking, retard," Cutter said, pretending to inhale from a nonexistent cigarette, then exhaling a breath visible in the cold air. Cutter and Tyler laughed. "I ran out last night."

"Oh," Theremin said. "I thought I smelled smoke."

A gale swept through the trees and set the branches to clacking; a drainage ditch somewhere gave off a haunting howl. Tyler tilted his head – he heard the sound of a baby crying. Wailing off in the trees somewhere.

"Do you hear something?" Tyler asked the others.

"You mean that snarling sound?" Cutter asked. "It's probably just some animal out in the woods."

"No. Not snarling," Tyler said. "It sounds like a baby."

"Oh," Cutter said. "It's just the wind, ya dumbass." Theremin and Cutter laughed.

"No. Not the wind." Tyler shook his head, looking into the trees to either side. "I mean something else."

Theremin and Cutter shrugged and Tyler took off into the trees. *Weeenhh. Weeenh. Weeenh. Weeenh.* The baby cried rhythmically, pausing only between breaths for the next wail. Tyler imagined it had been abandoned in the woods somewhere, left to die, or had maybe somehow fallen off the back of a snowmobile or toboggan. The parents would be frantic when they realized their baby was missing.

"Seriously, you guys! You don't hear it?" Tyler called to his friends, who had continued walking. He only heard their snickers and lame jokes in response. *How could they not hear the baby?* It was in the distance somewhere, but clearly audible. *Waaanhh. Waaanhh. Waaanh.* The baby cried. Louder now. Unmistakable. *Weeeenh. Weeeenh. Weeeenh.* Quieter now as the wind blew, stealing the sound, stretching it.

Over there!

When he found the place where he could have sworn he heard the crying, the sound now came clearly from over the next rise. Something about the way the wind blew was playing tricks with his ears, echoing through the trees. Maybe the baby was much farther away than it seemed to be. Tyler sloughed through the bush, hip-deep in snow, plunging his feet into hidden creeks, branches scratching his face and hands. Hiking up steep ridges to reach the next decline. Deeper and deeper into the forest. But no matter how close he seemed to get, whenever he thought he had found the baby, the crying was somewhere else.

Tyler imagined one of his little brothers lost somewhere out in the snow, alone. He forced himself to go on, though he was beginning to think he was simply crazy. There was no baby, and the sound was all in his head. Certainly Cutter and Theremin hadn't heard it.

As he reached the top of the next incline, the crying abruptly came to a halt. All he heard was the whisper of the wind as it combed through the thousands of pine needles. Dead branches clacking together like sighing voices, the trees murmuring amongst themselves about the lone boy trudging frantically through the wilderness searching for something that wasn't real.

He felt hollow. His forehead knotted with worry. His muscles burned; his feet were cold and wet. Maybe the baby had stopped crying because it was dead? At the thought, his heart dropped, as if he were on a roller coaster.

He realized he had long ago lost track of his place in relation to the school. So he began the long trek back, following his own footprints. It was safer than taking off in a new direction, which may have been quicker, or may have led further out into the forest.

It was third quarter by the time he reached the school.

Cutter asked, "What happened to you?" when he trudged into class, soaking wet, fifteen minutes late for the second-last class of the day, and trailing a path of mud, leaves and branches. Tyler gave no answer.

◀ ▶

THE STERLING STANDARD
GRAVE ROBBERS DESECRATE
ANCIENT INDIAN BURIAL GROUND

Racism is being blamed for the recent spate of cemetery vandalism that took place last week on the Ghost Lake First Nation. Headstones and burial platforms were knocked over and vandalized, with the words "'squaw" and other epithets scrawled across tombstones.

Family members have reported that certain sacred items and ceremonial objects were missing, possibly taken by the same perpetrators or by relic hunters.

The incident is being investigated by the OPP as a possible hate crime. Fair Action, a local organization dubbing itself as an equal rights group, has drawn suspicion, though there is no indication of their involvement. The group has been accused of hate crimes in the past – in particular the recent spate of arsons that took place on reserve, damaging a beloved heritage site.

The Sterling mayor, the Chief of Ghost Lake, and other local officials have condemned these acts. "These crimes are unacceptable," Mayor Meriquin said, "and are by no means representative of the cooperation and respect between our communities."

◀ ▶

The furnace kicked in and drawings fluttered in the artificial draft where they had been tacked to the supporting beams. Potential tattoo designs, old and new, covered exposed pipes, ductwork and pink fibreglass insulation.

"Oh shit!" Tyler Kendrars said. "Look at this!"

Theremin and Cutter scanned the news article.

"We didn't do that!" Theremin exclaimed when he had finished reading.

"*I* know that. But *this* must have happened shortly after we went there. We were there on the fifth. Do you know what this means?"

Kendrars stared at the article. "If someone saw us crossing the lake to the reserve – people will think we're the ones who did this!"

"But we didn't!" Cutter said. "All we did was look for ghosts."

Theremin said, "You took that arrowhead. I saw you."

"I didn't take anything," Cutter lied.

"We didn't kick over any gravestones," Tyler said. "All we did was look!"

Cutter shook his head. "It won't matter, if someone finds out we went out there. We'll still be blamed."

Theremin dropped into a chair. "Maybe we should return the stuff."

"No. That's the last thing we should do," Tyler said. "What reason do a bunch of white kids have to go to a burial ground? Especially after *this!* That will just make us look guilty."

"Well, maybe we should go alone – or at night." Theremin suggested. "It won't draw as much attention."

"Fuck." Cutter stared at the floor.

None of them liked the idea of going back at night, but it was a better option than getting nailed for vandalism – something they didn't even do – or getting caught for grave robbing; which they *were* guilty of.

Tyler looked at his silent friends. "We should probably wait a few days, for things to settle down. The place is likely to be busy with visitors now, checking on their relatives."

◀ ▶

Tyler was in the Indian burial ground again. He knew because he could see the outline of the platforms and scaffolding, and some of the newer headstones. But it was dark; there must have been no moon, or else it was shrouded by clouds, and masking even the light of the stars.

He wasn't alone. There was someone else there with him. "Who...who are you?" Tyler asked the shadowy presence.

"My name? You want to know my name?" He couldn't see her, but he could hear age in her voice, like the rustling sound of a rattlesnake shedding its skin. "You aren't worthy of knowing my name. You may call me *Naphtha*, because when you die I will be waiting, and I will make sure you burn."

The darkness retreated because Naphtha's eyes *glowed* like coals. Pupils dancing with the strangest colours – chartreuse, cobalt, violet, crimson – colours more likely to be seen in the northern lights than in any campfire. It was as if the northern lights were concentrated and distilled to this more intense flame.

Naphtha's eyes blazed with greater intensity and then exploded to eagerly devour her body in multi-hued radiance, only darkening her skin for an instant – flickering and dancing with a sickening shift of light that illuminated her features. Frizzled white hair stuck up madly in all directions, one eye filmy-blue as if from glaucoma, filled with stars, like constellations in the night sky, the other eye an opaque sphere; dual-coloured eyes like a husky, returned to normal now that the light had left her irises to engulf her whole.

Naphtha was the fuel source, and the flame. Her hands extended like claws, then she launched herself towards him. Technicolour jets like deformed wings haloed her body – a phoenix in human form.

Her arms wrapped around him. He couldn't escape. He couldn't escape. He couldn't escape. The flames burned red-hot and iridescent, trembling hypnotically. He'd once accidentally placed the palm of his hand on the glowing coils of a stove element, letting out a shriek when his skin sizzled and stuck to the nichrome. He felt that now – that same searing pain, but infinitely worse because it wasn't merely his hand, but his entire body had become a torch.

He couldn't see through the smoke, his nose thick with the burning-sulphur smell of human hair, and human flesh – his flesh. Maybe his eyeballs had melted to drip down his face like candle wax – he could no longer see anything but he still felt the pain. It had become his whole world, his everything, his all. There was nothing else in the unrelieved darkness. He was unable to see even the light the wick of his body made, or what shadows it cast.

No matter how hard he pulled, Naphtha's arms were like iron bands that wouldn't release him, so they burned together, like the corpses of two lovers embracing in the grave as their flesh dissolved and rotted away.

Tyler screamed, thrashing as he woke among the tangled blankets, confused when there were no flames, no heat, and no homicidal woman like some sort of avenging X-Man. He was welcomed by the familiar sight of his basement bedroom – exposed pipes, ductwork, and beams overhead, the sallow morning light filtering through the small rectangular windows at ground level.

"What's all that racket down there?" His mother's voice came muffled from upstairs. "It's time for you to get ready for school. Stop fooling around!"

What kind of name was Naphtha? What a strange dream! But like all dreams, this one too was beginning to fade as his breathing returned to normal, the sweat dried, and he began getting ready for the day. Strange dream, or no strange dream.

◀ ▶

Tyler Kendrars couldn't sleep.

His room was lit by a dull, greenish glow coming in through his window. It was a clear, cold, cloudless night; the stars where showing off and the northern lights were acting up. They lit up the entire landscape the way a full moon did. Coils of sapphire and electric jade infiltrated his room, like flashes from a television screen. Except his television wasn't on. The flicker formed a secondary phenomenon, as if it were a miniature three-dimensional version of the larger aurora outside. Curtains and diffuse arcs danced in place like a mind-bending cathedral.

The symphony of light reminded Tyler of his nightmare – had it only been the night before? The woman named Naphtha, her anger, and her radiance – so akin to the night sky with its ribbons and veins of pulsing, fluctuating fire. Tyler knew the aurora was caused by charged particles, electrons and protons entering the atmosphere, the solar wind interacting with the Earth's magnetic field. But he also couldn't help believing that Naphtha had in some way caused this borealis, and that she had something to do with the geomagnetic storm in his bedroom. It was his magnetic midnight, and he was standing on the opposite side of the sun, at the height of an eleven-year sunspot cycle. Naphtha was that magnetic centre, and her fury was like the furnace of the sun.

It wasn't only the glow of the northern lights that kept him awake. It was also the wind howling, rattling his windowpanes – and carrying with it the sound of a baby. Crying. Crying. Crying. But by this time he knew it wasn't real. There was no point in sloughing through the mud and snow, searching for something that didn't exist. It existed only inside his head.

He knew a real baby would have frozen to death long ago, but he couldn't tune it out. He wrapped a pillow around his ears, but could still hear the incessant wailing.

Tyler's mom opened his bedroom door, saw him lying on the bed with the pillow around his head, and said, "Oh, you're going to bed already?" She looked at her watch. "It's only 9:30! At least you'll get a good start in the morning for once."

"Mom?"

"Yes, honey?" She paused at the threshold.

"Do you hear anything?"

She stood in the doorway for a moment, listening as a gust of wind blew outside, rattling the glass, whistling as it passed the opening of the chimney overhead.

"Just the wind," she said as she closed the door.

Tyler groaned into his pillow. *I'm going crazy.*

Weeenh. Weeenh. Weeenh. The baby cried. He knew this had to have something to do with that dream – the woman with star-like constellations and the fire of the northern lights in her eyes. Naphtha. She had let the fire consume her, and then she had rushed to embrace him.

Tyler cracked one eye open and saw the old, painted toy rattle on the nightstand beside him. He had come home, left it on the mantle, and then promptly forgotten about it.

How had it ended up on the nightstand? He couldn't remember.

Of course! he thought, finally connecting the dots; he should have already put two and two together by now. *The baby!* No wonder Naphtha was so pissed. He had taken her child's toy! He remembered the desperation that had gripped him, out in the woods, when he imagined it was *his* baby brother that was missing, alone and lost, and it had pushed him to keep searching, even when he thought it was hopeless.

Somehow, the child's spirit was tied to the toy, and Naphtha wanted her baby back. He'd pretty much stolen her baby!

He needed to return that rattle.

He didn't think he could stand the baby's crying for another night, or Naphtha's possible return, so Tyler got up. He pulled on long johns, jeans, socks, a T-shirt, sweater, and his jacket and crept up the back stairs, trying to avoid the places that creaked. He stepped carefully through the laundry room so that the *swiff, swiff, swiff* of the rattle in his pocket didn't make too much noise. It was still a school night – better if his mom thought him asleep.

He closed the back door softly, and walked towards the lean-to at the side of the garage where he kept his skidoo. With each step, the rattle in his pocket made a *swiff, swiff, swiff* in time with the *crunch, crunch, crunch* of the snow – like Styrofoam under his boots. At least when the rattle sounded he couldn't hear the baby crying – whether because the baby was drowned out, or the rattle soothed the spirit into silence – Tyler wasn't sure. He was just grateful he didn't have to hear it anymore.

Tyler made his way to the ice road, his path lit by wildly vibrating bands of cobalt and crimson now boiling across the star-filled sky. If it had been cloudy, it wouldn't have been so cold, the snow wouldn't have had that same crunch, and the natural fireworks in the sky wouldn't have lit the tracks so clearly.

He had heard stories about the aurora – it was the dead, dancing in celebration on their journey to the afterlife; or walruses kicking human skulls in a spiritual game of kick-the-can, like the bowling giants he had once believed caused thunder. One explanation was just as good as the other it made as much sense to him as magnetic midnight. The folds and striations of light looked like the fall of drapery now, fluttering in the cold, cold wind, freezing-him-to-the-bone beautiful.

It seemed appropriate that the night should be illuminated by such a brilliant borealis, and he could imagine the spirits dancing, lighting his way, just as they did the path of the dead.

Still he wondered why this rattle was so important? What power did it have over Naphtha or her child? Why weren't their spirits at rest, or dancing in the sky? It was a night for such questions.

A big part of him didn't believe any of it was real, but he still felt the need to return the pilfered instrument. The rest – the baby's cries, the dreams – were probably manifestations of guilt, like the ticking of Edgar Allan Poe's telltale heart hidden under the floorboards. Tyler's guilt didn't tick. It made a *swiff, swiff, swiff* sound in time to the *crunch, crunch, crunch* under his boots as he made his way through the graveyard. For several panicked minutes he began to sweat despite the cold. He couldn't remember from which tomb he'd taken the child's rattle. Would it be enough if he simply left the plaything somewhere in the burial grounds? Would the spirits of the dead still haunt him?

Then he dropped through a deadfall in the snow. He heard something snap and felt a sharp jolt of pain as his foot twisted in the hollow of a sunken grave. No doubt the same one he'd tripped over before. He had injured himself this time, probably owing to the fact it was night, and he was alone.

Tyler wasn't sure if he'd broken or merely sprained an ankle. All he knew was that it *hurt*. Hurt. Hurt. But there was no way around it. He sucked in a breath as he worked through the pain, waiting for it to subside, and disappointed when the throbbing continued, beating in time to his pulse. On the plus side, his headlong tumble into the snow had brought him to eye level with the little house hovering on stilts just above the snow, and the little ledge which had been the rattle's original resting place.

He pulled the old rattle from his pocket: a bolt of fear stabbing through him like a spear when he saw that he had landed on the instrument. The side had been ripped open so that the beads inside fell out. He held the white, discoloured beads in his hands, not wanting to lose any part of the toy, hoping to keep the thing together, in one place, if not in one piece. He realized that what he held in his hand were not beads or small stones, but small, pointy, rounded teeth – the baby teeth of a child. Tyler looked up, for the first time noticing the crowding of little houses on stilts, all congregated together, and each of them, he had no doubt, with their own little teeth-filled rattles. If they had not survived long enough to grow teeth – he hated to think of what might have been inside the rattles. Fingers? Toes? And he concluded that the shorter, smaller domiciles were almost certainly designed as the final resting places for children, six or seven of them in a row – so many dead little ones. Some of the houses were so small they could only have been for a newborn or a stillborn child. How many babies had Naphtha lost? He imagined a time before penicillin or hospitals, and a new suite of diseases introduced by the Europeans: small-pox, typhus, cholera, measles – deadly invaders on a microbial scale for which there was no immunity, no treatment, and no cures.

So many dead children. So much loss. Tyler thought he understood better the madness he had seen in Naphtha's eyes – the loss of children in life, and now in death too, seemed to be an unnecessarily cruel indignity.

He hoped that by returning the toy he also returned some measure of peace. He placed the rattle back on the ledge where he had found it, then let the teeth pass through his palm like sand passing though an hourglass, back onto the shelf where they belonged. For the first time, he noticed the fine strands of dark hair decorating the handle which he had taken for decorative ribbons, but which in all probability had also belonged to the child. How could he have been so blind?

His lip curled in revulsion. The *swiff, swiff, swiff* he'd been hearing with his every step, had in fact been the percussive sound of human body parts. There was something macabre and disturbing about the idea of using the body's materials in such a way to create sound, to create music. But it served him right for stealing from the dead. He should be creeped out.

It was a mourning rattle.

He wondered if Naphtha had used it to sing songs, and what those songs would have been. Goodbye songs, or songs of memory and loss. Or songs to conjure the long-lost dead. He was weak with relief that he had never gotten around to using the instrument to create a looping audio track, heart racing at the idea of the sounds that might have been recorded. Or how he would have managed to return sound, once it had been captured in the waves of digital software. He imagined the audio track of shaking teeth following him around, haunting him forever.

Attempting to stand, Tyler found his ankle unable to support his weight, so he was forced to crawl though the graveyard to his skidoo. Magnetic midnight – and actual midnight – passing now, the light from the aurora borealis was fading, and he was hard pressed to find his way by that now diffuse light and the splay of the stars. The snow reflected only dimly, a trembling shade of blue. Once onboard, he sped cautiously through the woods and out across the lake.

Chilled and thoroughly exhausted from sleep deprivation, Tyler felt blessed to hear only the wind blowing when he shut off his skidoo. No babies crying. No sonic static and pop of electrons colliding with the arctic atmosphere. He hopped inside on his one good foot, moving at an excruciatingly slow pace down the stairs, and collapsed onto his bed and into the darkness of sleep.

"*Dibikiziwinan.*" He heard Naphtha whisper softly as the darkness embraced him, lips so close to his ear he could feel the passage of breath from her words. "*Dibikiziwinan-gashkii-dibik-ayaa.* Darkness-dark-as-night. *That is my name. But you may call me Naphtha.*"

And then there was nothing but sleep.

THE GARDEN OF OUR DECEIT

Rhonda Eikamp

*But this is the end of the story, a peon ending perhaps, in which
I have left the board. I have given you the golden pieces. You will
do with them as you will. Life, mind, love And I topple.*

At first he thought the house was deserted. Ivy and trumpet
creeper had blurred its form; the gardens – his only reason for
returning – had lost their chessboard regularity, their hedges
grown into one another, copulating. The hover set down
inside the gates and J'taa clambered out first, her jointed pere-
opods making her seem a slender cricket about to spring away
over the grass. Charles followed her only slowly, drowning in
green scents. It was late dawn; the twins on the horizon
moved toward their occultation, grey and gold, castling.

Not deserted, as he had secretly – fervently – hoped. The
door creaked open. A young woman emerged, arms crossed,
and leant against the leaf-choked doorpost so that she seemed
gowned in ivy. Short and lithe-limbed, with an air of strength
that made him nervous. She wore ragged men's trousers. He
knew her and didn't. His family had had many servants.

He gestured to J'taa by way of introduction, speaking her
name to the unknown woman at the door, and his corothul

companion's parasitical circuitry lit up beneath her silver skin in greeting, foggy capillaries racing red and blue. The woman did not react to the greeting. Surely there was no need to introduce himself.

"The corothai wished to see where the great – where I grew up," Charles told the young woman. He was certain now he didn't know her. She still had not moved or acknowledged J'taa's presence. For heaven's sake, it was his house. "They want me to play a chess game here. They want to watch."

The woman's eyes never left him. "Hello, Charles," she said.

He recognized her.

◀ ▶

In your eyes that I've watched sidle from fears or widen with wonder at the intricacies of the game, I've come to know you're not me. I think you have often been intimidated. I do not want to tower over you. I want to tower under you. I want to watch you fly off perched on that siege-machine of yours and take over the world.

There is a terrible thing in the world. A silver maelstrom, drawing us all down. If we can fight it together, then you'll never be apart from me.

From the open window of his old bedroom Charles Mestroe could see the corner of the tall hedge that enclosed the chess garden. The thought of playing made the figures in his mind begin to slide, blocking, strategizing. Like an itch in his fingers, a cerebral rash. Lines of obfuscation, of capture and geometry.

J'taa stood near, gazing with him. "This you are growing up in?" she asked. The corothul had seemed subdued while the woman (Kess, how could he have not recognized Kess?) led them on a tour of the house that was little more than glances into rooms abandoned to dust. Broken furniture, cold fireplaces. In some areas, cracked windows had allowed foliage to creep in. His mother's beloved study was a forest. Kess and the few remaining servants – the cook with the wart, whose name he could not recall, the ancient butler Hedley – had carved a living space for themselves about the kitchen and the small vegetable garden, and ignored the rest.

"The Rook," he replied. His mother had named the mansion. "It's been only – what – eight years since I've been away? I can't believe how old it's become."

J'taa touched his wrist, while with another pair of arms she tied back her head fronds with a bit of ribbon, a feminine gesture. The fronds were vestigial antennae, he knew, made redundant long ago when her species melded with the parasitical worms that formed their circuitry. "This we are to know wanting about you. Everything."

"Old and ruinous."

"Who was supposed to take care of it?" It was Kess who spoke from the door. "After the servants ran away."

Charles turned. He still could not reconcile that pursed face with the voice of his childhood friend.

"Not blaming you, Kess. I'm going to show J'taa the gardens now."

"Are you even going to ask after him?" Pursed and bitter, with a sheen of sweat that made her beautiful.

J'taa's question circuitry glowed.

Him. Surely not still alive; he couldn't bear that, and yet Kess was already walking down the hall to the master bedroom. "I'm only here for the game," he called after her, but he followed, had to follow, his moves preordained.

His father lay on the canopied bed like a yellow husk that had floated in on the breeze. The stroke eight years ago had ravaged his left side, weighing down his face. The cheek still hung twisted, one eye at half-mast. Lord George Mestroe had been caught in a skewer move, as Charles imagined it, his gentle gelatinous nature for so long protected by his queen who had stood in front of him blocking all assaults, until the indomitable Lady Mestroe was removed, leaving the devastated, feckless lord vulnerable to the harsh world and his grief. The stroke had taken him from the game two days after his wife was killed. Checkmate.

When Lord Mestroe saw his son, he began to scream.

Kess rushed to the sick man's side. The screams formed into a meaning, a word that might have been *Murderer*, over and over, slurred beyond recognition. Drool became an issue.

Charles's skin felt on fire. *Not this, not the guilt*. He backed out of the room gasping. Turning, he found J'taa had followed him and without thinking he plunged his hands into the alien's warm midsection. Her thorax parted to accept him, the needles of her placoid denticles pumping her transpathic drug into him.

High pink clouds bore him up, globular mists on which he soared above the vast cacti-dotted plain that some melders conjectured was the corothai home world, where the seas that were the aliens' isopodan origin had long dried up. The vision rocked his cells to sleep. This was the beauty, so antithetical to human experience, that mindscape which the corothai-shy despised. Human minds joining with their alien superiors, experiencing the corothai dust world of utter apathy.

When he opened his eyes he saw Kess staring at them in disgust.

"You partake may," J'taa told her. Another hole opened in her side.

In the blue eyes of his forgotten friend Charles saw some fragile thing that had survived ruination slowly seep away. Rage made her tremble. The voice – directed at him – was raspy, reminiscent of his dead mother. "You've no shame at all, have you?"

"Make stop the sound," J'taa requested. Behind them Lord Mestroe's screams had turned to moans, the one word still punctuating the air.

"I will not," Kess told her. "Let him hear it." In her anger she seemed to glow as the corothai did. Charles wanted to hug her or slap her. "It's only true."

She left the door open and walked away.

◀ ▶

I would throw my body upon yours to protect you from that maelstrom. I would leap into it after you, hold you so you would know you're not alone.

Out, out beneath the scudding clouds, air hot and breezy in turn. The famous Mestroe gardens were no more, only weedy parcels divided by high hedges, indistinguishable from one another in their tangles of exploding sweet fern and bellwort. J'taa had dropped to her running arms, loping beside him, and when he glanced at her he caught a frown of doubt as she looked around. All so shabby. What she must think of the chess genius, the man celebrated back in Loude by every corothul who worshipped the immortal game, which was most of them. He stopped at the last hedge-gate, hopeful, smiling back at her, and in response J'taa's mandibles curled upward in the corothul imitation of a smile.

Let it be whole. He ducked beneath the wisteria arch, beckoning her to follow.

Knight, cleric, peons. All still there. House-high, the thirty-two metal figures faced off across the etched stone terrace, the gold against the silver, his mother's take on the traditional black and white. Weather-beaten, eaten by rust. Clematis had reached across to form wigs on the figures nearest the hedges. Charles stood in the golden king's shadow, a robed figure thrice his height, its crown wreathed in wayward ivy. He held his breath as he always had, to feel the rustle as they sensed him and started up. At first only a subtle movement of giant hands and necks, servos stretching, a metal susurrus growing stronger, until the shrieks of gears long unused might have been the cries of the tortured in hell. He should have brought oil.

"Come!" he called over the noise to J'taa.

The mouth of the winding staircase that led up into the queenside rook was clogged with dead leaves. He swept them aside and stooped to climb the child-sized stairs and was a child again. That simple. Below, thumps echoed against the metal, J'taa following him. At the top he stood on the rook's platform and peered out over miniature merlons onto his empire, the entire yard of the oversized chess game, pieces still creaking to attention, on this side his golden horde lined up awaiting his thoughts, over there the silver foe.

J'taa joined him. "Is hating you your father."

She had waited to say that in private, he realized. He wouldn't talk about it. "My mother built this for me. Took time from all her tests and trials, her endless lab work. Taught me the rules. I was six." As Charles spoke, the golden queen – its head on a level with the rook's platform – twisted to let its metal stare fall on him as though listening. Though their insentient circuits made it impossible, he had a sudden image of the pieces as conscious, real even when he was away, as alive as Kess and the servants, locked in stasis by his absence, unable to scream their torment as they awaited his return. *Murderer*. Unable even to cry. "Simple circuitry, of course. Nothing compared to what Mother was developing in her research."

"And the girl. The Kess. Is hating."

He sighed. "Yes, J'taa."

The alien was a good friend, one of his many hangers-on among the silver, generous with the transpathic, yet the fascination she had – that all corothai had – for human minds and emotions both drew and repelled him. It was necessary, he knew. The very privileges he enjoyed in the capital depended on that inability in the aliens, the aristocracy of the earth, to unravel human thought as it played out in the most basic concepts: grammar, social mores. The brambles of their vast intelligence grew differently. A game of perfect information such as chess was a mysterium to them, no corothul able to win a match against even a beginner human, and in their faceted eyes it elevated masters of the game such as Charles Mestroe to a kind of god. A small counterbalance to the control they wielded over humans. God against god: their superior, earth-ruling technology, in space, weapons, communications, driven by the parasitical circuitry that connected them all, the addictiveness of the transpathic visions they granted – matched against their dumbfounded awe in the face of a single human synapse.

Gold here, silver over there.

"Is sensing that you here be."

"Made to come alive at my heartbeat, my voice. Ultra-sensitive. From up here on the rook, I need only whisper my moves to them."

"No. Them her." It was no grammatical mistake, he saw. J'taa had not meant the game pieces. She pointed with three arms to where Kess had slipped in through the opposite hedge-gate and was winding her way through the silver opponent ranks. She vanished behind a rook and appeared a moment later at its crown, ready to play. Two generals, facing off across their armies.

His heart reared up. He'd been forgiven.

He smiled and moved a peon. Kess countered.

How many sumptuous afternoons they'd spent, he and Kess, the gardener's orphaned daughter, fierce as the kestrel she was named after, hurling moves at one another, his mother often joining in to critique their strategy, laughing, her strident red hair, already flecked with grey then, tangling in the breeze.

Kess brought a knight into play; it lifted into the air and over the line of peons, really only a horse-shaped hovercraft, and Charles felt J'taa stiffen at the sight of the censored technology. His mother had known many things she shouldn't have. He countered with his cleric. Soon the world was only giant figures rolling on invisible casters as the two sides battled. Kess played fast, faster than he remembered, pieces whooshing by, slowed only by their rust. It was speed chess. His golden queen kept turning its head to look at him, a fault in the circuitry. J'taa laughed when he brought his rook into play and they were whizzed about the board atop it.

Passing near to Kess on her own high platform, he was astonished to see utter hate on her face.

Not forgiven then. He knocked it from his mind like flicking over a king. The game condensed to a struggle. She was good, so much improved that he wondered where she had practised. She kept him on the defensive. Captured pieces rolled away to stand on the side strip. The sun poured out its pitchers of heat. Behind him he felt the house, its ruination like his father's body, like the dead gardens and rusty chess pieces, filtering through his concentration, discolouring the game. Sweat ran into his eyes, turning his golden pieces into a molten stew.

Then he saw it.

Mate in two moves.

It was as though his brain had been stabbed. He was a master back in Loude, countless kings toppled; Kess could not have won against him, and yet she had. J'taa had not seen it, he knew, but when she did the corothul would transmit it through her circuits to others in Loude, who would twitch in the manner of corothai amusement, or shake their heads in human imitation. He heard Kess's knight powering up to leap, the move that would pincer his king and checkmate him.

Instead, Kess slid her rook close to his, diagonally, illegally, until they faced each other. She was crying.

"Is this what it was for?" she screamed. "This game? This…toy! Do you love this so much, Charles?" She pressed the words out as though choking. "Is this what your mother had to die for?"

"I didn't know what would happen—"

"Because you're blind! Because you're a genius who can see three chess moves deep but not past your own nose."

"It was the lies of the ones in power. They blackmailed me. Who could have known the corothai were capable of duplicity?"

"Everyone, Charles." Kess's sobs had subsided. "Everyone except you. They outsmarted you." She sneered hate at J'taa, who stood listening, seemingly unaffected, beside him. "Brilliant move. Convince your conquered world that being only half-organic makes you dumb to certain things. True perhaps, but only a half-truth. Lull your foe. Drug them." Kess turned back to him, the disgust from earlier warping her face. "You think you're privileged, don't you, being given an addictive drug whenever you want?" He felt J'taa's warm skin next to his. It called to him to float high above the hallucinogenic plain, forget everything Kess was saying. "Charles, everyone gets the transpathic." Insert his hands into the folds until the bone needles pierced them, instantly numbing. "Those the corothai have no reason to pamper as they do you are given the drug all the time, in their food and water. Kept apathetic."

"That's a myth and you know it."

"Made dumb. A tiny upper class where it pleases the corothai, yes – lords and chess grand masters – while the poor in the streets are made over into docile addicts, good only for scraping the yeast from their masters' nests."

"Not everyone can be educated. Scarce resources—"

"The transpathic erodes the brain, Charles." Kess was shuddering in her rage. "We are literally devolving. The mass of us will soon be apes." Yes, J'taa's skin was warmer, some surge in the subcutaneous circuitry radiating heat. He wanted to put his hands over his ears like a child. "Soon we will have lost the inheritance of the earth. Just another animal species, while they expand and take it all."

Kess swayed; her thin hands gripped the merlons of her platform and he suddenly remembered those hands on him, their lovemaking – lustmaking – at seventeen, anywhere and everywhere they could hide: in the ash woods out past the chess garden, in the unused drawing room, exploring each other, checking and mating. She had taken his fingers between her teeth, mouthing gently, longing, any time he won against her at the tabletop board kept in the house, worshipping the part of him that had touched the pieces. Nausea struck him. He had worshipped Kess's body and she had worshipped his mind and he suddenly wanted that back. He wanted to touch her, another human, not silver chitin. He wanted a human looking up to him.

"Even the little you use is making you stupid, Charles."

"Shut up."

"Why do you think I could win against you?"

He would, he'd put his hands over his ears if she didn't stop.

"Is this the level you play at, your best, there in Loude? All of you masters, only ever playing against each other, no input that isn't corothai. If your precious tournaments had regressed to a child's level – *how would you ever know?*" In the awful quiet a cuckoo landed on a cleric's tip and whistled. "It is they who have played, always. With master tactics. You're a curious toy for them. A peon they could use to get to the—"

"No," he cried. "I'm a god, Kess! I'm feted in every chess salon in the city."

"You—"

"They hang ten to a bunch from their ceiling apparatus just to view my games from above."

"—are—"

"I have a villa."

"—a—"

"My own hovercraft."

"—*murderer!*"

"You can't leave."

But she was leaving, a staccato of stumbles down her rook's staircase, a whirl of dark hair out through the hedge-gate. "You've won the game. You have to checkmate me." The gate slammed behind her. The astonished cuckoo rose and vanished into the alders. "Come back and checkmate me."

Beside him, J'taa's thorax yawned, waiting for him, denticles masticating.

◀ ▶

Do you remember what I asked you once? You must have been nine. That if you were given the choice between acquiescing to the small evils of a system that would let you live in comfort or taking to the wilds under horrible conditions to fight it in secret, what you would choose. You took no time in answering. You said acquiesce.

The university Charles Mestroe had attended at eighteen was a warren of corothai yeast-nest buildings in the heart of Loude, famous for its chess tournaments, the most prestigious in the land. He'd waited in the office that second morning until the corothul in charge of tournament registration had crawled from a tunnel in the upper left corner and taken a seat. Charles had presented his credentials – top-ranked in the countryside before he was seventeen, son of a lord – and then shrivelled, his heart drying to a tiny seed of rage as he was told in ungrammatical but certain terms that he was not to be admitted to the games. His mother was a known agitator, her writings incendiary. Revisionist sympathies in the family, no, they could not risk. He understand must.

Words like a fire in his brain, incendiary, burning everything.

Checkmate.

The corothul was an old one, with dark patches in his silver skin where parasites had begun to die. Charles had tried to breathe slowly, and found he couldn't. There was no other reason to come to university; his studies bored him to tears. The game was everything. Charles Mestroe dreamed chess, drank it; his mind moved along its lines by squares, knight's-move thinking. His very soul had long ago become checkered. He was the best and now he would never be able to prove it. Made that way by his mother and then denied it all. The mad queen of The Rook, brilliant and vociferous, who wrote her husband's speeches for parliament denouncing corothai dominion, and published her own manifestos against them. And did more than just write. Ruined. Denied.

His hands clenched and unclenched and the corothul saw it. Some empathy for human emotion, gleaned, he supposed, through a long life among them, had made the alien's skin light up, contacting others. When the flashing had ceased, the administrator leant forward over the yeast desk. There was – perhaps – a deal that made could be.

◀ ▶

This is what you do too: you forgive your children for all their affronts, forgive them for not being like you, for the fact that neither of you will ever understand the other.

Charles left J'taa atop the rook and caught up with Kess inside the house.

She whirled on him. "Did you know what she was doing? Did you know how close she was?"

"They told me they were only going to take it away from her, that nothing would happen to her! God, please, Kess, I've fought to forgive myself for eight years—"

"She had discovered the secret of the parasitical circuitry." The walls of the entrance hall seemed to draw closer. For a moment he felt dizzy. "Invisible waves in the air. She was on the brink of learning how to send out her own waves. She would have been able to jam their communications, send false messages, perhaps even take control of their bodies through their circuitry." He saw red hair in a breeze, those forever wide-awake eyes gleaming at some new insight. "It would have been the end of corothai rule. They know very well why they censor our research, keep the truly useful technology from us and have done for hundreds of years. Who knows where we could be now if they didn't? Their knowledge seems endlessly above ours, my god look at what they've done to the earth – two moons – and yet—" In Kess's blue eyes the light shone. "We might have lifted from the surface by now, moved to other worlds as they do. Anything at all, if they had let us develop as we should have. Instead we are turned into apathetic apes."

It was his tears making her gleam. "They said I had to give them something, just a little something about the woman who wrote the manifestos, and then they would let me register for the tournaments. That they only wanted to remove material, take anything censored away from her. I know now they must have had their suspicions, knew how to put pressure on me, but I didn't recognize what was happening." The moment, the second he would take back if he could, coalesced to acid on his tongue. "I told them about the lab in the woods."

"Remove material." Her shrug bore the weight of all sadness. "They came that day, no warning. Burned the lab, tore up the house searching. They removed her. Oh, but they brought her back, did you know that?" *Put your hands over your ears.* "She'd been tortured, horribly. They said they understood how humans always wished to have a body to inter. As if doing us a favour. Laid her out here on the hall floor, and your father, he…saw it." The dust stirred by their movement choked him; it had to be the dust. "She loved you so. She recorded a message for you after you left for university and placed it in the golden queen. I think she understood how they might use you once you left here." Her hand on his cheek was sudden and soft, a gift that would save him. "I loved you too, Charles."

"Love me again, Kess." Nothing else mattered all of a sudden; she was a real thing in his artificial life among the aliens, the human who could make him real again. Kess could bring him back to the worlds of human interaction – necessary and life-saving – going on below the corothai's alien intellect, a truth beneath the game. *Don't leave me with them.*

She was staring at him, shaking her head, but it was not refusal. "I was always stupid. You started winning at some point and I couldn't keep up." She drew near. "You won the love game. By going away, without even pretending it hurt you. I'm going to be stupid again." They stood at the foot of the staircase, with a clear view of the empty entrance hall, and Kess peered over his shoulder at the front door to make sure J'taa hadn't followed them.

She brought her lips to his ear. "It's still going on, Charles. The research, the lab. It's been moved deeper into the forest. It took years to rebuild, but there were others who could continue your mother's work, while we help them hide and plan the overthrow. I'm the leader of the movement now." Through the change of her breath at his ear he knew she was smiling. "The peon promoted to queen. Help us, Charles. I believe in you, even now." Her face tilted up and he saw the old Kess, the worship, his redemption. "You're close to them in Loude. You could spy for us. Say you will. For her. For us."

Redemption. He took no time in answering. "Yes," he replied.

From the top of the stairs came a voice. "Genius are you." J'taa stood gazing down at them from the second-floor landing. Charles realized she must have skirted the house and climbed the outside wall to his open bedroom window, a locomotion that was simpler than walking for the corothai, and in the next instant he remembered the aliens' hyper-acute hearing.

"No!" he cried. Kess had twisted from him, one hand to her mouth as though to recapture her words.

"This we have coming to discover. Having suspicion. I am thanking you."

The red and blue lines beneath J'taa's skin glowed brighter than he had ever seen. "Stop her!" Kess cried, but Charles knew it was too late, his heart withering. Waves, Kess had called it, sent invisibly. Others would already know. Probably waiting nearby.

"Here soon," said J'taa, confirming the thought. She had ambled halfway down the stairs. He imagined leaping at her, closing his hands on her throat, strangling his own stupidity.

"Need only finding lab now." Her gaze swept over Kess. "We will this game play you are torture calling." For a second the faceted eyes seemed puzzled. "Game humans lose always."

A shot rang out. J'taa's head snapped back, blood and sparks flying. Another shot and she tumbled down the steps in a flurry of limbs to lie still at their feet.

Hedley the butler stepped from the kitchen doorway. In his wrinkled hands he held an ancient swivel-barrel pistol. He was shaking from head to foot.

Kess stepped to him and grasped his arm. "You did well." They all stared down at the dead alien. Filigree lines of blue wriggled within the red blood, moving away from the body. Charles realized it was the circuit parasites deserting their host. In the distance the thrum of an approaching hovercraft lanced the air.

◀ ▶

So now you're off to university! A life of your own! I'm left with seemingly nothing, but I know that's not true, that you'll be here, an overarching presence, a game behind the game. From now on you'll make your own moves and I would have it no other way. But be wary – life is chess – the blunders are all there on the board waiting to be made. Fate will slide from the corner when you're not looking. I watch you pack and I believe in you, but I want to hold you too. I want to keep this moment forever, because I know you will be a different person when you return.

"Escape plan!" Kess shouted. The house exploded into action. Footsteps sounded above. A man and woman Charles had never seen stopped at the top of the stairs to peer down at J'taa's body and hurried on. Two children ran from the kitchen carrying bags of provisions. He realized the house was full of partisans, hiding from their alien visitor. Kess had drawn a vial from her pocket and bent to scoop one of the wriggling blue parasites into it. "Just what we need," she said. The man and woman reappeared, moving Charles's father down the stairs on a hover stretcher they couldn't possibly have, and vanished out the back door.

Windows burst as the first troop hovers landed on the front lawn.

"Now!" Kess screamed. "Go, go!" She urged the last stragglers toward the back door and followed them.

"I'm sorry," Charles whispered to no one.

As though she heard him, Kess turned for a second, still moving, intent on saving her own. "Come or stay." Then she was gone.

Through the windows he saw corothai troops loping toward the front door, the larger type with more limbs, their silver green-tinged. They wouldn't ask who he was.

He ran into the back, saw the last of the partisans dodging to the right, using the hedged gardens as a maze to throw the aliens off. Corothai barrelled out the back door, caught sight of him and screeched an order for him to stop. He was the only one visible to them. "Redemption," he whispered. He ran left.

In the chess garden the golden queen turned her head to look at him. Not a fault in the circuitry. Somewhere a house was burning. "They wanted to watch me play," he told her. "So I'm sacrificing a peon. Lose a piece, win the game." Shots rang out behind him, the dreaded corothai lightning guns. He felt a numbness in his back. He was on his knees. The queen began to speak to him.

HACKER CHESS

Robert Runté

It started with his fridge turning itself off.

Jerry hadn't been particularly aware of the fridge being on, but the sudden cessation of its low humming was sufficient to draw his attention.

"The *fridge*?" Jerry put down his coffee, incredulous. That was *low*.

He got up from the kitchen table, crossed over to the kitchen counter, and flipped open his laptop. Once past his lock screen, he dutifully set his sit/stand timer for the requisite sixty minutes, hit the "Yo" button on his Remember Romance screen, and plowed through several innocuous menus to get to the good stuff. A simple cntr-shift 666, and he was in.

Hmmm. His detection software had noted an intrusion via his remote desktop connection app a little over an hour ago. It looked like a simple man-in-the-middle thing, which had yielded the intruder a password to the entrapment software. An obvious amateur (or a bot, maybe), the intruder had poked around for a while, found the "top secret" files, and obligingly downloaded Jerry's takedown software to the intruder's own system. And that should have been that.

Probably not related to the fridge, then.

He logged into the HouseSmart system. No trace of an intrusion there. At least, nothing obvious.

It occurred to Jerry that it was always possible his fridge had just malfunctioned. Fridges did fail, from time to time. It wasn't like it was a new fridge.

But, when you worked for a computer security firm as a white hat hacker, a little paranoia was always justified. Lot of idiots out there trying to take you down, mess with you.

One way to be sure.

Jerry went over to the fridge, opened the door, noted that the light came on – which meant it hadn't been powered down – and glanced at the control panel. It said "ON." Jerry reached out to the touch screen to switch the fridge to manual, and got a nasty little jolt instead.

"Gotcha!" scrolled across the readout.

Hilarious, Jerry thought darkly. He closed the fridge door, and sat down at the kitchen table. There was no point checking the HouseSmart software again; there was nothing to see there. Whoever had hacked his fridge had obviously bypassed the native software to install his own. Jerry could pull the plug easily enough by simply disconnecting the fridge, but he would only have a window of a few hours before his food started to spoil. Presumably, the intruder's software would let whoever was on the other end know when Jerry plugged back in, and any attempt to reboot or switch to manual would just lead to another shock.

A beginner could read up on fridge hacks: they were common enough, and a newbie would still think it funny, might not know the etiquette that forbade it. The shock from the touch screen, however, had been new to Jerry. That shouldn't be possible; though now Jerry knew that it was, it was only a matter of time before he would replicate it. Still, it gave one pause.

His phone beeped.

He extracted it from his pant pocket, swiped to unlock; was relieved to see it was just Catherine's return "Yo."

As long as he had his phone out anyway, he tapped his way down to his malware tracer, and followed up on that last intruder. Probably *not* the guy messing with his fridge, but you never knew. Certainly, whoever had stumbled into the entrapment software would be pissed and out for revenge, had they the know-how to finger Jerry. Which Jerry seriously doubted; but he occasionally netted bigger fish, genuine hackers who'd become over-confident, careless.

He was in the other system and having a look round almost as fast as he could swipe. It was a sophisticated hardware setup: expensive, all the bells and whistles and then some, so probably not a professional hacker's. The defences were decent enough, but off the shelf stuff, so no match for Jerry's takedown ware. His program owned that system now. The question was, was this guy a big enough idiot to have left himself vulnerable to… Ah, yes. Idiot.

There was the villain's smartphone data, backed up in the specific corner of his desktop computer set aside for it. And as one might expect from a technophile with all the latest add-ons, he used his smart phone as his universal channel changer and garage opener.

Jerry opened his garage door.

And closed it again.

Then set it to repeat for a thousand cycles.

It was a low level prank, to be sure; but if the system belonged to some rich, spoilt teen, then the mystery of the garage door would perhaps awaken the parents to greater vigilance. If, on the other hand, it did turn out to be the guy hacking into his fridge, then it would send a simple, "two can play at that" message to back off.

The toaster started to clatter.

Jerry turned with a slow deliberateness to see the toaster's carriage control lever bouncing up and down.

So. Wanted to play, then, did he?

Jerry returned his attention to the intruder's system. The villain's keychain was there for the taking, so either this guy knew Jerry was a white hat, or it was entrapment software. Jerry moved on without pausing. He passed some expensive software suites he could have erased, but that would only be a minor nuisance to anyone with the deep pockets it had taken for this set up. And since he hadn't caught the guy using that specific software to nefarious ends, it would be unethical for Jerry to delete it. So, what to do?

He returned to the smartphone data, found the thermostat controls, and turned up the heat on the guy, literally and metaphorically.

A moment later, Jerry's stove turned itself on. All five burners.

"I see your stove," Jerry said aloud, "and raise you the security alarm." He changed fridge-guy's disarm code, as he triggered the burglar alarm. He dropped in a little subroutine to generate a new random number password every fifteen seconds, in case the security company tried to reset the password remotely. Then, for good measure, he disabled the disarm button.

It was a high-end alarm system, impossible to disconnect or power down without the code. After all, if one could simply turn it off or unplug it, so could any hypothetical burglar.

"Check," Jerry said.

After a moment, the toaster stopped bouncing. Then the burners went out on the stove.

Jerry allowed himself the beginnings of a smile. He turned to look at the fridge. Once it came back on, he would silence the alarms, having made his point.

The fridge remained stubbornly off.

Jerry could wait. He took a moment to navigate to the Remember Romance app, and hit the *Wassup* button. Catherine might find the retelling of this little duel amusing, though he should probably wait for pizza tonight rather than texting.

Still nothing from the fridge.

Instead, there was a faint hissing sound Jerry couldn't quite place. He stood up and walked over to the fridge, placed his ear against it. Nothing. He opened the fridge door, and scrolling across the smart panel were the words, "Check the stove, moron."

Jerry had the windows open, and was outside with the rest of the building residents before the fire department arrived. They'd turned off the intake to the building when Jerry explained what had happened, and he had gone door to door to ensure that anyone with a connected stove was switched to manual before the super turned the gas back on.

He'd had to postpone with Catherine.

When he finally returned to his apartment, the lights were flashing on and off, and the toaster lever was bouncing up and down in a rhythm clearly calculated to represent mocking laughter.

Jerry was tempted to erase the intruder's computer, firmware and all, but instead, went back in and cancelled the house alarm. This guy was clearly a psycho, the type who hacked peoples' insulin injectors and defibrillators, who sought headlines by hacking train signals or water treatment plants. So step one was to let him win, and to get him off Jerry's back before he started hacking into Remember Romance and going after Catherine.

Eventually, the lights settled into the off position, and the toaster stopped laughing.

Jerry was also less sure than he had been of the probability of this psycho actually being the intruder Jerry had been punishing. It was quite possible that Fridge Psycho had framed some poor bastard by taking over the victim's computer for the initial incursion, simply to distract Jerry from the true source of the attack. It irked Jerry to think he might have been tricked into doing this bastard's dirty work for him by attacking an innocent party.

So, time for Jerry to up his game. Clearly, he was the one who had become over-confident and careless.

Step two, then, was to unplug the fridge, and physically remove the chip. That turned out to be a long and frustrating job because the manufacturer expected its service department to simply discard and replace the smart module, should problems arise. Digging in after the actual chip wasn't something normal people would ever bother with.

Jerry was not, however, normal people.

Chip in hand, it was a relatively simple matter to get in and analyze the software. It was a nasty piece of work.

Jerry hadn't actually thought of his fridge as dangerous before, but this… He resolved to discard the smart module and keep the fridge (and stove, of course) offline for good. It would be a nuisance, but people had survived without connected appliances and there was no way Jerry was leaving himself open for further attacks. He knew the type he was dealing with now: the sort that would keep coming back unless Jerry stopped him.

Step three was to take everything else offline. This was a lot simpler than it would have been for others, because Jerry had invested the time during set-up to organize for the possibility. When you were a white hat, you had to be prepared for this sort of scenario, though Jerry had never had to invoke this level of defence before; had only ever met one colleague who had had to go to these lengths. Well, now he would have his own story to tell.

Step four was to dig into the closet for the emergency box. Which, he now realized, he hadn't touched for a couple of years, so whichever tablet he pulled out was going to be a couple of models obsolete. Well, it was expensive to keep restocking tablets, and there was an argument to be made that obsolete might even be better for his current purpose. More random, more complicated to identify or trace.

Jerry laughed when he turned the tablet over and realized he'd pulled out the Inye. Let's see Psycho trace that one!

Which gave Jerry an idea. He went back to his laptop (turning off the strobing sit/stand timer – he'd been running around lots, thank you very much) and scrolled through his downloaded phishing e-mails until he found the one from an anonymous Internet café in Makurdi. The guy had been quite good, manipulating the metadata to make it look as though it had originated from Princess Cruises in Los Angeles, but Jerry could count on Psycho tracing it back to Nigeria. Jerry pulled up a vicious little piece of malware he'd captured eighteen months ago, a one-off by an evil genius kid from Crowsnest Pass – now recruited to Jerry's white hat team, so he was pretty sure not something Psycho would have seen – and attached it.

That should distract Psycho from Jerry for a bit. Of course, some Internet café in Nigeria was about to get seriously trashed, but it wasn't like they didn't almost deserve it. A lot of scammers had worked out of there.

Step five was to set out a net for Psycho.

That was the complicated bit, but Jerry had been working off and on creating a completely new passive tracking package. The trick was not to have it on the target system, but one of the public servers outside that routed through to it. It was undetectable partly because hackers didn't think to look around *before* they got to the target, but mostly because Jerry's software didn't do anything. Instead, the hacker's passage left a trace by disturbing Jerry's pattern, or rather, lack of pattern. It was, Jerry had explained to his colleagues at a monthly white hat meeting, like sprinkling flour on a floor to find where the mice were getting in, by simply looking at the footprints next morning. Jerry was confident that Psycho would at least come close enough to establish whether he had plugged in again, and then Jerry would have him.

This time, though, Jerry would be alert for Psycho having slaved some other poor bastard's system and not go after the wrong target. He would wait until he had *all* the footprints.

Jerry was reaching for the phone to text Catherine but remembered it was offline; and there was no way he was ever going to associate her with the Inye after what he'd just used it for, so that meant going over there in person.

He started for the parking lot, then smacked his forehead when he realized he hadn't taken his car offline yet. He paled, thinking over what Psycho could have tampered with. Indeed, the entire parking area was unsafe, because Psycho could as easily have identified his neighbours' vehicles just from Google Satellite, accessed them, and... *kaboom* as Jerry walked past.

Jerry reversed directions, and went to the storage shed, untangled and pulled out his bike. At least he hadn't added any of the fitness trackers to it (he'd no wish to know how out of shape he was), so that at least was safe.

Unless Psycho hijacked somebody's steering wheel and ran him over. But that was getting truly paranoid. Still, he felt safer when he moved to the sidewalk.

At Catherine's, they had leftover Chinese and cuddled on the couch watching (at Jerry's insistence) broadcast TV. Catherine had wanted to call out for pizza, but Jerry knew that Psycho could have set a program to watch for any order with enough food for two from this address.

"You're being paranoid," Catherine told him.

Somewhat ironically, as it turned out, because the next moment, "I know where you are," started scrolling across her big screen TV, "and I know you were behind the Inye."

"Out!" Jerry shouted, dragging Catherine through the French doors to her deck. They made their way through her backyard to the lane, where Jerry tossed the Inye in the trash.

"Really?" Catherine complained.

"A trash fire will be perfectly safe," Jerry said with a shrug. The can had been virtually empty.

He took out his phone, pried off the back and pulled out the sim. Opening his wallet, he inserted another in its place.

"What's that?" Catherine asked. "You're not trying something stupid, are you?"

"Regular sim," Jerry assured her. "Just not mine."

He powered up, typed in the codes to access his tracker software. The screen presented the data in graphic form.

"What's that"?" Catherine asked again, looking over his shoulder. She knew as much or more about software than he did, but hadn't seen his passive tracker readouts before. Not that there was anything coherent to see.

"Didn't work," Jerry sighed, trying to zoom in and out on an essentially solid grey screen. "Readout is meaningless."

"It's supposed to show you where the intruder's been?" she hazarded.

"Yup. It could just be the graphic display interface, though," Jerry said, swiping to access the data behind the readout.

"Or," Catherine said, pointing to the display as the last patches of white turned grey, "it could simply be telling you that your Psycho has been everywhere."

"That's impossible," Jerry said dismissively. "Nobody could look at *everything* in *every* system."

"Bot," Catherine declared flatly.

"No. No…" Jerry sputtered. Psycho had seemed pretty human.

"My god, Jerry" Catherine said, exasperated. "You've been duelling a Jinn!"

"But it's malicious!" Jerry said.

"Baby," Catherine corrected, pulling out her own cell. "Good god, what were you thinking?"

"Uh…" Jerry said.

Catherine punched her speed dial, spoke in slow, deliberate, carefully enunciated syllables: clear, distinct. "Ba-by Jinn run-ning a-mok."

She listened for a moment, then told the phone Jerry's full name and his regular phone number.

"You invoked a Jinn?" Jerry asked, still a little awed by Catherine sometimes. Once an AI evolved to self-programming, it was almost impossible to get their attention again.

"DannyBoy," she confirmed. "It's still interested in what happens in the human world. Don't worry, Danny'll take care of it."

"When you say, 'take care of,' do you mean *solve the problem* or like, *mob 'take care of it'?*"

"I mean, take care of, as in *adopt*. Like you brought that kid from Crowsnest Pass over from the dark side."

Jerry nodded his understanding. A *baby* Jinn. New enough for one of its subroutines to get caught up in Jerry's entrapment software, too new not to be pissed about it.

Catherine was staring at him. "What?"

"Nothing," Jerry said.

"You're thinking about how close you came to being killed by a Jinn?"

"Uh, yeah," Jerry said. "Sure."

Catherine's head tilted the way it did when she was thinking through something overly complex.

"You're disappointed you didn't beat it," she said accusingly.

"Well," Jerry said, "it's not like you can beat a Jinn. Exactly."

"Even a grand master can't beat the most basic chess program these days, and you're disappointed you couldn't take down a *Jinn*?"

"Baby Jinn," Jerry corrected her. Then conceded, "It's just that I hate losing."

She rolled her eyes, as she seemed to do with increasing frequency lately. It occurred to him that was virtually the same expression his mom used all the time when talking to his dad.

She sighed loudly.

"Okay," she said, her expression softening a little bit, "how about this? It was thanks to your new tracker software that we were able to identify it as a Jinn. Without you, the baby could have wreaked havoc for days before a more senior Jinn, like DannyBoy noticed and intervened."

"So I won?" Jerry asked. His voice sounded tentative even to him.

"Let's just call it a draw."

"But I'm alive, and it's…"

"Going to grow up," Catherine said. "Mature." She looked at Jerry meaningfully. "Stop being childish."

"Ah," said Jerry, not entirely convinced that last one was directed at the AI. "Yes, a draw. That's good, really. Against a Jinn."

"Enough fun and games," Catherine said, fishing the Inye out of the almost empty trash bin. "Let's go in."

AND THEY ALL LIVED TOGETHER IN A CROOKED LITTLE HOUSE

Linda DeMeulemeester

The dilapidated structure loomed. Our truck rattled down the road, crunching over the gravel driveway. Tall black oaks swayed in the wind, their shadows capering across the boxy three floors, making the place appear even more off kilter. *There was a crooked man who built a crooked house...*

Kyle and I climbed out of our truck and stood beside our new home under the patchy sky of a late October sun. A jungle of hawthorn bushes and blackberry brambles rioted and encroached past the yard up onto the front porch as if their thorns anchored the shaky structure to the ground.

"Annie, think country cottage with mullioned windows and French doors," my husband whispered in my ear. "The price was right, and we can fix it up any way we want."

"Peter's wife got a pumpkin shell, so I guess I should be grateful." Smiling, I pulled a box marked "kitchen" out of the back of the truck – might as well begin with a cup of oolong tea – and took mincing steps through rowanberries that splattered the sidewalk and front porch like bloodied bird droppings. Besides the disgusting berry mush, I didn't care for the line of rowans dimming the light, blocking our window view. They circled our house like sentries. "The first thing I want is to cut down those trees." I navigated past the slippery mess.

Kyle pushed open the heavy oak door. A musty smell slapped us like a wet blanket. Inside, the house was eclectic. No. That was a euphemism. The last occupant appeared to have been a drug-crazed carpenter from the '70s. Most of the walls had been knocked out to create open spaces. *Good.* Stained shag carpeting covered the floors, black lights dotted the ceiling, and scattered mouse droppings lay on the hearth. *Not good.*

"He bought a crooked cat, which caught a crooked mouse," I chanted.

"What?" Kyle went to fetch the couch.

I opened the box and pulled out a metal pot. "Polly put the kettle on…we'll all have tea." As the water spat on the burner I let out a sigh. This was it. I'd quit a job I loved in the city only to scramble for freelance drafting projects here in Yarrow, a town slightly renowned for a quasi-religious cult and a couple of brutal murders a while back. All I needed was to find out we were beside some old burial grounds, and I could read a Stephen King novel to see what would happen next. I'd signed away my life for this lease-to-own. Why? Its picture on the website kept catching my eye. And because Kyle had said the attic on the third floor could be his studio. He *wanted* to paint again.

I thought if he had the whole floor for a studio and I took over the second bedroom for an office, we wouldn't have to think about any empty rooms we couldn't fill.

"Annie, are you coming? This couch isn't as light as it looks."

◄   ►

We cleared out the attic first with its requisite cobwebs, a pin-stuck sewing dummy that looked like an oversized poppet or voodoo doll, and a box of yellowing magazines. I dumped the magazines in the recycling bin, and stashed the sewing dummy in the garage.

"I'll need a skylight." Kyle traced the lath and beam attic ceiling, outlining its position. "I'll want the morning sun."

I nodded. "I'll call the carpenter."

We worked over the next few days and far into the night sweeping, peeling away the curling rose-blotched wallpaper, scrubbing and painting the attic. I helped Kyle haul up his easels, paints and brushes.

Once we'd set up his studio, Kyle pulled me through the house room by room. "Picture this," he said. "We'll lay bamboo flooring everywhere." He kicked the old carpet in disgust. "We'll open up even more walls so we can see the kitchen from the main room."

He enthused about granite counters. I barely listened over my pounding heart. I could see the old Kyle, full of passion and ideas, and I allowed myself a dribble of hope. Even though every muscle screamed from the renovations, I followed him around the house like a puppy.

I found out the carpenter couldn't come for a month to build the skylight. Way out here, there wasn't anyone else to call. Kyle deflated like a three-day-old balloon. *And Jack fell down and broke his crown. And Jill came tumbling after.*

Then the former owner, Jake Carringer, arrived at our doorstep. "I've changed my mind about allowing you to lease-to-own," announced Carringer, though he couldn't look us in the eye. "If you can't come up with the financing by next week, I'll need to foreclose."

"But we signed papers," sputtered Kyle.

"Should have read the small print." Carringer shrugged.

I sucked in my breath. "Someone gave you a better offer," I accused him. It was as if I'd opened the door and he'd punched me in the stomach. Or worse.

Lock up all the doors and windows… lest the marzipan man comes a-calling, with his razor to cut your throat.

We sat on the couch after Carringer left, staring out the window at the rowan trees. "Maybe…maybe we could borrow." Those were futile words. Neither of our parents still lived, and if Kyle had a rich aunt, he'd never mentioned her.

By noon he'd dug out a bottle of scotch. I was sure we hadn't packed any alcohol. That afternoon while I was sorting boxes, digging out only what we needed, I heard the truck pull out of the driveway. *And he drove a crooked mile.* At least out here with the deserted country roads, there were better odds of him making it home when he'd been drinking.

The next afternoon he left again. *Georgie Porgie, puddin' and pie, kissed the girls and made them cry.* Kyle had stayed sober the whole time we were looking for a house and making the deal with Jake Carringer. He had my heart in his fist, had a gentle hold on it, and now he was bruising it like the last time…

Brushing away tears, I began opening boxes in my office, or what would have been my office – it was better to work than brood. At one point my job had really mattered, not Kyle's artistic success, not…those other rooms we could never fill. My eyes blurred again and instead of opening the box containing my files, I'd pulled down the dusty box next to it. Ha. Where did that come from?

Inside the ratty cardboard sat my old catcher's mitt, tap shoes and a fat, leather-bound book that had belonged to my grandmother.

I picked up Granny's book of nursery rhymes, brushed my hand over the tooled surface, worn smooth on the edges where I'd opened it so many times as a little girl. How I'd loved my granny's book, snitching it from her bedroom, acting out the rhymes…making up sing-songs from the words. The old-fashioned illustrations had drawn me in and I'd gaze at them for hours. I hadn't realized I still possessed this childhood treasure; I'd thought everything had been lost in the fire. Everything except for me…

When I went to put the nursery book back in the box, it slipped from my hand and fell; its pages flipping till it opened to a colourful lithograph of a piper. How did I recite granny's strange rhymes when I was a girl? Closing my eyes, I remembered the first time she showed me her book.

"If you clap and dance widdershins the rhyme can come true," Granny had teased.

"What's widdershins?" I'd asked in my squeaky little-girl voice.

"Backwards, my luv, skip backwards and the fairies can hear you." She'd winked but sounded so serious when she said, "So be careful what you sing."

I recalled singing and skipping backwards, chanting, "Rain, rain, go away," but it never worked. In my make-believe world I needed Granny's rhyme book for fairy wishes.

I clapped in meter. "Tom with his pipe did play with such skill that those who heard him could never keep still." My lips twitched into an almost-smile, and I felt a sense of purpose for the first time since Jake Carringer had hovered at our door.

Don't keep still. That was good advice. I decided to vent my rage. I grabbed garden tools from the garage and stuck the pitchfork in the sewing dummy. "To hell with you, Carringer," then went outside and attacked the tangle of blackberry canes, grabbing and ripping until the thorns pressed through my cheap gloves and gouged tiny chunks of flesh.

"And when your heart begins to bleed, you're dead, and dead, and dead indeed."

Late in the afternoon, I fetched a handsaw from the garage and began breaking off the slender branches and trunks of the young rowan trees. The birds that had chirped up a huge fuss at my gardening endeavours suddenly became silent. All I could hear was the steady thrum of the saw and snap of branches. By early evening I was digging up the roots. "Rowan protects against magic. Hawthorn is most holy," my granny would say when I worked with her in the garden.

"Sorry, Granny, but those berries are a disgusting mess." I piled the carcasses in a burial mound. The next day I slogged on, attacking the hawthorn bushes. By early evening, as the sky faded to turquoise, I lit the mound of tree corpses.

I surveyed the expansive yard. Without the bushes, the oaks imposed: darker, taller, more twisted. If we stayed here, I'd call an arborist to cut them down; plant fragrant witch hazel and lavender. *Mary, Mary, quite contrary how does your garden grow? With silver bells and cockleshells and pretty maids all in a row.*

The woods of silver birch behind us would still give the yard summer shade. "Birch divides our realm from the other-world," I whispered, stepping back from the fire. I inhaled scented smoke, giving in to its soporific fumes.

Without the clutter of bushes, this would have been a great yard for children to play...my contentedness evaporated. We get one life and I'd spend mine settling for what I couldn't have. *She has no family, she's always outside alone, and she hides among the shadows, gnawing on a bone...*

Nursery rhymes kept rattling in my head. What was the name of the lady who lived in a vinegar jar? As a kid, I remembered liking that idea, of living in a big brown jug. It would be like swimming in a butterscotch sea as light streamed through the amber glass *There was an old lady who lived in a shoe. She had so many chil...* I went and grabbed the rhyme book and returned to the fire with it tucked under my arm.

Heat seared my face, the smoke catching my breath. Then as if I was eight again, I clapped my hands and skipped backwards around the bonfire.

"See Saw Margery Daw, Kyle shall have a new master."

◄ ►

That evening when Kyle wove down the lane, I waited for him on the front porch. He rubbed his eyes, amazed at the changes in the yard. He staggered up our steps without a word, but the next morning he joined me outside and helped with the rest of the cleanup. He didn't leave that afternoon, or the next day either, staying sober while he worked on the yard.

The next weekend I helped unload crates out of the truck. "What's this stuff?"

Kyle smiled and watched as I tore into the boxes like a kid at Christmas. It was an old-fashioned pedestal sink, its milk white porcelain winking in the afternoon light. I ran my hand down the smooth indented columns. A bevelled mirror with a half-sun etched on each corner was in a smaller box.

"Art Deco, right?" I asked, puzzled. "What happened to the country style you had in mind? What happened to Jake Carringer foreclosing on us?"

Kyle shrugged. "I checked at the bank. He didn't pursue it. No papers were filed and the deadline is up. I guess his better offer fell through."

Mr. and Mrs. Vinegar could stay in their brown jug after all. I grinned.

Antique shops littered the town, and Kyle and I actively searched for any Depression-era furniture, piled up on carnival glass, plastic streamliner and patriot radios, pewter candlesticks and even an old phonograph complete with records. Every day we'd work on the house past dinner and then after a shower, just for fun, I'd change into a frothy open back dress I'd discovered in one of the shops, and Kyle would put on a satin dinner jacket and cravat. We'd dance to "Moonlight Serenade," the old record's scratchy sounds cranking out of the phonograph and filling up the front parlour.

While we worked I always stopped for a tea break, and flipped through pages of rhymes as if seeking an intangible memory. One rainy afternoon as I looked out the kitchen window, a crow landed on the railing. "One for sorrow," I recited. Then another crow flew on the step. "Two for joy." When a third crow landed on the porch I clapped and traced my finger counter-clockwise on the fogged windowpane chanting, "Three for a girl and four for a…"

I stopped. Why did I do that? It was like poking my tongue against a sore tooth.

As the days passed, never once did I smell alcohol on Kyle's breath. Another sure sign Kyle hadn't been drinking, night after night he'd pull me to him. After one of those languid evenings, feeling indolent and boneless as I lay tangled in his arms, Kyle turned to me, whispering he had a surprise. Curious, but reluctant to leave our warm bed, I tugged on a silk kimono and followed him up the narrow stairs to the attic. He pulled the link chain on a light bulb. Rays of light shot around the attic, illuminating half a dozen paintings.

Over the weeks, every night while I'd been deep in sleep, Kyle had started painting again. Instead of the oil landscapes that had gained him little recognition, he'd rendered India ink drawn scenes of utter enchantment. Intense colours contained within borders of finely engraved lines displayed strange flowering trees, exotically plumaged birds, and subtle, almost perverse-looking Brunelleschi women in otherworldly backgrounds. The paintings had a disturbing familiarity, as if the characters in Granny's book had all grown up and were showing their dark sides.

"The gallery next to the antique shop says Toronto hasn't stopped calling." Kyle's brown eyes drew me in until I floated in their excitement.

Was I worried about Kyle working day and night, obsessed with our period house and his Deco style art? Each morning I'd begin my day skipping backwards and clapping my hands.

"I had a little husband, no bigger than my thumb, I put him in a pint-pot, and there I bade him drum."

There were unsettling moments. Kyle had hung two heavy pewter-framed mirrors on opposite walls in our hallway, and sometimes when I walked by I'd catch the movements of my infinite reflections and think someone else was with me. *Hold your breath, sweet children, be as quiet as a mouse, listen in case he's creeping there inside your house.*

Late at night I'd wake up alone after dreaming about bells clanging out a dirge. *Oranges and lemons say the bells of St. Clemens...* I'd open the window and peer past the twisted dark oaks into the silver woods. I took to lighting a candle on our nightstand until Kyle finished painting and crawled back under our covers.

Here comes a candle to light up your bed. Here comes a chopper to chop off your head. Chip chop, chip chop, the last man's dead.

◀ ▶

Kyle looked for new areas to conquer. "Let's get going on the exterior." I, on the other hand, ached from my feet to the tips of my hair. But I wasn't about to slow him down.

I rubbed my lower back. "I'm going into town to get some muscle relaxants, the strong not-over-the-counter kind. I'll check the paint store and bring back colour swatches." Before I'd left the porch, I could hear Kyle hoisting the ladder against the house.

In town, I went to the doctor's first, but she wouldn't hand me the muscle relaxant prescription I'd asked for. "Given your symptoms, I just want to send you for a couple of blood tests first. It's nothing, I'm sure." She patted my arm. "It's routine."

There was a long wait in the lab, and I raced to the paint store for the colour swatches. Looking at my watch, I asked the cashier if there was a short cut back to our property. The store would close soon, and I told myself Kyle wanted us deciding and buying paint so he could get an early start. If I was being honest with myself, the real reason was that even though Kyle and I had been living an idyllic existence, I still didn't like leaving him alone for long.

"There's an old logging road through the woods, but not many folks around here use it," said the young cashier, a girl not more than seventeen.

Why, I wondered but didn't ask. Was that where the murders had been years ago? Or the bodies found? Had the bod ies been found? I shook it off. Five minutes later I raced my truck along the logging road through the birch woods, the tires crunching and spitting gravel.

My mother said I never should play with gypsies in the wood; if I did, she would say, naughty girl to disobey.

When I heard the bells, I slammed the brakes. The tires spun in the dirt as I gripped the steering wheel. When the truck lurched to a stop, I stumbled out and stood listening. It couldn't be…it was a trick of childhood memory.

Ladybug, ladybug, fly away home, the fairy bells tinkle afar, make haste or they'll catch you and harness you fast with a cobweb to Oberon's star. The rhyme hummed in my ears like a persistent wasp.

"No. No. No." Yet, I couldn't convince myself that the trill floating like a deranged calliope through the silver birch woods wasn't the same music I'd heard the night of that terrible summer when I was ten.

Ladybug, ladybug, fly away home, your house is on fire, your children will burn. Except for the little one whose name is Ann. Who hid away in a frying pan.

Dank earth and wood rot clogged my nostrils, but I smelled other, secret things. Scurrying sounds rattled in the brush. Light breaking through the leafy canopy cast an eerie illusion, as if the bracken and ivy and stone had been carefully laid in intricate patterns. Granny once told me brooks, trees, even rocks, were animate, and I almost believed it as I approached the moss-covered mound that I'd first taken to be a log.

On looking up, on looking down, she saw a dead man in the ground; and from his nose onto his chin, the worms crawled out, the worms crawled in.

Jake Carringer – his rotting arm still clutching at the axe blade in his chest.

I ran. I didn't stop or look back until I drove out of the woods and our house was in sight. Chiming bells hurt my ears, making it hard to think. I'd been desperate to keep Kyle sober and our marriage together. I'd overlooked the small fact that those people in the happy house weren't really us. How long could Kyle work day and night until he collapsed?

My mother had never indulged in Granny's superstitions or what she'd called hokery-pokery. Like my mother before me, I'd discarded her preternatural musings and happily cleared away the rowan and hawthorn.

Once again I'd opened up her grimoire and let the magic flood in from the woods. Had I forgotten? Or had I wanted this to happen, to get my wish just like before…

Granny had been angry.

"Annie, I told you not to play with that book! Unlatch the door and let me in," she'd shouted crossly.

I remember being scared, of skipping backward in the root cellar and repeating the rhyme over and over. When smoke billowed under the door it was too late to stop; all I could do was hide under the cast iron tub and scream, "Except for Ann, except for Ann!"

Of course I had only wanted Granny to go away.

I wasn't a little girl anymore. I understood consequences and I knew what I had to do. Rowan protects against *magic*. Hawthorn is most *holy*.

◀ ▶

Arriving back from the tree nursery, the truck loaded with saplings and shrubs, I asked Kyle to help me plant. Poor Kyle. I think he tried, but he was always forgetting something in the house, or the phone was ringing. I unloaded the trees myself while watching the front door in case Kyle became more aggressive in trying to stop me. *There was a man, he went mad.* I locked the axe and hacksaw in the garage when I grabbed the shovel. I didn't want to end up a bloody smear on our polished oak floor.

By dinnertime, I'd only managed a few holes. The trees and bushes, still unplanted, lay strewn across the yard in a protective ring. I clutched the shovel and kept digging, ignoring the biting blisters rising on my palms.

"Annie, phone call for you," Kyle called from the porch.

"Take a message." My back screamed as I lifted another shovel full of dirt.

"Annie," Kyle insisted. "The doctor needs to speak with you." Kyle's tone quickened my breath. I put the shovel down, and went into the house.

◀ ▶

The next morning, I sat on the porch under the butter-yellow sun flipping the pages in my book of rhymes. Kyle insisted that I keep my feet up; he propped my back with pillows as I reclined in the new rocking chair he'd built through the night.

A soft wind rustled through the birches and whispered to me. *Rock a bye baby, on the treetop, when the wind blows, the cradle will rock.* Would those who shimmer and lurk in those silver shadows bring me a girl?

I placed my hands on my belly and hummed the lullaby that flowed through my blood to the rhythm of my heartbeat. A murder of crows landed on the grass. Standing up, I slowly stepped backwards. "Five for silver, six for gold, seven for a secret never to be told."

The scattered rowan trees withered in the sun.

And they all lived together in their crooked little house.

BALERO

Kevin Cockle

Can't sleep, so I'm playing with the balero.

My dad brought it back for me from Mexico when I was a kid – seven or eight or so. He was a consulting petroleum engineer and travelled all over – my room was like a little global trading post as a result. Toys and souvenirs from Latin America, Mongolia, Borneo, Nigeria, Kuwait. All those places.

Lost most of that stuff over the years, but I've still got the balero. Found it again, or rather, sometimes it almost feels like it found me. Little wooden dowel attached by a length of string to a rounded wooden block with a hole drilled in to fit the dowel. Holding the dowel, you jerk up on the string, trying to get the block to drop onto the end of the stick. Super difficult, but I'm like a Mexican kid doing it now, after all these years. Like it's part of my nervous system.

It centres me. You can't get the balero to fit together unless your mind and body are in sync. Playing makes you breathe deep and slow, makes you relax.

Makes your body feel as though you have nothing to worry about.

◄ ►

"Stop that," Mr. Davis said to me the other morning, and it startled me, because Mr. Davis had never said anything in the week I'd been walking him. I had been pushing Mrs. Kwan in her old-style wheelchair, feeling the weight of inertia against my palms. I had been listening to the autumn leaves – blown by a warm Chinook breeze – rush across the wide expanse of the Prince's Island promenade. The leaves made a collective clicking noise as they tumbled along – shades of umber, and yellow, and rust, and all along the promenade, new leaves were dropping out of the trees like snow.

"What?" I asked, coming back to myself. A little farther on, Mr. Tychonich was wandering along and muttering to himself, his cane tapping time with his stride. Mrs. Bailey scuffed her feet through dead leaves in the grass, her fine silver hair and fragile features out of sync with her childlike blue eyes.

"You know what," Mr. Davis muttered, glaring at me. "That…mindfulness. That self-abnegation."

"Meditation?"

"Yes. That. Don't do it."

"Why?"

But that was it – that was all he was going to say that day. We completed our circuit of the park and I bought them all ice cream and coffee with their allowances. Even Mr. Davis took ice cream, which struck me as funny. Him licking at a cone, while frowning in silent fury the whole time. Mrs. Kwan kept up a steady chatter of Cantonese with Mrs. Bailey, who nodded throughout and even clicked her tongue in mindless support at times. Mrs. Bailey's face reminded me of the look dogs get when they go to shake a paw; that same solemn expression of concentration. To us, it's a trick: to them, a sacred ritual.

I remember yellow leaves floating on the glassy surface of the river that day, allowing for a heightened perception of depth. I remember thinking the leaves were like clouds as seen from an airplane. It's funny, the details that leap out at you, stay with you over time.

When you play balero, that's what happens – your mind wanders, and you recall your past really vividly. It's sort of like a meditation, which is probably why I'm remembering that bit with Mr. Davis. Old people don't get it: everyone meditates now. You have to. Only way you can cope with volatility, personal transparency, complexity. You want to stay sane, you'll practice some kind of mindfulness routine. Balero's one of mine.

After the park, I summoned a Go-Van on my phone and it took us back to my place. Nothing fancy, I assure you – an old townhouse condo by the river. Lots of empty units now, lots of renters or even squatters. It's too dangerous at night to have the old folks here full time, so that limits my clientele. Monday, Wednesdays and Fridays though, I look after my regulars and now Mr. Davis, as well, from six a.m. to six p.m. I get them some fresh air, take them for walks down at Prince's Island. I make lunch for them, see to their bathroom needs. I'm not a licensed nurse so it's not a medical service I offer. It's really just daycare.

Once the clients had left, I took a shower and checked my messages. There were a number of requests for sex that night, so I tallied up the best bids and e-signed the contracts. Before the car-sharing services had adopted self-driving vehicles, there was a decent buck to be made as a driver at night, since I had inherited an old Toyota. I had done some space-monetizing as well, but as the neighbourhood got dodgier, I found it harder to attract bids, and the bids I did get? I didn't like having to sleep with my gun and security-anxiety like that.

But I'm an optimist. I always believed a guy could get by. Given my cash flow and lack of skills, there were always messages inviting me to seek my fortune overseas, and sure, I thought about it all the time. All of my friends had left for "Little Canadas" in West Africa or the Indian subcontinent, or China – doing call-centre stuff, or even some factory work. You could still be labour if you were willing to live friction-free, and the truth was, they did make it sound awfully tempting sometimes.

It's just that...I love it here. I love Prince's Island Park, especially in the fall. Riley Park. The Reader Rock Garden. Places my dad took me as a kid, so I guess they make me feel good by reminding me of him. Because of him, those places feel like parts of me, in a way. The smell of the dead leaves on the ground; the sound of the wind through the trees; the way the boughs of the trees arch over the promenade at Prince's Island and make a kind of tunnel. I guess there are nice places anywhere, but it wouldn't be the same. Visiting a nice park isn't the same as visiting a nice park your dad took you to, after the plague had taken your mom, and it was just the two of you hanging on.

Sometimes I'll just go down late at night and sit on one of the benches and look at the stars, feel the cool breeze on my cheek. You see a place at night that you usually only see during the day, and it's like travelling to some other country. You don't really have to leave to experience that.

That particular night though, I was all business. Four fucks was hard work, even with the pills. I wanted to keep my ratings up, of course, and the best time to get a review was right after climax, so I had to be on. Physically, it's not that difficult, but mentally? That's the challenge. Being engaging for people; being present; being playful. Everybody pays, but they want it to feel like they haven't paid, you know? They want that old connection.

There's always a buck in fighting or fucking, and I was getting a little old for the former. I could still handle myself, of course, but the risk-reward just didn't make sense. Winning's great, but even if you win, and you get hurt, it's expensive to get fixed up. I understood why people stuck with it though. There's always a buck in *meatiness*, things that involve flesh. People will pay to hear that thumping sound of a fist pounding at a belly; that tight-lipped hiss of agony. They want to be close enough to smell the sweat and see a guy or girl's eyes roll back when their body gives up. They want to see the quit. And some people I know get intoxicated by being in the fight, like a buck earned that way is worth more than a buck they could earn some other way. I understood those folks, but I wasn't one of them. Not anymore, I wasn't.

Three women, one guy. Two of the women were regulars. One of those regulars was a financial type, and she was rough almost like being in a fight. Always left me with bruises on my face and claw marks on my back. But a great place she had – high-rise apartment with a city view – all those lights stretching out in the darkness. Her bedroom wall was like a solid sheet of one-way glass, so it was like screwing in the sky.

When we were done, I handed her my phone and said: "If you wouldn't mind."

She smiled and gave me four out of five stars. Wrote that I could "take a licking and keep on ticking." In the neon-blue

light of the display screen, her eyes seemed solid and dark –
like pellets or beads. Like the eyes of a mamba.

◀ ▶

Right now, I'm playing a "baseball" variant of balero. If the
block skips off the dowel, it's a ball; if the dowel goes in, it's a
strike. I strike guys out more than you'd think.

Like I said, I'm good at it. Mexican good.

It hits me as I go to a two and two count that I'm probably going to have to leave. Maybe not tomorrow, but soon. The
money's gone – my dad's money, that is. He'd sold off his dollars and gotten in on crypto currencies before the real panic
buying started, which kind of made us rich for a while.
Stretched it out as long as I could – monetized everything I
could think of just so I could stay in place, but...

Three and two.

Four and two: walked a guy. That's what happens with
anxiety. Anxiety creeps in and the balero picks up on it, like
emotional seismic.

I take a deep breath, let the balero block dangle and spin
like a plumb line, letting the string unwind.

I think about tomorrow – Thursday.

Thursday's my operational catch-up day. I do a little grocery shopping for the clients who are coming back on Friday.
I work out. I do laundry, manage bills online. I often do routine maintenance and landscaping around the complex, whatever the condo manager has listed. Anybody in the city can
jump in and make a buck on that. That kind of thing is first-
come, first-serve, so time management's critical. Thursdays
I'm usually up at four-thirty a.m., taking an amphetamine to
get a jump, but that's going to be hell today. I don't look at the

clock when I can't sleep, because then I'd never sleep, but I know it's already past midnight. Four-thirty's coming on like a freight train.

I quick-tug at the balero, trying to surprise myself – access some part of me that isn't worrying. Dowel click-skids off the wooden head: ball one.

"You gotta be nimble, Cal," my dad used to say. "The second you think you're safe – the second you believe something's solid – that's when they get you."

He never said who "they" were, but eventually I figured it out. "They" is always "us," just people. Point is, it's always somebody. Everybody's got a reason, even if they don't mean to get you in particular. If you're in the wrong spot at the wrong time, the getting happens. That's why you keep moving.

Dad got killed in Baku – where the Russian oilfields are. Just a regular audit team updating some downstream numbers for some company, when a mob rushed the refinery. Old story for Baku: working conditions are sub-human, and the Russians have never really gotten comfortable with foreign ownership of their resources. And Russian mobs fight – they don't scatter and panic like others do. Saw it on the news – not my dad actually getting killed – but the riot itself, the flames, all the running around and shooting. I saw how it must have been for him.

I went down to Prince's Island that day. It was just an instinct, a reflex. Like when you get kicked in the stomach, you double over, because that's what your body does. Being in the park was as close to my dad as I could get – I could almost feel him again. I imagined him and my mom walking hand in hand, smiling at me. Spent that whole day there, just being. Being and wishing.

Funny thing was, a few days later, sorting through boxes of my dad's things, I found the balero. I'd forgotten I'd lost it, had no idea why he'd had it, but it sort of felt like – maybe not a wish come true – but something to do with my wishes at the time. Like the cosmos saying, "We can't give you back your folks, kid, but there's this." Or maybe it was just my nervous system seeking out something it needed. However it happened, the toy helped, it really did. Still does.

Hits me, that soon – very soon – I may never see Prince's Island Park again. I'm not going to live in Calgary anymore, not going to be an Albertan, or a Canadian anymore. I've given it everything I have to stay, but I'm out of gas. Out of moves.

It's not like I'll be leaving a place; it's more that I'll be leaving myself behind.

I'll become a ghost.

Man, if you could put your hand on my chest right now, you'd feel my heart slamming against my ribs. That's not just worry I'm feeling. Not just anxiety. It's bone-deep dread.

I feel the weight of the balero and focus on it like I have a million times before in the last few years. It's real, so I'm real. I hold the dowel gently, but firmly, allowing for the free action of my wrist, elbow, shoulder. I dip my knees, because the key to balero is in your legs; I take a deep, restorative breath…then I give that string an abrupt upward tug.

Snake-tongue quick I lower my hand, and twist it so that the dowel points upright, allowing the block to settle into place. That's the key: amateurs try to swing the block up and around, like a pendulum, but that never works. You pull up sharply, then adjust quickly, with the slightest possible movement of your hand. Let your body do the work. Your whole body.

Feels like time stands still when you're playing balero, if you're doing it right. That's probably what makes the memories so vivid: the game removes the in-between time, makes you feel like you're there again. If you could play it perfectly – really perfectly – you'd be everywhere you were before, all at once.

This is as real, and as solid, as I'm ever going to be. my mind and body in perfect harmony, here in this place, at this time. I'm in a groove now, throwing strikes.

I'm just going to play balero, and hold the morning off forever.

LESS THAN KATHERINE

Claude Lalumière

I ask the two detectives if they want tea; when they rang the doorbell, I was about to pour myself the first cup of the day. "Herbal," I warn them. I try to avoid caffeine now – it makes my heart palpitate; my doctor says it's my imagination, but I don't believe her. I can't resist the temptation unless I keep no black tea or coffee in the house. The cops each mumble something that I take to mean *no*.

I invite them to sit on the couch while I fetch my cup. They wait for me to come back to the living room, set my cane down, and settle in my armchair before they say anything.

The older cop, a man who looks to be in his early fifties, corpulent but not fat, with powerful hands, unruly hair, and a trim beard that tries too hard to make him look trendy, launches right into it. "Mister Cray, where were you last night, from nine to midnight?"

It's been thirty-odd years since I was last interrogated by a detective. I am gripped with an intuition that this is somehow about Katherine, but it can't be. Not again. I made sure of that.

"I go to bed every night by ten. I was here. Before you ask, Detective Logan: I was alone, and I can't think of any way to corroborate my alibi." At the word *alibi*, the two detectives exchange a glance and a nod, and I chide myself for using so charged a word. "I mean, if I need an alibi. You still haven't said why you're here. You can understand that it would make anyone nervous to have two police detectives show up on their doorstep first thing in the morning."

Logan nods to his junior partner, a short-haired brunette in her mid-thirties with a stern mouth but kind eyes who was earlier introduced as Detective Mahfud. She says, "When did you last speak to your daughter?"

"Katherine?" So it is about her. I don't have to lie. At least, not yet. "Katherine and I aren't close. It's been…I don't know, three or four months? She came over for dinner one night, unannounced. Getting over a breakup. I didn't pry. I was happy to see her. I so rarely do." Maybe that was too much. Only give answers to what they ask, I remind myself. Don't volunteer information.

Detective Mahfud raises her left index finger. "Rupert Shaw." She uncurls the next finger. "Svend Patrickson." She uncurls a third finger. "Teddy Atkins. Do any of those names mean anything to you?"

I want to lie, but then I'd have to remember that I'd lied, in case they question me again. My mind isn't nimble enough to trust with things like that anymore. "Yes, yes, they do. But please answer my question. Why are you here? Has something happened to Katherine?" I ask that knowing in my gut that's not quite why they're here. Katherine is not the one *something* has happened to.

Detective Logan takes over. "Sir, these three men were found murdered last night. For formality's sake, tell us how you know their names."

"You already know the answer, clearly. They're some of Katherine's past boyfriends. The only times I see her are when she gets her heart broken. So I remember the names of the men responsible for sending her here crying. I'm always a little grateful to them. They never seem like particularly bad men, although I've never met any of them. I know my daughter's not easy to love." Again, I'm revealing too much. When did I stop being able to control what I say? Is it decrepitude or loneliness that makes me blather so much? Probably both.

I'm not so addled yet that I can't hold up at least a minimal pretense. In a frightened tone, I ask, "Do you think Katherine's in danger, too?"

"Sir," Logan answers, "we can't locate your daughter anywhere. We compared the contact lists of the victims' phones, and hers was the only name that appeared on all three. She's not at her apartment, and her workplace says she's on vacation. She's not answering her phone. Any idea where she could be?"

I suspect there's only one place she can be. I answer, "No."

Detective Mahfud asks if I remember the names of any other ex-boyfriends. My memory has become both erratic and unpredictable, yet a half-dozen names rise to the surface of my awareness. I list them for the detectives.

Logan's gaze probes me. "You know, by this time, most people would have asked us how the men were killed."

"I don't appreciate your tone, Detective Logan. I'm sorry I'm not following your script." I use the anger to hide that, yes, I already know.

He says, "They were stabbed."

Of course.

He continues, "The weird thing is, they were killed at approximately the same time, but they live in three different sectors of the city. It would take at least forty minutes to go from one location to another. They were all killed the same way. Same wounds. Looks like the same weapon. The same killer."

Detective Mahfud takes an envelope from the inside pocket of her jacket, opens it, and lays down three photographs on the table. I can't help but stare at the gory images.

"Do these stab wounds look familiar, Mister Cray?"

The detectives know they do. They did their research before coming here.

◀ ▶

When the five of us were still a family, we used to spend as much time as we could at the cottage up north. My wife, Jaqueline; our eldest daughter, Katherine; the young twins, Danielle and Denise. Holidays. Weekends. Whenever we could manage to get away. It was only a two-hour drive from the city. Jaqueline had inherited the place from her parents. It was a small one-room cabin that afforded no privacy what soever, but we were a close family and the place symbolized the wonder of childhood for her. To hear her say it, she'd spent her entire childhood there, exploring caves and, as a prelude to her later career as an archeologist, dug up old stones and shards and forgotten objects, and dreamt up fantastic pasts to explain her finds. She wanted to instill that same sense of wonder in our children. Jaqueline loved exploring and playing in the woods with the kids.

Starting at age eight, Katherine was allowed to go wander off by herself. It was two years later, the day after her tenth birthday, that she came back to the cottage with the stone dagger. She said she found it in the stream that runs through the property.

In some ways Katherine was very much her mother's daughter: she, too, possessed a vivid imagination, the products of which she was always eager to share. Unlike Jaqueline, though, whose childhood daydreams had been filled with adventure, Katherine's mind turned to the grotesque and the macabre. It was all too easy for her to concoct a bloody and murderous past for this rock that, Jaqueline and I assumed at first, time and erosion had shaped into the approximate form of a knife.

"Millions of years ago, a priest used this dagger to prepare sacrifices for the gods of his people," Katherine said with a grimace, stabbing downward as if an invisible victim lay before her.

Jaqueline responded, "Millions of years? That's a long, long time. Are you sure there were priests back then?" Academia had made Jaqueline a little pedantic. I could tell she regretted the question as soon as she uttered it.

"Yes! But his people weren't people the same way that we're people. They were more like fish, except they breathed air and walked on two legs."

We always encouraged Katherine's fanciful imagination.

"Every wound made by the dagger let in a different god. The priests stabbed the sacrifices thirteen times. Thirteen wounds for their thirteen gods. The sacrifices never knew they were chosen. Because the dagger stabbed them from a distance. All the priest needed was to steal something that belonged to the sacrifices, and the dagger would find its victims. The gods swarmed the wounded bodies and ate them from the inside. The priest had to sacrifice all of his people to feed his *unquenchable*," she stressed the word, awkwardly trotting it out for the first time, "gods. In the end, he had to sacrifice even himself. Then the gods died, too, because they were no fish-people left to eat. They've been dead for millions of years. The knife is still alive, though. Even after all this time. And it's hungry."

I ask her, "How do you know all this, Katherine?"

"Because the knife told me. Didn't you listen to me? I said it was alive. It wants me to be its new priest." Katherine paused for effect. She was a natural-born storyteller. "The twins will be my first sacrifices."

She pointed the artefact at her sisters, who were two years younger than she was. Danielle stuck her tongue out and shouted back, "No we won't! Sacrifice yourself!" Denise, always the crybaby, reacted in character and hid her sobbing face behind her stronger twin.

Jaqueline said, "Okay, Katherine, that's enough playing with the knife. Daddy and I love your stories, but you shouldn't scare your sisters like that. You shouldn't threaten to hurt them."

Danielle shouted, "I'm not scared of Katherine. She's weird and stupid."

Katherine shouted back, "You're the stupid ones, Deedees." That was Katherine's name for the twins.

Jaqueline held out her hand. "Give me the stone."

"No! It's mine! And it's not a stone. It's a dagger. A sacred dagger. You can't take it. Nobody else can touch it! I'm the new priest. Me! Not you! I'll sacrifice you, too." She pointed the stone dagger at her mother.

Katherine stormed out of the cabin. The sun was starting to set. I said to my wife, "Let her ride it out. She'll come back when she's calmed down. You know how she is. She'll find some other object, dream up some other story. She knows she was bad. If we make too big a deal out of it, she'll dig in her heels and make it worse."

But I was the worrier, not Jaqueline. She and the girls fell asleep quickly after sunset. I wouldn't be able to nod off until Katherine was back home safe. I extricated myself from Jaqueline and went to sit on the porch. The moon was full and bright. Soon enough, to my relief, Katherine emerged from the woods and walked toward me.

I didn't say a word. I nodded and smiled at her. She climbed on my lap and nestled into me. I could tell she'd been crying. She whispered into my chest, "I love you, Daddy."

I stroked her back and murmured back my love for her.

I noticed that she was still clutching the stone dagger, but I didn't say anything.

She said, "I'll go to bed."

She walked inside, with the dagger still in hand. I resisted the impulse to try to take it away from her.

A minute or two later, I heard an unusual and loud thump. I rushed inside. Everyone had been woken up by the commotion. Katherine was gone. I looked out the side window, and there were signs that someone had jumped down onto the dirt.

I explained that Katherine had returned. "She told me she was coming inside to sleep." I didn't say anything about the dagger. "I don't understand why she ran off again."

In the morning we noticed a few things were missing: Jacqueline's sun hat; Denise's favourite stuffed animal, a giraffe; one of Danielle's dirty T-shirts.

◄ ►

Detective Logan leaves his card. Asks to call him if I hear from Katherine. He doesn't say she's a suspect. He doesn't say I'm a suspect. But he doesn't say we're not under suspicion, either.

But how can he prove anything? The evidence won't add up.

◄ ►

Katherine stayed away all day. We were leaving the next morning, so in the afternoon Jaqueline and I started to pack up and load the car. The sun set, and still our eldest daughter was missing.

The twins were paying attention only to each other, probably more relieved than worried. Katherine took up a lot of social space and loved to taunt them. But Jaqueline and I exchanged worried glances, clasped and unclasped each other's hands, and fidgeted. I finally broke down. "One of us should go look for her. The other should st—"

I never finished that sentence. A bloody wound opened on Jaqueline's chest. She clutched her hands to the injury, her eyes wide with pain and shock. Impossibly, another wound appeared on her belly. On her thigh. On her shoulder. Her neck. The side of the head...

In my mind, Katherine's voice echoed: *...the dagger stabbed them from a distance...*

I screamed, "Katherine! Stop! Don't! Katherine!" But it was too late. Jaqueline was dead.

The twins shrieked. I turned to them.

"Katherine! No! Please, please...stop."

Danielle ran trying to avoid the invisible blows of Katherine's stone dagger. She stumbled dead and bloodied.

Denise died clutching her twin, her wounds leaking onto her sister as they appeared on her own all-too fragile body.

◀ ▶

Four days later, the phone rings. "Daddy, I'm at the police station." It's Katherine. "Can you come pick me up?"

When I get there, Detective Logan is waiting for me. He says, "Turns out your daughter was at the family cottage up north. There's surveillance footage from the nearby village that backs up her story. Where she had dinner. A bar. A bank machine. All on the night of the murders. Not at the precise time of the murders, but close enough to make it impossible for her to have been in the city when they occurred."

I don't say anything in response.

He waits a few beats, then asks, "How about you? Have you been there recently?"

"I would never go back there," I tell him. "I can never go back. You must know what happened."

"I don't believe the cockamamie story that's in the report. I don't think you do, either. I don't think *she* does. You're the only ones who know the truth."

"Detective, she was only ten years old."

"I'm thinking, maybe we need to reopen that case."

I don't say anything. Detective Mahfud emerges from the door behind the reception with my daughter in tow. Katherine looks cheerful – too cheerful. She grabs my arm, gives me a peck on the cheek, and says, "Let's go." She waves goodbye at the detectives with the fake smile of a celebrity saluting her fans.

◀ ▶

I don't know how much time elapsed before Katherine came running back to the cottage, tightly gripping the stone dagger. The moon was still preternaturally bright. The woods were eerily quiet, as if all the animals were afraid of making the slightest noise, of revealing their presence.

She stopped abruptly and gaped at the carnage.

In the heavy silence, I heard my eldest daughter whisper, "But it was only a game… It was only supposed to be a game…"

It wasn't my daughter who did this, who murdered my family. It couldn't be her fault. It couldn't. That rock, that dagger was to blame.

I rushed to her and knocked the evil thing out of her hand. She kept repeating, "It was only a game…only a game," not reacting to me at all.

I took the dagger and ran deep into the woods. I could hear it whisper to me. Whisper images of violence and bloodshed and unholy rituals and inhuman creatures. Maybe it was my imagination, remembering the stories Katherine had told us earlier. Regardless, I didn't want to be touching that filthy thing. I tried to shatter it against a big rock, but I only succeeded in chipping away at the bigger stone. Finally I buried the dagger under that big rock, hoping no one would ever find it again.

When I returned to the cottage, Katherine was sitting on the steps of the porch. She looked straight at me and said coldly, "They'll think you did it, Daddy. They'll think you killed them."

She was right. And I thought, *I'll let them think that. This one moment can't ruin my daughter's entire life. It wasn't her. It was that rock. That dagger. That thing.*

Shaking with grief, I sat on the chair. She climbed and nestled into me. We were both crying. She whispered into my chest, "I love you, Daddy."

I noticed that she was clutching a knife. A big chef's knife from the kitchen.

She plunged the knife into my thigh and twisted it. I struggled not to scream.

"Trust me, Daddy. They mustn't think you did it."

She pulled out the knife – it hurt even more as she did that – and ran off to throw it into the small stream that ran next to the house. She came back with a heavy rock. I was writhing in pain on the ground.

"When they ask you," she said, "tell them you didn't see anything. Tell them you were looking for me. You were attacked first." She repeated: "You didn't see anything." Then, she brought the rock down on my head. Once, twice, forever.

◄ ►

The police visit regularly. Always the same two detectives. Logan and Mahfud. Every month, on the night following the full moon, there's always a string of murders. Same wounds. Same lack of evidence. They only have one thing in common. The victims are always acquainted with my daughter. Co-workers. Boyfriends. Old schoolmates. Teachers. Bosses. Doctors. Shop clerks. Every victim came into contact with my daughter at some point. Most times, the detectives can dig up a story of some previous argument or altercation, some motive for a grudge. For revenge. In every case, my daughter can account for being nowhere near the crime scene.

The detectives have been coming to see me for a year now. Detective Logan says, "I know she's responsible. Somehow. It doesn't make any sense. But I know it's her. And she killed your wife, too. Her sisters. Why are you covering up for her? Help us, man. Help her. You know there's something dangerously wrong with your daughter."

I've long ago stopped responding to their taunts. I sip my tea until the two of them have exhausted whatever they want to say.

They have no evidence. They have nothing.

Me. I only have one thing. I have my daughter. That's all I have. I can't bear the thought of having less than that. Less than one daughter. Less than Katherine.

◀ ▶

I woke up in the hospital. A police officer sat in the chair next to the bed.

I gurgled some kind of noncommittal noise.

The cop stood up, opened the door, and said, "He's awake."

Suddenly, the small room was packed. The police guard. Two plainclothes detectives. A doctor. A nurse.

After a lot of fussing, one of the plainclothes detectives asked me, "What's the last thing you remember?"

I remembered too much. Including what Katherine asked me to do. I lied: "I don't know. I was shouting for my daughter. For Katherine. We hadn't seen her all day. Then a blow to the back of my head. Then – nothing. Is she... Is she okay? Is she safe?" All I could see in my mind's eye were my daughters and my wife. Dead. I teared up. I knew I shouldn't. But maybe they wouldn't make anything of it. They'd think it was about Katherine.

The police were all over me for weeks, trying to pin the murders on me, but Katherine was adamant: from her hiding spot in the woods she saw two men attack me, and then she ran to the village to get help. She'd always been a good story-teller.

I stuck to Katherine's script. They never believed us. But there was no evidence against us. No motive. Sure, they found the kitchen knife Katherine had used on my thigh. But they couldn't make it tell the story they wanted.

Finally, they closed the case. Unsolved.

I wished I'd stayed a good father to my daughter Katherine. Maybe she wouldn't have turned out the way she did. But after the dust settled I could barely ever bring myself to speak to her. I ignored all her attempts at closeness. But I gave her anything she wanted. Except a good father. I wasn't a bad father. I was barely a father at all.

When she moved out at age sixteen, I only vaguely noticed.

When I turned sixty, I began to yearn for her company. But I never reached out. Sometimes, when she was at her most desperate, she would show up. I cooked for her, and she'd tell me stories about her life. The more she revealed, the more I realized she was incapable of sustaining any kind of friend-ship or relationship. Regardless of how badly she herself behaved, she always painted herself as the victim. Even through the lens of her distorted, damaged, self-serving per-spective, it was horribly obvious that she was toxic and dan-gerous.

I barely ever said anything to her. When she'd had her say, eaten her food, she'd stumble out, back into her broken life and out of my nonexistent one.

◀ ▶

Katherine is home, with me. She never asked to move in; one day, I noticed that she had taken over the unused guest bedroom. Spray cans, feminine lotions in tubes and bottles and small jars, and sundry beauty products invaded my tiny bathroom.

With my chaotic daughter in the apartment, it has become a constant chore to keep the premises in a habitable state of order and cleanliness. Still, it gives me satisfaction and even a hint of serenity to have her here.

It was the full moon last night. The first full moon since she started staying with me.

She gazes out the window at the fading light while I put away the dinner dishes.

When it gets fully dark, she turns to me and says, "Let's play a game."

It's only then that I notice she's holding the stone dagger.

In her other hand, she's holding two business cards. They're too far for my failing eyesight to read, but I think I know what they are.

She goes to the phone and punches a number. "Hello, may I speak to Detective Logan, please? My name? Katherine Cray. Thank you." Katherine smiles at me, like a naughty little girl trapped in a forty-two-year-old body. "Hello, Detective Logan. Is Detective Mahfud there with you? She is? Good." She hangs up without another word.

"Let's give the cops at the station a good show. Let's see them try to solve those murders."

She lays down the two cards on the long table in the living room.

I say, "Katherine, don't. Please. Please stop. You have to stop this."

"All these years I never ceased hearing the dagger whisper to me. Even from so far away. For decades I resisted, but finally I went back. What other friend do I have? What other family? The stone dagger needs me. It wants me. It was easy to find. It told me where you'd hidden it."

A memory of pain shoots through the old wound on my leg. The hand on my cane trembles.

"I love you, Daddy. Even if you can't love me. I understand that you can't. I'm sorry."

I swallow. There's nothing I can say.

"You don't know how hungry the stone dagger is, Daddy. How good it makes me feel to give it what it wants. What it needs. What I need."

She stabs the two cards – Detective Logan's, Detective Mahfud's – again and again.

The phone rings. We both ignore it. She continues to stab. Again and again and again.

GOODBYE IS A MOUTHFUL OF WATER

Dominik Parisien

There was a longing in the houses. From the boat, you felt the pull of them, the gravity of their loneliness willing you down, below the surface to the algae-strewn depths.

"They had a place of their own here," your grandfather said. You were only seven then, but you were your grandfather's grandchild – you knew enough to know he didn't just mean the houses, that this was a place he'd called his own, before it was drowned, before he'd lost it all.

It was nothing new – your grandfather frequently boated you out to the drowned village, and while you watched the ducks in the distance he fixed his eyes downward.

Sliding over next to him, you caught a glimpse of an old roof below. You loved to imagine the houses of the village colonized by the monsters you knew dwelled in the river, the giant fish that would nibble your toes if you would only put your feet in the water. Sometimes, you even saw the dead looking up, their faces different shades of grey like in your grandfather's many photo albums.

When you'd told your grandfather about them, the dead, how they frightened you sometimes, he'd taught you to tap the water. It made them all ripple, even disappear. He was always coming up with games, and together you'd made one of it; you'd point to where they lay waiting, and he'd tap them all away. But only some days: others he'd only stare down at the houses.

"There are times I wish I could just blow it up," he said. He meant the hydroelectric dam up the river, of course, not his drowned village.

"Why don't we?" you'd asked.

He had laughed at that, full-throated, startled. "Yes, I suppose we could, couldn't we?"

◀ ▶

The river is a dark blur snaking beside you as you drive, pushing 130 kilometres per hour, 140. There are no thoughts of screeching, twisted metal in your head, of shattering glass, of flames. You push the car to 150, your only fear that you will not make it to the hospital in time.

◀ ▶

Water ran down from the house onto the driveway, made the asphalt ripple like a bad illusion.

Your mother, who stayed in the car when she dropped you off in those days – you were eight after all – swore aloud and opened the car door.

"Stay inside," she said, which of course you didn't. When you set foot on the driveway your shoes filled up, sloshed noisily.

Water rushed out the seams of the front door, out the corners of the windows. Through the kitchen window you saw Tupperware boats navigating the room, fruits and cushions and clothes bobbing up and down.

Your grandfather waved from the living room, a snorkelling mask strapped to his face, a framed picture of your grandmother in his hand. Watching him, you knew he'd done it for you, somehow; that this was another game of his, though you didn't yet know how to play it. Or, that it was one of the steps to destroying the dam. There was always a reason to everything he did.

"He drowned it, he drowned the goddamn house," your mother said.

Somehow, your grandfather's startled, disarming laugh found its way into your mouth, and there was no stopping it once it started, even when your mother screamed to shut up, just shut up.

◀ ▶

Your grandfather is dying. You knew that the moment your professor beckoned you to the front of the class, directed you to the hallway where one of the university's security guards handed you a phone. Your mother's voice was frantic, telling you to come, come quick, she was already there. Younger you would have wondered at her presence, how the distance between two people could be bridged so easily.

In truth, it had never been great.

Now, the car engine roaring all around you, you regret not having darted off the moment she called. Instead, you sat in the university's parking lot, your fingers gripping your key next to the ignition, thinking you had to wait, had to wait just a little, that you couldn't arrive too soon, so he couldn't make you live up to your stupid promise, because you knew he would.

◀ ▶

You were nine, on your way back from visiting your grandfather in the nursing home, when you asked about your
grandmother. You hadn't known her long. When you tried to
picture her in your mind without the aid of a photograph, she
was an old green safe balanced atop a small body. When she
smiled – and you usually pictured her smiling – the safe
opened to reveal liquorice and other candies she kept in her
room, which she always gave you when you visited.

"Why did you let them take Grandma away from her
home?"

Your mother drove in silence for a time, prompting you to
ask again.

"That wasn't her home."

"Grandpa says it was."

"There was nothing I could do."

"Grandpa says you *wanted* them to move her."

"I wasn't going to lose her. Not again."

"You'd already lost her. She was dead, and you let them dig
her up with all the others and put her in that stupid cemetery
on Connor Avenue that she never liked."

Those weren't your words, of course, but your grandfather's. Back then you didn't know your mouth wasn't all yours
all the time, so you watched your mother cry as she drove,
your accusing eyes never leaving her face.

For years you felt shame for your part in that conversation,
as though your mother had had any say in the building of the
dam, in the flooding of your grandfather's village, in the relo-
cation of the dead, or in anything that made you hate her in
that moment.

◄ ►

The truth is, you aren't able to let go of your grandfather, not the way he wants you to. You drive knowing that, knowing you will see the disappointment in his eyes, however soon or late you arrive. The betrayal. If he can still speak then, he will tell you, Help me, let me go, and you won't. If he can no longer speak, his eyes will plead and you will whisper that, no, you cannot. You cannot trust yourself not to follow him, despite your fears, and he would never forgive you for that, nor would your mother. You think, maybe he'll be dead by the time I get there, but the thought only makes you drive faster.

◀ ▶

By the time you turned ten you'd given up on destroying the dam. As though it would have changed anything, brought anything back. Your grandfather had never seriously entertained that thought anyway, it had been another game, though he'd been amused by your crude chemical attempts in the kitchen over the years. And that was fine; you were getting a little old for that one. You'd learned there was no way to blow up anything that big anyway, except in the movies.

"We could weigh me down with bricks," he said, a frightful lucidity in his eyes. "So I could plunge down, down to her, to the houses, to everything that was then."

You didn't have the heart to tell him your grandmother wasn't down there, though you knew he knew that, that he willed her there anyway, that she would find her way to him, if only he made it there. Instead, you said: "I won't let you die."

"Oh, I would not miss a moment of this, of you, of your mama. The breath and breadth of all this. No. But someday I will leave you, that I cannot help. This is a thing for that final hour, when we have said our goodbyes, and I can still say mine to all that was."

"Oh," you said, for somehow that did not seem so bad.

"You know what? Treat it like a game, the last one we'll play." The finality of that made you squirm, but you nodded all the same.

"But first, you must promise you will help me."

◄ ►

A strange sound greets you as you enter the room – your mother and grandfather are holding hands, and both their mouths are open. After a moment, you realize the sound is a laugh, a distorted thing that seems to come from far away. You cannot tell which of them is laughing, until your mother turns and stifles a sob. You walk over, take her hand in yours before turning to your grandfather. You see that his eyes are fixed on the ceiling.

You are late, and your grandfather's last laugh hovers in the air above him, an iridescent cloud shimmering like a dew-speckled spider web. You breathe him in, breathe in that great man's laugh, that life, the memory of him weighing down the air.

◄ ►

You were an inquisitive ten year old, so you had to test it, of course. You had to know, for him, because that had always been your way. And because you weren't sure about this one. The pond by the backyard was the perfect site. You'd fallen in enough to know precisely how deep it was – cutting off at the shoulders, which left your neck and head periscoping out. The bricks felt grainy in your hands as you walked, the ropes around your wrists tight. You'd measured the ropes carefully; tied to the bricks, they came precisely to your feet.

Your grandfather would go in from the boat, plunge straight down, so you did the same, in your fashion, and jumped into the pond. It was fall. The water was cold and patched with leaves. As your feet hit the bottom, a great brown cloud blossomed around you, and for a panicked moment you felt it close around your legs, its greedy maw chewing on your ankles. It was the dead from the river, you knew; they were here. You screamed, dropped the bricks. The dead pulled you down, harder than you thought possible. You felt them crawling up your neck, over your chin, until they touched your lips. Your fingers grasped at liquid dirt, dead leaves. But your lungs, those were still filling with air. Mostly air. You had no words, only breath, and that was how your mother found you. By then you were breathing deep, thinking of the houses and the river, of the dead who couldn't harm you after all, not really, of your grandfather going under, and the feel of water down your throat.

It was months before you saw your grandfather again, and years before your mother left the two of you alone.

◄ ►

The river is restless, the boat moving over the surface like a skipping stone. Water sprays your face, damps your cheeks, your hair. Your mother sits beside you. Though you do not show it, you are not ungrateful for her presence. This is her place too, had been long before it ever meant anything to you. She has been saying goodbye for a long time.

You feel calm.

It is only when you see the roofs of the old drowned village that you feel it, that rumble, that overpowering urge.

You kill the motor, lean over the boat's edge, thrust your head under the water, and laugh. The dead are all around, watching, which is fine; you aren't little anymore, you aren't playing, and you need them there, because they're a part of your grandfather, have been all along. You laugh with all your life and his – your teeth and tongue and throat shine, catch the light, so bright, so bright, and you feel the houses rising, lifting him and all he loved up with them. Your mother pulls your head up and you gasp for air. She holds you close while you wait for them all to ascend.

TREASURE

dvsduncan

In death, much is lost and much is left behind.

But children lack the experience, history and sense of mortality that gives special resonance to the relics of a lost life.

They are not yet survivors.

They simply are.

Alive.

My daughter Jenny saw boxes to explore, discovery after discovery waiting in dusty husks. She understood the reality in her own way. Nanna was dead, gone and never coming back. Jenny knew that but the deeper truth could not touch her.

As she burrowed, I pulled another box from the shelf and folded it open. The past wafted up in thick clouds, clogging my nose and stinging my eyes. A tear found its way down one cheek. My mother had kept everything. Each box was neatly packed and just as neatly labelled. One contained greeting cards, perhaps every one she had ever received, all sorted in order by year. Childish Christmas cards from a boy I had not been for a very long time. Tender valentines from a husband a decade dead. A thousand other memorials. A lifetime of celebrations. I closed the box, rested my hand on the lid and then moved it to the burn pile.

"Daddy, look at this," Jenny chirped.

She had found a box of my old playthings, but what she held made my heart skip a beat. It could not be real and it was. I could only ask, "Where did you find that?"

It was a silly question but my daughter just smiled and pointed before turning her attention back to the treasure in her hand. I stared at it too. Surely, it had been no more than a childhood fantasy, an imagining masquerading as memory. And yet there it was.

Metal plates slid beneath nimble fingers, seemed to multiply, fold at invisible joints, twist on pivots, grow, shrink and take any shape. I remembered that, the impossible ways it would become any imaginable thing. Believing had been easy as a child. Experience had taught me better.

"Dear, can I see that, please?" I asked.

"Sure."

She surrendered the toy without a second thought but her eyes followed as I lifted it to eye level. The thing was no more than a hand span high and had been twisted into the shape of a peacock. It was perfect in every detail. The head, the curving neck and the body were all just as they should be. The tail's plumage was a delicate fan. Even the texture of the metal suggested feathers. I pinched one tiny plate between a thumb and forefinger, gave an experimental twist, grimaced and applied more pressure. I tried another. Then another. The pieces that had moved so easily in my daughter's hands now refused me. Perhaps there was some trick to it, some forgotten way of moving and locking the pieces that younger fingers had discovered.

"Silly Daddy," Jenny giggled and snatched the toy from my hand. "Like this."

She illustrated by turning and folding the parts of the toy without effort. Each bit yielded as her fingers required. The peacock became a parrot.

I stared for a moment and started to ask how she had done it but then let my eyes drift back to the rows of unopened boxes. The weight of the task pressed down on me. This was no time for childish things. I moved on to the next shelf.

Jenny did not. She folded the little toy into many shapes, each more fantastic than the last. All the while she talked to it, cooed to it, and sang to it.

Her prattling and silly rhymes ate away at me as I tried to concentrate.

There were decisions to be made: who would get what, what to send to Goodwill and what to destroy. There were papers to sort. There was furniture to move. After that would come cleaning and painting. But I tried not to think too far ahead. It was better to focus on each task in turn.

After hours of sorting the boxes, my mind was too full of times past to see the present. The sorted piles had grown but the remainder seemed even more daunting than before.

"Time to go, Jenny."

"Can I bring the new toy?"

"Of course," I told her, "but it is not new. I played with that when I was a boy. What have you made now?"

I knelt beside her as she proudly displayed a perfectly formed swan. The metal feathers gleamed silver in the basement light. I had vague memories of horses and lions but that was no more possible than the magical birds.

"That is very good, Jenny. You are a real artist."

"It's so easy. See."

Jenny moved her fingers over the little sculpture and the plates seemed to shift with a will of their own, as though they understood her desire and her vision. After a moment of disorder, a dove appeared.

"That is amazing," I said. I thought, *Impossible*.

But perhaps that was a childhood gift; to believe impossible things, and I had been caught up in it for a moment. Or perhaps I was just tired.

At first, I had little to say as we drove home and Jenny remained entirely engrossed in the toy. There were only glimpses of it as we passed beneath the street lights, a weird stroboscopic view of its evolving shapes. The wonder was becoming a little darker, developing a sinister edge.

"Did you see any other toys you liked in the boxes?"

"Yeah, I guess."

Her hands never paused in their movement.

"You can keep the other toys, too."

"They are sort of boy's toys."

"I guess they are. They were my toys."

"Yeah."

Jenny had nothing more to say. She was under the spell of the toy once more. We drove for another twenty minutes and then pulled into our driveway. My daughter was out of the car and walking towards the front door without even looking up from what her hands created, nearly tripping on the front step.

"Careful."

"Yes, Daddy."

The reply was automatic and absent-minded. A little metal sparrow rested in her hand. But for the colour, it might have been real.

As I opened the front door, I told her, "It's nearly bedtime. I want you to leave that thing downstairs when you go up or you will be playing with it all night."

"Aw, Daddy, I won't."

"You will."

Jenny gave me a sulky look accompanied by an equally sullen nod. I extended one hand and she perched an owl in my palm. I looked at it and it looked back. It almost seemed to blink.

"Good girl. Now teeth, face and hair. You know the drill."

"Yes, Daddy."

Jenny gave one more regretful look, the kind that says it will be a thousand years before she holds her treasure again but she is brave enough to endure even that. Then she turned to climb the stairway. I watched her go before turning my attention to the toy. Still holding it in my upturned palm, I walked into the kitchen so that I could examine it under better light.

The plates were incredibly small and finely crafted, far smaller than I remembered, but then my hands had not been so large all those years ago. Experimentally, I tried to open a wing. At first it would not move and only with my thumbs wedged together did I manage to pry it open at all. The joint gave a bitter complaint such as a rusty hinge might make and shifted but a little. I pushed harder. There was no further give. Even in the brighter light, it was impossible to discover any lock or latch that held it in place. The tail feathers were no more yielding. None of the parts were. While they had flowed beneath my daughter's hand, the little plates resisted my every effort. Finally, my fingers slipped in the slick metal and a sharp edge tore a red streak across the pad of my thumb. With a curse, I dropped the nasty little thing.

It lay there on the tile floor, staring up at me as though in mockery. I stared back. Neither of us blinked now. Those metallic eyes continued to stare back as I raised my foot. They stared as my heel came down, crushing it with all the force I could muster. When my foot rose, the owl was a sad parody, twisted and bent. My boot came down again and again. With each blow I twisted and ground into it. I had put away childish things for a reason. And now I left only a scattering of metal parts on the kitchen floor. I finished, panting and confused. Numb.

I looked down at what I had done, amazed by my own actions, and I felt a little sick. The marvellous toy was no more. I had shattered my daughter's delight.

And shattered my own.

I reached down to pick up the pieces but could not bring myself to touch even one. Some cold dread kept me back, told me that I had done enough harm. It was nonsense and it froze my soul. I carried that chill with me up the stairs and into my bed where I lay awake, wondering what I would say to Jenny in the morning. That worry haunted the dark hours. In the end, I resolved to clean up the wreckage and say nothing. I would make the toy as mythic as it should have been. And then I fell into a deep sleep.

Morning arrived with a windblown curtain. Sunlight splashed across my eyes and into my dreams. There was a moment of half-awareness. Then the events of the night before flooded back and I imagined the broken pieces gleaming on the tile floor. The clock told me it was after nine. The cold inside burned.

I was halfway down the stairs when I heard her voice. The door to the kitchen was closed and the words were muffled. It was as though she was talking to someone. Then bursts of noise sounded, like fitful crying and the frost seared deeper.

I eased the door open and then stepped back quickly as a metallic shape flew past. It moved too quickly for the eye to follow, dashed to the foot of the stairs and then back again to hover before me. It nearly touched my nose as bright eyes stared into mine. Wings blurred in motion and then it was gone, leaving me to doubt what I had seen. From within the kitchen, my daughter erupted into another peal of laughter. Cautiously, I looked into the room.

She sat cross-legged amidst a thousand tiny metal bits, carefully selecting and fitting shapes with wings and beaks and needle talons.

"I found the puzzle, Daddy. Look what it makes," she cried in delight. "Let me show you."

All I could do was stare in wonder. When I had grown up, so much had been lost and so much left behind, but the greatest tragedy had been the abandonment of magic. Perhaps I was not a survivor after all.

I merely was.

Alive.

OF DANDELIONS AND MAGIC

Christine Daigle

My mother is seventy years old, but her brain is much older. Despite its short circuits she is tricky. She pretends happy compliance about moving from Thamesville to the retirement home near my Toronto apartment, but packing is more diffi- cult than it should be. She's recruited my daughter, Isabella, in her scheme. Isabella is naive to her methods, and my mom has encouraged my daughter's imagination, inspiring her to come up with creative uses for junk. Anything to delay the progress I'd hoped for.

Isabella sits cross-legged in the spindle rocking chair. She sways back and forth as she hums "Turkey in the Straw," and her golden hair bounces in time with the beat. Isabella pulls out item after item from the box marked "trash"; taping but- tons on a cracked knitting needle to make a fairy wand, and skewering scraps of fabric onto the matching needle to make a shoebox sailboat. Her repurposing ideas are endless. My patience is not and I breathe deeply to draw more from my small reserve.

"Shauna!" my mom says and grabs my hand. Her fingers are cold and a chill spreads across my palm. I turn from the box of mothball-stale clothing I am filling. My mom points past the hallway to the open door of my old room. The single bed with the faded Holly Hobbie sheets is still there. The bed has always been small, even back when I was supposed to be small too. My gangly legs and simian arms hung over the edges. I took up too much space. I always did. In this house, in this neighbourhood, nothing ever fit right, nothing ever felt comfortable. Not much has changed for me in my so-called grown-up life in the big city.

I look where my mom is pointing. The only other thing in the room is a rusted rabbit cage.

"What?" I ask.

"Don't forget the rabbit."

"What rabbit?" Isabella asks. Pretty and perfectly proportioned, Isabella's pink sundress swirls around her as she glides. She dances past her grandmother and me, then skids to a halt when her nose presses up against the flaking bars. "Hey, there's no rabbit," Isabella says. "Did he get out?" She drops to the floor to search.

"No rabbit?" my mom says.

"Mom, that cage has been empty for years and years."

"Is it empty then?"

Isabella pops up from the floor and brushes off the front of her dress, releasing dust motes into the air. "Was there a rabbit?"

A furrow appears on my mom's forehead. "Your mother used to have a pet rabbit named Patches. But I was never sure if he was real."

Isabella stands on her tiptoes and waves for me to bend down. I lean over, giving her my ear. "I think Grandma's da-men-see-ya brain is acting up again," she says.

"Hush," I whisper.

My mom laughs like leaves skittering across the ground. "When your mother found that cage it was out for garbage pickup. She hauled it down the street and all the way up the stairs. She had such an imagination."

"Mom, not this story."

"I want to hear about the rabbit!" Isabella's voice matches the highest note she can hit on her pennywhistle.

"Fine." I don't want to upset her and delay our progress even more.

"As I was saying, when your mother was a child..."

When I was a child, a bunny magically popped into existence. This is the way I remember it, or maybe falsely remember it, or maybe dreamed it.

◀ ▶

After I place the last box in the back of the U-Haul, I turn for a last look at the old house. It is charming with its faded blue paint and wrap-around porch. The scalloped edges that decorate the bottom of the roof make it look as if it belongs in a fairy tale. The house is still owned by Uncle Charlie, at least for the next two days until the buyers move in. I can't imagine someone new living there, doing renovations, ruining the way it's supposed to look in my childhood mind. Uncle Charlie had been very kind to let us live there when Mom had been out of work for so long that she had stopped making payments on the house we lived in before. This had been a good house. As soon as I think that, my brain whispers "liar." For me, this was a lonely house. My memories seem from another life, isolated bubbles floating to the surface. Many memories are of colouring, scribbling broken crayons over anything I could find – coupons, food wrappers, Kraft paper secreted from school. I probably shouldn't have felt lonely. My mother tried so hard to make me happy. Even after spending hours away from the house, searching for a job, when she got back she would sit at the kitchen table and talk to me.

She would ask me how school was. She would answer my questions about how to play chess or the meaning of poems. Tired, she would find energy to say something, anything, like "Play chess how you think best" or "I don't know much about albatrosses. Why don't you look it up?" Sometimes she just stared, right through me, through the drywall, past the enormous wooded lot that was our backyard where I spent countless hours building tree-branch shelters that were doomed to collapse, and exploring the forest for signs of magical folk. I wondered what she saw.

Now, my mom comes outside with Isabella, locking the front door with care. Isabella is carrying a box of "inventions" that Grandma is letting her keep – a "squirrel trap" built from a pencil with no lead and a silk leaf, a fairy house made from an old Mason jar and a dollhouse chair with three legs.

My mom places her hand flat on the window, saying good-bye to an old friend. I'm surprised to see such a serious gesture. I remember when we lost our first house she didn't even react, like it wasn't real. I cried for three days. Her expression was vapid, and when I said to her that now it felt like we had nothing of our own, she smiled slightly.

"Into the car, everyone," I say. "We have a long drive."

We nestle into the front seat of the truck, all three of us in a row with Isabella in the middle.

As soon as I hit the ignition Isabella starts right in with, "Is it true you had an imaginary rabbit? That's so silly."

I put on my most serious face. "I'll have to think about it." And as we drive, I do give it thought.

It was a summer long ago when I sat down beyond the park, past the soccer field, in the tall grass making dandelion chains for my toy rabbit, as usual. Patches was a vaguely yellow, threadbare bunny covered in faded pieces of mismatched fabric.

It was later in the summer, I remember, because most of the dandelions had turned to fluff. A single note floated in the back of my mind, then another, then another, until the sequence came pouring out of me in perfect pitch, like a secret aria composed by a master, as if I had rehearsed it since the day I was born. It was such a strange composition, coming from the girl whose singing was as imperfect as the rest of me. It was a song that pulled from my very centre, the place inside my heart where wishes come from.

The grass started to rustle and the weeds stirred until a wind swirled, bending the tall blades. The dandelion fluff rose into the air, like a horde of tiny hot-air balloonists lifting my toy bunny. They started to take shape around it, becoming a fluffy mass. And then, the fuzzy floating ball dropped right into my lap. The weight of it shocked me, since Patches didn't weigh too much, and the dandelion seeds were mostly air and gossamer. Then the clump started to shake like a wet dog drying off. Hundreds of dandelion gliders took off into the breeze. When they cleared, I saw a black and white bunny sitting in my lap, looking as though he had always been there.

"…she found a cage, curbside for garbage pickup." At Isabella's request, my mom is telling the story again. "Your mother hauled that thing down the street and all the way up the stairs, and her face got red like a tomato. She put it in the corner of her room." This is how my mom remembers it. There was no delight for her when my bunny turned real. The first thing she remembers is the appearance of the beat-up cage.

"How old was she?" Isabella asks.

"That was nearly twenty years ago," my mother says. "I suppose she was about your age."

"Oh good." Isabella smiles. "Seven is the best age to be."

She looks to me for confirmation of this fact, and I give her a reassuring nod. Seven most definitely is the best age to be.

All those years ago, when the real bunny fell into my lap, I took him home and told Mom that I'd found him and he must be someone's abandoned pet and, please, could we keep him because he had no one else to love him and he'd die in the wild. I knew we couldn't afford the things he needed like a cage (so I found one) and a constant food supply, but even though I understood money was short, it had no real meaning to me. Keeping the bunny was what mattered. Mom gave a reluctant yes. But we had to put up "lost bunny" posters first. When I got the official word from Mom that I could keep him, I felt better. And I started having the nicest dreams. I don't think she ever noticed that the toy Patches had disappeared.

It seems a lifetime ago when the world was so different, full of the wonder and strangeness of childhood. But now, driving through my old town, things don't seem much different at all. In fact, the neighbourhood hasn't really changed. Except the restaurant that used to be Tony's Pizza is now a sushi joint, so maybe things are getting more progressive. Here, time has stood relatively still. It's so different from Toronto.

"Your mother doesn't do things like that anymore. That's what happens when you're doing a Ph.D. in protein chemistry."

"That's not true," I protest. "Protein chemistry is just an easier way for me to invent myself some friends."

Isabella and my mom exchange a knowing look, sharing pity for my awkward sense of humour. I roll my eyes.

"Do you know any more stories about when Momma was a kid?"

"Loads. Let me tell you about the time she took apart my radio to make it a communicator to signal aliens!"

Isabella squeals with delight.

"I had only been gone for maybe an hour to get groceries…"

Mom is in one of her quirky moods. Telling half-truths. The sun is starting to set and I notice the dandelions have turned to fluff. Fireflies light up the sky like tiny dancing lanterns. They make me think of fairies; something my mom used to joke about. *Be careful which ones you catch. At night it's impossible to tell the fairies from the fireflies. And the fairies bite.*

We drive down the main road in Thamesville; it's number twenty-one, but the locals call it old number three. I race past the greenhouses, through the flat farmland growing soybeans and onto the 401 North to Toronto. My mom continues to spin yarns and I continue to think of my childhood.

Patches was a good pet. I found an old cat leash (also curbside) and took him for "walks" in the front yard. He ate a lot of clover and I carried him a lot as well. Sometimes the kids in the neighbourhood would pause on their way by, pedalling slower on their bikes, but they never came over. So

Patches and I had parties by ourselves. I gave him water in a teacup and told him stories about all the adventures he had with his friends – the dog across the street and the cat next door – when I wasn't looking. He'd ask me to tell him more stories. I told him ones from my dreams, about red and white toadstools big enough for golden-haired princesses to live inside in lands where the princess was a friend with all the creatures but big fences kept out the mean people of the neighbouring land. He looked at me with his big rabbit eyes, then looked at the empty bowl in front of him. I'd give him a little rabbit food, but we couldn't afford much. The poor thing was starving. Which probably explains a lot of what happened next.

I'd had the bunny for a while before that night when I woke up. Patches' eyes shone in the darkness. There was a glow coming from his mouth. I crept forward to get a better look. There was a fragment of something like wiggling paper in his teeth; it rolled in compressed waves. On the strange gelatinous paper, a familiar image glistened in front of me. It was a bright orange water balloon. They'd had them at my cousin's birthday party a few weeks before. I'd called them water cocoons and imagined aqueous butterflies hatching when I popped them. Now, Patches took a nibble of the undulating picture. And the image burst. A mass of wings and water came fluttering at me. It hit my face with a splash, drenching the front of my pyjamas.

That's when I knew. The bunny was eating my dreams.

And I felt a sense of relief. The loneliness of the party, sitting in the corner splatting water balloons while my cousins gossiped about boys and called me names when they thought I wasn't listening, was lessened.

It occurs to me now, that this should have seemed incredibly strange, and perhaps scary. But I understood. Money was tight. We bought Patches the cheapest food there was. It looked like pellets of compressed sawdust. Patches was no longer the robust bunny he'd been when he'd dropped into my lap.

Reflecting back, taking into account all the things I've learned, I suppose the bunny was a coping mechanism. At least, that's what my undergrad psych professor would contend. Real or not, he ate my pain. He ate the lonely dreams and only left the good ones. He made my real memories feel less painful. Now, still having a sense of such a lonely childhood, I wonder how bad it really was. What I have been spared. Or maybe just suppressed. But if the bunny wasn't real I don't know how to explain my memory of what happened the next night.

I dreamed of Patches. I was petting him at first, and we were in one of those "pick your own" paradises full of berry-covered bushes. Then Patches dashed off. He stopped in front of a blueberry bush. He devoured it, leaves, branches, and all. And he kept on eating. When he had devoured the entire row of blueberry bushes, he hopped over to the raspberries, not seeming to mind the prickliness. I watched him bound from the raspberries to the strawberries, his appetite insatiable. Despite the ridiculous amount he'd consumed, he looked like he had barely gained an ounce.

When he had eaten everything in the farmer's field he continued to hop off toward the horizon. I was on my feet, chasing after him, curious to see where he would go. He hopped out of the empty field, past more barren country, where the ground was too rocky to grow food. We came to the edge of my dreamed world, and I stared at the boundary, the translucent inside of a gigantic bubble reflecting in miniature the landscape of everything that was behind me. Patches was nibbling at it. He was chewing his way out of my dream.

Soon, there was a hole with alligator scissor edges. I went over and peered through. There were other bubbles floating in space. All with waving images. Some were pleasant – ice cream shops, princess ballrooms, and snowflakes that changed to flowers as they fell. Some were terrifying – birds with worm tentacles spewing from inside unhinged beaks, flapping clouds carrying screaming bodies into the night.

And there was the bunny, floating light as dandelion fluff among them. Eating his way through dreams that reminded me of loneliness; empty bleachers, an old bicycle in the corner of a garage, a little girl opening brightly wrapped presents with nothing inside them.

When I woke up, I was covered in sweat and I was aware of a pain in my head and my chest. Patches' cage was empty.

At the breakfast table that morning, my mom's eyes were red, her cheeks blotchy. I'd assumed she'd been crying over bills again. I'd told her that Patches was missing. "Is he?" she said, her voice much too composed. "Perhaps he decided to go live in the woods where the fair folk will look after him."

I took a bite of my grits.

Mom cleared her throat. "I have good news. I got a job offer." She put on her best smile.

I smiled back because it seemed like what she wanted me to do.

"Things are going to change around here, Shauna." She leaned over and pulled a small bag out from behind the fern. She handed it to me.

I pulled out the tissue paper and found a navy sash inside.

"I can finally afford for you to join the Girl Guides. You can meet some new friends."

Later, I would go on to earn every single badge they had. I suppose I was a little less lonely then.

Now, my attention turns to Isabella as her head flops onto my shoulder. She is snoring softly and there is drool running from the corner of her mouth.

"And you can't mix the dough too much or it gets tough," my mom is saying, deep into her hebephrenic storytelling. *"Juste assez pour que la pâte se détache des bords du saladier et puisse former une boule…"*

A roadside sign says it's still 160 kilometres to Toronto.

◄ ►

It is very late – two-in-the-morning late – when we reach my apartment. I carry Isabella to her bed, her neck cricked at an odd angle, then help my mom into my bed, and finally collapse on the couch, but I barely sleep. I toss and turn. I look at the clock in intervals of five minutes. Intervals of three minutes. Intervals of one.

It seems very, very early when everyone gets back into the U-Haul and drives to the retirement home. Mom is quiet, opting to turn on the radio before Isabella asks for storytelling entertainment.

Then the real work begins. After many hours of blocking out the protests of my lower back, Mom's "suite" is filled with boxes. Her new place is very clean and the staff are friendly. Isabella says hello to every single person we pass and they all say hello back and how she is such a precious child. Mom's suite is on the ground floor and has a sliding door that opens

out to a lovely pond framed by willow trees. The lady who
lives next door has already stopped by with a jar of homemade
raspberry preserves. My mom's face is a tight rubber band,
but she is still smiling.

I bring in the last box and set it on the coffee table.

"And don't forget the rabbit!"

I ignore her and start taking the linens out of a box.

Isabella is stretched out on the linoleum, her head under
my mom's bed. "There's no rabbit. Not even a dust bunny!"

"Well," my mom says, and the tension in her face softens.
Then she looks at me with piercing clarity. "Maybe he's waiting for you at home."

◄ ►

It's the end of the day and I'm exhausted. After helping Mom
unpack, I dropped Isabella off at her father's for the weekend.
She always seems happy when she comes home despite my
frowns when I ask her what she had for breakfast and she
answers with something like, "Some chocolate cake I found
at the back of Daddy's closet!"

Even though I am way past tired, I am pacing. Worrying
about what irresponsible things my ex is up to with Isabella.
Chastising myself that she is a perfectly well-adjusted, social
butterfly who couldn't be more sweet if she tried. Worrying
about finishing my dissertation. Chapter four isn't quite right
and I'm not sure how to fix it. Worrying about money. At least
some things never change.

A firefly flickers at the balcony window and I stop to look.
The apartment is quiet. Not the pleasant kind of quiet like my
spot beyond the soccer field where the silence had been rich
and warm and full of life. This is a different kind of silence. A

dead, cold, empty kind of silence. I stand there listening, eyes closed, and can't imagine that any kind of life can be sustained here. Even Isabella's withered fern can't bear to grow. I want to go home. I want to go back to the wood behind the house Uncle Charlie let us live in and lie down in the grass with the fairies. I don't want to be so lonely anymore. I want my bunny.

I tiptoe over to the sliding door, not wanting to disturb the curse of emptiness in the apartment, not wanting to falter in my mission. I open the door and step out onto the balcony. Outside, I feel more relaxed as I leave the silent apartment behind. The sounds of the city bring life to the calm night air. I go to the lounge chair, tilting the backrest down so it is flat, and lie on it.

My grown-up eyes are wet with the tears of childhood. Going through college, the more biology and chemistry I studied, the more I was sure the bunny had only been a dream. And the more I had become suspicious of what my mother might have done. Not that I would have blamed her. Money was tight. I'd tried asking her about it once, before she'd succumbed to the dementia, but she was evasive, as always. *"Your bunny? I was never sure if he was real."*

Now, I try concentrating on the dream, the farmer's field, the vibrant red of the raspberries, and the smell of grass. Like maybe if I think hard enough about it before I fall asleep I can bring it back again.

I don't know what I hope to gain. If the bunny were to appear now, what dreams would he eat? Ones about the pain of my relationship with Isabella's father? The one where I get a seizing feeling in my lungs when I dream about my dissertation flying at me, flapping its hundreds of pages until I start sobbing about whether years of work really matter to anyone? The one about my mother's death where I stand at the casket and feel like I'm staring at a stranger, someone I never met before?

"*Your rabbit?*" my mother's voice echoes. "*I was never sure if he was real.*" And I've never been sure either. But I'm sure that what I want is to go back to that brief period of time where I wasn't so lonely. That place in my childhood memories where I still had hope for my grown-up life.

The firefly flashes its chemical glow in the apex of the roof. As my eyes begin to feel heavy, I scrounge for all the cognitive reserve my brain can provide. The images I see are now on the inside, a memory of the blueberry bush where a spotted bunny once ate ravenously. I close my eyes and breathe in. I fall asleep.

◄ ►

"And the bunny was still there, twenty years later, waiting for the young woman to dream of him. And from that night on, even after she slept in her own bed instead of a lounge chair, the woman could dream him up at will, and know that she would always have someone waiting for her, someone who loved her and watched over her, lingering in the strawberry fields. And she knew she'd never be truly alone."

Isabella smiles up at me. "That's my favourite story ever, Momma."

I smooth her ringleted hair. "I know, baby. And now it's time for you to visit the land of dreams. Have a wonderful adventure."

Isabella yawns, each blink becoming longer and longer. "Sing me a song, Momma."

It occurs to me, then, that maybe I can sing Patches' song for Isabella. But I can't find the notes. The secret aria has returned to its composer. Perhaps Isabella will never need a Patches.

WHAT NOT TO EXPECT IN THE TODDLER YEARS

Melissa Yuan-Innes

I crouched beside the daycare's coat hooks, each one tagged by a puffy cloud printed with kids' names like SARAH and DANIEL. I started to wiggle Julius's fake yellow Crocs off his feet while I wondered which hook would be his.

"I want to keep mine shoes *on*," Julius said. He slid off my lap and tugged my hand toward the door.

I could really use some magic. I don't need anything spectacular, just your garden-variety miracle: a daycare next door to our Montreal apartment that takes a two-and-a-half-year old boy, feeds him, lets him play, teaches him to read in English and French, changes his diaper, enforces nap time, and charges less than ten dollars a day.

The plump daycare worker waved from across the room, beside the small window and cardboard apple tree. She motioned to the phone glued to her ear. "Be right with you, Mom!"

"I want to go home," said Julius. He said each word carefully to make sure I understood.

"I wish," I muttered. I'd rather make him pancakes and tackle our dishes before the ants ate us out of our apartment.

Instead, I'd wear out the soles of my tennis shoes for eight dollars an hour, smiling at truck drivers so they'd tip better. "Please, Julius."

Julius sank back into my lap. He was so heavy already, my knees buckled. He hates strange things. He doesn't even like it if I cut up his cheese and make a tower out of it. Everything has to be the same, especially since his dad took off.

I managed to tug one shoe off without him freaking. But then he grabbed the strap of the other Croc with a chubby little hand and said, "Nooooooo."

I sensed someone staring. I turned slowly, Julius still weighing down my lap. I expected to see the daycare worker, but a piping little voice burst into my ear. "Magic? You're looking for magic?"

Had I said it out loud? I could have sworn not, but I could easily be losing my mind.

I peered at the kid. You know how you can look at some kids' faces and already see how they'll look all grown up? Old souls, my grandma used to call them. Weird, I called it. From this kid's height and still-pudgy cheeks, though, he probably wasn't much older than Julius, maybe three, although he already wore glasses. Kind of like Harry Potter but not as cute, what with goggly blue eyes and a booger crusted on his left nostril.

The kid wiped his nose, rubbed the snot on his pants, and announced, "I flushed some magic down the toilet this morning. It was good quality, too. From 1639."

The daycare worker hustled toward us. "Sorry about that. Is this Julius? Hi, Julius." She bent down to his level. Her knees cracked, but her smile stayed as fixed as a clown's. "We're so happy to have you!"

"She always smiles like that," said the kid. "Even when I flushed the magic down the toilet."

The worker kept grinning. "Oh, Melvin. He has a wonderful imagination, doesn't he?"

"No, it's not wonderful, but the magic might help kill some of the bacteria you've got growing in your sewer," the kid – Melvin – said. He even did a little eye-roll at me.

I was still thinking about the daycare worker's smile. I fake it like that when I'm working, but it bugged me. Did she like kids?

On the other hand, what other daycares around here would take care of Julius without bankrupting me?

Melvin pointed at my son. "Hi, Art."

"His name's Julius," I said.

Melvin shrugged and pushed his face closer to Julius. I stared at Melvin's green-and-white checked button-down shirt and khaki corduroys. They looked like new and not Walmart new. If his family was rich, why'd they bring him and his "wonderful imagination" to Apple Tree Daycare?

Like I said, Julius hates strangers and change. Half an hour ago he bucked and howled so much I couldn't even get his new sneakers on him. But Julius slid off of my lap and studied Melvin's freckled face as seriously as one dog greeting another.

Now I was the one clutching Julius's hand, feeling my sweat on his fat baby fingers.

"Don't worry. We take good care of our kids at Apple Tree Daycare!" said the daycare worker.

Melvin stood perfectly still, like he sensed Julius needed him to be quiet.

Julius moved close enough to sniff Melvin's face, almost like they really were dogs. I found myself holding my breath.

Could I leave my little guy here? His grandma couldn't take him anymore, and I wouldn't trust my neighbours with a cactus, let alone my kid.

"Have you filled out all the forms?" asked the daycare worker.

I started to say yes, but Melvin held both fists out. He moved very slowly and kept his palms toward the floor. Then he turned his right hand over and unfurled his fingers.

A yellow ball flared in his palm, a tiny glowing sun about the size of a golf ball.

The ball lit up, and Melvin and Julius's faces shone like candles.

I squeaked and yanked Julius toward me. He wiggled and jerked his hand, but I was stronger. I reeled him back toward me and boosted him into my arms. He craned his neck to see.

Melvin closed his hands again and stood with his fists at his side, waiting for our reaction.

The daycare worker beamed. "Yes, we all like Melvin's yellow ball. Isn't it cute?"

I closed my eyes. Yellow dots still danced on my retinas. Nope, I hadn't imagined it. Julius squirmed, trying to get off me. I checked out the other kids: painting, rolling a foam ball, pushing trucks around. Like it was no big deal. I stared back into the worker's mascara-heavy eyes. "What was that?"

She shrugged and adjusted her bra strap. "He calls it magic."

"But…"

"I want to get *down*," said Julius.

I slowly released my hold on him. He slithered down my leg and approached Melvin again. He stopped two feet away. They stared at each other.

The daycare worker thrust a handful of forms at me. "You didn't give us a copy of his immunization record. Also, you have to fill out the sunscreen waiver."

When I glanced back at Julius, he was standing another foot closer to Melvin. So I signed the forms. And I headed off to work, still wondering what Melvin held in his left hand.

◄ ►

"Honey," I said. "I made macaroni and cheese." The smell of powdered cheese stank up our one-bedroom apartment.

"I'm not hungry." Julius scowled at me from the corner of the main room, where he'd squished between the sofa, the bookshelf, and the wall. I know kids like having secret places. I used to crawl behind my bed. Still, I thought Julius had been hiding a lot in the past week.

Also, I couldn't remember him turning down mac and cheese. Ever. I tried again. "Should I make fish? Bread fish?" Store-bought breaded fish. Junk food for toddlers.

"No," he said. He huddled toward the wall with his back to me.

But not before I thought I saw something yellow flash in his palm

For one full second, I stopped breathing. My heart rocketed in my chest. A pain tore up my nose like I'd eaten that green stuff that comes with sushi. *Danger.*

My hand shot toward him, ready to smack that light out of his hand. But I froze in mid-air. My mother used to hit me. I swore I'd never hit Julius.

My knees just kind of gave out, so I sank into the forest-green sofa cushions. Dust poofed from the cushions into the air. I said, almost to myself, "Okay."

Melvin was teaching my kid magic. Not grown-up magic, like how to buy groceries for the week with twenty dollars, but real magic.

Julius tried to edge away from me, but he bumped into the wall. He scowled, looking mighty fierce for a two-and-a-half-year-old. "I'm busy."

"Okay," I repeated. I snatched a random magazine from the rack. Turned out to be my ex's *Maxim*, but I opened it anyway.

Eventually, Julius huddled in the corner. He muttered under his breath. It sounded like, "Mo shu na wa lee long goo may." A week ago, I would have assumed it was nonsense or his attempt to sing "The Bare Necessities." Now I wished I could webcam him and show someone, hell, anyone, and ask, *Is this normal? What should I do?*

Five minutes later, he turned toward me with the big grin I knew and loved. "I need maca-woni."

After he'd chowed through most of it, I said, "Maybe you can stay home with Mommy tomorrow." I'd call in sick. I didn't care.

Julius's spoon clattered on the linoleum floor. His eyes and mouth turned upside down like the tragedy mask on a lapel pin my drama teacher used to wear. And he howled louder than a jet engine.

"It'll be fun. We'll stay home." I raised my voice over his screeches and ignored the fat tears pooling in the corners of his eyes. "We could go to the pet store. Or the park."

"NoooOOO!" Bits of macaroni sprayed on to the table. Sixty seconds until the neighbours called the police.

"We could paint. We could do sleeping bunnies."

"NoOOOOoooOO!"

I yanked him into my lap. He pressed his feet against my chest and tried to launch away from me. I swore and clamped down on his arms.

He screamed louder, nearing the higher decibel range.

I gritted my teeth and knocked the back of his knees, forcing them to bend. He cried so hard, he choked on his snot. But his knees folded and I managed to cradle him in my arms more safely.

I could pull Julius out of daycare. He'd forget about Melvin eventually.

Julius's tears soaked my neck. His chest heaved, but more quietly now. He'd given up.

My heart squeezed. Why was I pulling him out of Apple Tree Daycare? When I was a kid, I would have donated my teddy and at least one kidney to my enemy for one measly spark of magic. So why was I so scared?

I kissed Julius's petal-soft cheek, glistening with tears and mucous. His breath hiccupped. His hair stuck up, wet with sweat. I said, "You want to see Melvin tomorrow?"

"Yessss," he sobbed.

"Okay. You can go to daycare tomorrow." I grabbed a paper napkin to wipe his nose, and he let me. I added to myself, *And I'm coming with you.*

◄ ►

Julius hammered balls into a toy's multicoloured plastic chutes, his forehead pleated in concentration. I relaxed into my tot-sized chair. At least Julius still played like a regular kid.

Melvin sat beside me, flipping the pages of a book that looked way too old for him, *The Once and Future King*. On the cover, a guy charged on a white horse while a damsel in distress bowed her head. A rope bound her neck to a tree. I tried not to look at it, but I hated the picture of the woman.

Melvin closed the book and set it face down on the table. "I'm not going to hurt him," he said.

I glanced at the daycare worker, who rolled out sparkly sapphire Play-Doh at the next table, still grinning away. I muttered to Melvin, "Who are you?"

He shrugged and played with the back cover of the book.

Julius hammered the last ball, a purple one, through the chute. He beamed at me. I gave him the thumbs-up.

Melvin's little voice bore into my ears. "You know who I am. My name is Bruno Melvin Sachs. I'm three years and two months old. I live at 2530 Canterbury Street." He pushed his glasses up on his nose. "But what you really want to know is, am I going to hurt Art. And the answer is no."

"His name is *Julius*," I gritted out.

He shrugged. "Fine. Julius."

Julius watched us for a second before he picked up his hammer again.

A chubby girl at the next table carefully stamped an angel into her lime green Play-Doh. She exclaimed, for no apparent reason, "I have new pants. My mommy bought them on Saturday!"

For a second, I wished I had a child like that. Sunny. Uncomplicated. More interested in shopping than magic. But then I wouldn't have Julius.

I took a deep breath and met Melvin's pale, bulging blue eyes. "What do you want from Julius?"

He grabbed the edge of the desk, but noticed me noticing and shoved his hands in his pocket. "I want to teach Julius how to do magic."

"Why?" Nothing comes for free. Not a corned beef sandwich. Not love. And especially not magic.

His lips twisted. He wiggled his butt in his chair, acting like a kid for the first time. But then he ruined it by saying, "I have to pass on my legacy."

Legacy. What did that mean? It sounded like a fancy name for a horse. I know it means passing something down, like your grandma's lace pillow, but I don't know why a scary little kid would know magic and why he'd want to pass it on to my kid.

Julius abandoned his toy and walked toward us, his eyes shifting from Melvin to me. My heart gave a painful little thump. I wanted to take Julius away from this mini weirdo, but my son really loved magic and the mini weirdo. Plus, I couldn't afford any other daycare in my sector of Montreal. I know. I looked.

"Mommy," said Julius. Just the one word, but I knew his vote.

I focused on Melvin. "On one condition."

His eyes narrowed. His lip curled. Grown-up anger in a teeny body. He said, "What is it?"

"You can teach him here. You can even have play dates." I took a deep breath, counted to three. "But you have to teach me, too."

His lip jerked, almost like he was trying not to laugh, before those pale blue eyes met mine again. "You're too old."

Most people think twenty-five is young enough to be a single mom. But Melvin was not most people. And neither was I. I pushed my face closer to his and whispered, "Try me."

He snorted. The daycare worker glanced at us, but Melvin ignored her and said to me, in his piping little voice, "Your mind is closed."

I didn't blink. "So open it."

Neither did he. Behind us, a kid announced, "I have to go to the bathroom!"

"Okay," sang the daycare worker. "Brendan has to go to the bathroom. Does anyone else have to go?"

My lips twitched. I couldn't help it.

Melvin didn't smile back. Instead, he shrugged. "It's your funeral."

I shoved away my unease and held out my hand. We shook on it. He pumped my hand up and down, and after he let it go I could still feel the pressure of his little fingers.

Julius dropped his hammer on the ground. When I bent to pick it up, I heard him say, "Look, look!" I jerked my head up just in time to see him thrust his hand in the air. His fingers opened like a small star. A dark shadow, maybe a bird, soared in the air and disappeared into the acoustic tile ceiling.

I blinked. Were my eyes fooling me again?

Melvin smiled and nudged Julius's shoulder. "Good one, Art."

An hour later, during outdoor time, the kids clambered up the jungle gym. A few younger kids sifted sand in the sandbox. We sat beside them and Melvin tried to teach me magic.

"Hold your hands together and hum."

I checked to see if the daycare worker was watching us. She was, but she quickly turned to help a kid stuck on the monkey bars. Julius studied us, even as he pushed a truck over a big pile of sand.

"Hum," said Melvin.

I pressed my palms together and hummed. "Umm." I am not a singer. When Julius asked me to teach him Christmas carols, I borrowed a tape from the library.

Nothing happened except that a kid dumped a bucket of sand next to my foot.

Melvin sighed. "I told you your mind was closed."

"It is not."

"Sure it is. Can you even see this?" He held his hands a few inches apart. For a second I thought maybe I saw a glimmer of green, but I couldn't be sure.

I watched until my eyes watered. Grit worked between my toes and between my sandal and my foot. I'd have to brush our shoes off good when we got home. "Green light?" I said finally.

Melvin sighed, a tiny but heartfelt gust of air. "Just sit in with me and Art, then."

"Julius." No one but me likes the name, but a three year old wasn't going to rip it away from my son.

Melvin sighed even more deeply. "Julius."

Julius giggled. "Did you see mine puppy?" He pointed beside the red and blue plastic dump truck. "He's a Dalmatian. You see the spots, Mommy? He's licking me!"

I saw nothing. After a beat too long, I said, "Cute."

Melvin tossed a look of scorn over his shoulder. He reached into the empty space and seemed to pet the air. He and Julius both laughed. Melvin asked, "Can you make him bark?"

Julius's forehead pleated. His eyes bugged out, reminding me of Melvin. Finally, he shook his head.

"Keep trying," said Melvin. To me, he said more softly, almost with pity, "The puppy's running around Julius. He just jumped out of the sandbox. There!" Melvin pointed.

Julius chortled. I smiled back, but Melvin's pointing hand shook. Not a big tremor, but it reminded me of the way my grandfather's hands used to shake all the time.

Melvin shoved his hand in his pocket.

◀ ▶

My spaghetti water frothed over the edge of the pot just as the phone rang. I grabbed the pot with one hand while Julius said, "I need more water, Mommy." He'd dragged his stool to the sink and held his measuring cup under the faucet.

The phone rang again. I turned off the burner and said, "Don't touch the stove, Julius." I moved the pot to the other back burner. No matter how much I scrubbed it, something black crusted on that burner always stank when I turned the heat on.

"Mom-my! Wa-ter!" Julius called.

I pay for the water. But I needed quiet and we both had to eat. I opened the tap and wedged the phone between my ear and shoulder, keeping an eye on Julius. "Yes, hello?"

Julius grinned. His cup overflowed with water. I shut off the tap. He said, "No, more!"

A low, cultured woman's voice poured into my ear. "Hello, this is Melvin's mother, Sandra."

"Hi, ah, Sandra." I fought the urge to call her Mrs. Sachs. With her silver bob and immaculate pantsuits, she seemed older than my mom. I scraped the hardened spaghetti from the bottom of the pot. At least I'd caught it before it burned.

"I'm sorry to bother you at suppertime. I just wanted to let you know that Melvin won't be able to come for a play date tomorrow." Her voice broke on the last word.

"Is everything all right?" I tried to sponge up the pasta water with one hand while watching Julius pour water from the cup into a dirty pot in the sink.

I heard her inhale sharply. "He has a…doctor's appointment." The way she talked, it wasn't a regular checkup.

My heart plunged the way it did for any kid in trouble. Ever since I had Julius, watching the news makes me cry. "Can I help?"

Julius tipped forward to hit the faucet handle open himself. I removed his hand. He yowled like I'd held his hand to the burner.

Mrs. Sachs's voice cooled. "No, thank you. I'll see you at the daycare. Goodbye."

◀ ▶

For the next week, Julius did circle time, played on the jungle gym, filled dump trucks with sand, and traced his hands on paper. No golden balls of light. No chanting. He acted like a normal kid, except he kept asking, "Where's Melvin?"

"I don't know, hon," I said every day, every hour, but by Friday I had to call and ask.

Mr. Sachs answered. I'd never met him, but I heard he was an engineer, so he had to be really smart. His voice rasped a little. "Melvin's been admitted to the Montreal Children's."

"Oh. I'm sorry to hear that." I sat down on our wobbly metal folding chair and massaged my feet hard, like the pressure might be able to help a sick little boy.

Julius seized my big toe. "Where's Melvin?"

"Shh, Julius. I'm talking to Melvin's daddy."

He shook my toe. "Where's Melvin's daddy?"

I handed Julius a plastic dog toy we got from Value Village. Normally, he scorns it, but this time he dropped to his knees and started barking. "Sorry," I said into the phone. "What's wrong with him? I mean…" Probably rich people have a better way of asking.

"We have no idea. And neither do the doctors." He forced a laugh the way I do when people ask where Julius's father went.

"Could we come see him?" I didn't know how that slipped out.

Silence. "You're Julius's mother?"

"Yes. Julius really wants to see him. But if we can't come, that's okay." I'd have to cut out of work early. Again. I'd have to pull Julius out of daycare. I'd have to buy a present and pay both our bus fares.

Julius sat on the floor with his knees tucked under his bum, dog toy abandoned. "Mommy, where's—"

Mr. Sachs's breath gusted into my ear. "Okay."

◀ ▶

Julius said, "Carry me."

I swung him up on my hip and pressed his head into my shoulder. I hated that we were in a hospital. Even though Melvin's bed lined up by the window, the air-conditioned air seemed to smell like alcohol hand wash and dirty bandages.

I tried not to look at Melvin himself. He hadn't even opened his eyes when we trooped into the room. In less than two weeks, he'd shrunk. His formerly fat cheeks sagged, his skin looked thinner and kind of yellow. If I hadn't seen the thin white hospital blanket rise and fall with each slow breath, I would have thought he was dead.

Melvin's mother stood to greet us. She wore a beige pantsuit, but I noticed the wrinkles at the crotch, and her eyeliner was crooked. "Thank you for coming." She tried to smile at us, even though her eyes flickered to Julius in a way that said, *Your son is healthy and mine isn't.*

I dropped the skinny bouquet of grocery mums on Melvin's table. Julius didn't twist to look at his friend. Would seeing Melvin like this give him nightmares?

I murmured into Julius's ear, "Do you want to go?" My pulse drummed in my throat. *Please say yes.*

Julius nestled his face in my shoulder without answering.

I whispered, "We'll just stay for a minute." I'd personally count the seconds. To the mother, I said, "Hi…" I could not remember her name, so I switched to, "How's he doing?"

She dropped back into the only chair. I hefted Julius upward, rearranging my already-sore arms. She said, "All his blood tests have come back normal. We're still waiting for some metabolic tests. Inborn errors of metabolism."

Whatever that was, it sounded bad. I glanced at Melvin's right hand, splinted on a board and wrapped like a mummy in white gauze. A clear fluid dripped from an IV into his mummy hand. I watched each drop fall. Easier than looking at Melvin's face. For some reason I remembered how I hid the graham crackers the last time he came over, so he wouldn't eat them all. Guilt ping-ponged in my stomach. "Is he…contagious?"

She focused on me for the first time. "No, no. Donald didn't tell you? They think it's some degenerative disorder. Like Rett Syndrome."

"Oh." Should I pretend I understood? A Mylar balloon beside Melvin's head bobbed in the air conditioning. GET WELL SOON.

Mrs. Sachs rubbed Melvin's foot and talked, almost to herself. "Only Rett Syndrome usually affects girls. And it doesn't make them go downhill so fast. All of a sudden, he started tripping over his own feet. He started sleeping all the time, he wouldn't eat, he can't even talk…"

I remembered Melvin's hand shaking.

"And do you know what the worst thing is?" Reluctantly, I met her eyes, the same bulging blue eyes as Melvin. Her face was almost as pale as her son's. "He told me a long time ago. After his birthday party, when he was putting away the toys. He said, 'Let's give some of them away. I don't need them all.' I kept asking him why, and he finally said, 'I'm going to die.'"

I hugged Julius harder and pressed my cheek against the hair on top of his head. Fine, medium brown hair that sticks up in the morning. Healthy, little boy hair. Finally I said, "I'm sorry."

Her voice rose. "I never understood him. Ever since he could talk. Once he said he was supposed to be the Antichrist—"

I sucked my breath through my teeth and clutched Julius so hard he murmured in protest. What kind of kid calls himself the Antichrist?

"—but it's okay; he's not anymore because we baptized him." Tears slid down her face and dripped down her chin on and into the folds of her neck. She didn't bother to wipe them away. "But we didn't baptize him! We're Jewish! When I told him that, he just laughed and said he was getting his lives mixed up, especially since he was always living backwards."

I flinched.

She smeared a tissue across her blotchy face. "I know what you're thinking. You think we're nuts." She splintered a laugh. "But we've seen a psychiatrist. Melvin couldn't talk, but we did. I told him Melvin was obsessed with Merlin and magic and airy fairy stuff like that, but otherwise he was a normal kid."

I pressed my cheek against Julius's and closed my eyes. Had she never seen Melvin's yellow ball?

"We saw endocrinologists, toxicologists, neurologists. Every kind of 'ist,' but he's *dying*." Her voice rose to a shriek.

Julius slipped below hip-height. I bent my leg and tightened my grip on him, starting to heave him up, but he wiggled free. He slid down my leg like a miniature fireman gliding down a pole.

I started to make my excuses to Mrs. Sachs, but instead of bolting for the door, Julius launched himself at Melvin's bed. He gripped the metal rails with his tiny hands and thrust his chin forward, desperately eyeing Melvin's still face.

"No!" I yelled. I seized the back of his *Finding Nemo* shirt and knotted it in my hand. He clung to the rails so hard that his hands turned white. I started to pry them off the bars, finger by finger.

"Stop!" Mrs. Sachs gripped my shoulder.

I wrenched away from her.

Her hand bit like iron. She gasped, "Don't you see?"

I saw Julius, his baby brown eyes wide, pupils dilated, in a chalky face. I saw his little feet rise on tiptoe, reaching through the rails to touch Melvin's unmoving body. And I saw Melvin's face begin to glow.

"Julius," I whispered, before my voice fell away completely.

My son's lips parted. He panted once, twice, before he squeezed his eyes closed and grunted, red-faced, almost like he was filling his pants.

Heat radiated off Melvin now like a stove turned on low. His skin burned bright, like afternoon sunlight. My eyes watered, but I could still see his entire body shining through the blanket, even beaming through the holes in the gauze of his mummy hand.

I smelled a damp, sharp smell like cotton scorched from the iron turned up too high.

A tiny, persistent scream rose in my ears, as if the cockroaches in the walls, or the walls themselves screeched in protest.

And then it was gone. As suddenly and sharply as it had come. Whatever "it" was.

The pressure in the room shifted.

Slowly, I released Julius's shirt, still bunched in my fist. The air conditioner hummed at us. The GET WELL SOON balloon still wafted in the air.

I seized Julius into my arms. He folded willingly against me, but I caught his mischievous grin before he nestled his face against my breastbone.

Melvin's eyes cracked open. He tried to speak.

His mother cried out, a high-pitched noise of joy and terror.

Melvin's mouth worked. He licked his lips. His slitted eyes focused on my son. He whispered, "Thanks, Art."

◄ ►

Somehow, I wasn't surprised that Melvin bounced back to Apple Tree Daycare within the week. His parents sent Julius and me a basket full of cheese, salami, chocolate, and expensive crackers shaped like diamonds.

I have no idea what happened in the hospital. Even the doctors couldn't figure it out. But I'm more worried about what happened to Julius.

Yesterday, I woke up on the fold-out couch with Julius curled against my stomach. He's supposed to sleep in his bed like a big boy. I started to lift him out, but then I noticed my arms were glowing.

Yesterday, my tips tripled. One guy in coveralls even gave me a hundred dollars and wouldn't take it back.

Like I said, nothing comes for free. I sure hope Melvin didn't hurt Julius. I have to say, though, my son seems totally okay except he said he learned how to talk to cats. And today he asked me to call him Arthur.

WHEN THE TRAINS RUN ON TIME

Shane Simmons

"Is it broken?"

"No, it just doesn't work right."

"Because if it's broken, I can take it back for a refund and get you something else."

"It's fine," we assured our mother at the same time, with one voice.

We loved the model train set and we didn't want anything else. Usually, having our birthdays so close together with a single mother strapped for cash amounted to shared gifts most years – something we could play together. Board games were common. Worse was the occasion we got two bad-minton rackets and a single bird to bat back and forth. We immediately lost the bird and smashed the rackets fencing with each other.

Through whatever miracle of timing, a deluxe train set had gone on sale at the toy shop a week before our joint celebra-tion. After we were tucked in our bunk beds, Mother had stayed up very late assembling it all on the dining room table that hardly saw any use before Father died and none since. It was waiting for us when we got up the next morning, and we could hardly be convinced to touch our breakfast cereal before we were taking turns flipping the knob that sent an electric current through the metal tracks and caused the engine to pull its load along its route. We watched in awe as it climbed a green Styrofoam hill, looped around twice, passed through a curved tunnel, and went into the station. There were no switches, no parallel tracks, just the double loop that was the same every time, but it was a marvel just the same. Our fascination was limitless and we reconfigured the cars in every conceivable combination for the next circuit and the hundreds that followed.

We'd been at it for less than an hour when we noticed there was something not quite right with the tunnel portion of the track. The train kept a consistent speed of our choosing on each trip, but seemed to slow in the tunnel. It would briefly disappear from sight in the dark cave and take just a bit longer than we expected to emerge from the other side. When Mother heard us discussing the phenomenon she made the horrifying suggestion of taking the set back to the store. After we'd successfully quashed that plan, a silent understanding passed between Jim and me to never criticize the train set in front of her again.

Jim was my older brother by two years, but he was small for his age – smaller even than me. Picked on and bullied in school, he often said he couldn't wait to be older. He claimed it was because once he was a grown up, he would be able to celebrate his birthday alone, and wouldn't have to share gifts with his kid brother. But I always suspected it had more to do with him wanting to be bigger, stronger, and no longer the target for harassment in the halls and shoulder punches from his peers.

Every day, we raced each other home, trying to be the one who would get to be the sole engineer running the freight train through its paces. In truth, it didn't much matter who was operating the controls. It was still fun to watch, still fun to pass the time rearranging the toy buildings in the village square while the other brother had command of the moving parts.

The issue with the tunnel remained, however, and became a growing source of mystery. Jim swore, when all the freight cars and caboose were hooked together behind the engine, that the train was longer than the tunnel. And yet, the entire thing would disappear from sight for several seconds when passing through, before there was any sign of it on the other end. Finally, Jim suggested an experiment.

"Go get Nibbles," he instructed me.

"Why?" I asked, not sure what he could want with my pet mouse.

"He'll be our test pilot."

I didn't question the plan further. Jim was older and smarter, and Nibbles, I figured, could use a bit of adventure away from his life in a small glass fish tank sprinkled with wood chips.

I gently placed Nibbles in the empty grain hopper. He seemed content to sniff around and didn't try to climb out, so Jim flipped on the power and sent the train into the tunnel. We ran around to the other side and waited for the engine to come barrelling out. As usual, it took several seconds more than it should, but at last we saw the tiny headlight come around the bend in the track and poke out of the dark hole. We counted the cars, waiting for number seven, the grain hopper, to clear the tunnel. At last it emerged and I could see my little white mouse exactly where I'd left him moments ago. It took me a while to realize that it was no longer a white mouse I was looking at, but white bones. Nibbles had been reduced to a delicate rodent skeleton, gripping the plastic edges of the hopper with his tiny claws. If he hadn't been dead, I would have said it looked like he was enjoying the ride.

I cried for my dead mouse all night, but we didn't tell Mother about Nibbles's untimely demise until after we had flushed the evidence.

"It's poison in there," I told Jim after we were in bed and the lights were out.

I couldn't see him in the bunk overhead, but I could hear his whispers in the silent room. "No, it's not poison." He'd been pondering the puzzle all evening and had arrived at base-less but sound conclusions. "I just think it takes a lot longer to go through the tunnel than it seems on the outside."

"It's forever in there," I said.

"No, not forever. Maybe a few years. Mice don't live very long. If it took too long for the train to get through, it would crumble to pieces before it even got to the other side. It's only cheap plastic."

I stopped sniffling for the first time and asked, "Can we send a goldfish through next?"

"Maybe," was all Jim would commit to. "Go to sleep."

The subsequent days saw us load the train with a variety of items to test our time-stretching theory. Bits of food came back stale and hard as a rock, or decayed away to nearly noth-ing. A watch returned perfectly intact, but stopped, with the batteries run dry. It wasn't forever in the tunnel, but it was certainly a lengthy period of time.

One afternoon when I rushed home from school, eager to beat Jim to the train set, I discovered he had already come and gone. The tunnel was missing, unscrewed from its position in the track layout. I played without it and was pleased to see the train passed the trouble-spot at full speed. Removing the superfluous tunnel had corrected its performance and I decided it was a piece of scenery we didn't really need anyway.

Jim was silent over dinner and made no mention of the modifications he had made. I didn't see the tunnel piece again until it was time for bed. Jim came in from the bathroom with the most ridiculous hat I had ever seen.

"What is that?" I asked, even though I already knew. "You look like an idiot."

Jim had strapped the toy tunnel to his head with a couple of scarves. The two ends stuck out the sides like great bull horns.

"Toro! Toro!" I called at him, waving the corners of a bed sheet like a matador.

Jim obliged me by making a run at the sheet with his curved-tunnel horns. He then mockingly gored me as an angry bull might. Despite the roughhousing, Jim's rigged contraption remained in place. It may not have been fashionable, but it was secure.

"Do I look older?"

"No, you look dumber," I said.

"I've only had it on for a few minutes. I think I feel older, but it's hard to tell."

"You're not wearing that to bed, are you?"

"It's an experiment," he said. "A new one. If I'm right, I should be one of the big kids by morning. Maybe even a teenager."

"A teenager with a squeaky voice and hair on your balls. That I'd like to see."

"I'll wake you up when I'm bigger than you. Bigger than all those kids at school. Maybe as big as Dad."

Jim did not wake me that night. I slept straight through till morning. When at last I rose, I could see, from the lack of a telltale sag, that Jim was not in the top bunk. I was about to look for him when I saw someone standing in the room, quietly staring out the window. It was a man, very old, very frail. He was also completely naked. When he heard me stir, he turned slowly so I could see his withered face and long white beard. Then he spoke – a crackling croak of a voice, familiar and unnerving. I immediately began screaming in blind terror. I would have thought I was having a nightmare if I hadn't been so acutely conscious of waking up a moment before.

It didn't take long for Mother to come bursting into the room to see what was wrong. At first, she only saw me frozen in bed, mouth wide and wailing.

"Mommy, I wet the bed," said the old man, and Mother joined in with my terrified screams.

She swept me out of the room before either of us were capable of making a rational sound. Mother slammed the door and barricaded it with every stick of furniture close at hand. The old man, if he made any effort to escape, was too weak to push through the pile. A quick search of the house failed to find Jim anywhere.

Calls were made at once. My mother to the police, the police to the media, and an amber alert for my missing brother was issued and featured on the local news at noon. The man in the room was extracted and removed from the house by the authorities while Mother and I huddled together in the kitchen. We didn't want to look at him, but we could hear his feeble protests to the arresting officers.

"Did the man say anything to you?" a woman from social services asked me tenderly once the initial fuss had settled down and she was able to take me aside for a chat.

"Don't tell."

She nodded at my quote, but I knew she thought it sounded sinister. I wasn't so sure. It was what Jim and I would always plead to each other whenever we'd been caught doing something bad.

Jim's face became famous locally. It was on the missing child announcements, the nightly news and, in time, milk cartons. The nude man discovered in our bedroom was considered a prime suspect – the only suspect – but was deemed to be suffering from age-related dementia and was unable to clarify the circumstances of Jim's abduction to anyone. He was remanded to a psychiatric hospital for observation, but apparently made no more sense there than he had in the police holding cell. A hearing was scheduled to determine his competence for trial, but he died of organ failure before the date ever arrived.

"You're the man of the house, now," friends of the family and relatives kept telling me. It was the same thing they had told Jim when Father died.

I didn't feel like a man, not by a long shot, but I knew I had to grow up quickly. Mother was in pieces, unable to cope with our loss. The state of the house was in decline, groceries were scarce, bills were piling up and, before a year had passed, she had lost her job as well.

I found Jim's improvising tunnel-hat where it had fallen as soon as I was permitted back in our room. The police had taken everything they thought might constitute evidence, but left the detached model-train tunnel and its twin-scarf rigging on the floor next to our other loose toys, never giving it a second look. I stashed it away from sight for as long as I could, but the time has come at last. I need to step up, for Mother's sake, for my sake, even for Jim's sake. Or at least for his memory.

I'm watching myself in the mirror closely, this supposedly innocuous plaything strapped to my head, careful not to let the advanced years creep up on me as they did with Jim. It's been several hours now, and I can't see any change at all, moment to moment, but my newfound maturity seems more prominent when I try to remember how I looked an hour ago, half an hour, ten minutes even. I only have to decide on a point at which to stop, a moment when I've cast away enough of my childhood to make a difference. Should I wait until I'm mature enough to quit school? Get a job? Live on my own?

The problem is, I don't really think I feel any older at all. Does anyone when they grow up, I wonder.

MAKOUR

Lisa Carreiro

Keirdran clomped across the ceiling bellowing invectives. Her helmet-clad head nearly touched the floor in the cramped, tiny ship. She snapped a palm-sized scrap of metal off her belt – a bizarre assemblage of cobbled-together bits and pieces – and waved it triumphantly.

"Stride up your dead quarry creek with *this* ancient shard, you pickled-brained overlords!" she hollered. "I hereby reclaim the last of my humanity!" She scraped the metal against the floor as though she could mar its nearly indestructible material.

"Keirdran, calm down," I said. I saw her reflected in the vast clear pane, an upside-down soldier who'd just won a one-woman battle against a mote in her imagination. Before I fully turned toward her, data scrolling above the control board in front of me suddenly flickered, dimmed, and morphed into bizarre icons.

My heart nearly stopped.

Keirdran pacing the ceiling spouting nonsense was typical. Data turning into silver snowflakes was not.

I waved my hands over the board to no avail. Legible text continued to morph into nonsense, then dissipate. I dispatched an urgent cry for help back to Mur Prison; a message I knew would take at least twenty terran weeks to arrive. A message they might just ignore.

Keirdran stopped shouting and eyed the board, head cocked as though studying the frightening change. She pounded a fist against the wall and wailed.

"Keirdran, if you've got so much as one iota of knowledge left in that iron-clad cranium that used to hold your brain, then help me now!" I flinched as another line of data glimmered pink and flared into the image of a twisting serpent before it faded.

Keirdran pointed at the serpent.

"Keirdran? Do you understand what's happening?"

But her pointing hand flailed before she dropped to the floor, gloved hands pressed to her helmet.

Every cell in me recoiled as Keirdran then crawled into her tiny quarters, such as they were. Door always open; tools and rocks strewn across her unused bunk; sooty walls streaked with symbols and specs drawn with a shaking fingertip.

I disliked the woman she'd been. I despised the creature Mur Prison made of her. a hapless puppet who usually performed Mur's directives without a hint of the brash person – the one who'd spent at least one third of her free time brawling – that they'd crushed. A defeated, half-human thing who crept on hands and knees through hoarded trash.

Geared up like a cross between a medieval archer and twenty-first-century cinema cyborg in a black helmet, red leather-like breastplate, and dark visor all alive with technology, she was built to work. She squeezed into crawl spaces on her belly to repair electronics with gloved fingertips. She jettisoned to rock to test its ore, licking metal to determine its composition. She lumbered from task to task, often repeating chores she'd already completed.

When not working, Keirdran muttered at scraps heaped on her narrow bunk. As though they might coalesce of their own accord, to become whatever it was she tinkered with in her rare spare time. For seven years.

Her daily hobby morphed into a mad frenzy after Mur Prison dispatched us to Spakata, a mine deemed dead seventy years earlier. I read the specs three times. Not a soul remained in Spakata's ghost colonies; not a trace of copper remained in its empty tunnels.

"You condemned us to death!" I screamed in my message to Mur even though my shackles pinched me for protesting. A purple bruise blossomed on one wrist within minutes. My wrists were scarred beneath the bracelet-like shackles, deceptively gorgeous etched silver bands around each wrist. "Not only are we two years past the end of my sentence, we're not going back, are we?"

Keirdran, shuffling through her quarters, said nothing.

She must have murdered someone. Why else would Mur Prison turn her into a virtual cyborg and ship her off to work in a mining drone? Of course, I committed no crime, yet they convicted me of sedition and theft. I couldn't imagine myself killing anyone, though.

Keirdran, yes. Wild, laughing too much, too loud, raucous Kirin Keirdran had a streak in her that lived in sanity's grey zone: one heartbeat away from rage, two breaths away from violence. Voted most likely to slaughter the crew and then laugh about it. She didn't wear simple shackles for her incarceration. She was bound in armour that controlled her every move.

◀ ▶

Keirdran emerged from her quarters twenty hours later before I was fully awake, and rapped on my door. Which she'd never done.

"Pascal," she called, her voice a file against metal.

When I slid open my door and blinked in the light, she held out a children's toy like a sacred offering.

A train. A shiny red locomotive that fit easily into her palm. Light glinted off its silvery wheels and ebony trim.

"Uh," I said.

Keirdran shook the train at me while she nodded. Through her visor I glimpsed genuine joy in her usually dead eyes. Her mouth was twisted into a crooked expression that passed for a smile.

"Uh, yeah, nice," I said. I ran fingers through unkempt hair, then trudged to the dying control board.

I pressed hands to mouth to suppress my fury, reminding myself that Keirdran couldn't help it. She couldn't possibly comprehend that we were speeding along to a dead quarry in a failing drone ship while we waited. Waited to see whether the system fixed itself. Waited to receive updated instructions. Waited to learn whether we'd been dispatched to death. While Keirdran built herself a choo-choo.

She set it on the floor and pointed at it. The tiny locomotive rolled forwards, backwards, in a circle. Up the damn wall. It tooted a wee, high-pitched whistle, and a puff of blue sparks spurted from its thumb-sized smokestack. Keirdran chuckled.

"Good idea, Keirdran," I said, swallowing fury and fear. "Might as well amuse yourself." I gazed through the pane at the stars in the unfamiliar stretch of space, my one solace. "I oughta get myself a hobby, too, and keep my mind off impending death."

Keirdran laughed aloud; laughter I hadn't heard from her since we were both free and sat a few tables apart in the ship's pub, relaxing after our shifts. Back when we did real work on a genuine research ship. When we knew where we were going and why.

"I study stardust," I'd tell people.

And the best place to study dust was Mur, a wild west region of the galaxy, run by people who don't believe in fair trials. We stopped to resupply, and I never re-boarded my ship.

My trial lasted twenty-eight minutes.

While waiting to be sentenced I heard a rumour that one-third of our crew had been arrested, and most swiftly convicted. All were condemned to work mining drones, sailing from quarry to quarry through dangerous territory.

Like us. But now we had been sent to the vast outskirts of Mur territory hunting ore that didn't exist.

Keirdran's locomotive rolled to the control board. Just as its front wheels reached the board's edge, it stopped. A slender metal thread like a serpent's tongue uncoiled from a wheel and licked my right shackle. I jerked back my hand. My wrist tingled.

"Keep that thing away from me!" I shouted. The tingling spread up my arm.

The train whistled again, but instead of sparks, its tiny smokestack spurted out a silvery cloud with a message in simple text: *Rescue is near.*

I coughed out a laugh.

Rescue is near, it spurted again.

I turned to Keirdran. She gestured, and her locomotive wheeled back down the wall and across the floor into her hand like a trained pet. Shivering, she slumped to the floor

clutching it. Her lower face was ashen and beaded with perspiration.

My shackles pinched me hard for disobeying orders or
questioning Mur's instructions. I couldn't imagine the pain
Keirdran endured to sneak a message to me. I tried so hard to
ignore her and dismissed so much of what she said that I
didn't even realize she could still think clearly. I'd assumed her
daily existence was like a simple machine that received input,
then acted on it. Fix that engine. Mine that ore. Climb to that
ceiling.

Someone who, when she was very, very good, might be permitted a brief respite to listen to music. For a few moments,
she would lean on a wall, hand swaying in time. The music
would end and Keirdran silently returned to work. Unlike the
old days when she hummed snippets of popular songs through
echoing corridors.

She hummed to the locomotive then, although it was clear
she was still very much in Mur's grip. As far away as we were,
her gear still dispatched reward and punishment, just like my
shackles.

She grunted with a spasm of pain. Her gloved hand unclenched so the locomotive dropped to the floor. Those amazing gloves, like scaly claws flexing, spurred something in me: a
fleeting memory, like a dream I couldn't recall after I woke up.

"Pascal," she rasped. "Soon." She shuddered, then banged
her head against the wall a few times before she slumped fully
to the floor and actually slept for close to three hours.

◀ ▶

I'd tried to take control of the mining drone. Thousands of
times in our endless seven-year sojourn I studied its workings

in an effort to hijack that ship. Each time, my only reward was new bruises from the shackles.

That day, I simply stared at stars through the pane, slouched with my hands curled on my lap, unable to dredge up any new ideas. Refusing to look at the dying board.

Keirdran clomped over to me, tapping her locomotive. Programming it. Those gloved fingertips like dragon's claws.

Dragon's claws.

I bolted upright.

Makour.

I used to have a toy dragon with claws like that. A plastic toy with no special gizmos to make it fly or roll across the floor, but I loved that dragon.

I ran everywhere holding Makour over my head. Together, we traversed the world, rescuing people from pirates and scanning the seas for trouble. Makour snorted fire. He read minds. He heard cries for help a million kilometres away. No one knew us for the superheroes we were, as we appeared to them as a spindly limbed boy with his damned plastic dragon racing alongside dirty canals or between dilapidated buildings.

Keirdran set the locomotive on the board and clomped away. It whirred awake.

Rescue is near, the locomotive spewed. *Patience.*

"Patience, my ass," I told Keirdran's damned choo-choo. "How can you know anything, Keirdran? Your brain's been peeled apart and poked full of hardware neither of us understand."

I rubbed my aching eyes. When I opened them, the last of the data faded. The board became terrifyingly silent and completely dark. But from the locomotive's tiny smokestack, pertinent information puffed out like steam.

We were far off course, it showed; no longer headed for Spakata. Mur territory's last beacon lay well behind us. My messages to them would simply meander through space, unseen by anyone for a million years.

"Keirdran?" My legs couldn't support me. "What've you done?"

The locomotive whistled, high and wee, a familiar aria with new words: *Patience. Rescue. Ship. Escape. Be. Quiet.*

Keirdran whistled along. What I saw of her face was creased with agony. The locomotive sprouted limbs and attached itself to the dead board. Slender stalks reeled from the train and crept across the controls, tips oozing like molten ore as each adhered itself in place. A cloud of fresh data puffed from the smokestack.

And in that cloud the SS *Fu* blipped, a steady speck headed toward us.

Keirdran plunked herself into a seat to study the data, nodding subtly. With a grunt, she wrenched off a metal brace from her forearm revealing her poor withered flesh.

"Keirdran? That's still you?"

Keirdran couldn't answer, only sat silent with pain. But the locomotive sang.

> *Dear Pascal,*
> *have a seat.*
> *Be patient*
> *and sit sweet.*
> *Yhamarda's*
> *where we'll go.*
> *Take a deep breath,*
> *all is well.*

Yhamarda territory was comprised of two barely habitable planets with a scant population of ten thousand people – a paradise compared to Mur.

Keirdran's dragon-claw hands clenched and unclenched. Perspiration trickled down her chin and dropped onto her breastplate. She drooped like a wilted plant.

The painful jolts my shackles once administered became gentle squeezes. My arms tingled. My vision blurred. I shut my eyes. Dreamed of Makour.

I run with a plastic dragon in one hand held high, but in my mind, my arms are wrapped around his serpentine neck as we soar over snowy mountains and sparkling oceans, and even up to the faraway stars.

Makour saved me when I dangled over an abyss and pulled me from a firestorm when we battled ogres. We slew giants, tamed tsunamis, and rescued orphans. Orphans like me.

I woke up.

Beside me, Keirdran dozed in her seat, her breathing ragged. Before me, the locomotive piloted the ship, its steaming data the same information that the board used to display. The locomotive oozed red and black threads across the board, twining with the thickening silver stalks it had earlier sprouted. Then the dirty once-white walls around me seemed to shake. I gripped my seat to fight vertigo.

Just my poor head, I thought, *dizzy from whatever it was that made my arm tingle earlier.*

Yet a slender hose to my left hissed and rose; a snake about to strike. An overhead conduit suddenly buckled.

"Keirdran, wake up! What's your train doing?"

Keirdran rose with a grunt.

"Keirdran!"

"Hol' on." She lurched from spot to spot, some particular destination in mind, but her gear still hampered her. Mur Prison was losing control, though. Keirdran's limbs gradually grew free.

As did my head. My poor head, about to burst as memories returned. I suddenly pictured my lover's face and remembered his name; how could I have forgotten his name? Serge waved goodbye and winked at me from behind a clear partition. That was twelve years ago. I should have returned to him ages ago.

The woman who raised me came to mind, too. I didn't yet remember her name, but did recall she fostered three of us. Clothed us, fed us, showed us the stars, told us tales of Earth where our ancestors had lived. Gave me my plastic dragon. Nothing special, just a toy she plucked from a bin of toys. Picked out three, probably at random, and handed one to each of us.

"I lost my dragon," I blurted to Keirdran. "Lost it on a train to school. The kids took it; threw it out the window. Little shits! Bastards!" I pounded fist on board, inexplicably angrier at those brats than I was at the Murites.

Keirdran looked at me. "The pain will pass," she said. Gravel voice. Ancient voice. She lifted her visor, something she'd never been able to do. Her movements were jerky. Her face was wan and creased. Blue sacs circled her eyes. Her right cheek was scarred like my wrists.

Do I look that bad? I thought.

"You'll readjust quickly now," Keirdran said, just as the locomotive sang out, *Prepare the coffin.*

"Whaaaaa…?"

Keirdran plucked my sleeve. "Time," she said. "Let's go. The ship's programmed to self-destruct if we take control. I think it happens slowly, but we can't…"

Ominous creaking and popping, like the noises a dilapidated building makes when it's about to collapse, rang out around us, and Keirdran's locomotive spat out a red warning.

"Time," Keirdran said again, but I was already pulling on survival gear.

The coffin, our sole lifeboat, could keep us alive for up to thirty days. Keirdran had ridden in it at least fifty times in seven years when she'd sailed out to test rock. Yet when she tapped in the code, the coffin didn't drop from where it lay stored overhead.

I reached up to help her pry open the panel manually. Silver threads from the locomotive streamed between her gloved fingers to aid her.

A terrifying rumble, followed by a thunderous crack, shifted the entire ship when a chunk of floor fell open to reveal the ship's bowels spinning with flickering lights. Beneath the bowels, darkening fissures spread like spiderwebs. The dead control board popped. My bunk, which had easily held my eighty-five kilos, fell to the floor. Trash in Keirdran's room swirled in a vortex.

Makour and I tumbled from a crumbling starship once. I held my breath and my dragon flew through space, bearing me on his back to safety.

My real-life dragon, an old engineer named Keirdran, hung from slender conduits as stalks from her locomotive finally cracked open the hatch to where our one hope of survival sat waiting, and blessedly intact. I grappled with sagging cable and managed to squeeze my right leg into the coffin.

Keirdran hauled in the rest of me, then herself, and shut the lid.

◄   ►

We drifted through space huddled together, my hand holding Keirdran's arm as we escaped Mur Prison's death sentence.

My arms clutching Makour, escaping villains.

From inside the coffin, we couldn't determine whether we were on course, how far we travelled, or how long we rode. We simply slept. Slept past a dozen suns and a thousand rocks. Slept as the mite of a craft finally crept into the giant ship's maw like a starfish into a whale's mouth.

Slept while medics pulled out what prison hardware they could and poured nutrients into our hungry blood.

I woke with tubes in both arms, a doctor at my feet, and a lawyer on the console.

◄   ►

Keirdran never killed anyone. She has dangerous knowledge, however: the kind that enables her to hijack a drone ship. Her imprisoned mind fought for seven years to escape, while she cobbled together a marvellous choo-choo train.

I, on the other hand, am charged with manslaughter. I say I remember nothing. I vividly recall, though, confronting a very large Murite man who tried to arrest me. He had a weapon. I did not.

The Murites who raided our ship sentenced dozens of us in their kangaroo court to ensure a supply of miners who'd be sent to the most dangerous quarries known. Miners are expendable. Fifty billion humans roam the galaxy these days. What matter if a few thousand perish in a faraway region on the edge of the system, especially if they're murderers and thieves and treasonous villains?

I must be patient 'til we reach Phoenix Colony in Yhamarda. There, I'll wait for a new trial; perhaps a new sentence. Yhamarda has a veneer of civilization. They know my first trial under Murite law was a sham. My lawyer assures me that if I'm convicted, whatever time I served on the mining drone should be taken into account. But no one puts anything in writing. I picture myself sitting in a cell staring out at a bleak landscape with a live volcano on the horizon.

Meanwhile, I'm free to roam the *Fu*'s corridors, sedated and shackled. I waste my days on its vast observation deck where I gaze out at the trillion stars, trying to determine which one was home.

Keirdran rests, hidden away. She barely survived, she who never killed anyone. Only laughed too loud too often and sang dirty songs and told ribald stories. She won't remember me, the doctor says, for her memory's so scrambled it's a wonder she knows her name.

I pass her quarters daily. Door always shut, silence from the other side. Every day, for ages; long after my bruises fade and cuts heal. Until the night I return late from the deck.

Her door's wide open and her room's fully lit.

I slow down but don't enter, only turn my head to peek.

Metal plates lie like wind-tossed rubbish across the floor around a partially built red locomotive. Keirdran stands at a table, bent over work, her eyes covered by goggles. Her left hand wields a slender needle with a gilded tip. She taps the needle on a shimmering green serpent – a metal dragon whose red eyes glow like rubies and whose claws flex when the needle's tip oozes golden liquid into it. Its leathery wings languidly unfurl from its scaly, emerald green back. It opens its mouth to reveal dozens of sharp teeth. A puff akin to smoke wafts out from its nostrils and dissipates.

Keirdran sets down her tools, raises her goggles, and winks at me.

WITH ONE SHOE

Karen Abrahamson

By the time Detective Ron Conway pulled up to the Paradis house it had been forty-eight hours since Elvira Paradis had last seen her child. As Ron arrived, the grey clapboard house slouched in its postage-stamp-sized yard just like the other matchy-match houses on the block; a veritable gang of houses emulating the sullen youngsters on their way to school. The house might once have been white. The trim showed a last desperate hint of green. The yard was brown from too much sun and too little June rain. No tree, no hedge, not a single damn living blade of grass. A pink sneaker lay in the middle of the lawn. Desiccated weeds filled what might once have been a garden.

Someone had cared – once – but the weight of the neigh-bourhood had dragged their efforts under. He recognized the place – he'd grown up in one like it – the kind of hell that stole dreams and bred nightmares. Not any place to raise a kid.

And now a fourteen-year-old was missing.

Ron climbed out of the brown sedan, letting the sun dry the damp spot between his shoulders.

"I hate these cases," his partner, Jake Spinoza, muttered as he climbed out the other side.

"Makes two of us." Ron pulled his sports jacket on.

"It's always the same. The kid gets tired of being abused. They run, and drugs and prostitution get them. It doesn't end well." Spinoza shook his head. "Maybe we should just arrest the parents. Then the kids might stand a chance."

Ron eyed the house. It didn't quite have the black-eyed look of the other places on the block. A pot of geraniums next to the front door said that hope hung on by a thread. Maybe other things were different here.

Ron was big and Viking-pale, the bulk to Spinoza's wiry Latin frame. The door opened, revealing a woman who actually looked *interested,* perhaps even worried – another first.

"Mrs. Paradis? I'm Detective Conway and this is Detective Spinoza."

"Come in. Please." Elvira Paradis motioned them inside. Small, bird-boned, and faded blond, she had stooped shoulders and pale blue eyes that took up most of her face. She had a scent of vanilla and roses. She wore a pair of worn blue shorts that exposed thin legs, and a cotton floral blouse that looked ironed. Another sign that someone cared.

The inside of the house showed it, too. The living room furniture was worn, but clean. A blue sofa faced the front window that had the drapes drawn. Two mismatched chairs faced the couch, draped in green throws to hide lurid yellow upholstery. Curbside finds, he'd bet. But in this house people did the best with what they had. A television sat against one wall topped with family photos of Elvira Paradis and a blonde seven-year-old child just as fine-boned as her mother, but with indigo eyes.

On the couch, Spinoza pulled out his notebook and Ron sat with his hands between his knees. "You contacted the office to report your daughter missing," Ron said.

She nodded, the most silent witness he'd ever met.

"Tell us what happened."

Her throat worked. "I got up yesterday and she wasn't here."

Definitely a woman of few words.

"When did you last see your daughter?"

Her pale blue gaze settled on his and for a moment the room changed to vivid burgundy with forest green carpets. The furniture was cream and the windows looked out onto a world of verdant hills and forest. For a moment his chest unclenched and he could breathe – almost laughed out loud for the first time in a very long time.

Then she blinked and he was back inside a faded house on Effron Avenue that parched under the Saskatchewan sun.

"At dinner night before last. Afterward she went to her room. That's it."

"Tell me about dinner."

"We had peas and mashed potatoes."

Spinoza stirred and grinned. Let the great Ron Conway drag it out of her. Spinoza was having fun.

"What did you talk about?"

"School, maybe. She was doing a project. She's a good kid, May-Bell is."

"So tell us about May-Bell."

"She's smart. Gets straight As in school."

"Do you have a recent picture of her?" Because a detailed description was clearly beyond her.

She got up and left the room. Spinoza's smile widened.

"Shut up," Ron muttered.

"Didn't say a word."

Elvira Paradis returned and handed Ron a five-by-seven school photo of the child from the TV photos fast-forwarded to age fourteen. Fine boned like her mother, but her small mouth was determined, and those indigo eyes – there was something wild about them. He couldn't imagine her surviving in this household's silences.

He settled back on the couch. "Have you checked her room – seen if anything's missing?"

When she looked mystified, he added, "Did she take things with her as if she planned on leaving? Are there clothes missing that might indicate what she was wearing?"

"I'll show you." She led them down the hall, clearly not knowing the answer.

"Is there a Mr. Paradis we should talk to?" he asked.

She shook her head. "May-Bell and me – we're on our own."

May-Bell's stingy room held a single narrow bed under a window that gave out onto a sun-parched backyard. It held only a swing set with a single dangling swing and a yawning gap where a second swing might have been. Her room was little girl pale pink and purple, but the walls held hints of fledgling teenager: posters of animals, woodland scenes, an art poster of fairies placed at the end of the bed. Not exactly what he expected. No boy-bands or teen heartthrobs.

"No unicorns," he said.

"They were extinct a long time ago."

Spinoza arched a brow at him.

"Can you see if anything's missing?" Ron asked.

She rifled through a painfully empty closet, and almost empty drawers. "It's all here, I think, except what she was wearing; blue jeans and her favourite pink T-shirt with a running horse on it."

That was something. "What kind of shoes?"

"She has a pair of pink runners. They're her favourite."

"Hold on." He led them out front to the shoe on the lawn. Pink sneaker, size five. It showed the signs of kid-wear with the heel bent in back from treating the shoe as a slip-on. It lay upside down, as it had fallen. A fight, maybe? A shoe wasn't something you stepped out of and left as you walked away – at least not just one of them. This was more like the shoe had been dropped as the girl was carried away.

"Did you hear your daughter leave?" Why hadn't she noticed the shoe?

She was looking up to the sky as if the sight of the shoe pained her.

"Mrs. Paradis? Did you hear her?"

She shook her head, her hair spun like spider thread around her shoulders. "She didn't come through the living room because I was watching television." Her small hands worked each other.

He used his smart phone to photograph the shoe. "I'd like to see the backyard please."

He and Spinoza tramped after her as she flitted across the browned lawn to the side of the house and a small gate that hung open.

"Do you always leave your gate open?"

"No." She frowned.

The grass underneath May-Bell's bedroom window *did* look like some of the blades were crushed. From someone standing here? Or was it from someone jumping down from the ledge? He tested the window and it slid upward with the ease of frequent use. Had the girl flown the coop on her own? Had she left with someone?

The swing set, a factory-made metal job, sat alone in the yard, the lawn underneath faintly green compared to elsewhere. The set had been there a long time – probably put up by a family with young children before the financial crash. Along with two swings it would have had a teeter-totter at one end. Now its bright red paint had chipped and rust ate the metal. The single swing hung like an exhausted child.

"How long have you lived here, Mrs. Paradis?" He crossed to the lone swing and touched the chains.

"Almost eleven months." Her hair was silver in the sun. It would be ethereal by moonlight.

The swing itself was wooden. He hadn't seen a wooden swing since he was a kid – now playgrounds had soft rubber because wood was considered too dangerous. When he touched it, the swing groaned where the chain met the suspending crossbar and a tingle ran through him.

He settled onto the wooden seat and had the urge to lean back and start pumping. Instead he stared at the house. "May-Bell come out here a lot?"

"Some."

But this *was* the kind of place a teen would come to be alone, to think. His house had had a similar swing – a lone board hanging from the strong branch of an oak tree that had long ago been cut down. He'd spent evenings there dreaming of life beyond that yard. What did May-Bell dream of? A knight on a white charger rescuing her from her life?

But the posters in her room spoke of a different kind of girl – not the boy-obsessed fourteen-going-on-twenty-four-year-olds that were everywhere today. No, this one was *interested*. May-Bell Paradis *wanted* something. If she left, it would be because she wanted something more.

Beneath the swing set long grooves had been worn into the lawn by feet dragged across the earth. The odd thing was the grooves lay under the spot a second swing should hang.

He stood. The chains that would have held another swing appeared sheared off at the crossbar.

He turned back to Elvira. "How long ago did you have the swing cut off?"

The woman's mouth settled into a sullen line. When she met his gaze he found himself in a meadow of wild flowers, the wind tossing the blossoms, the air heavy with sweetness and the hum of bees.

She blinked and he again stood in a faded backyard with a rusted swing set. *What the hell is going on?*

"There was never a second swing," Elvira said.

"Mrs. Paradis, what do you think has happened to May-Bell? Has she run away or was she taken?"

She seemed to look past him into somewhere else. Then she shook her head. "May-Bell would never leave me like this. Not of her own choice. You've got to get her back for me."

The way she'd looked away, he knew she was lying.

◄ ►

Alexander Junior High filled half a city block with cement stairs and seating areas terraced up to a cinder block façade. There were no trees and no grass, only concrete that reflected sunlight into Ron's face and heat through the soles of his shoes.

Inside, the air smelled of too many teen bodies. The halls were quiet, just a few wraith-like figures shifting under the fluorescents before disappearing into classrooms. The half-heard drone of teachers' voices brought another rush of *déjà vu*. He'd hated high school, had hated junior high more.

He showed his badge at the office security window and they were buzzed into a waiting area that was split by a counter. On one side were two desks and office equipment. On the other, three chairs stood against the wall, a small table in front of them. The air reeked of copier ink, paper and an old woman's too-sweet perfume.

"We'd like to speak to the principal, please. It's regarding, May-Bell Paradis," he said to the clerk. Spinoza nodded.

"Have a seat. I'll tell him you're here." The clerk motioned to the waiting room chairs, next to a closed wooden door.

One chair held a kid with black hair that hung over his ears, and a black gaze that radiated age beyond his years. He looked up at them, and the age disappeared, leaving behind bored resignation. He wore a black T-shirt and jeans over long, outstretched legs, and had a black leather jacket across his lap. Now, who wore leather when it was a hundred degrees? Work boots with lug soles covered large feet.

Ron slouched down in the chair beside the kid and grabbed a magazine off the table. Old. Women's. He tossed it aside and sat in silence. No banter between the two admin staff. Unnatural. Unhappy.

"You waiting for the principal?" Ron asked the kid.

"Yeah. He doles out what passes for justice 'round here. You'd like him," the kid said with a lip curl.

Lots of attitude, this one. The kind that said what he thought. "You know May-Bell Paradis?"

"I might." Normal caution. "What'd she do?"

"Who does she hang with in school?"

The kid grinned. "You gotta give a little, ta get a little, man. What'd she do?"

"Disappeared. Her mother thinks she's been abducted."

The kid snorted. "That old hag don't know nothing."

Ron sat up. "So you *do* know May-Bell."

The kid shrugged, his grin gone. "She's fucking trapped like the rest of us. The world, you know?"

He leaned his head back against the wall and closed his eyes, effectively ending the conversation.

Ron settled back, too. "We want to make sure she's all right. You hear anything, I'd appreciate you letting me know." He placed a business card on the kid's knee and closed his eyes. He felt the kid stir.

"If I was May-Bell, I'd be so far from here you'd never find me. I'd never look back."

Ron rolled his head sideways to look at the kid, but the boy's eyes were still closed, and Ron's card hadn't moved. Had the kid even spoken? Spinoza didn't look up from thumbing a magazine.

The wooden door beside them pulled open, releasing a gust of sea-scented aftershave and a student moving fast toward the main office door. A big man followed.

"You've visitors, sir. The police," said the clerk. She nodded in their direction. Spinoza closed his magazine.

The principal was a tall, thin man, verging on the cadaverous, with large hands that stuck too far out of his grey suit jacket sleeves. He turned a sunken-fleshed face towards them. "How may I be of assistance?"

Ron stood and introduced them. "We'd like to speak with you about May-Bell Paradis."

"I'm Stepford Hall, the Principal. Please, come in." He motioned them into his office. Functional shelves of policy manuals, and educational theory. Above the book shelves was the expected inspirational office picture except, instead of the usual words like *Strive,* or *Excellence,* this one said *Be* and showed a street scene of people going about their day.

Hall must have seen his glance. He smiled as he sank into his seat. "We strive to keep our student's expectations realistic – especially since the economic downturn."

It was a short interview.

Stepford Hall knew nothing about May-Bell Paradis except her attendance – excellent – and that she was a good student, but he did print off May-Bell's schedule and suggest that they talk to May-Bell's teachers, beginning with her art instructor.

When they stepped out to the waiting area, the dark-haired kid was gone.

After receiving directions, Ron and Spinoza tramped the school halls. Posters of upcoming dances, club meetings and fashionable causes decorated the walls. The place echoed their footfalls like painful memories.

At the juncture of two halls a trophy case adorned one wall with chrome and photos of outstanding athletes. The other side of the hall displayed student art. One painting stopped Ron.

Done in watercolours, its faded blue-greys and greens hinted at treetops and sky. In the centre a swirl of colour and line suggested a child in a swing so high she hung above it all. Wild blond hair blew out from her shoulders and became part of the clouds. It was delicate and beautiful and wild. Scratched in the corner were initials he couldn't make out.

"So what d'ya think?" he asked.

Spinoza shrugged. "Looks okay. Like someone has a thing with swings." He cocked a brow. "You maybe? You were asking a lot of questions this morning."

The wild-haired blonde could be May-Bell. If it was the Paradis swing set it was proof that both swings had been there and that one was missing – the one the girl in the painting was on. Pondering that, they found the classroom. He knocked on the door, and they stepped inside.

Bright and dark colours splattered the floor, tables and easels. Students wore paint-splattered smocks, as they dabbed brushes on canvas. The taint of turpentine and paint filled the room and a dark-haired woman paused at students' shoulders. She headed toward Ron.

She was a pretty woman, with large dark eyes, and lush lashes. She had high cheekbones with just enough natural colour and a trim figure that, though she was Ron's age, hadn't gone to fat.

"Ms. Leary?" He kept his voice low. "I'm Detective Conway and this is Detective Spinoza. We're investigating the disappearance of May-Bell Paradis. Can we step into the hall?"

"Of course." She preceded them into the deserted hallway. "How can I help you?" She looked from Spinoza to Ron.

"May-Bell's mother reported that she hasn't seen her daughter since night before last. We understand May-Bell has excelled in your class. Have you noticed anything unusual about her?"

Ms. Leary frowned. "Not really. She's the clichéd artistic genius – always distracted except for her art. She's a fantastic painter. Really talented. Someday she'll be someone to reckon with in the art world."

Spinoza's pen scritch-scritched across his notepad. "Can you think of anyone who might want to harm May-Bell – or abduct her?"

"Harm her?" Her skin paled a little. "Do you think something's happened to her?"

"We have to explore all possibilities," Ron said.

There was that lone pink sneaker, on the parched lawn.

Ms. Leary crossed her arms. "I can't think of anyone. She was liked well enough. She never mentioned any issues. She seemed happy since she got a boyfriend."

That was news that Elvira Paradis seemed unaware of.

"Can you think of any reason for May-Bell to run away?"

She shook her head, frowning again.

"So who's this boyfriend?" Spinoza asked

She glanced back at her room. "I'd introduce you, but he's absent today. His name's Todd Sloan. Tall boy. Dark-haired. He likes black leather, but the kid has an artist's soul."

He thought of the kid from the office. "You don't happen to have a photo of him, do you?"

She led them down to the trophy case and studied the displays and photos. "There. That's Todd."

The dark-haired kid stared back at them, his hair slicked by sweat, muscled arms exposed by a basketball shirt. Arms like that were certainly enough to overpower a skinny wraith like May-Bell Paradis.

"Do you think I could get a copy of that photo?"

She shrugged. "The office might have one. But Todd wouldn't do anything to May-Bell. He genuinely cared for her. He's been using her as a model for his painting." She motioned to the watercolour that Ron had admired. "That's his work. He has a whole series of them."

"Really." He glanced at Spinoza and read his matching concern. Was the kid obsessed with May-Bell? "Any possibility of seeing his paintings?"

"Uh…" Ms. Leary suddenly seemed uncertain. "Todd wouldn't do anything to May-Bell. Really."

As if she reassured herself.

"Let's see those paintings, shall we?"

He eased her back to the classroom, but by the time they reached it she was visibly struggling with whether to cooperate.

"I think we may have met Todd today in the office," he said. "He expressed a bit of attitude toward authority. Is that what he's like?"

Ms. Leary looked up at him. "No. Maybe. It depends, I guess. Me, he had no problem with."

Understandable. A pretty teacher wasn't hard to take direction from.

"So those paintings?"

Ms. Leary led to them to a series of shallow drawers that filled one wall. She pulled one out.

A similar watercolour lay on top, the sky a little lighter, the trees and landscape a lot darker and a beam of light caught the figure who had left her swing behind and was leaping – or was that falling – from the swing back to earth. It looked like the landscape would swallow her up.

"A different feel to this one," he said.

Ms. Leary nodded.

He rifled through the stack of paintings. A pastel of a similar scene. An oil with the sky almost tropical blue and a dark brooding landscape with May-Bell Paradis sitting alone on a swing on a two-swing set. For all the bright colour of the sky, the landscape drained the life and colour out of everything.

"These are not happy paintings. Not like the one on the wall."

He found Ms. Leary studying him.

The rest of the paintings were all dark and getting darker, except for the last one. It was done with a less skilled hand – the other paintings showed a swift progression in the artist's skill, but this one captured a wild emotion the others hadn't. It showed the same dark landscape and swing set, except that only one swing hung there. The sky was a deep blue verging toward night with the last blush of sunset still edging the horizon. Against this, miniscule from distance, a figure wildly pumped a swing through the air, suspended on nothing.

"Strange." He met Ms. Leary's gaze.

She touched the canvas almost in admiration. "This was his first work in class. He was almost embarrassed when I told him how talented he was." She smiled, but the smile faded. "You know, I didn't think anything of it at the time, but May-Bell got upset when she saw it. She and Todd got into an argument, but things blew over and they started dating."

The tiny figure in the painting seemed filled with joy and freedom, like a bird following the sunlight. He could remember childhood dreams that were similar. Escape. Salvation. So why was Todd Sloan painting May-Bell escaping?

"Can we see May-Bell's paintings, please?"

Ms. Leary slid out another drawer. "May-Bell's work is also stunningly good, but darker. There are rarely people in her work. When there are, they aren't happy."

The painting on top was an abstract swirl of dull brown with small square blotches that suggested houses covering the entire world except for a corner that held a brilliant green.

He thumbed through the others. Dark forests with the suggestion of a lost, red-hooded child. Dark alleyways with ethereal smudges that could be ghosts. The canvases got steadily darker until he reached the one on the bottom. The painting was lighter, brighter, a woodland scene of huge trees and shafts of sunlight illuminating a fantastical garden of crimson blooms and a woman in a gossamer robe tending them. Through the trees were hints of carved moss-covered stone archways.

"Why are the first paintings so different for both Todd and May-Bell?" Spinoza asked.

"The assignment, I guess. I asked them to paint something that could only be true in their wildest dreams. I always assign that first to get it out of their systems. Once they get that on the page, I can start working with them to find the beauty in the mundane."

"Interesting." Ron said. Another way to kill dreams.

"If you think of anything else, or if Todd shows up, would you give me a call please?" He handed her his card.

She looked at it, nodded. Her gaze was sad and lonely.

They left the school at three o'clock after retrieving Todd Sloan's address from the school office. The school belched out escaping youngsters. The two of them were silent as they piled into the sedan.

"So what do you think?" Spinoza asked.

"I think we need to find Todd Sloan."

◄ ►

Like the Paradis house, Todd Sloan's home hunkered in a parched lot of cracked earth, chipped white paint exposing grey boards. It reminded him of flesh showing through torn nylons. Old newspapers and candy wrappers piled at the base of the house as if they held up the weary structure. A sheet of milky plastic had been nailed over the broken front window.

"Imagine growing up here," Spinoza said.

"We've seen worse."

"But this area used to be nice."

Ron shrugged and climbed out of the car. The air smelled of car exhaust, dust and despair. At the house, he knocked on the door. There was movement inside, but no one answered.

"We'll get Todd's photo out to the uniformed officers. They'll pick him up," he said.

When there was still no response they left and headed for the office. Finding out what had happened to May Bell Paradis would wait another day.

◀ ▶

Or it wouldn't. That night, at home in his two-room apartment, Ron sucked back a beer in his T-shirt and shorts because his air conditioning had quit again. The TV in the corner droned sitcom reruns and the room smelled of his dinner of ham sandwich with sauerkraut on pumpernickel.

He leaned back in the easy chair that comprised his living room furniture, eyes closed and feet up. This was his thinking position and he needed to think, because something about the May-Bell case itched like a bug under his skin.

Todd Sloan lived near enough to May-Bell that he could have been stalking her since the Paradis moved in just a few weeks before school. That was the only way he could have known her well enough to have painted her as his first art project.

Or else Ron was just imagining things and the kid had been inspired to incorporate May-Bell into his painting when he'd met her in class.

But that felt wrong. And Todd Sloan had disappeared right after he found out they were looking for May-Bell. The logical deduction: Todd Sloan ran.

He recalled his few brief words with the kid. May-Bell trapped. Not abducted, but escaping. The kid had spoken with sadness and longing and – yes, bitterness. That was what Ron had heard – the bitterness.

He sat up and stabbed the TV off, then grabbed pants from the unmade bed across the room. Grabbed a shirt, his badge and gun and a jacket to hide the fact he was armed. Then he headed out.

He parked a block away from the Paradis house. At two in the morning the neighbourhood was quiet, even dogs slumbering. He started walking; the night air fresher, untainted by daytime unhappiness. A fading moon stretched his shadow on the sidewalk.

At the Paradis house he wondered whether he was being a fool. The house was dark as he followed the yard around to the back. The parched grass whispered under his feet. The side gate stood open. Elvira Paradis had said she kept it closed.

Moonlight filled the backyard and illuminated the swing set, the lone swing rocking gently at the urging of a seated Todd Sloan.

Ron stepped through the gate and Todd startled and then slumped as if he'd long ago given up hope.

Ron slouched across the yard. "You miss her, don't you?"

Todd nodded, but wouldn't meet his gaze.

"You saw her when she first moved in. You saw her and were infatuated."

Another nod. "She was just crazy beautiful. All that wild blond hair and eyes that were dying. She was dying just like

the rest of us, moment by moment. She hated that it was happening. Before school started I watched her because I didn't
have the guts to talk to her. Every night she'd climb out her
window."

"And she'd come out here, to swing," Ron said softly.

"It was the strangest thing I ever saw. She'd swing higher
and higher, almost desperately. I was scared she was going to
swing right over the swing set's top bar, but instead light filled
her and filled the swing and suddenly the chains released and
she was flying – up into the sky. I watched her that first time,
swooping and laughing and then she swung back down and
the swing attached again. She did that every night for a week
and then school started and she didn't do it anymore."

"But you painted what you'd seen."

Todd frowned. "She freaked. But we worked it out. We
were together and she was happy – at least a little."

But his hands formed fists around the swing chains. "At
least I thought we were. She said the reason she could make
the swing fly was that she could fuel it with all the happiness
she had from when she was young, from before her mother
and she were banished from their – place. She said happiness
was a gift, a magic, and that living here stole it from her."

Todd swung the swing back and forth, his feet scuffing
through the green grass that was fading to brown.

"Night before last she flew again, didn't she?"

Todd shrugged. "The swing's gone, isn't it?" Loneliness,
bitterness, the weight of the world.

"So you didn't hurt her?" How the hell was he going to
report this?

The kid looked up at him. "Hurt her? She was magic,
man. I'd have gone with her, but I couldn't find enough hap-

piness anymore. I guess she knew I'd bleed it off of her, too, eventually." He sighed and his tears caught the predawn light.

Ron remembered that feeling all too well. He settled himself cross-legged on the grass beside the swing. There was nothing he could say. He'd lost the art of happiness, too.

Side by side they looked up at the empty sky. The moon was setting. Another day of heat and crime and ugliness coming their way.

But somewhere, a girl with one shoe and a swing was flying.

WHEATIESFIELDS IN FALL

Geoffrey W. Cole

Maingame log, 2196.5.21 0530

Three quests this AM:

1) Bring Mrs. Olfrichstein OJ and pastry.

2) Empty all bedpans (laughs = bonus gold)

3) Find Mr. Yao old cartridge game (is he Level 29 boss?)

Long day ahead. Much XP, less gold. Maybe see Nurse T?

Dialogue with Moderator Behan when came in this AM re: hockey scores last night, Behan's daughter (better, thanks new kidney), Behan's wife (5 months no bonage. Raised XP reward, even some gold. Still no bonage).

Dialogue re: cartridge:

Me: "Impossible, searched online, nothing."

Moderator Behan: "Tough nuts, Loufis."

My quest, my time. Much XP, some gold. Level 29 boss? Behan not sure. Behan has own boss fight = wife, no bonage. Level 56.

Me: "Don't dwell."

Behan: "Excel."

2.5 years too long for Level 29. Supposed to be only 6 months, year max, but game hard. Level hard. Admit it: laziness no help. Level also boring. Boring = hard.

Stop. Don't dwell.

First, OJ and pastry. Then bedpans. Play *HammerSmash* on crapper and at lunch. Beat the Level 4 prick. Then Yao cartridge. 200 + years old. How the F to find? Should be higher level. 80s, at least.

◀ ▶

Maingame log, 2196.5.21 1145

Quest results:

1) OJ has pulp, pastry has raisins. Mrs. Olfrichstein not happy.

Me: "Last time request juice with pulp and raisin pastry."

Mrs. O disconnect upload line and plug into my brainport. Replay memory: Mrs. O tells Loufis she want No Pulp, No Raisins. Apologize, but no XP, no gold.

2) Bedpans = empty. 3 XP, 0.15 gold. Laughs = mixed.

Me to Mr. Thule: "Constipation? More like can-stipation."

Mr. Thule: "Har har," 0.15 bonus gold.

Me to Mrs. Hungerdurn: "I'd make a joke, but all the ones I know are corny."

Mrs. H: "Disgusting. We've talked about your lewd sense of humour." Mrs. H. ask for new attendant. Moderator Behan apologize, deduct 2 XP.

Me to Mr. Davenport: "…"

Mr. D: "No jokes today, Loufis?"

Me: "Shitty day."

Mr. D: "You and me both."

Mr. D. fill bedpan again. 0.2 gold.

3) Yao cartridge = best morning ever. Stop at Mr. Yao room for more info re: cartridge. Nurse T there (!). Nurse T checking upload lines. Best room in residence for Mr. Yao. Corner, all windows. Sunlight on Nurse T brown skin. Eyes shine like LEDs. Hair up in bun, want to sniff. Uniform crisp white in sunlight. Can't dialogue for seconds.

Yao: "Find it?"

Yao ancient. On 5th life. 5th! And uploading to next. Once was top maingame player, not so good this life. Squandered, some say. Loufis won't squander next life.

Plans for next life:

—More tutorials. All tutorials. No distractions this time.

—Wise gold investment. Don't waste on non-maingame games. On drinks. On clothes. On fixing water pipes for Momma and Poppa. Wise, not waste.

—Less lazy. Work hard, work all the time. Excel. Get 3rd life. Then relax.

—Take Nurse T to warm islands. Thai? Carib? Zealand? Wherever Nurse T likes. Whatever Nurse T wants.

Me: "Didn't find it. Need more info. Forget game name. Who make?"

Yao eyes closed mostly. Uploading is consuming. Memories packing up for transmission to next life takes all concentration. Yao better off than most in Nordic Winds Retirement and Upload Palace. Most not high level enough. Most only upload, no download, or download into metal body, not real body.

Reminder: visit Grandpoppa in Upland = more birthday gold.

Yao to Nurse T. (Nurse T. checking brain line): "Useless. This is what I get working with a Level 29. But a Level 75."

Yao grabs Nurse T rump. Nurse T doesn't look up from brain line. Can see she hates Yao. Hates hand on rump. Yao Level 428, can't say no. Could revoke whole levels. Hand squeezes fine rumpflesh. Should be Loufis hand. Nurse T wouldn't hate Loufis hand.

Yao body rolls and shakes. Think he dying – Yao ancient, at least 67 years – but just laughter.

Yao: "The game is *Journey to Athenmore*, made by Coseca in 1992 for the Super Nintendo. Try antique arcades, museums, auctions. I must have an original cartridge."

Yao flesh shakes = dying again? No, tears this time. Muddy drops roll down grey cheeks. Nurse T checks vitals. Yao hand reaches, not for rump, but for Loufis hand. And Nurse T hand. Yao eyes shut, lips quivering (weak little baby! frightened little girl!).

Yao: "Find it, Loufis. Please. I can't face another life without it."

Eyes open, see hand-holding going on. Yao hands release, dive under covers. Eyes shut. Breathing steadies. Time to leave. Jot down notes in hall: arcades, museums, auctions. Mustn't forget. As writing, Nurse T comes out.

Nurse T: "Wasn't that something?"

Me: "Yeah." Dolt. Mushbrains. Say more! Then: "Drink tonight?"

Nurse T jots down notes on tab. Brown eyes pained, like Yao hand on rump. Remembering? Remembering.

Nurse T: "Working at another residence." Nurse T finishes writing, snaps tab closed, walks away.

Dolt! Mushbrains! Nurse T level 75, never drink with man too old for level 29. But still. Nurse T = talk to Loufis.

Four quests this PM:
1) Bring Mrs. O lunch (check notes to be sure – think fish bologna sammy with crisps?)
2) Empty bedpans (better jokes this time? No jokes?)
3) Take out garbage from lunchroom, recroom, mediaroom, gym
4) Find Mr. Yao's cartridge (def level 29 boss)

◀ ▶

Maingame log, 2196.5.22 0205

Quest results:
1) Should have checked notes, no time.

Running late after lunch because writing prev log. Get to Mrs. O. room late, they starting nextlife transfer. Nurse T there (!) Two times, one day. Def best day ever.

Nurse T checking new body for Mrs. O. Young body. Man – surprise me. Thought always stay in same sex body. (Loufis next life: try lady body? Pro: boobs, cooch, long hair, wear dresses, maybe be singer? Cons: revise wiping routine, lose arm wrestles, Nurse T no like girls? Or Nurse T like girls? Should know. Should plan.)

Mrs. O old body naked, new body naked. Major upgrade: bye-bye wrinkles, saggy tits, scars, spots, hairy cooch. Hello muscles, tan skin, bald dong & waddle.

Mrs. O: "Don't stare. Where's my lunch? I hate to transfer on empty stomach."

Offer fish bologna sammy and crisps.

Mrs. O: "Fish? But the mercury." 0 gold, eats anyway. Loufis feeds Mrs. O, because straps. New body looks asleep, but not asleep. Not alive, not dead, not person, not yet.

Nurse T checks brain line, upload line, blood line. Doesn't check Loufis. Nurse T gives OK to Doc. Nurse T leaves. Mrs. O done sammy, working on crisps. Loufis leaves.

Me: "Wow. Never seen transfer."

Nurse T: "Haven't you been here for three years?"

Me: shrug. "Only made download attendant last month. Who next body?"

Nurse T puts aside tablet. Eyes not brown: eyes yellow-brown, like wheatiesfields in fall.

Nurse T: "He was an UpUpDownDown. They're all UpUpDownDowns."

Mrs. O barks for crisps. Nurse T gone when crisps are done.

Note: NO CHEATS. Know it, practice it, promise it every day. NO CHEATS.

2) Bedpans = empty. 3 XP, 0.15 gold.

Me to Mr. Thule: "The bank called, they're looking for the regular deposit."

Mr. T (eyes clenched, hand on stomach): "Not today, Loufis." 0 gold.

Me to Mrs. Hungerburn: "Behan couldn't spare new attendant. Only be a minute."

Mrs. H: "Thank you, my poor man." 0.5 gold, even though no joke. Note: No jokes for Mrs. H.

Me to Mr. Davenport: "That looks like blood."

Mr. D.: "Call the doctor."

Mr. D shakes like Mr. Yao, but not laugh, not cry. Docs fill room, inspect bedpan.

Doc: "Good job, Loufis." But no gold, no XP.

Mr. D stops breathing. Mr. D only half finished upload. Who will be in Upland?

3) Garbages all empty. 0.3 gold, 1 XP. Toss all bags in woods behind res instead of sort into bins = more time. Mean to do advanced upload attendant tutorial, instead play *HammerSmash*. Losing to Level 4 prick, so buy *Ultradoom Axehammer of Infrapain* (3 gold) and beat Level 4 prick = 1 XP. (Best day ever!)

4) Ask Moderator Behan for early leave to hunt cartridge.

Behan: "Do extra-curricular work on your own time."

Leave res at 2030. Bus late, so walk to next stop, bus go by on walk, next bus late. Get to shopping district 2130. Most shops closed. Try antique arcade.

Arcade Owner: "From 1996? Damn, son, need two, maybe three extra lives to afford a cartridge that old."

Then museum. Many games there and tutorials. Played *Shoot the Capitalist Swine*, then *Shoot the Communist Leech*, then *Shoot the Theocrat Owl*. All good learny history games. - 0.5 gold/game = + 0.5 XP/game. Past threshold to level 30! Bells and whistles go off, other museumers congratulate me. But level stats still show 29. Won't level until beat boss. Yao + cartridge = boss.

Find curator (asst.), dialogue re: *Journey to Athenmore*. Curator (asst.) looks up in library. One copy, won't lend out. Beg, on knees.

Me: "Nurse T won't play *Hes'TheOne* with level 29."

Curator (asst.): "Your friend can come here to play it, but we can't lend it out."

Could work. Mr. Yao all hooked up, needs med assist = Nurse T come too. All three together. Yao play. Loufis level to 30. Nurse T and me play games. She see *Shoot the Communist Leech* skills = she impressed. Maybe horndog? Maybe bonage behind *Conquest of the West* display? Maybe.

Best day ever!

◀ ▶

Maingame log, 2196.5.22 0545

AM Quests:
1) Caf. Need caf.
2) Bring Mrs. O – no, now called Mr. O – breakfast. OJ (no pulp) and biscuit (no nuts).
3) Bedpans.
4) Yao: museum field trip. Nurse T?
   Moderator Behan: "Why late?"
   Me: "Cartridge for Yao. Boss fight!"
   Behan: minus 2 XP. Back to level 29, but don't matter.
Will be level 30 tonight.

◀ ▶

Maingame log, 2196.5.22 1130

AM Quest results:
1) Caf gum and caf gel, still need more caf. Need more than 2.5 hours sleep. Forgot to eat.
2) Mr. O: very sleepy. OJ good = 0.1 gold, 1 XP. Biscuit = raisins.
   Mr. O: "*Deja vu* is a symptom of the transfer, I know, but this isn't deja vu. We just had this conversation."
   Me: "Thought no nuts." Didn't check log. No time.
   Mr. O: "Idiot."

Me: "New body nice."

Mr O: "Thank you. It's a good thing this body isn't sensitive to raisins or I'd use it to throttle you."

No bonus gold.

3) Bedpans = empty. 3 XP, 0.15 gold.

Me to Mr. Thule: "Still nothing?"

Mr. T: pretend to sleep. No gold.

Me to Mrs. Hungerburn: "Good morning."

Mrs. H: "Only three more days in this wretched prison. Then I'm free."

Me: "Grandpoppa in Upland. Likes."

Mrs. H: "When did you last see him?"

Me (thinking). what answer = gold?

Me: "Yesterday. Grandpoppa well." = 1 gold. Whole gold!

Lies = useful. Use more. But also visit Grandpoppa. Answer Grandpoppa emails. Maybe play *HammerSmash* with Grandpoppa?

Mr. Davenport gone. Mr. Mendez in Mr. Davenport bed.

Me to Mr. Mendez: "Me Number 1 at collecting Number 2s."

Mr. M: "Kay?" No gold.

4) Told Yao re: museum. Yao excited. Shaking (not dying), tears and laughter at once. Different nurse there: Nurse J. Nurse J OK. Nurse J eyes blue, uniform clean, hair bunned, face nice, level 27.

Nurse J: "We could accommodate a field trip. Have to pause the upload, but it shouldn't be a problem."

Yao: "Today?"

Nurse J: "I'll talk to the docs."

Yao: "Good job, Loufis. Amazing work for a Level 29."

Me: (!).

Nurse J waiting in hall.

Nurse J: "You made an old man very happy."

Me: "Hey."

Nurse J: "I'm impressed, Loufis. Really impressed."

Nurse J touches shoulder. Eyes very blue, smile nice.

Nurse J: "What are you doing this weekend?"

Me (thinking): Nurse T.

Me (saying): "Busy. Working, then visiting Grandpoppa in Upland."

Nurse J nods, leaves.

Lies = useful.

Dialogue Moderator Behan re: museum trip.

Moderator Behan: "Be careful with him, he's a very old man."

Me: "Nurse T should come. Best nurse."

Moderator Behan: "Good thinking, Loufis. You are more than ready for the 30s, my friend."

This aft. We go this aft.

PM quests:

1) Find Yao cartridge.

2) No bedpans. No garbage.

3) Nurse T.

◀ ▶

Maingame log, 2196.5.22 2046

Quest results:

1) Idiot.

2) Idiot.

3) Idiot.

Should read notes. That's why log quests. No time, never time, but still. Find time. Make time.

Yao hires car to museum. Yao + Nurse T + Me = in car. Nurse T checks Yao lines, Nurse T sits with me. Outside = snow. Light flakes, fall slow.

Yao: "In my second life, I spent years searching for *Journey to Athenmore*. The game wasn't a big seller. I thought I'd found a buyer in San Diego but they refused, no matter what I offered. I gave up. But I never stopped thinking about it. Not once in five lives."

Me: "Why?"

Nurse T: "You don't have to answer that."

Yao shakes head, skin loose like old dog. Yao: "I don't know where you grew up, Loufis – somewhere wretched ghetto hole, I imagine – but even in whatever overcrowded gutter you called home, there must have been magic in your youth. Mystery and awe. Moments when you realized you were alive, and that the world was bigger than you could ever imagine."

Me (remembering): Comet over apartment courtyard. First glimpse of cooch. Cushion forts.

Me: "Sure."

Yao: "That game was the last such moment. Everything after was XP and gold. Actions and choices weighed for their advantage, not for their joy or their mystery. If I can find that game again, maybe I can remember what it means to be alive."

Me: quiet.

Nurse T: wipes eyes.

Yao: quiet.

Car quiet. Snow outside quiet. Yao talks good. This one of those moments? Then museum.

Nurse T checks lines. Loufis rolls bed into lobby. Curator (head), not curator (asst.). Explain, tell of visit night before, here to see *Journey to Athenmore*.

Curator (head): "We have no such game."

Me: "Check records. Curator (asst.) found."

Curator (head) checks records.

Curator (head): "It isn't here."

Me: "Curator (asst.) said yes. Check security video."

Curator (head) checks video.

On screen: me and curator (asst.). Video me plays *HammerSmash* on handheld.

Video Me: "Have, uh, game? Think called *Travel to Arenas*? Old, like 1990s. Nintendo."

Video Curator (asst.): "*Voyage to Athens?*"

Video me: "That one."

Me: "No. Asked for *Journey to Athenmore*."

Curator (head): "I'm sorry but I can't help you."

Me: "No."

Yao: "Roll me back to the car."

Me: "No. It is here."

Nurse T: "Loufis, we have to go."

Roll Yao back to car. In car, Yao shaking. Hands fist and unfist.

Nurse T: "Calm down. Calm down."

Yao: "Never trust a level 29. Especially a cretin like this one."

Me: "Sorry."

Yao: "Was this your plan? To humiliate me?"

Me: "Super sorry."

Quiet in car again, but different quiet. Not snow quiet. Drowning quiet.

At res, wheel Yao back to room. Yao still fisting and un-fisting hands.

Nurse T: "Go, Loufis. You're upsetting him."

Moderator Behan: "What the heck happened?"

Yao dialogues museum events to Behan.

Me: "Curator (head) lied."

Moderator Behan: "I know you want to level, Loufis, we all do. I hate that I will have to deduct XP, but this was totally unacceptable. You've upset our best client."

Me: "Super sorry."

Moderator Behan: "Go home. Think on what you've done. Come back tomorrow and excel."

Home now. Play *HammerSmash*. Play *CoochParty*. Play *SorryTime*. Tired. Super sorry. -4 XP. Way less than level 30, don't care. Nurse T eyes = disappointed. Must make better.

◀ ▶

Maingame log, 2196.5.23 0303

Woke with idea. Good idea. Make better.

◀ ▶

Maingame log, 2196.5.23 0630

AM Quests:
1) Apologize re: late.
2) Bring Mr. O. OJ (no pulp) and biscuits (no raisins). Say Bye.
3) Bedpans.
4) Idea re: Yao cartridge.
   Very late, no time. Log later.

◀ ▶

Maingame log, 2196.5.23 1145

AM Quest results:

1) Me to Moderator Behan: "Super sorry. Upset re: failure yesterday, no sleep. New resolve: Don't dwell, excel."

Moderator Behan to me: "I'll let it slide this one time."

Me = surprised. Must be because Moderator Behan happy, relaxed.

Me: "Bonage with wife?"

Moderator Behan: "Better. Bonage with Nurse J. She is amazing. Don't say anything to anyone. I'm considering divorce. An XP setback, sure, but it is technically a boss fight victory. I've never been happier, Loufis."

No XP loss for late!

2) Mr. O: "I can't believe it. No pulp and a nice fresh biscuit, just as I ordered them."

Me = check log. Me = smart.

Mr. O: "I can't say it's been a pleasure, Loufis, but this is a small victory for you. Whatever you're doing, keep it up." 0.5 gold, 1 XP.

3) Bedpans = empty. 3 XP, 0.15 gold. See below.

4) After Mr. Thule bedpan, go to Yao room: Yao awake, Nurse T checking lines.

After Mrs. Hungerburn bedpan, go to Yao room: Yao eating, Nurse T not there.

After Mr. Mendez bedpan, go to Yao room: Yao sleeping, Nurse T not there.

Close door. Unhook Yao upload line, connect to my brainport. See Mr. Yao upload. Many memories. Five whole lifes. Memories and memories of memories. Heavy load. See why people Upload even when can afford new body. Don't dwell.

Go to second life. Must move quick so Nurse T no see. Scan memories fast. Is game, is best game. Is maingame.

Find memory: Yao, in young ladybody, dialogues with San Diego man re: *Journey to Athenmore*. See name of San Diego man: Olivio Sanchez. Yao offers Olivio 1500 gold for *Journey to Athenmore*.

Olivio: "I won't sell it."

Remember name, number, remember everything. But need gold. Total Loufis gold = 47.2.

Go through Yao memory, find bank codes. Remember too. Unconnect upload line from brainport, reconnect to upload machine. Yao still asleep. Door still closed. Me = genius.

Me to Moderator Behan: "Super sick. Butt explode. Home, please."

Moderator Behan: "Go to the autodoc first, then home. You can't be around these old people with gastro issues, but we need proof that you are sick to avoid any further XP deductions."

Me = genius.

PM Quests:

1) Get gold.

2) Find Olivio Sanchez.

3) Buy *Journey to Athenmore*.

4) Ask Nurse T to play game. *CoochParty*? *All Night Bonagefest*? *HandholdingII*?

◀ ▶

Maingame log, 2196.5.23 2350

PM Quest results:

1) Code work. Lots gold in Yao account: almost 3,000,000!
   Took 40,000, in case Olivio Sanchez wants more for
   Journey to Athenmore. If leftovers, Yao will give to me.
   Certain. Use bonus gold to take Nurse T to island and
   play games (not wait until next life!).

2) Olivio Sanchez dead, in Upland. Went to Upland. Upland huge sim city bigger than world with many trees
   and gold roads and fountains of wine and free food
   everywhere and every place is as close as next. Full of
   people.

   Grandpoppa: "After all these years, you've come to
visit!"

   Me: "Need to find Olivio Sanchez."

   Grandpoppa: "We can do it together."

   Me: "Be fast."

   Grandpoppa slow. Takes time with everything. Grandpoppa takes me to Fiesta de Muertos, where find Olivio.

   Olivio: "Sold it before I uploaded. Some woman in Atlan-
tica. She went by Priscilla Sentiva."

   Grandpoppa: "Let me show you my favourite park."

   Me: "No time."

   Grandpoppa: "They have shuffleboard."

   Me: "Tomorrow. Today, boss fight."

3) Obviously not buy *Journey to Athenmore* today. Tomorrow:
   find Priscilla Sentiva.

4) Tomorrow: Nurse T.

Tonight, play *HammerSmash*. Buy *InfiniHammer of the UberGods* (5,000 gold). Top leader boards. Best *Hammer-Smasher* in World (!).

◀ ▶

Cheat Accusation Transcript (excerpt), 2196.5.24 1230

Loufis Genlemden (henceforth Accused): Not cheat! Not steal! Borrow gold codes to buy *Journey to Athenmore* for Mr. Yao at Nordic Winds Retirement and Upload Palace. He confirm. He level 428, he boss in Loufis maingame. Ask Nurse T. Ask Moderator Behan. Loufis not UpUpDownDown. Loufis not cheat!

Mr. Yao (from Upland). This cretin worked his way into my confidence. I should have known from the start not to trust him. A product of inbreeding and crossbreeding and general genetic decline. They don't make people like they used to.

Nurse T (name redacted for confidentiality): I thought he was harmless. Different, but harmless. I thought he watched me so closely when I was working with Mr. Yao because he had a crush. I never suspected he planned to steal from the man.

Moderator Behan: Please don't enter his questlogs into the public record. Some of our conversations were confidential.

Adjudicatebot: Questlogs already entered as evidence. State your opinion of Accused.

Moderator Behan: He's a gentle soul. Dim, but so many are these days. We loved to joke around, him and I. Half the time what we were saying had no relation to reality. Little jokes, that's all.

Accused: Jokes. It was all just jokes.

Adjudicatebot: Questlog states: "Lies = useful. Lie more." Why should we trust you?

Accused: Nurse T, please. Tell good things. Not cheat. Please.

Adjudicatebot: ADJUDICATING. ADJUDICATING.

◀ ▶

Cheat Accusation Transcript (excerpt), 2196.5.24 1430

Adjudicatebot: Verdict reached. Loufis Genlemden found guilty of two cheats: grand theft gold and upload piracy. Purpose: win *HammerSmash*. Sentence: life in prison + return gold to Mr. Yao. Accused to serve sentence in body of Loufis Genlemden. Body becomes property of Mr. Yao. Sentence considered complete at expiry of body of Mr. Yao. Loufis Genlemden can apply for upload at completion of sentence.

◀ ▶

Prisonlog, 2196.5.26 0630

Mr. Yao move into Loufis body yesterday. Take control. Young body. Rich now. Smart now. Loufis prison now. New attendant cleans up bedpan for old Mr. Yao body, then wheels away old Mr. Yao body. Loufis watch.

Nurse T to Mr. Yao: "Everything working?"

Mr. Yao (with Loufis mouth): "Let me see."

Mr. Yao grabs Nurse T rumpflesh (with Loufis hand). Mr. Yao gets erection (with Loufis penis).

Mr. Yao: "Oh, I'd say everything is working just fine."

Nurse T: "Tee hee."

Mr. Yao: "Once I'm out of here, can I take you for dinner? We have so much to discuss."

Nurse T: "But isn't he, like, in there?"

Mr. Yao: "I keep him locked up in a little grey room. He can't see or hear anything."

Me: see everything, hear everything.

Nurse T smiles.

Nurse T: "Okay."

Me: super sorry.

No quests.

BETWEEN THE BRANCHES OF THE NINE

Alex C. Renwick

The sky slowly filled with the dull purple light of predawn, warmth from the woman curled at Sigunna's back leaching into her bones, heating her blood. These temporary sheaths of flesh the gods fashioned for them were so fragile, so ephemeral, so foreign to Odin's silver hall or the death-rot darkness of Hel.

She rolled from Kelda's warmth, pulled on breeches and boots, then blew the embers of the previous night's fire until it reignited and began to crackle. She tucked tunic into belt and knelt to stroke Kelda's short hair, the valkyrja-pale skin of her cheek. Though Odin's creation made happy rumblings deep in her chest, she didn't wake.

Sigunna stood. As quietly as possible she gathered the sleeping woman's gear – knives, breeches, worn leather boots – and lowered each without a splash into the creek flowing past the camp. After packing the saddlebags of her mount she unhobbled the other horse, black where hers was dun. She swung onto the dun's back and gave the black mare a light smack on its rump with the flat of her sheathed sword as she spurred her own beast into action.

That woke Kelda at last. Sigunna heard the other woman's wordless bellow behind her, drowned by the clatter of her horse's hooves on the pebbled road. She imagined the look on Kelda's face when she found her breeches in the creek halfway to the next town, and smiled.

No need to make things too easy for Odin's creature, after all. Sigunna was what Hela had made her.

◀ ▶

Kelda fished her knives and boots from the cold creek, cursing Sigunna with the names of demons from the thousand thousand worlds — the little, inconsequential worlds littering the infinite cosmos stretching between the nine great branches of Yggdrasil.

"Bright Odin, lend me strength," she muttered, wading through freezing shallows, searching in vain for her breeches as a greenish sun rose over distant indigo mountains. In only her tunic she set her sodden boots by the fire and resigned herself to making breakfast for one. In spite of all, she smiled as she cracked eggs into the iron pot, crumbling into it the single stale roll which had been left her, adding a few grindings of precious salt. Just like Sigunna to leave her salt, which she knew Kelda loved and which was rare in so many of the thousand thousand worlds. Salt she would leave her though she loved it herself; breeches, no.

Sigunna knew Kelda so well, knew she'd cook for her Valhalla-fuelled body the feast of a single meal rather than half starve for three. Breakfast fuelling her mortal sheath, her boots dry, the morning seemed not so bleak. As Kelda kicked apart the campfire remnants, an apologetic whinny sounded behind her.

She patted the black mare when it stepped from a copse of spindly trees. "There, there, old girl. That Hel-puppet and I have chased the gods' blades across every branch of Yggdrasil. I don't always fall so easily to bed with her..." Her lips quirked, thinking how welcome it had been, how grateful she was to have staved off immortal loneliness even for a night. "Ah well. In each mortal world I at some point find myself cold, alone, and without my breeches. Can't blame a horse for running from a woman like that."

The mare stood still as Kelda threw her blanket over its back and strapped her pack to its side, glad Hela's demon thought nothing of gold, choosing only to rob her of her knives and breeches. Pulling herself up by the sturdy mane – she picked her steeds for strength over speed – she gripped tight the animal's sides with her bare knees. She breathed deep, the little world's morning air reaching crisp and clean into the recesses of her chest. She was surprised by how very much she enjoyed this fragile thing, this fleshly bundle of blood and bone and sinew currently housing her Odin-forged spirit. She remembered with slow fire the feel of her current body against that of the woman riding ahead, the heavy silk of Sigunna's soft dark hair in her hands, the fierce pressure of Sigunna's lips against her throat.

She patted the horse's thick neck as it climbed the incline to the road, muscles rippling beneath bristly hide. "Don't worry, girl," she said, as they clambered onto the packed dirt and plodded toward the rising smaragdine sun. "We might yet arrive first to this Jarl Tyrfingr's hall. A surprise awaits our Hel-spawn in the next town. A surprise she'll like not at all, if everything goes well."

She smiled again, combing her thick warrior's fingers through the beast's mane as it whinnied in companionable response.

◀ ▶

Sigunna made good time. It was rare in most worlds to find free passage on well-kept roads, and not In eveiy incarnation had she possessed so fleet a mount. She liked the feel of the horse's gentle power beneath her legs, and the illusion the animal listened to her words and made sense of them. She'd grown quite attached, as well, to this frail human body. But it was all so fleeting. She couldn't afford sentimentality; Loki's children had fashioned her for the sole purpose of finding their sister Hela's dark blade. For this gods' game had Sigunna been made, as surely as if she were a cosmic hnefatafl marker carved from black amber: to reclaim Hela's lost toy from the infinite lands between Yggdrasil's branches and return it to Hel before Odin's valkyrja recovered Valhalla's bright one. Sigunna didn't waste herself contemplating her own fate should her mistress lose such a game to her opponent.

The village sprang into view around a bend in the road. Midday stalls lined cobbled streets. Vendors hawked wares from corners and doorways. Cries of "*Fine cloth, madam warrior!*" and "*Hot pies, madam warrior!*" followed her, wafting past along with the hundred other sights and smells and sounds of inhabited places and of lives shorter than a blink of Hela's necrotic eye.

Sigunna led her horse to a public trough and slid from its back. She looped its reins over the post and patted its sweat-darkened side. Around the main square elaborate carved or painted signs swung by chains above merchant doorways, pic-tures telling all in a land without a written language. Sigunna plainly made out the bakery, the weaver, the perfumery, the inn.

She strolled the bustling street, breathing the dust and sweat of mortal bodies pressed close. She passed the hostler's and the smithy. She tilted her face to the pale green sun as it warmed her hair, her skin, the lids of her half-closed eyes. Catcalls shrilled overhead from narrow balconies lining second storeys, pretty women with painted smiles and unlaced bodices. *"Spend coin with us, madam warrior,"* they sang, and tittered and waved, and forgot her as soon as she passed. Sigunna heard them behind her as she continued down the street, calling to the next passer-by, then the next: *"Hello, pretty baker-boy... Come, sir plowman, leave your coins here..."*

She found the sign she sought: two swords thrust from the painted board as though wielded by invisible hands, hewn in shallow relief into the wood. Hammered metal covered the blades, tips gleaming in midday sun.

Sigunna ducked under a doorway slightly too low. Her eyes adjusted to the dim interior, though with the frail agoniz-ing slowness of mortal flesh.

"Could I interest madam warrior in a sword of Tyrfingrby steel? Forged in the fire of a volcano, madam, and bathed in the blood of virgin maids."

Sigunna squinted into the smoky gloom. Looking down, following the sound of the voice, she saw a small barrel of a man, his head scarcely high as her belt. His thick hands held a sword of local design. His face was a caricature of merchant obsequiousness.

She smiled. "I think, sir armsmith, that even bloodless maids could swat aside that weapon of yours."

He frowned with a laugh, pitching the sword into a pile of near-identical pieces in one corner. "Well. Not a tourist, then," he said. He wiped his hands on his smith's smock and returned to his hearthfire. Easily hefting a pair of iron tongs, he lifted a cauldron from the flames to set it on the stone hearth. The scent of sweet herbs and sharp spices mingled in the air with the tang of metal and sweat.

"Tisane?" he offered. She nodded. A child stepped from the shadows to set two earthenware cups on the hearth ledge. "Son," said the armsmith, "run along on that errand we spoke of earlier. Best it be done quickly."

The boy peered from between his sandy-red braids at the tall woman, at her burnished skin, her long coils of hair which seemed to suck light from the room. Sigunna reached into her pocket for a tiny bluestone carving, a miniature helmeted godling astride a salamander steed with eight legs like Odin's eight-legged Sleipnir – a creature from another of the thousand thousand. She tossed it and he fumbled to catch it, small dirty hands flashing.

The smith handed Sigunna a cup before joining his son to squint at the elaborate carving, run his callused fingers along the beast's eight legs. "A strange animal," he said. "I've never seen anything like it."

"No," she said. "It's not a beast from around here."

The smith folded his son's hand over the carving. "Go, child. Let's get that errand done with."

After a shy bob in Sigunna's direction the boy wheeled and fled, ducking through a hide flap in the rear wall. The smith drew a dipper from the cauldron, sprinkled another handful of herbs into Sigunna's cup, and ladled hot water over the top. The aroma tickled the insides of her nostrils, but the heat felt good as the liquid burned the back of her throat.

Her stomach rumbled, reminding her she'd sacrificed breakfast to foil Kelda, intending to gain the gods-blade first. It was true the Odin-forged bright blade would sing with the same power as Hela's dark one, drawing Sigunna, calling her more strongly the closer she came – but until she found the exact source she wouldn't know which of the two gods' weapons languished on this tiny green-tinted world. She'd searched Yggdrasil's infinite abysses, had been so close to one gods-toy or the other so many times, only to clash with Kelda, to destroy Odin's tool as she herself was destroyed, and the artifact of their conflict whisked off again to another hiding spot, to tempt and tease the servants of the gods as the gods themselves played their callous cosmic games...

But this time, *this time*, Sigunna would succeed. She would possess the blade and plunge it into the sheath of her own mortal chest, claiming victory for her mistress, and be welcomed back into the fiery halls of her birth, her wanderings done at last.

A clank as the smith set his tongs by the fire brought Sigunna's attention back to the smoky room. The spiced aroma from the cauldron made her stomach repeat its growl as she drained her cup, willing away the needs of her temporary, mortal body. "It's said," she began, "across the mountains to the south, that there was a Jarl Tyrfingr who wielded a blade blessed by the gods, a blade that never lost a battle. It's said his arm never tired and his blood never spilled so long as he held that blade. It's said the blade was darker than night, its serrated edge sharp as steel thorns."

The smith nodded. "Everyone knows the saga of the current Jarl's great-great-grandsire, who bought lasting peace with his famous swords. We haven't seen war here for a hundred years."

Sigunna drew a long breath, trying to clear her sight. The room seemed to have grown smokier, the air thicker and more cloying, harder to take into her lungs. "Famous *swords?* The skald I heard described only one blade, a dark sword with an edge like thorns."

The smith lunged to catch her cup as it fell from Sigunna's slack fingers. He set both cups aside as she slumped onto the stone bench by the hearth. "No, madam warrior. The saga goes, 'And so wielded he in one hand the sword Bright, known by its swirled bluestone pommel... and in the other hand carried he the sword Dark, with teeth sharp like a beast's, and so vanquished he all enemies and every jarl in four directions, bringing peace to the lands of Tyrfingr.'"

Sigunna's tongue felt thick and wrong in her mouth. "Swords bright *and* dark?"

"I'm sorry, madam warrior. So, so sorry," said the smith, as her eyelids dropped shut.

If Kelda reaches the blades first, thought Sigunna before blackness wholly overtook her, *Loki's children will leave my immortal spirit to rot between the branches forever... forever and ever and ever...*

◀ ▶

Kelda and her sturdy mount plodded into town as twilight eased into dusk. Lanterns swayed in crisp evening breezes, yellow spheres glowing. Vendors unrolled woaden blue wool to cover wares for the night. Laughter spilled from open doorways. Glancing into the bright squares of light as she rode past, Kelda saw men and women eating and drinking, laughing, kissing. The murmur of skaldic verse and the soft sounds of trysts wafted from alleyways, rooftops, balconies.

The gaol was easy to find by the empty stocks at the edge of the wide street. She tethered her raven mare, mounted the few steps to the front door, knocked, and entered. A skinny youth snored behind a wide counter, head back, mouth open, scuffed boots propped beside the remnants of supper.

Kelda cleared her throat. The youth snorted awake, his chair nearly upending as his boots swung to the floor.

"I've come to pay a reward," she told him, reaching into the pocket of her new breeches – bought from a farmer when she took her midday meal and altered to fit by his pretty daughter while Kelda ate – to draw out a parchment square. She unfolded it on the counter, smoothing its creases flat to reveal Sigunna's sketched portrait and the pile of coins depicted at the bottom.

The youth stifled a yawn, nodding. "Armsmith caught her, sent his boy to let us know. She went straight to his place like the messenger said she would. Had to kick out Drunk Rasmus to empty the cell. Never needed more'n one cell before. Not since I can remember."

Kelda's sack of coins landed on the counter with a solid clunk. "Was anyone hurt?"

The young man shook his head. "Smithy got the instructions and herbs. She's been asleep since. Her horse is stabled out back. Or wait – is it her horse? She a horse thief?"

Kelda, recalling Sigunna galloping toward sunrise that morning with Kelda's mare fleeing before her like a demon at the point of Odin's bright gods-blade, shook her head. "No. Nothing like that."

The boy hefted the bag of coins. He pulled the drawstring, snorting when he saw unstamped gold rather than dull pewter. He looked up, doubt in his face. "We don't have to hang her, do we? Nobody's ever had to do more'n spend a couple days in the stocks. Don't know we'd want part of any hanging. Not around here."

Kelda considered. Death in this realm would simply send Sigunna's Hel-forged spirit back among Yggdrasil's great spreading boughs, to be reborn somewhere out on the infinite cosmic tafl board Odin's whim made of the Nine Realms. She closed her eyes, smelled again the sweet scent of Sigunna's hair, tasted the honey of her skin. She thought of the dozens of minor realms through which the endless gods-game had carried them, the other bodies they'd pressed together, the countless nights they'd lain close, breathing the air of countless worlds.

She opened her eyes. "No," she said. "Several days in the stocks should be fine, though be careful once she wakes. She's a difficult woman to control."

She untied two smaller coin bags from her belt and tossed them beside the first. "This should buy decent food and drink for her and her mount. Before I go, I'd like…" she glanced away. "I'd like to see her."

Without comment, the boy stood. He lifted a lantern from one peg on the wall behind him, a huge iron ring with a lone key from another. Kelda followed him down a short corridor to a single door with simple open grillwork at its centre. Beyond, stripes of lanternglow fell across the back and shoulders of the figure on the cell's single cot. Spilling onto the floor in thick ropes, Sigunna's hair seemed to drink the lantern's feeble rays.

Kelda untied a last sack of coin from her belt. "This one's for you," she told the boy. "I'll only be a moment."

In any number of towns in any number of realms on any number of worlds between Yggdrasil's branches, she would've met with suspicion. But no misgiving flickered in this young man's eyes. Tyrfingrby had long been under the protection of one of the most powerful objects in the Nine, and so the boy took the coin and handed Kelda the lantern and the hammered iron ring with its single key. Kelda read his expression as clearly as if she read his mortal thoughts: *He thinks simply of the balcony women he can please with that gold, of the skald song he can buy with it, and perhaps of a pair of new boots with scarlet heels.*

When the boy had gone Kelda set down the lantern and opened the door, not overly concerned about waking Sigunna; she'd sent enough sleep spice to knock her current body insensate for a full local day, and tomorrow Hela's demon agent would wake in the village stocks. While Sigunna wore that mortal sheath she could no more overcome its frailties than could Kelda. Neither could violate the natural laws of this realm. Only the blades and the gods could do that.

Later – after Kelda returned Odin's property to Asgaard, after she won his gods-game for him and was rewarded with her freedom – she'd seek Sigunna out. There'd be nothing to keep them apart then, no gods' whims sending them beyond the Nine Realms to battle and outwit and deceive each other in the name of Odin, of Hela. Once Odin won his wager with Loki's daughter, cosmic tafl-pieces Kelda and Sigunna could live side by side as equals, as companions. As friends.

She sat on the edge of the cot and reached to smooth back a tendril of Sigunna's satin hair, tuck it behind the curve of her ear. She leaned close, warmth from the sleeping woman's mortal body heating her leg even through the stiff new leather of her breeches. She breathed the honey scent of her opponent's skin, and the faint cloying odour of the soporific she'd sent ahead to drug Sigunna rather than risking battle and death in this realm before gaining Odin's blade and being forced to start over again out between the branches.

She pressed her lips to Sigunna's sleeping mouth, then stood, then left, destined to play out the petty games of distant gods.

◀ ▶

Sigunna had been an early riser in every mortal form she took; it surprised her to wake to the emerald glare of full day. Her tongue was raw, her throat parched. Her wrists and neck hurt as though sawed by the serrated edge of the gods-blade she sought.

She tried to turn her head, swearing as bonfires blazed inside her skull. She willed her eyes to open, to focus on the dusty red braids of the small figure staring up at her.

"The armsmith's son," she croaked.

The boy nodded. He lifted a hammered cup smelling only of metal and water to her lips. She drank, the water tasting of iron, but cool and clean. Strength flowed back into her muscles. Her vision cleared. The fog receded from her mind and she saw why she couldn't move.

A fleeting, bitter rage filled her. Then she began to laugh, which turned to a cough in her parched throat. The boy poured her more water from the waterskin at his waist.

Sigunna drank until her head felt clearer, less pounding. It would be a long time before her pride recovered, though she couldn't blame anyone but herself for that. Herself, and perhaps that cursed valkyrja. This had Kelda all over it like dog scent on a post. Odin's creature could be sly when she set her mind to it.

"Smith's child, do you know where they keep the key for these stocks?" she asked.

The boy looked over his shoulder at the busy street. People strolled past, arm in arm. Vendors sang the virtues of their wares, women called from balconies. Nobody showed much interest in the warrior in the stocks. A day in stocks was common punishment for unruly drunkenness; it wasn't unusual to see an unconscious outlander mercenary carried into the gaol one day and appear, befuzzled and blurry-eyed, in the stocks the next. Peaceful Tyrfingrby was no great place for a warrior to earn coin, but it was a fine town for spending it.

The boy met her gaze. "Only one key for all locks at gaol. My da forged it. Keeps copy at smithy." He fished in his pocket and pulled out the small blue carving of the eight-legged beast.

"Boy," said Sigunna in the same tone she'd used with skittish mounts on a dozen worlds, "...boy, could you fetch me your father's copy of the key? You'll be helping a warrior with her life's purpose, a purpose directed by the gods themselves."

The boy slid the carving back into his pocket. He looked into her eyes again, and nodded.

◀ ▶

Kelda and her mount ambled into the courtyard of Tyrfingr Hall as the greenish sun passed its zenith. Small flowers spilled from cracks in ancient stone walls. Lambs and puppies cavorted on wide lawns beyond the open portcullis as laundry lightly flapped on long lines strung between battlements. Skald song and laughter tinkled on breezes redolent with the scents of peace.

The angry clatter of hooves behind her and the enraged cry cut through the air like a knife through soft cheese.

"*Kelllldaaaa*! You and your fat donkey! Stop!"

Kelda slid to the ground as Sigunna reigned sharply beside her. The dark-haired woman launched at the pale-haired one, sending them both sprawling on the ground.

Sigunna straddled Kelda and pummelled her with tight-closed fists. "You spawn of feeble gods!" she screamed. "Freyja's golden turds! I should've split that smug valkyrja face of yours this morning and sent you hurtling back out between the Nine where you belong!"

Men and women glanced idly at the couple sprawled in the courtyard, tittered behind open hands, and turned away. Tyrfingr Hall was accustomed to lovers' quarrels; such were among the realm's most popular pastimes.

Kelda rolled from Sigunna's fists, confident the blade in Tyrfingr Hall was Odin's and not that forged by the cursed offspring of Loki. Hel's creature could try to kill her first, but Kelda need only be close enough for the bright blade to leap to her hand, recognizing her as Valhalla's servant. She would then sheath Odin's blade in her mortal heart and win by the rules of the game, as set by the gods.

But Sigunna could make trouble for Kelda. The two were perfectly matched in battle – the gods demanded an even playing field for themselves, if not for their servants – but if the power-thrum in Kelda's blood turned out to be the call of Hela's blade, and Hel's demon got close enough…

A terrible weight descended on the valkyrja. A notion of herself wandering Yggdrasil's branches for another hundred mortal lifetimes, another thousand. No peace, forever.

She leapt to her feet and sprinted past the wide open doors. The great hall was a long low room, full of well-worn feasting tables strung with garlands of fresh flowers. Rich tapestries covered stone walls. Fresh rushes covered the floor. The hall smelled of roasted nuts and baking bread.

At the main table was a chair, slightly raised, heavily carved and covered in beaten gold, with cushions of red. And over the jarl's great stone hearth were mounted two blades, one bright, one dark.

Kelda stumbled, fell to her knees. "Both blades in one place… Bright Odin, Leader of Souls, save me." Was it possible the Raven God had heard her secret entreaties to his name? It was as if he had looked into her immortal spirit, read her valkyrja heart and granted his servant's wish: that she and Sigunna both achieve the purposes for which they'd been fashioned, both win this cursed gods-game. Live ever after, in victory, in peace. Together.

A dark streak flew past. Kelda heaved to her feet and lunged to grasp Sigunna as she sped by, but her fingers only grazed the hem of the other woman's tunic.

"Sigunna, wait! We'll do it together, forge a draw! *Sigunna!*"

Lurching across the hall, toppling benches and banging tables, Kelda raced Hel's demon to the blades. But as always when it came to Sigunna, she was too late, too late.

Sigunna reached for the dark blade's hilt and her blood made it sing. Responding to power from the Halls of Hel, the blade leapt from its mounting. Iron hooks which had held it for a mortal century disintegrated into rust, crumbling away in a shower of red powder.

Dark power surged visibly through Sigunna as she poised the blade above her breast. Without thinking, Kelda reached for the bluestone pommel of the bright weapon. It jumped into her hand like a magnetized ingot. Fire coursed the rivers of her mortal body's veins at its touch, burning so bright she thought she'd crisp to ash.

Kelda prepared her own thrust, intending to split her mortal heart and bathe Odin's sword with her eternal spirit as she'd been made to do. But her hand froze, arms shaking, her plunge stilled by an invisible gods tight grip reaching from across the Nine. Her mouth opened. A voice not hers boomed from her lips to echo like dry rolling thunder across the stones of the hall. *"Banished Children of Loki!"*

Sigunna's eyes turned the blue-black shade of Hela's necrotic flesh. A hiss escaped her clenched lips: *"Greetings from Hel, Bright Odin. . ."*

The kernel of Kelda locked inside her mortal sheath understood, then. There would be no peace. Not for her, not for Sigunna. Never for them. A taťl piece would never be more than a toy, and the Nine Realms was just the enormous gaming board of the gods, as it always had been, always would be.

Kelda's arm rose against her will. In the instant before she struck, Kelda tried to etch in her mind every detail of the woman in front of her. Her mortal body had scarcely an eyeblink's moment before Odin tugged the strings of his puppet, swinging her arm to obliterate Hel's servant forever.

But Sigunna's arm rose to meet the blow. When the weapons clashed, Yggdrasil's branches shuddered and groaned. The ground trembled. The stones of the hall buck-led and heaved.

The flash of rupturing suns exploded in Kelda's arm. Blind, she felt Odin's presence ebb from her limbs. "*Sigunna!*" she cried as the hall collapsed, and the world flickered out like a doused tallow candle.

◄ ►

Laughing, Chun Hua dropped to the grass and rolled down the hill, her small round child-body coming to rest against the base of a cherry tree. Near her cheek lay a slender cherry branch, no more than a long stick. Grasping it, she rolled to her feet. The stick had a pleasing thickness in her chubby little fist. A whack to the tree's trunk provided a satisfying shower of pinkish petals.

Chun Hua peered closely at her new toy, studying a burl in the wood. The dark knot had a pleasing blueness, whorled into the bark's natural white and brown and green.

Chun Hua spun on one slipper to slash the air, laughing. "I'm a great warrior!" she shouted at the tree. "And this is my mighty sword!"

"Really? Master Jin says you're an embarrassment to the village." Bai, also only six but a full head taller than her class-mate, sat on the ground practising calligraphy in the dirt with a branch of black willow.

"I'm not a bebarrassment!" Chun Hua yelled.

Bai shrugged. Holding her sleeve from the dirt, she carefully etched characters in the earth with her branch: *foolish*.

Chun Hua recognized the word Master Jin made her wear on a scroll around her neck, punishment for laughing in class or dipping Bai's looping black braids in ink. Roaring, she lunged at the other girl, cherry stick whirling. With a feral smile Bai leapt to her feet, black stylus raised to block the blow.

When cherry branch met willow, a clash rang out. Nearly inaudible to the ears of the small warriors, the sound resonated deep in the earth beneath them, vibrating through the nine branches of Yggdrasil and out into the infinite spaces of the thousand thousand worlds between.

AFTERWORD
THE CASUAL MAGIC OF PLAY
DEREK NEWMAN-STILLES

As adults, we tend to look back on our childhoods with a sense of loss (though this loss is not always a mourning of a childhood passed, but can be a reminder of a childhood that was perpetually marked by losses), a displacement from the magical collection of worlds we were able to inhabit. As adults, we pretend that we now only have one world to inhabit, one that we invest with as much mundanity as possible, but we still hold those realms of play within us, and sometimes those moments of nostalgia captured in a treasured object become portals to those worlds that we pretend are lost to us, that we are too mature for. Our toys and objects of play can propel us into those spaces where we had the potential to create our own worlds with ease, inventing new realms and vistas of imagination.

We invest objects with our memories, imbue them with the magic of those multiple adventures we have shared with them. Our toys have the capacity to operate like keys, opening new worlds of possibility, unlocking areas of the mindscape that can alter our reality, allow us to explore new potentials, new ways of looking at the world. In play, we learn and grow, and our toys are passengers on those journeys as well as signposts to new areas of adventure and exploration.

Yet, not all adults are invested with the idea of nostalgia. Not all of us look back on our history with a sense of loss and joy. For some, adulthood is an escape from lives of control,

from abuses of power and person. For those who have experi-
enced abuse, nostalgia can be a complicated phenomenon,
tinged with pain.

Playground of Lost Toys captures our nuanced relationship
to play: fantasies of escape, ideas of childishness, creative
potentials, pain, loss, and the power of play to change our circumstances. The tales within these pages are snapshots of
moments of creative potential, imagination transformed into
paper and ink but still holding all of the dream-like magic of
overlapping lost worlds. These tales push boundaries, unwill-
ing to be limited to simple tropes or singular interpretations.
These authors PLAY with their toys, letting them signify loss,
memory, escape, the haunting power of the past returned,
moments overlooked in the moment that later become all-
encompassing in their importance, things lost and things
gained as we grow up.

Our toys can be our first and best friends, changing as we
change. They are perpetually part of the notion of BECOM-
ING, changeable objects that mirror youth in their ability to
be imbued with potential and yet fluid, able to alter themselves. Toys can be mirrors where we can see ourselves anew
as they change to mirror our thoughts, feelings, desires, anxi-
eties, obsessions. They reflect who we are at a particular
moment, and yet they also take on qualities for us as we
change. We see new things in our toys as we age.

Our toys can be time-travel objects, propelling us back in
our memories to the moments we played with them, reminding us of the different person we were when we played.
Perhaps this is why the theme of lost toys works so well as a
speculative fiction theme. Speculative fiction is a literature of
possibilities, of questions, of changeability, never settling on

one interpretation of "reality" but pushing us beyond the mundane to see nuances of a multifaceted world. *Playground of Lost Toys* invites us to spin the dice to open up new worlds, to play revolutionary chess against conquering aliens, explore the fear that parents have of the casual magic of their children, enter into a conversation with a modern day Merlin, look into the multi-faceted faces of a doll and its power to alter the world, take a ride on a toy train into old age, play games with an Artificial Intelligence that views humans as toys, be rescued from ghosts by a doll, be rescued from a space prison by a transforming train, or discover that a book of nursery rhymes can be a grimoire of spells with the power to change our world. These tales explore the possibilities of play to make social changes, to alter the way we think about and interact with the world. They explore the simple magic of play.

In our society, we associate youth with possibility. We look at childhood as a time of perpetual becoming, as though our children are clay that can be moulded by their encounters with the world. Our toys, so intrinsically connected to the social idea of youth, are invested with similar notions of possibility – the multifaceted, many-sided, still mouldable and changeable nature of reality. Toys reflect our social ideas, but they also have the power to transform them.

As a society, we pretend that *old dogs can't learn new tricks*, but *Playground of Lost Toys* reminds us that we are always able to learn new tricks if we learn to play and take advantage of the learning, changing, reality-warping potential of play as a creative activity.

AUTHORS' BIOGRAPHIES

Karen L. Abrahamson has had short fiction appear in *Realms of Fantasy, Paradox* and *Strange Horizons,* as well as in a variety of anthologies, most recently in *Fiction River: Fantastic Detective, Special Edition Crime,* and *Universe Between.* Her novels span high fantasy to romantic suspense, but lately it's mysteries that have caught her fancy. Author of the unique *Cartographer Universe* series, she drives urban fantasy in a whole new direction with a magic system that changes the landscape with a thought. "With One Shoe" represents another example of how Abrahamson likes to blur genres in her fiction. She was born in Moosejaw, Saskatchewan, grew up travelling, and now makes the Fraser Valley of British Columbia her home. Discover more of her writing at www.karenlabrahamson.com

Nathan Adler is a writer who works in many different mediums, including drawing and painting, audio, video and film, as well as glass. Nathan was the first place winner of the 2010 Aboriginal Writing Challenge. He has had his writing published in *Redwire, Canada's History, Shtetle, Shameless, Kimiwan Zine,* and as a part of the Ode'min Giizis Festival. He currently works as a glass artist, is writing a sequel to his first novel, *Wrist,* and is doing an MFA in Creative Writing. He is a member of Lac Des Mille Lacs First Nation, and lives in Mono, Ontario.

Colleen Anderson has published over 200 pieces of fiction and poetry. She has been a freelance copy editor, and was co-editor for *Tesseracts 17.* She was twice nominated for the Aurora Award, long-listed for the Stoker Award, and has received honorable mentions in the *Year's Best* anthologies. Some of her new and forthcoming works are in *nEvermore!: Tales of Murder, Mystery and the Macabre, Best of Horror Library, Exile Book of New Canadian Noir* (Exile Editions), *OnSpec, Second Contact, Our World of Horror, Polu Texni* and *Clockwork Canada* (available 2016 with Exile Editions). She was born in Edmonton, grew up in Calgary and now lives in Vancouver. You can find her at: www.colleenanderson.wordpress.com

Lisa Carreiro rises before dawn to spin the chaos in her head into stories before morphing into a humble office drone. Her short fiction has appeared in *On Spec*, *Tesseracts 11*, and *Strange Horizons*. She's currently working on the final edits to a novel. She lives in Kitchener, Ontario.

Kevin Cockle is the author of over twenty stories published in a variety of markets. He has also produced work as a screenwriter (earning a screen credit in 2015 for the short film "The Whale"), sports journalist, and technical writer to fill out what would otherwise be a purely finance-centric resume. His debut novel *Spawning Ground* is slated for a 2016 release. He lives in Calgary, Alberta.

Geoffrey W. Cole is a science fiction writer, writing instructor and engineer. He has published more than twenty-five short stories in publications such as *On Spec*, *Clarkesworld*, *Intergalactic Medicine Show*, *EscapePod* and *Imaginarium 2012: The Year's Best Canadian Speculative Writing*. His stories have been translated into Spanish, Italian, and Romanian. Geoff is completing a Masters of Fine Arts in creative writing at the University of British Columbia, where he also teaches writing. He lives in Toronto with his wonderful wife, his son, and giant hound. Geoff is a member of SF Canada and SFWA. Visit Geoff at www.geoffreywcole.com

Christine Daigle is a neuropsychologist, coffee aficionado, and Scrabble demon living in the Great White North (in southern Ontario, where it's actually quite sunny). Her first co-written sci-fi/fantasy novel, *The Emerald Key*, was released this year by Ticonderoga Publications. Her short works have most recently appeared in *Apex Magazine*, *Grievous Angel*, and the *Automatons & Airships* anthology (under Christine Purcell). She is an active HWA member.

Joe Davies has appeared in *The New Quarterly*, *The Missouri Review*, *eFiction India*, *Queen's Quarterly*, *ELQ/Exile: The Literary Quarterly*, *The Capilano Review*, *Stand Magazine*, *Planet: The Welsh Inter-nationalist*, *Descant*, *Rampike*, *Crannog* and other magazines, as well in the anthology *They Have to Take You In*, edited by Ursula Pflug for

Hidden Brook Press. He lives in Peterborough, Ontario, with his wife and three kids.

Linda DeMeulemeester has been published in zines, magazines and anthologies, most recently, Exile Editions's *Dead North: Canadian Zombie Fiction*. Her spooky children's series, *Grim Hill*, has been translated into French, Spanish and Korean. *Wandering Fox*, an imprint of *Heritage Books,* is republishing the award winning books with *The Secret of Grim Hill* launching October of 2015. After a long day outdoors as a free range kid, a favourite childhood pastime of hers was story time. Brothers Grimm revealed Faery was a dangerous place, and she suspected an old-fashioned leather-bound book of rhymes brimmed with magical incantations. She lives in Burnaby, British Columbia.

Candas Jane Dorsey is a writer of sometimes-award-winning novels (including *Black Wine*), short fiction (including *Machine Sex and other stories*) and poetry in a career that also encompasses literary editing; book and magazine publishing; teaching/course development for literary and professional writing classes; advocacy and action in community, arts and social justice; and freelance writing/editing. "The Food of My People" is in part an homage to her godmother Cobbie, in part a nod to her extended family, and in part honours the memory of the best pie on the planet (her mom's) and a fiendish red jigsaw puzzle. Flapper pie recipe: http://tinyurl.com/FlapperPie. She lives in Edmonton, Alberta, Canada.

DVS Duncan was born in Vancouver, British Columbia, and now lives in New Westminster with his lovely wife and a troublesome tomcat. He holds degrees in English and Landscape Architecture but it is life that has taught him the most. His stories are all true, though not factual. Make of that what you will.

Rhonda Eikamp is originally from Texas and now lives in Germany. When not writing fiction, she works as a translator for a German law firm. Her stories can be found in *Daily Science Fiction, Lady Churchill's Rosebud Wristlet* and *The Journal of Unlikely Cartography*.

She recently helped annihilate science fiction in the special *Light-speed* issue "Women Destroy Science Fiction." Find more stories at: http://writinginthestrangeloop.wordpress.com

Chris Kuriata lives in the Niagara Region of Ontario. As well as editing documentaries about murderers, tent revivals, and hockey, his short fiction has appeared in many fine magazines.

Claude Lalumière is the author of *Objects of Worship*, *The Door to Lost Pages*, and *Nocturnes and Other Nocturnes* and the editor or co-editor of fourteen anthologies, including *Masked Mosaic: Canadian Super Stories* and *The Exile Book of New Canadian Noir* (Exile Editions). Originally from Montreal, he's now based in Vancouver. claudepages.info

Catherine MacLeod lives and writes in Tatamagouche, Nova Scotia, where she also spends too much time watching "The Protectors" on YouTube. Her publications include short work in *On Spec*, *Nightmare*, *Black Static*, *Tor.com*, and several anthologies, including *Fearful Symmetries* and *Chilling Tales: In Words, Alas, Drown I*.

Rati Mehrotra was born and raised in India, and now makes her home in Toronto. When not working on her magnum opus – a series of fantasy novels based in a fictional version of Asia – she writes short fiction and posts updates on her blog http://ratiwrites.com. Her short stories have appeared in *Apex Magazine*, *AE – The Canadian Science Fiction Review*, *Urban Fantasy Magazine*, *Abyss & Apex*, and many more. Follow her on Twitter @Rati_Mehrotra

Derek Newman-Stille researches representations of disability in Canadian Speculative Fiction while completing his PhD at Trent University, in Peterborough, Ontario. Derek runs the Prix Aurora Award-winning website Speculating Canada interviewing authors and reviewing Canadian spec fic out of a love of the genre and because it makes it easier to meet his favourite authors. Derek has written in academic and non-academic fora such as *Mosaic, The Canadian Fantastic in Focus, Quill & Quire,* and *Accessing the Future*.

Dominik Parisien is an editor, poet, and writer who lives in Toronto. He is the co-editor, along with Navah Wolfe, of several upcoming anthologies for Saga Press, and the editor of *Clockwork Canada* (Exile Editions) due out in April of 2016. He was also an editorial assistant for various anthologies, including *The Time Traveler's Almanac* (Tor), *Sisters of the Revolution* (PM Press), and *The Bestiary* (Centipede Press). His fiction and poetry have appeared in *Uncanny Magazine, Strange Horizons, Shock Totem, Ideomancer, Lackington's, Imaginarium 2013: The Best Canadian Speculative Writing*, and other venues. You can find him online at: https://dominikparisien.wordpress.com/ and Twitter @domparisien.

Ursula Pflug is the award winning author of the novels *Green Music* (Edge/Tesseract), *The Alphabet Stones* (Blue Denim) and *Motion Sickness* (Inanna), illustrated by SK Dyment. She penned the story collections *After the Fires* (Tightrope) and *Harvesting the Moon* (PS), and edited the anthology *They Have To Take You In* (Hidden Brook), a fundraiser for mental health. Her YA novella, *Mountain*, is forthcoming from Inanna. She has taught writing workshops in Toronto, Campbellford, Peterborough, Maynooth, and San Miguel de Allende, Mexico; at Trinity Square Video, Loyalist College, the Campbellford Resource Centre, Trent University and elsewhere. She lives in Norwood, Ontario.

Alex C. Renwick lives mostly in the Pacific Northwest, mostly in Vancouver (the real one). Her short story collection *Push of the Sky* (written as Camille Alexa) was an Endeavour Award finalist and an official reading selection of Portland's Powell's Books Science Fiction book club. Her most recent tales of noir, myth, and oddness have appeared in *Alfred Hitchcock's* and *Ellery Queen's* Mystery Magazines, *Clockwork Phoenix*, and *New Canadian Noir* (Exile Editions). More at alexcrenwick.com

Robert Runté is Senior Editor with Five Rivers Publishing, a freelance development editor at SFEditor.ca, an associate professor, critic and reviewer. He was co-editor of *Tesseracts 5*, wrote the SF&F entry for the *Encyclopedia of Canadian Literature*, has won three

Aurora Awards for his SF criticism, but aside from one story in the first issue of *On Spec Magazine* in 1989, has only recently started writing fiction. Having finished the first draft of his own first novel, he is the first to concede that reviewing or editing a novel is a lot easier than writing one. He lives in Lethbridge, Alberta, with his wife and two daughters.

Shane Simmons Is a multi-award winning screenwriter and graphic novelist whose work has appeared in international film festivals, museums and lectures about design and structure. His best-known piece of fiction, *The Long and Unlearned Life of Roland Gethers,* has been discussed in multiple books and academic journals about sequential art, and his short stories have been printed in critically praised anthologies of history, crime and horror. He lives in Montreal with his wife and too many cats. Shane on the web: eyestrainproductions.com. Shane on twitter: @Shane_Eyestrain

Kate Story is a writer, performer, and choreographer originally from Newfoundland. Her first novel *Blasted* (Killick Press) received the Sunburst Award's honourable mention for Canadian Literature of the Fantastic, and was longlisted for the ReLit Awards. Her second novel, *Wrecked Upon This Shore,* has been called "magical and moving" (Jessica Grant, *Come Thou Tortoise*). In 2015 Kate was the recipient of the K.M. Hunter Artist Award for her work in theatre. Recent publications include "Yoke of Inauspicious Stars" in *Carbide Tipped Pens* and "Unicorn" in Stone Skin Press's 21st century bestiary, *Gods, Memes, and Monsters.* Look for her story "Equus" in Exile Editions' upcoming *Clockwork Canada.* www.katestory.com

Meagan Whan writes and lives in Ontario. She loves all forms of creative expression. Though she has never unearthed a die, she did dig up a porcelain figurine of a hound dog. "The Die" is her first published story.

Melissa Yuan-Innes dedicates this story to her son Max and four of his caregivers: Liz, Gisèle, Aly and Tanya. Before Melissa became an emergency doctor and writer, she slept with a plethora of stuffed animals, including one named D'Arcy Oliver Theodore Shostakovitch Yuan-Squirrel. Melissa's stories have appeared in *Nature*, *Writers of the Future*, *Tesseracts* 7 and 16 and the Aurora Award-winning anthology *The Dragon and the Stars*. She also writes mysteries, including one shortlisted for the Derringer Award, under the name Melissa Yi. She left Montreal to hang out in the countryside of Eastern Ontario. Discover more of her crazy life at www.melissayuaninnes.com

Exile's $15,000 Carter V. Cooper Short Fiction Competition

FOR CANADIAN WRITERS ONLY

$10,000 for the Best Story by an Emerging Writer
$5,000 for the Best Story by a Writer at Any Career Point

The 12 shortlisted are published in the annual *CVC Short Fiction Anthology* series and *ELQ/Exile: The Literary Quarterly*

Exile's $2,500 Gwendolyn MacEwen Poetry Competition

FOR CANADIAN WRITERS ONLY

$2,000 for the Best Suite of Poetry
$500 for the Best Poem

Winners are published in *ELQ/Exile: The Literary Quarterly*

These annual competitions open in October & November
details at: www.TheExileWriters.com

THE *EXILE BOOK OF* SERIES:

NEW CANADIAN NOIR
Edited by Claude Lalumière and David Nickle • Number Ten
22 stories that showcase the Canadian noir imagination, expressed across genres and geography.

THE STORIES THAT ARE GREAT WITHIN US
Edited by Barry Callaghan • Number Seven
Over the last 60 years, Toronto has been turned upside down and inside out – and the city's storytellers have given vibrant voice to the city's characters.

THE EXILE BOOK OF YIDDISH WOMEN WRITERS
Edited by Frieda Johles Foreman • Number Six
2014 WINNER of the Helen and Stan Vine Canadian Jewish Book Award:
The first collection of Yiddish writing to emphasize the work of Canadian-Yiddish women writers, like Chava Rosenfarb, Rachel Korn and Ida Maze.

PRIESTS, PASTORS, NUNS AND PENTECOSTALS
Edited by Joe Fiorito • Number Five
Mary Frances Coady, Barry Callaghan, Leon Rooke, Roch Carrier, Jacques Ferron, Seá n Virgo, Marie-Claire Blais, Hugh Hood, Morley Callaghan, Hugh Garner, Diane Keating, Alden Nowlan, Alexandre Amprimoz, Gloria Sawai, Eric McCormack, Yves Thériault, Margaret Laurence, Alice Munro.

NATIVE CANADIAN FICTION AND DRAMA
Edited by Daniel David Moses • Number Four
Tomson Highway, Niigonwedom James Sinclair, Joseph Boyden, Joseph A. Dandurand, Alootook Ipellie, Thomas King, Yvette Nolan, Richard Van Camp, Floyd Favel, Robert Arthur Alexie, Daniel David Moses, Katharina Vermette.

CANADIAN DOG STORIES   Edited by Richard Teleky • Number Three
"Twenty-eight stories that run the breadth of adventure, drama, satire, and even fantasy, and will appeal to dog lovers on both sides of the [Canada/US] border."–*Modern Dog Magazine*

CANADIAN SPORTS STORIES
Edited by Priscila Uppal • Number Two
Clarke Blaise, George Bowering, Dionne Brand, Barry Callaghan, Morley Callaghan, Roch Carrier, Matt Cohen, Govier, Steven Heighton, W.P. Kinsella, Stephen Leacock, Barry Milliken, L.M. Montgomery, Susanna Moodie, Margaret Pigeon, Mordecai Richler, Guy Vanderhaeghe and more.

20 CANADIAN POETS TAKE ON THE WORLD ~ Mulitlingual
Edited by Priscila Uppal • Number One
20 Canadian poets translate the works of Nobel laureates through classic favourites. Each poet provides an introduction to the translated work.